ON EARTH

AS IT IS IN

HEAVEN

ON EARTH

AS IT IS IN

HEAVEN

DAVIDE ENIA

TRANSLATED FROM THE ITALIAN BY

ANTONY SHUGAAR

FARRAR, STRAUS AND GIROUX | NEW YORK

Farrar, Straus and Giroux

18 West 18th Street, New York 10011

Copyright © 2012 by Baldini Castoldi Dalai editore S.p.A., Milano

Copyright © 2013 Baldini&Castoldi S.r.l., Milano

Translation copyright © 2014 by Antony Shugaar

All rights reserved

Printed in the United States of America

Originally published in 2012 by Baldini Castoldi Dalai editore S.p.A., Milano

Published in the United States by Farrar, Straus and Giroux

First American edition, 2014

Library of Congress Cataloging-in-Publication Data

Enia, Davide, 1974–

[Così in terra. English]

On earth as it is in heaven / Davide Enia ; translated from the Italian by
Antony Shugaar. — First American edition.

pages   cm

"Originally published in 2012 by Baldini Calstoldi Dalai editore S.p.A.,
Milano"—Title page verso.

ISBN 978-0-374-13004-6 (hardback) — ISBN 978-0-374-70915-0 (ebook)

I. Shugaar, Antony, translator.   II. Title.

PQ4905.N53 C6713 2014

853'.92—dc23

2013034091

Designed by Abby Kagan

Farrar, Straus and Giroux books may be purchased for educational, business,
or promotional use. For information on bulk purchases, please contact the Macmillan
Corporate and Premium Sales Department at 1-800-221-7945, extension 5442,
or write to specialmarkets@macmillan.com.

www.fsgbooks.com

www.twitter.com/fsgbooks • www.facebook.com/fsgbooks

1   3   5   7   9   10   8   6   4   2

CONTENTS

ON EARTH

AS IT IS IN

HEAVEN

here I stand
at the peak of my beauty
still on my feet
hands spattered with blood
in front of me the dark grain of her mulberry mouth
and she takes my bloody fingers and raises them to her lips
and kisses them
one by one
her name is Nina
she is my love
she's nine years old

There are two of them in the boxing ring.

One weighs 145 pounds, stands five foot five, and is twenty-six years old.

The other one? Nobody knows his weight and it doesn't matter how tall he is, he'll grow.

No one has bandaged his wrists, he's wearing boxing gloves, he's bouncing on his toes in the ring.

He's nine years old.

There's a man at the far end of the room, smoking and talking on the phone.

"Zina, don't worry, he's with me, everything's fine, half an hour, no more, and we'll be home, ciao."

He hangs up the phone, picks up a paper from the table, and studies the horse-racing odds, looking to place a bet on an unforgettable trifecta and win big enough to turn his life around, at least for a couple of months.

At the edge of the ring, leaning on the ropes, a man with a flat cap on his head yells: "On the count of 'three.'"

The other boxers stop doing push-ups and turn away from the heavy bag.

"One, two, three."

The kid keeps a comfortable distance from his opponent. His footwork is beautiful to behold: the tips of his toes leave the ground together and touch down in unison.

At the far end of the room, the man who's smoking slaps the back of his hand against the newspaper.

"What a fucking trifecta: Asansol, Regulus, Mastiff the Third—I'm making this bet right now."

He tears out the page, stuffs it in his pocket, and comes over to the ring.

The twenty-six-year-old fighter is named Carlo. He's focused: his guard is up, his legs are bent, his gaze is trained directly on his opponent's eyes.

The kid feints to the right and then makes a surprise leap to his left. He's not even aware of the moves he makes; he just makes them. Carlo maintains his defensive stance. He's locked up tight, like the front doors of a church in the middle of the night. The instant the kid touches down, he throws an uppercut with his left glove. Carlo blocks the punch with his right elbow. The man in the flat cap at the edge of the ring is about to shout something but the words catch in his throat: unexpectedly, without warning, the kid has converted the uppercut into a double punch.

His left glove just grazes Carlo's face.

He gave it a shot.

He failed.

The smoking man issues the order without feeling: "Drop him."

The front doors of the church open wide.

Carlo unleashes a cross that slams into the kid's cheek, sending him to the mat.

A couple of seconds later, the kid gets to his feet, staggers, and loses his balance immediately.

He clenches his teeth to keep from toppling over again.

The man in the flat cap asks him: "You know how to jump rope?"

"My head's spinning."

"That's not what you were asked," the other man points out, calmly, exhaling a stream of smoke from his mouth.

The man in the flat cap has the eyes of the hunter just as the shot's about to be fired.

"I don't know how to jump rope."

"Teach yourself."

The kid pulls off his gloves, steps out of the ring, picks up a jump rope, and does his best. He gets it wrong every time.

"So," the man who's smoking says to the man with the flat cap.

"You saw it yourself, he threw a double punch."

"And he's got a pair of feet on him."

"Yeah."

"The time has come."

"Like father, like son."

"See you tomorrow, Franco."

The man with the cigarette in his mouth takes the jump rope out of the kid's hands after watching a series of unsuccessful attempts.

"You'll learn to do that, too, in time. Now let's go home. Listen to me carefully, you can tell your mother everything that happened, except the part about me taking you to the gym. Swear it."

The kid swears.

"But tell your grandpa everything."

"Can I?"

"Not can you, I'm telling you you have to."

They leave the gym just as the man named Franco, whipping the flat cap off his head, shouts at the boxer named Carlo to feint to the left and block that right uppercut, again, do it again, you miserable son of a bitch, again.

Outside, the sound of police sirens comes wailing through the hot, stagnant air. Little knots of people stand in the shade pointing to someplace in the distance. One person tells the version of events he overheard, someone else asks questions, another person ventures an answer, and everyone crosses themselves at the word *Mafia*.

The man who's smoking walks along with his hands in his pockets.

He answers to no one but himself.

He never turns around.

His name is Umbertino.

He's my great-uncle.

The nine-year-old kid is me.

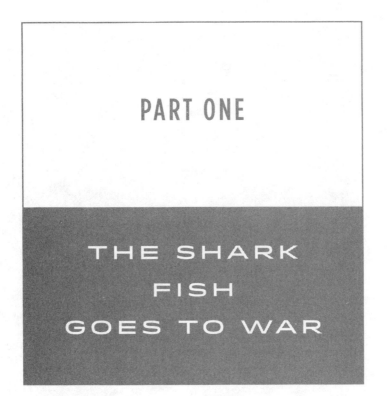

PART ONE

THE SHARK FISH GOES TO WAR

N o, it's the way I say it is. The first time you fuck, the string tears off."

Nino Pullara was adamant. He was the oldest, the tallest, the strongest boy in our gang. He was bound to be right.

"That's how it is, my cousin Girolamo told me, he's already fucked twelve times, he's fifteen, and the first time the string on your cock always breaks."

"Does it hurt?" asked Lele Tranchina; he knew that asking if something hurts was a sign of weakness, but he didn't give a damn.

"Yeah, it hurts, it bleeds, but Girolamo says that if you fuck the way you oughta, it feels so good that the pain don't matter."

Rebellious teenagers with jackknives have carved slogans into the benches in the piazza.

THE POLICE SUCK
GOVERNMENT = MAFIA
LESS COPS, MORE HEROIN

Nino Pullara pulled out a pack of cigarettes, lit one, passed it around.

"Gerruso, you dickhead, when you inhale, you have to hold all the smoke in, otherwise you don't feel a thing, and there's no point to smoking."

"But it makes me want to cough."

"Because you're a total pussy."

As long as we let him stay in the gang, Gerruso would put up with anything: we could kick him, spit on him, scratch him. He was so resigned to the idea of being beaten to a pulp that he didn't even resist anymore. The fun of beating him up was starting to fade.

"When I grow up," Pullara continued, "there's two things I wanna do. The first is fuck Fabrizia."

"The one at the bakery?" asked Danilo Dominici, wide-eyed.

"That's her."

Fabrizia, seventeen and spectacular, a pair of firm tits. After she took a job there, the whole neighborhood started buying bread at that bakery.

"I've never seen so many men willing to do the shopping," my grandmother Provvidenza had quipped.

"I'm definitely going to fuck Fabrizia, but only after my string's torn off."

Pullara was boasting with the confidence of someone who'd already turned twelve.

"What's the second thing you wanna do?" asked Guido Castiglia.

Guido Castiglia never missed a trick. Guido Castiglia wasn't someone you wanted to cross. One time he asked Paolo Vizzini for a stick of chewing gum, and Vizzini said uh-uh, he wasn't giving him any of his gum. Castiglia didn't say a word, didn't blink an eye, just walked away. Two months later, Vizzini fell out of a carob tree and landed on his left leg. His flesh was all ripped up, and you could see clear through to the white of the bone.

"Help me! Help me!" he was shouting.

Guido Castiglia appeared on the dirt lane.

"You want me to go get help?"

Vizzini begged him.

"Hah, that'll teach you: next time give me the stick of gum."

And he left him there, his leg fractured, crying like a little girl.

"What I want is to have the same job as my dad: at a gas station."

Pullara's statement resounded like a decree. His voice rang with a tone that underscored the inexorable future awaiting him. No job could compare with working at a gas station: there you sat in the shade, immersed in the magical scent of gasoline; a dog tied to a chain to keep you company, and, if you got bored, you could always beat the dog with a stick; in the back pocket of your pants, a fat, impressive wad of cash.

"I want the same job as my dad, too," Danilo Dominici announced. "It's great, you're always outdoors."

His father paved streets.

"Me, too; I want the same job as my father. He's a traffic cop."

We all glared at Gerruso with hatred: being a traffic cop was pathetic, they didn't even have sidearms.

"Gerruso, look over there."

The minute he turned around, Pullara landed an open-handed slap on the back of his neck. Then he turned to look at me.

"What about you, Davidù? What kind of job you want?"

I spoke the first true words that came into my head, without stopping to think.

"Me? Oh, I don't know, I'm not like you guys, you all want the same jobs as your dads. Me, I can do whatever I want, I'm luckier than all of you: I'm pretty much an orphan."

In front of my house I saw my grandmother, seated on a bench in the shade of the jacaranda tree. She was smoking a cigarette, leaning comfortably against the rusty green backrest.

"Light of my life, come sit next to me, Grandpa's upstairs, he's cooking lunch for you."

"Mamma's not home from the hospital yet?"

"No. It looks like a bomb went off on top of your head."

She started laughing, between a hacking cough and a mouthful of smoke.

Grandma smelled of tobacco and chalk.

She was an elementary school teacher.

She taught me to read and write.

I was four years old.

She had pestered me.

"Davidù, shall we learn how to read and write?"

Every goddamned day.

She was relentless, and I finally gave in. In part because she promised that once I learned, she'd teach me how to burp on command.

She was as good as her word.

"What did you do today?"

"At school, nothing, the teacher let us draw because she's working on our report cards, then in the piazza me and my friends talked about when we would be grown up."

"When we *will* be grown up."

"Okay, but you knew what I meant."

"Davidù, it's not enough for someone to understand the things you say. Words need to be treated with care. What did Grandma teach you? What are words?"

"The expression of our thoughts."

"Why do we use the future tense?"

"To give a direction to our plans and hopes and all that kind of stuff."

"Bravo, light of my life, if you were a little older I'd offer you a nice cigarette."

"Why aren't you upstairs with Grandpa?"

"I wanted to smoke in blessed peace, as if it were six forty in the evening."

"What do you mean?"

"It's something I've done since I was a girl. Back then, the war was still going on and the Americans had reached Capaci. They were giving away chocolate bars and cigarettes. I met this soldier, Michael. He gave me my very first pack of cigarettes, in exchange for a dance."

"Did you kiss him?"

"No, silly. Back then I had a job, I'd already been working in Palermo for a few months, at the city library, and I was studying for the civil service exam."

"Because in those days, civil service exams were tough, you always tell me that, Grandma."

"I even know Ancient Greek."

"The story, Grandma."

"The library is next to the church of Casa Professa. Bombs hit them both during the famous raid of May 9, 1943. In the wing of the library that was still intact, I spent the day archiving books that had been dug out of the rubble. I wrote down title, author's name, missing pages. Bombs don't just sweep away people, houses, and hopes. Bombs erase memories, too. When the workday was over, I leaned against the sycamore tree in front of Casa Professa and lit my favorite cigarette, the six forty evening cigarette. I'd leave the workday and my job behind, savoring that nice pungent taste and relaxing, from the first puff to the last. While I smoked, the crowds streaming into and out of the Ballarò market kept swelling. Back then, the market was especially crowded at the end of the day. So crowded you had to hold your packages high over your head to get anywhere. The houses didn't have refrigerators back then, and they had to sell everything before it went bad, so they cut prices in the evening. The kids would stand in line to buy salt, playing rock, paper, scissors. The women gossiped about love affairs and girls who had eloped. Here and there, a man, scented with cologne, stood in line for potatoes, singing the first few notes of an aria and winking at anyone who met his gaze. I couldn't say how many cigarettes I smoke every day, twenty, maybe twenty-five, but the one I really enjoy, my favorite one, is the cigarette of six forty in the evening, and even when it's not six forty in the evening, say right now, I pretend it is, I stop whatever I'm doing, I walk away from everything and everyone, I savor my cigarette, and to hell with the world."

Grandma taught her pupils bad words, too, secretly; she said it helped prepare them for life. "Life is more than verbs and arithmetic, it's mud and dirty words, too, and knowledge is better than ignorance."

A police car came toward us, slowed down, looked us over, drove by, and went away.

On the bed, a note from my mother, in her distinctive nurse's handwriting.

"Your uncle wants you to go someplace with him at 4, he'll come by to pick you up, goodbye, light of my life."

In the kitchen, Grandpa was cooking lunch. Whenever there were strangers around, he was practically mute. Grandpa Rosario talked only to me and his old friend Randazzo. He worked as a cook.

"What are you cooking?"

"*Pasta ch'i tenerumi.*"

He blanched and peeled a tomato, then sliced it. Grandpa's hands were lightning fast.

"How do you know how long to cook everything? Are there tables, like for multiplication?"

"You just have to learn to get the ingredients right."

"And how do you learn that?"

"By getting them wrong."

———

On the shelf in the dining room stood a photograph of my parents on their wedding day. My father's right arm protectively encircled my mother's shoulders, his hair was parted to one side, his suit was dark. He was smiling. In his blue eyes there was a fierce note of hope; he could hardly have known he'd be dead within the month. In the photograph, my father was as handsome as his nickname implied: the Paladin. Mamma wore a white dress and held a red rose. Her eyes were shut as she breathed in the scent of the flower: serene, a definitive serenity.

"So that's that: I'm bettin' on this fine trifecta: Pirollo, Little Frenchman, and Abracadabra. A fabulous combination. Let's go on home now."

"Aren't you going to watch the race, Uncle?"

"Why on earth would I wanna waste my time watching the race?"

"You made a bet."

"Davidù, get this into your head once and for all: once you've gone and made your bet, it's none of your business no more. It's even written in the Holy Scriptures: first you size things up, then you lay your bet, and after that, to hell with it."

The calm detachment with which my uncle had made his bet. That's what I was thinking about on the piazza, in the sweaty aftermath of lunch, while we subjected Gerruso to a firing squad of slaps and smacks.

Nino Pullara had issued the order: "Let's play neck-slap; Gerruso, you're it."

That pathetic loser, unaware that the game was nothing more than a pretext to beat him up, started over to the wall without a word. He dragged his feet as he walked. An inexorable march. He knew he was headed toward certain pain, but he was so stubbornly determined to be part of our gang that his sense of personal dignity had long ago lost its battle against his resignation. Why didn't Gerruso just look for other friends, friends who were as fat and worthless as he was? Why did he accept all this misery? I felt not a scrap of pity for him. He was a weakling. Weaklings deserve no respect.

Gerruso reached the wall, covered his eyes with his right hand, wedged his left hand under his armpit, and held it open, flat. He was ready to play the game. But Pullara had decided to twist the rules.

Even if Gerruso did guess who'd slapped him, we'd say he was wrong, he'd have to turn back around, and he'd get another smack on the back of his neck and then another and another, over and over again.

The goal wasn't to play.

The goal was to slaughter him.

The first slap was thrown by Danilo Dominici.

Gerruso took it, suppressing a groan of pain, then turned and looked hard at us.

"Danilo Dominici."

"No."

Pullara had answered for the rest of us.

Gerruso wasn't cheating.

Pullara was.

Lele Tranchina took a running start and slapped with every muscle in his body. Gerruso throttled a cry of hurt deep in his throat. He turned around, without looking at anyone in particular.

"Tranchina."

"No."

Gerruso turned back to the wall without a word. He was a weakling. He deserved all the pain in the world.

I spat on the palm of one hand and rubbed it into the other, the way they did in the movies I'd watched at the theater with Umbertino, who would say after every killing: "Finally a movie the way they oughtta be made, not one of those French pieces of garbage for people who are sick of living. Look at that beautiful explosion! Now this is art."

The truth is, Gerruso, you were born for French movies.

I hit him with such extreme violence that I even surprised myself. The slap didn't erupt into the ringing sound of a smack; instead it was muffled at impact by his entire body into a single, cavernous moan.

Gerruso looked at me instantly, ignoring everyone else.

"Pullara."

Why, Gerruso? Why? What possible reason could you have for being such a loser? You'd guessed who it was that time, too; you should have said my name; that's not how the game is played.

"Wrong!"

Drops of saliva sprayed out of Pullara's mouth. His pupils gleamed with fire. He would be the next one to deliver a neck-slap—it was obvious.

"Turn around, you dumb baby. Now I'll bet we make you cry."

Pullara didn't state the challenge with detachment; he was ferociously committed. He was hopping in the air, waving his hand to warm it up. Once again he broke the rules, bringing his clenched fist down straight onto Gerruso's ear. Gerruso bent over like a snapped twig. Pullara burst into an animal howl, one finger pointing straight up at the sky. Gerruso stood back up, both arms dangling at his sides.

"Pullara," he said.

His eyes hadn't wept a single tear.

As I walked home, a powerful white Vespa roared past, cutting across my path. Two men, both wearing full-face helmets. I saw myself reflected in the visors. My expression was relaxed, even though both hands had leaped to cover my mouth. It was an instinctive movement. The body bent over in anticipation of danger, warning the senses to react. In Palermo, the defensive crouch is an art handed down from one generation to the next. It becomes more refined as you grow in the city's womb. It was the helmets that made me crouch. No one wore helmets in the city, especially in that heat. Grandma said that heat waves made people lose their minds.

"Have you ever wondered why people kill each other over a parking space in the summer? It's the heat."

"Does that worry you?"

"Not in the slightest, light of my life, nothing can happen to me, I don't even have a driver's license."

Uncle Umbertino was already waiting out front.

He was bouncing on his toes.

"You're late, I've already been standing here for a hell of a long time, two minutes at the very least."

"We were all smacking the fool out of Gerruso."

"Who's Gerruso?"

"Just a kid."

"You rough him up good, so he felt it?"

"Yes."

"Good, there's always some good reason to beat the fool out of a body. But listen, there's been all kinda uproar in this neighborhood: engines roaring and screeching tires, more'n I'm used to."

"What does it mean?"

"How the fuck do I know, I'm no mechanic."

"Isn't Mamma home yet?"

"Do you think for one second that if your mother was upstairs, I'd be waiting here in the middle of the street in all this heat?"

"But don't you have your own keys to our apartment?"

"Yes."

"So why didn't you use them?"

"For two reasons. First of all, I wanted to make sure you had your keys, like you oughtta."

"Here they are."

"Make sure you don't lose them."

"What's the second reason?"

"I left the keys to your house at my house, absurd, ain't it? Now, let's go to the barbershop."

"But I don't want to get my hair cut, Mamma cuts my hair for me."

"Davidù, what the hell do I care about your hair, you'll come to the barbershop with me because I'm asking you, nice and polite, to come with me. Now get moving, because I'm already sick and tired of waiting."

There was a sign in red paint on the front of the barbershop.

TONY: SHAVE and HAIRCUT

Inside, sitting in the revolving chair, was an old man, his face coated in white foam. Standing next to him, straight razor in hand, was the barber, Tony.

"Is there much of a wait?" my uncle asked.

"This shave, haircut for the gentleman, then you."

"Do you have a horse-racing sheet?"

"What do you think? Would it be a barbershop without it? Right over there."

Umbertino took a seat, began reading intently about the ponies. I sat down next to him, on a red chair that creaked all over. In the stack of newspapers, a glossy magazine. On the cover, it said ADULTS ONLY. The pages were wrinkled and torn.

"So you're telling the truth, Tony?" the old man asked the barber. It seemed as if the foam was talking.

Every movement of Tony's body spoke eloquently of his sincere concern.

"I swear it's true, he was a certified genuine faggot."

"But didn't you notice at first that he was queer?"

"Now to look at him, he looked normal, an upstanding citizen, I even talked to him about the game, you understand? We talked 'bout soccer together, that's what I'm telling you."

"Ridiculous."

"Exactly."

The customer whose turn came before ours was sitting to my left. He had curly hair and a bristly mustache. He felt called upon to break into the conversation at this point in the story.

"But Tony, are you sure he didn't infect you?"

"Right! That's exactly the problem. This momosexuality is one hell of a disease."

"The worst thing there is," the customer with the mustache agreed.

"No laughing matter, that's for sure," the barber reiterated.

Finally Umbertino's voice. He spoke without lowering the racing sheet.

"I hear that them as get infected wind up taking it straight up the ass."

The whole shop burst into laughter.

"Shit, I done picked the wrong trifecta yesterday, oh well, what the hell," my uncle observed without a hint of irritation.

Now that Tony had had a laugh, he seemed more relaxed. He began using the straight razor on the old man's face.

"Listen, you all want to know how I found out he was gay? I swear it's God's own truth, on my mother's sainted head: he told me himself. He said: Now, friend, I happen to like men."

"No!" exclaimed the customer with the mustache.

"Yes."

"This world is going to hell."

"Right."

"They're the curse of all creation," murmured the old man, but gently, because if he moved his jaw too much he might get a new crease in his face. A straight razor doesn't take indignation into account.

"But wait, it gets even worse. Then I realized that this monster had gone and offered me a drink from his bottle of beer. The selfsame bottle he'd been drinking from all this time with his diseased mouth, I mean."

"So then whaddya do, Tony?" the old man asked with vivid concern.

The barber faltered for a moment. He squinted, raised the razor, and decided to go ahead and confide in his little audience.

"From that infected bottle of his, I had gone and taken a drink."

"Fuck! Disaster."

"Fuck is right."

"Infection!" said the old man, in a shrill voice.

The straight razor hovered in midair, a warning.

"Listen, I'm gonna tell you the truth, I was terrified. That momosexuality of his might have infected me, an oral infection straight from the bottle. I was terrified."

"So what *did* you do, Tony?"

"What do you think? First things first: I broke that bottle right over his head, that piece-of-shit queer."

"Good work, Tony!"

The old man's voice had regained confidence; breaking bottles over the heads of faggots is the behavior of true men.

"I thought I was 'bout to lose my mind."

"I can imagine."

"I had to do something to cure myself, immediately. So I thought it over and . . ."

Tony looked around, as if he were taking care to shield the information from prying ears. He pronounced each syllable solemnly.

". . . and I realized that I had to get cured, sooner than right this second, and so . . ."

Each person in the barbershop listened with a heightened intensity. Tony filled his lungs to give greater emphasis to the rest of the story: the old man's ears craned in the direction of the barber's mouth to capture the words of revelation at the earliest possible moment; the customer with the mustache stood up and began tapping his foot to an irregular beat. Only Uncle Umbertino remained unruffled. He read his racing sheet and blithely ignored everything and everyone. A burning curiosity to learn whether and how poor Tony had recovered from this momosexuality swept over me, just as it had all the others. I lowered my magazine.

Tony kept his eyes fixed elsewhere, staring out the shop window.

"I."

He reckoned the time needed for his words to clarify. Each time he sensed that the tension had become unbearable, he deigned to dole out another word or two.

"Done."

The old man's neck craned tautly; the mustachioed customer's foot trembled.

"Went to see."

Tony watched us. When the silence had grown deafening, he laid down his ace.

"Pina."

"The whore?" the old man and the man with the mustache cried in chorus.

"Yes."

"The whore in Vicolo Marotta?" they sang out in unison.

"Yes."

"One has the bedroom filled with mirrors?" they drove home the point.

"Yes."

At last Uncle Umbertino folded up his racing sheet and laid it on the pile with the others. Tony had one more spectator now. Flattered, he went on with renewed zeal.

"'Pina,' I told her, 'I gotta make love now, right this second, or else I'm in danger of catching a bad case of momosexuality, and that right there's a fate worse than death, iddnit?'"

"Blessed words of truth," the old man decreed.

"Luckily, I thought of the perfect remedy: get me a good fuck right then and there and get cured of that disgusting mess. These fucking queers, they all just need to be killed."

"Blessed words of truth," the old man seconded. Apparently, by the time you come to the end of your life, you're so tired that you have the same thoughts over and over again and you just go on repeating them.

"Boys, I look her straight in the eye and, 'fore we started to fucking, I said something to her that I never say to a whore: 'Pina, go rinse out your mouth, 'cause that's where I gotta kiss you, it's out the mouth that a disease can get going, you get me? I took a drink of beer from the same bottle as that faggot, come on, hurry up.' And Pina did things right, boys, she rinsed her mouth, nice and clean, even used toothpaste, and the minute she came back I shoved seven feet of tongue down her throat, fuck, I'd never even kissed my wife that deep."

"And then?"

It was Umbertino who spoke. He'd gotten to his feet without my noticing. I never saw him move.

"And then, seeing as I'm a gentleman, I can't exactly go into details, let's just say that I cured myself by fucking her like heaven above, and I needn't say another word to you men of the world."

Tony the barber was chuckling complacently, unaware of something that had become clear to everyone else. My uncle was there, in his shop, because of what had happened, the subject of Tony's story. He moved toward Tony soundlessly, light-footed in a way that no one would have expected from a man of his bulk. Leaping, little steps, quick and silent. When he loomed up in front of him, Tony vanished, hidden from view by his shoulders.

"Listen up and listen good, you dickhead, I'll tell you exactly how the story ends: you tripped, you fell, and shitty luck that you were having, you broke your arm. Or you broke your leg. Take your pick."

"I don't understand."

A second later, Tony was on his knees, keening in pain. My uncle's right hand was crushing the fingers of his left hand.

"Tony, it's either you can't understand, or you won't understand, which is worse. You tripped and fell, now take your pick: an arm or a leg."

Tony was sobbing. The old man and the mustachioed customer said nothing and did nothing, it was all they could do just to breathe.

Umbertino raised his left fist.

"Uncle."

My voice was calm.

Tony managed to mumble a single word: "Stop."

"But when Pina told you to stop, whaddya do, Tony, did you stop?"

He snapped Tony's left forearm with a single motion: his left hand grabbed Tony's elbow, his right hand grabbed Tony's wrist, he twisted both hands, crack.

"Now you remember, Tony, you tripped and fell, uh-huh? You broke your arm. Someone call this boy an ambulance. Davidù, let's get out of here. This place stinks of shit."

I was so overwhelmed that I forgot to leave the magazine. I didn't know a forearm could snap like that.

"You didn't see nothin', right?"

"Right."

"Swear to it."

"I swear."

"What's that you're holding?"

"A magazine, it was in the barbershop."

My uncle leafed through it carefully.

"Good boy, nice stuff you read; just don't let your mother catch you."

"Why not?"

"What do you mean, why not? It's a dirty magazine, if your mother catches you, she'll yell. Listen, here's what we do, I'll hold on to it, and when you wanna look at it, you just come see me, we good?"

Without waiting for my reply, he folded it in half and stuck it in his back pocket.

"Uncle, who's Pina?"

"She's a sort of friend of mine."

"What's that mean?"

"Well, let's just say she's cooked me dinner, once or twice."

"She a good cook?"

"Not as good as she used to be."

The street was cordoned off by a line of police cars.

"Another killing?" Umbertino asked an officer. The policeman lowered his head without saying a word.

I spoke to my uncle under my breath. I didn't want a cop to hear what I was saying to him.

"Why'd you take me with you to see the barber?"

In his face, not even a speck of joy.

"You were the only one that could stop me."

"From doing what?"

"You want a delicious ice cream?"

"Yessss!"

I ordered a cone, with pistachio and mulberry gelato.

"You heard him," Umbertino told the ice cream man. "A nice big ice cream cone with pistachio, mulberry, and whipped cream. Lots of whipped cream."

"But Uncle, I don't want any whipped cream."

"It isn't for you."

He devoured the whipped cream in a single bite.

Outside the front door, unexpectedly, we ran into Grandpa. Umbertino lengthened his stride and approached him. I hung back, it was too hot to hurry. Cars went past, the passengers looked around, their faces sweaty behind the closed windows. Umbertino and my grandfather shook hands, in complete silence. Then Umbertino came back toward me at a dead run.

"Davidù, hurry, gimme the keys to your apartment."

"Ain't Mamma home yet?"

"No, and your grandpa is leaving, come on, let's git upstairs, hurry!"

"I don't want to, I'll stay down here with Grandpa, then I wanna play with my friends on the piazza."

"Gimme your keys, then, and on the double!"

"Why?"

"I gotta take an Olympic-size shit. Come on, the keys, I'll take you to the piazza afterward, gimme the keys now!"

And off he gallopped upstairs to our apartment. The minute the street door swung shut behind him, Grandpa started talking.

"I came by to bring you some dinner, at work we had leftovers: potato gateau with ground beef filling. Come on over here, now, your face is filthy with ice cream."

He pulled out his handkerchief, raised it to his mouth, dabbed a corner of it against his tongue, and used it to clean my chin.

"Grandpa, Pullara says that if you want to be a real man you have to get yourself dirty. The filthier someone is, the more of a man he is."

"Pullara must have his head full of filth."

"What do you mean?"

"Look out."

A sudden screeching of tires caught us off guard. Grandpa's hands were already around my shoulders. The car swerved quickly, vanishing down the first street on the left.

"Calm down, Davidù, you can put them down."

Both my hands had leaped up to cover my face, without my even noticing.

"There's a lot of uproar," Grandpa mused aloud.

"Uncle said the same thing, the exact same words."

In the distance, the sound of police sirens was incessant.

"Grandpa, I know what it is: Fabrizia!"

"Who?"

"Fabrizia, the girl with the huge tits, works at the bakery. Everyone's coming to the neighborhood to buy bread; I hear all my friends say that Fabrizia is a hot mama."

"Do you like her?"

"Fabrizia? Well, she's a girl, I don't know if I like girls, they're always crying, they can't throw a punch to save their lives, they see blood and start screaming, they're weak."

"They're not weak."

"No?"

"No. I have to go to the train station to meet my friend Randazzo, why don't you go upstairs?"

"No, I'm going to go play with my friends, ciao."

The first thing I saw when I got to the piazza was Pullara bent over Gerruso, forehead crammed against forehead. Why didn't Gerruso just stay home? Couldn't he see that Pullara hated him, that Pullara was bigger and stronger than him?

Lele Tranchina and Danilo Dominici had their asses planted on the backrest of the bench and their shoes on the seat. Standing in the sun, Guido Castiglia had both hands jammed into his pockets. His shadow merged into the larger shadow of the magnolia tree. He was observing the scene with the remote indifference of someone watching ants. A couple of yards behind him, a girl. She must have been more or less my age.

No one noticed I was there.

My legs decided not to take another step.

My body was assuming a defensive crouch.

The girl was wearing a light-colored dress with a hem that hung just below her knees.

Red hair.

Pullara was shouting.

"Pass the test!"

Gerruso was whimpering incomprehensibly. Pullara spat a single gob of spit into his face, a gob that clung to his skin without sliding off. Then he ground his forehead even harder, with greater determination, against Gerruso's, shoving him downward, forcing him to his knees. Pullara's voice was piercing and strident.

It was too hot to get as worked up as he was.

"You have to pass the test!"

Pullara pulled a jackknife out of his pocket, opened it, and placed it in Gerruso's hand. He was so sure of himself that it never crossed his mind for an instant that he might be stabbed. Lele Tranchina tried to say something. He couldn't get the words out. Danilo Dominici was white as a sheet. Guido Castiglia kept his arms folded across his chest. The only voice that could be heard in the piazza was the girl's.

She spoke: "Stop it now." And then, "Why don't you take it out on me?" she went on. "I ain't scared of you," she concluded.

The last few words rang out for Pullara as a mortal insult.

"Wha'd you say?"

"I ain't scared of you," she said again. She spoke decisively, firmly, proudly.

Pullara moved jerkily. Like a human hiccup. He was about to lunge at the girl, but thought better of it, went back to Gerruso still kneeling on the ground, and delivered a sharp slap to his cheek.

Pullara's body language made it perfectly clear that some threshold had been crossed. Enough hesitation, no more fooling around, no more games. Now we'd entered the world of adults.

"Pass the test right now or I'ma cut your cousin's throat!" he threatened, pointing to the girl.

Gerruso, suddenly, stopped being a weakling. He raised his head without a whimper, just like that, from one instant to the next.

"Don't touch her," he said. His voice was cool and steady. Not a hint of begging.

"Pass the test or I'ma cut her throat!"

Everything about Pullara was wild, restless: legs, eyes, words.

Gerruso stood up.

The knife he held was no longer trembling.

"Swear to me that nothing bad will happen to my cousin."

Pullara, electrified, was waving both arms.

"Sure," he shouted, increasingly frantic.

Pullara was possessed, the world outside of the test no longer existed. He hadn't even noticed that he wasn't the one who was being asked to swear the oath. Gerruso's eyes, the only eyes in the whole piazza, were staring into mine.

"Yeah, yeah, yeah, I swear it, nothing'll happen to her, now you just pass the test, go on and cut, go on and cut."

Gerruso, unperturbed, insisted: "Swear to me that nothing bad will happen to my cousin."

Before I knew it, my mouth uttered a reply.

"I swear it."

Gerruso stopped staring at me. He gripped the knife firmly in his right hand and placed the blade carefully on the knuckle of his left forefinger. Tranchina gripped Dominici's hand and gnawed at his lip. Dominici was folded over, bent by abdominal cramps. The cousin lunged forward.

"You bastard."

Castiglia decided to step in. He grabbed her and pulled her close to him.

Pullara was jumping up and down in place.

"The test! The test!"

Gerruso swiveled his gaze back to me. He wasn't crying, he was no longer shivering. He took one last look at his cousin, saw that Castiglia was holding her back, concentrated his gaze on the jackknife, and just for an instant he reminded me of my grandpa, sitting at the cutting board slicing mushrooms, the knife held clear of his finger, the thumb pressing down on the stalk of the mushroom, the cap being sliced away, the jet of blood spraying into the air, the last section of forefinger tumbling as it fell, Dominici vomiting, Tranchina weeping, the cousin shouting, Castiglia gripping her close to him, Pullara howling, the bloody blade bouncing off the ground, Gerruso with the tip of his left forefinger gone, fainting away backward.

In the midst of all this, I thought I heard someone calling my name.

A dark blue car drove onto the piazza, kicking up a cloud of dust and gravel behind it. There was no time to admire the strip of dust that rose through the muggy heat. Another car, painted a metallic silver, appeared behind it. Through the open window on the passenger side an arm emerged, a hand gripping a pistol. I glimpsed my reflection in the window of the rear door. Once again, my hands had flown up to guard my face. Tranchina was sobbing. Dominici was holding his belly. The girl was looking down at Gerruso unconscious on the ground. Castiglia continued to hold her tight. Pullara, who hadn't noticed a thing, was bellowing.

And as I became more fully aware of that amputated finger, it dawned on me, for the first time in my life, what power and focus the sudden epiphany of a gunshot brings with it.

The shot was perceived first by my ears, such a deeply penetrating sound that the body needed to immediately contract every single muscle in order to absorb it. That lasted no more than an instant. Like a wave, it was followed by the physical consequences that came hard on the heels of the crack of gunfire: the thundering shot unleashed a sharp stab of pain in my eardrum, and the world seemed to stretch out. Everything seemed to slow down, like when you're underwater. It lasted a few seconds, then the bubble slowly popped.

A second shot rang out.

My shoulders shot forward, huddling together as if my body were trying to shrink.

The back window of the dark blue car shattered into a hailstorm of glass pebbles.

The number of shots kept climbing. Three, four, seven, ten. Hard to keep track of them all. Over near Castiglia and Gerruso's cousin, the window of a parked Alfa Romeo Alfasud exploded into shards. Broken glass flew in all directions, hitting the magnolia leaves with a sound like a sudden squall. In this jagged score of breaking glass, crumbling walls, screeching tires, punctured leaves, and rattling gunshots, I heard someone shouting my name, like an echo in the distance. On the far side of the piazza I saw Umbertino. He was running straight toward me. Long strides, torso angling forward, arms pumping the air. Meanwhile, they were returning gunfire from inside the dark blue car, bullets hitting the windshield of the silver car. The windshield collapsed. Swerving crazily, the car thudded against the side of the parked Alfasud. At the moment of impact, seeing the car hurtling in his direction, Castiglia lost control of his nerves and threw his hands up to grab his own hair, letting go of Gerruso's cousin. He started moving erratically back and forth, within a few yards' radius, like a fly trapped in an overturned water glass. Danilo Dominici was still throwing up. Lele Tranchina had pulled his head down, clamped tight between his elbows and knees. Umbertino was running. The gunshots continued to dominate.

Pullara, drunk with rage, was still sunk in his delirious visions. He leaned over and grabbed the knife and then strode in the direction of Gerruso's cousin with the smile of someone about to do harm.

The dark blue car swerved left, beyond the piazza. The silver car followed it unhesitatingly, vanishing around the corner. More gunshots could be heard, but now they were elsewhere.

Umbertino was no longer shouting my name. His eyes were on Pullara.

"What the fuck are you doing?"

Pullara was singing under his breath, gripping the jackknife.

Gerruso's cousin wasn't running away.

She held her gaze level, meeting his.

"I ain't scared of you."

Pullara seemed to be invincible. He seemed to be the shark fish going to war.

I was wrong.

The shark fish wasn't him.

The shark fish was me.

But I didn't know that yet.

Umbertino was about thirty feet away from us.

Too far.

Pullara raised his fist, gripping the jackknife still smeared with Gerruso's blood.

She didn't back down.

He threw his head back, poised to drive the stabbing blade as deep as possible. It was only then that the danger became concrete, and in that instant no other possibilities remained, and the shark fish remembered the oath he had sworn and finally surged onto the battlefield.

The body acted on its own.

A distant urge.

A seed sown a lifetime ago was suddenly sprouting.

My legs took me straight in front of Pullara.

Umbertino was cursing the names of the saints.

I alone stood between the girl and the knife.

She had dark eyes.

She smelled of salt and lemon.

I felt no fury, I felt no anger.

I was as calm and unruffled as the wrath of God.

I plunged my fists into Pullara's face, once twice three times four times. He tried to stab me but missed. A leap back and away, that's all it took. Pullara was off balance. A push with both feet and my right fist sank deep into his belly, forcing him to bend double toward me. My left uppercut rose dizzyingly, shattering his incisors. Before his back could hit the ground, I was already hurtling through the air. I landed with both knees on his gut. I clenched my fists and pounded him over and over again until my uncle managed to drag me off his body. He lifted me with both arms and clutched me to him.

My hands were bloody, my knuckles were skinned.

Beyond my filthy fingers, there she stood.

In the street behind the piazza: shouts, ambulances, and police sirens.

The sound track of Palermo.

Uncle checked what was left of Pullara.

"That'll teach him to treat women like dirt; what a dickhead."

Danilo Dominici and Lele Tranchina sat riveted to the steel bench.

Castiglia, motionless somewhere not too far from us, had a lifeless gaze.

Umbertino stopped Gerruso's bleeding with a handkerchief.

Gerruso finally seemed serene, now that he'd fainted.

My uncle spoke to the girl.

"Honey, are you all right? An ambulance and the cops are all coming, can I leave you here? Can you take care of yourself? My nephew and I have to get out of here, right this second."

"Wait," she replied.

Calm and confident, she stopped looking at Gerruso and came over to me.

"Ciao," she said.

I couldn't utter a word.

She took my filthy fingers in her hands.

"Ain't nothing but blood," she murmured, "it washes off."

She lifted my fingers to her lips.

One by one.

She washed away the pain.

I had a hollow feeling in my stomach, as if I were on a swing.

"I'm Nina," she said. Then she smiled and I fell off the swing.

My uncle tousled my hair.

"Let's go before the cops get here."

My fingers fanned open, clamped shut, then I was done saying goodbye to her.

A few minutes later, I was back in the gym, putting on my boxing gloves and climbing up into the ring, for the first time in my life.

I thought about her the whole time.

My grandfather Rosario came home to Palermo after being held as a prisoner of war in Africa. There was nothing left for him; the war had swept away his family, his house, his friends. The field of the present day was swept clean of the tumbleweeds of the past. His life was a blank sheet of paper. He wore a military uniform two sizes too big for him. He was sleeping in the ruins of bombed-out buildings. He spent his days at Cape Gallo. He would peel an apple and save the peel in a handkerchief: that would be his evening meal. He stared at the sea.

Provvidenza's curiosity was aroused by his skinny profile. He looked like a statue. She shut her book and studied my grandfather while her cigarette burned between her fingers, then she opened the book again; her final exam was drawing nearer, and the bus for Capaci was always late.

The next day, the same scene. The young man carved in stone was still there, on the bench, as if he'd never moved. She sat down, on a low wall, a dozen feet away from him. She watched him for a long time. He didn't look around. She did her best to concentrate on the textbook she was studying, but my motionless grandfather had become a puzzle that demanded an immediate solution.

"Soldier, what are you looking at?"

He turned around and stared at her, in absolute silence.

"What did he say to you?"

"Davidù, it was your grandpa. He said nothing, and just looked at me."

"What was he like?"

"He was young, thin as a rail, and had these indecipherable, light-colored eyes. He was confused, poor thing."

"And did you fall in love with him right then and there?"

"Not in the slightest. When I first saw him, to tell you the truth, I just thought he was odd. And so skinny, too skinny. Still, there was something about him."

"See? You were in love."

"I already told you I wasn't. Even though . . ."

"What?"

"He had these eyes that—well, you know it yourself—it's something you all have, you, your father, Rosario. Men with light-colored eyes and a very dangerous gaze."

"Dangerous how?"

"Your gaze troubles the soul of anyone you look at."

"Really? I never noticed."

"Neither did your grandfather or your father. That's why you're such lady-killers, damned light-colored eyes."

"I don't understand."

"Of course you don't, you're not a girl."

"Soldier, did you hear me? I asked you: What are you looking at?"

Silence and nothing more.

"Hey, can you understand me when I talk to you? Are you from around here?"

He tipped his head forward in a sign of assent. A small movement, the very minimum required. Better than nothing. Suddenly, amid that growing silence, she had a hunch.

"You aren't mute, are you?"

A tiny smile escaped his lips, a more than satisfactory response. He wasn't mute, just stingy with words to the point of miserliness.

"What are you up to? I've seen you here for two days now, motionless, staring out to sea. What are you looking at?"

No answer. A sphinx. Nothing she liked better than a puzzle. She tried looking at it from another angle.

"What's your name?"

"Rosario."

Heavens above, he had actually spoken. In fact, he'd even added an extra syllable: "You?"

"My name is Provvidenza."

Her lips parted in a smile, spontaneous and inviting.

His face showed no reaction.

"But he did gesture for me to come sit next to him. There was room to sit down, I was on my feet by that point, he didn't seem to have the slightest interest in standing up, so I sat down next to him."

"Did you talk to each other?"

"Do you really think we talked, Davidù? I asked the occasional question, and he would mumble, dip his head, things like that. Non-verbal communication. 'Were you in the war?' and he'd dip his head in my direction. 'And where were you stationed?' and silence. 'Do you smoke?' and he'd shake his head no. 'Wait, are you sure you're not mute?' and then he'd smile, but softly, and never a sound that passed his lips. Why I didn't start slapping him is still a mystery to me."

"You were head over heels in love."

"No, knucklehead. Really, I was just curious about him. Seeing that he hardly bothered to look at me, I pulled out the book I was studying for my exam, Lucretius's *De rerum natura*, because back then, school was serious, if you wanted to teach elementary school you had to know Latin. It's important to know Latin, in that language you'll find the past of our own language, its whole logical structure. Come on now, declension of *rosa*."

"I don't want to."

"Come on, I told you."

"*Rosa*, first declension: *rosa, rosae, rosae, rosam, rosa, rosa*."

"*Lupus*."

"Grandma, you were telling me about Grandpa."

"Latin is important, very important."

"*Lupus*, second declension: *lupus, lupi, lupo, lupum, lupe, lupo*."

"Good boy. Now, where was I?"

"The book."

"So, I pull the book out of my purse and the minute I open it, Davidù, I swear to you, I felt his gaze pierce me through."

"Grandpa's."

"He was staring at me with a new expression."

"Like how?"

"I couldn't say, Davidù, but in that instant his gaze had a light to it that was—how to put this?—gentle and sweet."

"And you fell in love."

"Yes."

He had taken her fingers in his hands, as carefully as you would pick up a green sprout, and yet as desperately as you would if you were grabbing the only handhold that stood between you and a deadly fall.

"Teach me to read and write."

And in the presence of that unexpected revelation of vulnerability, when faced with the humility of that unexpectedly straightforward request, the instant the fragile reed of his voice fell silent, Provvidenza found that she, once so facile and fluent, was suddenly at a loss for words. She was simply smiling at the man who would become her first pupil, the silent love of her life.

"Whores, all bombs are whores."

Salvo Pecoraro was cursing; his house was gone. The bedroom where he'd been born, the round table made of dark wood, the cane-bottom chairs, the bed with a wrought-iron headboard, the photograph of his mother, Assunta, may she rest in peace, amen. Nothing had survived. To clutch at material certainties is not of this life. Umbertino watched him dig through the rubble. The surrounding buildings were intact, only Salvo Pecoraro's house, bull's-eyed by the bomb, was gone now, collapsing in upon itself, dying a mortifying death. It had not been transformed into a myriad of fragments hurtling murderously in all directions. Amid misfortune, a memorable piece of dumb luck.

Umbertino had lost his own house four days earlier. A chunk of stone weighing an eighth of a ton from the building across the street entered the house without so much as knocking, and went on to demolish the kitchen, the bathroom floor, two load-bearing walls, the bedroom where, fingers knitted behind the nape of his neck, my great-uncle would lie dreaming of women with clean, fragrant skin. The dining-room balcony remained intact, with his mother's red geraniums still proud and present, as if nothing had happened. Those flowers reminded him of the lipstick traces left behind after sex. Umbertino decided that shrapnel and hurtling fragments just weren't his friends. He'd been saved from death in that explosion because he was elsewhere, fucking. That realization filled him with pleasure. He even managed to smile in the face of what from that day forward and forever after would no longer be his home. The only relative who remained to him, his sister, my mother's mother, had been evacuated to Terrasini, a small village twenty miles away from the city. He had chosen to remain behind: I'll survive, don't worry about me, Sis, I always get by. He had no one to answer to. He was the sole master of his fate. He was almost nineteen years old.

He asked a stranger for a cigarette with a glance and was given one, ducked his head in thanks, lit it, sucked the smoke into his lungs. All around him, people were digging, cursing, finding friends, consoling one another, weeping, and shouting that all bombs are whores.

But bombs aren't whores.

Bombs don't have feelings.

Whores, on the other hand.

They have feelings, and how.

Feelings to spare, if not to sell.

Not all whores, of course.

But some of them.

Some of them could be entrusted with a life during a bombing raid and keep it intact. They'd give that life back, all sweet-smelling and safe.

The way Giovannella the whore did.

She had told him that she'd gladly give her life for him.

And in fact.

It happened one night. The bombs were raining down out of the sky. Yes, it's true, it was the grip of my uncle's hand that pulled her along in an exhausting panting race to the door of the bomb shelter, still mercifully left open. But when the air turned incandescent and the sound drilled into the ears so furiously that it made you lose your balance, it was Giovannella who shoved him to the ground, just as an eighteen-inch-long section of shrapnel tore into her chest, coming to a halt inside her love-warmed heart. Giovannella flew backward, fell to the ground, and slammed her head against the smooth stone slab of the road's surface, but it didn't matter—she was already dead. Umbertino couldn't seem to get out a single word. Not a single word of love.

It's not time that creates the hierarchies of love. One might feel a once-in-a-lifetime, precious love for a prostitute met just two weeks earlier and then lost, just like that, during a hail of bombs falling from the heavens. And since all around him he heard cursing, screaming, thundering collapses, weeping, roars, and sirens, Umbertino decided to say to hell with all the sounds of war, caressed Giovannella's still-warm forehead, carefully closed her eyes, and went away, leaving her there. The dead cannot save their own lives.

Giovannella had never asked him for money. She really loved him. Umbertino was handsome, with a harsh and melancholy beauty. When she undressed in front of him for the first time, Giovannella felt a hint of shame to be seen naked. Maybe I'm not so beautiful after all, she thought to herself. She was seventeen years old. It was a single instant, a tiny fragment of time, that made her fall in love all the more, one of those rare moments remembered forever, expanding in one's memory. It was an unexpected, unclothed pirouette that Umbertino performed in front of her. Giovannella the whore laughed with the fullness of her lips, her eyes, and her heart. What came next—my uncle's rough embrace—dispelled all doubt, all fear, all shame. Their kiss was shameless, moist. The way it ought to be. And they loved each other. It lasted two weeks. Fourteen days. Fourteen nights. A roaring, sweaty, passionate love. Happiness within reach.

Then the bombs came.

In Palermo, there were corpses everywhere. Every courtyard, every street, every family was mourning a loss. Umbertino felt his own shoulders, once so broad and powerful, suddenly narrow and become measly. His shoulders had failed to protect Giovannella.

That's war, he told himself.

It happens.

The only way to outsmart war is to survive.

Don't let yourself get attached to anything.

Or anyone.

Follow your instincts.

He started to spend practically all his time with whores. One had already saved his life. Now another did. A certain Mariù, flaming red hair just like Giovannella. She was the one he was fucking when a two-hundred-pound chunk of concrete thundered into his bedroom but failed to find him in. Mariù the whore. He'd been looking everywhere for her for four days. Slowly. Like in any self-respecting exodus. In no particular hurry. One step after the other. Rain soaks you, wind dries you out. The road to Golgotha is always an uphill climb.

There was no way to bury people anymore. They'd already used all the wood to make coffins. There were no tools left to dig graves. Dead bodies were abandoned, heaped on top of one another. The corpses were rotting. Insects danced on them. The streets reeked of death. The center of every square was piled high with rubble from collapsed buildings. Sometimes, if you dug down, you might find a human limb.

In Borgo, a man was singing: "Down will come cradle, baby and all."

He might have been thirty. Clutched tightly to his chest he held a hand attached to a ragged shred of arm, which had been severed below the shoulder joint. The end of it was white: a jutting bone. That was all that was left of his daughter. The man was singing, wobbling back and forth, back and forth, then an epileptic fit swept over him and he stopped singing. When they came to his aid, no one paid any attention to the arm that tumbled into the dust.

Umbertino came to a halt for a few seconds too long in a place he couldn't seem to recognize. He lacked landmarks. He raised his eyes and saw the light of the sky. A curse welled up in him from the depths of his heart. He managed to tamp it down. That's not the sort of thing you do if you want to survive, you have to train yourself to feel nothing. He went on walking but after seven steps he stumbled over all that remained of a leg. It was crawling with flies and worms. My uncle said to hell with all his resolutions about self-control and let out a mighty curse, a furious despairing oath, inveighing against everything and everyone, with the sole exception of Saint Rosalia.

It made him feel great.

———

The house with the rose garden was in Piazza delle Sette Fate. A perfect place to take women. But now it was gone, struck by a bomb one afternoon while a March downpour was pounding the city, sudden and fierce. Water was manna from heaven in those days of misery. So everyone ran out into the street to gather as much water as they could. Almost immediately, an unexpected air-raid siren announced an impending attack. The sound ripped through the air, scattering the joy of standing upright in the rain. Bombing raids at this time of day—what fresh hell was this? As the fear rose, they gathered pails and basins and hurried toward the nearest shelter, where those present were counted, and as time passed, they prayed, hoped, embraced, and swore.

The sky darkened with aircraft and, in the space that separates Palermo from the clouds, the bomb had already been dropped. In the instant of impact, it created a small sun that struck the falling rain, forming a beautiful rainbow, and then the house with the rose garden no longer existed.

The silence of Piazza delle Sette Fate was shattered by a roar drawing closer, as Umbertino cursed all the saints on their crosses.

"Did you know what was gonna happen next, Uncle?"

"How the fuck could I, Davidù? I'm no fortune-teller."

"Were you afraid?"

"You want the truth?"

"Obviously."

"I was just dying for it to happen. Wasn't nothing I wanted more: fists crunching into ribs, the fury of battle."

"But how'd you know, Uncle?"

"Same way you knew."

"Instinct?"

"Blood don't lie."

At the sound of that avalanche of curses and oaths, the people who were in Piazza delle Sette Fate stopped excavating. Maybe it was just tension, or perhaps it was a sincere desire to defend the faith, or else the simple need to let off steam. For those who were digging in the piazza, that stream of profanities was more than they could take.

"Shut your mouth," a voice called out in warning.

Umbertino slowed to a stop. Enveloped as he was in dust, no one could sense the actual dimensions of his body.

But his voice.

Firm, calm, sharp.

Like the well-honed blade of a knife.

He savored that silence. Then he let loose again, cursing God and the Virgin Mary.

Sensing his contempt, everyone decided to forget that under the rubble there might still be something to find. Or perhaps it was simply that the time to stop digging had come. Their hands hurt and their lungs burned.

"I told you once: Shut your mouth."

"And if I don't?"

They wiped their eyes to get a better look at the man on whom they'd be taking out their violent impulses. His outline was vague, hard to see.

"If you don't I'll break your ass in half."

"So will I," added someone else.

"And maybe I'll join in."

"Me, too."

Umbertino looked up, spread his arms wide, and offered his breast up to the clash of battle.

"Let's go."

There were eleven of them. No one moved a muscle.

In that silence, it was impossible to hear anyone breathing, no rumors of war.

My uncle's hands clenched into fists.

"How'd you feel?"

"It felt like nothing I'd ever felt in my life."

"What do you mean?"

"I felt as free as a murderer."

They couldn't make up their minds to attack him.

That wasn't right.

What was missing was battle.

What was missing was blood.

What was missing was slaughter for everything to be perfect.

Umbertino made perfection attainable.

He cursed the uncurseable.

Umbertino cursed Rosalia, patron saint of Palermo.

He was as calm and unruffled as the August sea.

"Now come at me, you assholes."

Emotion overwhelmed all sense of strategy. All eleven of them went for him, lunging as one. A pack without a leader. They attacked him, ready to devour him, without a glimmer of understanding that the prey wasn't him. They were the prey.

He used his fists.

He needed nothing more.

The men collapsed the way sand collapses.

He drove his fists into the flesh of one and then of the next and then of yet another.

A ravening and contented beast.

The fight hardly lasted a minute.

He shattered arms, jaws, ribs, teeth, cheekbones.

When it was over, five men lay sprawled on the ground, and six others stood staring at Umbertino. My uncle looked at his hands and in them he read the future.

He found Mariù with the red hair two days later, at the Sant'Orsola cemetery. She wore a filthy dress. He called her by name. She turned around and failed to recognize him. He explained to her that fucking her had saved his life. She pretended to find that interesting. The story came to an end and was followed by a silence that failed to fill anything up. He came straight to the point and asked her how much. She named her price.

"Too much."

"How much do you have?"

They went past the last row of headstones, behind the larch trees. As soon as he was done, Umbertino stood up, buttoned his pants, and left without a word. He never saw her again.

He was the first boxer in my family.

Il Negro.

No one knew what his real name was.

Umbertino met him during a street fight. A round of bets was placed, and on the basis of how much money was in the pot, a prize was set aside for the winner, and when the word was given, fists began to fly. Umbertino was the last man standing, all his adversaries were flat on the pavement. That's how he made a living until the middle of 1945. He was twenty-one years old, his fists were deadly weapons, and he had no technique whatsoever. That's how matters stood the day he met *Il Negro*.

When he spoke *Il Negro*'s name, Umbertino paused in mid-sentence. He listened to the silence that followed the name he had uttered. His respect for his maestro is a sentiment that has remained intact, despite the passage of time.

Il Negro landed in Sicily with the U.S. Navy. Less than a week later, he deserted. He spent his days in the taverns of Palermo, soaking up alcohol like a sponge.

"Of course, it's not like he went unnoticed, Davidù, he was completely black. Why didn't they come arrest him, you ask me? Shit, first they had to catch him, and even if they caught him, they'd still have to stay on their feet. *Il Negro* was too damned murderous, he bruised my ass red, white, and blue."

In their first fight, *Il Negro* punched him so hard and long that Umbertino fell in love with him then and there. He was skinny and gnarly and he reeked of booze. My uncle was bigger, stronger, and soberer. A heavyweight up against a middleweight. It should have been no contest. Instead, not even a minute into the bout, there was no mistaking the foregone conclusion—and it wasn't the one everyone expected. Umbertino couldn't lay a glove on him. Big as he was, all it would have taken was a punch, a single roundhouse and he would have decked him. But the other guy was a grasshopper. He kept hopping out of the way. Umbertino couldn't seem to get him in his sights. He'd throw a right cross and with an agile hop *Il Negro* was already somewhere else. The instant that Umbertino pulled his fist back toward his torso to recharge it for another slug, *Il Negro*'s fists were hammering away at his face, his chest, his forearms. He'd never met anyone as fast as that. Umbertino stayed put, feet flat on the mat, dealing out punches in all directions. *Il Negro* danced around him and disfigured him. No, he wasn't a grasshopper. He was a butterfly. After seven rounds, Umbertino had a shattered eyebrow, a swollen upper lip, bruises on his chin, a cut over his left cheekbone, and pristine knuckles on both hands. *Il Negro* just kept fluttering. His feet made no noise. The bout ended in the tenth round; Umbertino hadn't had the chance to land a single punch. *Il Negro* took the money, clenched it in his fist, and said: "Booze." Umbertino was devoured by shame. He lunged at him and grabbed him by the arm.

"Teach me to box."

Il Negro shook him loose, spat on the floor, and went off to get drunk.

That was the first lesson.

Humiliation burns worse than the punches you take.

"That was my first real boxing match. I thought that a fistfight was just a matter of strength. Hitting harder, hitting meaner. But not only did *Il Negro*'s punches grind you down, they were beautiful to behold. What destroys you is precision, not just strength. He'd destroyed my face. He had to become my maestro, there was no other way."

He searched all of Palermo. He found him at the Taverna Azzurra. *Il Negro* was getting drunk on Sangue di Cristo wine. His hands were shaking. He was so befuddled that it would have been child's play this time to lay him to waste.

"You understand, Davidù, there in front of me, reduced to a wine-soaked rag, was the man who had clobbered my face with fists that felt like a couple of bricks."

"So what'd ya do?"

"What could I do? The only reasonable thing: I swallowed my pride and went over to talk to him."

Il Negro hated everyone. White, yellow, black. Everyone. He took my uncle on as a pupil only because he gave him the right answer at the right time.

"Teach me your movements, your feints, all your technique, come on, teach me how to box."

He wouldn't so much as look at him. He reached out for his glass of wine. Umbertino grabbed his wrist just as he grabbed his wineglass.

"Crying all over yourself like this is for women."

"Is there a manly way of doing it?"

"Sure, while you're crying you can always beat someone bloody."

Il Negro trained him till he could barely stand. He taught him that when you throw a punch, it doesn't start from the arm, that you don't plant your foot on the ground—it should barely graze the floor, that sliding motion gives you room while keeping your eyes on your opponent's. He changed the way Umbertino walked and how he held his shoulders, his posture. He positioned him in front of a mirror, telling him to punch the empty air over and over again, following a specific sequence of crosses. He showed him how to release muscle tension by jumping rope. He decided what and how much Umbertino could eat. He forbade him to drink water at the end of each sparring session. He prohibited alcohol. Once in a while, laughing hoarsely, he would throw an empty beer bottle into the air, and the instant the broken glass littered the floor, "Take off your shoes and jump all over it." That's how Umbertino learned to land on the mat lightly: by slinging his feet onto broken glass.

Il Negro transformed his body. That's how my uncle became so agile. He was a heavyweight forced to become light on his feet because he was being trained by a middleweight. But the real metamorphosis was taking place inside his head. Day by day, Umbertino clad himself in an increasingly glacial calm, the result of a growing self-awareness. He was learning to fully appreciate his talent for mayhem.

Il Negro taught him to do push-ups and knee bends. He taught him a series for the abdominals, the upper, middle, and lower, then the dorsals and the extensor muscles. He designed choreographies of attack and counterattack just for him, strategies for occupying the center of the ring. And, more than anything else, he made him run. Speed, resistance, sprints. In the hot sun and the pouring rain. Before and after sparring sessions. In the morning, first thing. Every goddamn day, several times a day, until he fell to the ground, cramping, vomiting from the effort, trembling with sudden spurts of diarrhea. Still, in spite of everything, he went on running just the same. My uncle possessed an indestructible will.

Il Negro spoke Italian. His father was a Lucanian emigrant and a complete bastard. Someone stabbed his old man to death when he was just seven in a fight over women; so much the better, he deserved all eight inches of the blade that plunged into his heart. His mother was black. She cleaned house, worked variously as a cook and a streetwalker, and did anything she could to put bread on the table. She died of scurvy when he was twelve. *Il Negro* explained to Umbertino that in America there are couples like his parents, of different colors, that they are few in number, and that being born into such a family is terrible luck. He told him that his boxing skills were noticed by a Campanian emigrant in the street one day. *Il Negro* was fighting with a young Irishman who objected to the sight of a Negro walking on a public sidewalk, and he was pounding the Irishman's face in. He was thirteen years old. He walked into the gym as a nobody, but when he left he was a champion. He said that it would be feasible, if challenging, to teach Umbertino to box, he had grit and talent and maybe, someday, who could say? He added that it was beyond anything the Good Lord ever intended, though, to teach Umbertino to speak English. That's when he stopped talking and ordered him to start running.

Il Negro was twenty-seven years old and there wasn't a mark on his face.

"You should have seen him box, Davidù. He moved toward the center of the ring, jumping and turning like a racehorse, stretching his neck to uncrick it, raising his right guard, and then suddenly, as if by magic, he was gone, and a butterfly had taken his place. Was all that work worth it? If only you could have seen him even once. *Il Negro* didn't box. *Il Negro* floated; he flew."

His first fight with *Il Negro* as his trainer came seven months later. It was held just outside of Palermo, in Bagheria, in the courtyard of a school, with only a few spectators. His opponent was a father from Siracusa, age thirty-three, tipping the scales at 298 pounds, with broad shoulders, giant hands, a hairy chest, and good eyes. Umbertino was no longer the trash-talking youngster who until just seven months earlier was slaughtering citizens in the alleyways of Palermo. He'd discovered new muscles. He was acquiring an impeccable technique. He danced on the tips of his toes and he was damned fast. He fought like a veteran, focused and measured. His maestro had made a few offhand comments to the effect that he might actually have a shot at winning something big.

Il Negro didn't show up in Bagheria. Umbertino never found out why. He finally tracked his maestro down late that same night at the Taverna Azzurra, drunk as a skunk. He sat down at his table without asking a thing. He sat there in silence, watching his maestro steadily destroy himself. The minute *Il Negro* finally passed out, Umbertino threw him over his shoulder and carried him home.

He'd won the fight by a knockout in the second round. The Syracusan's eyes were two puddles of blood.

Il Negro stopped drinking, cold, the next day.

"He was all boxer in his head, so when he set out to do something he just did it, in a way that left everyone else with no option but to suck his dick."

He was there for Umbertino's next twenty-one bouts.

Unlike many other trainers, he almost never said a word. When they met at ringside between rounds, he'd ask: "How are you doing, Umberto?" The arrogance of the answer was enough to reassure him. *Il Negro* delivered his orders with a calm that would brook no transgressions. Generally speaking, his instructions never varied: to take a specific punch in a specific part of the body in order to test his opponent's power.

"And then?" Umbertino asked.

"Kill him."

Twenty-one bouts.

Twenty-one knockouts.

Il Negro explained the rules of boxing to him and the underlying logic of the division by weight into different categories. Umbertino trained and listened. *Il Negro* told him which attacks scored points and which didn't and which ones were necessary to demolish the opponent's fortress. Umbertino got better and stronger, growing from one fight to the next. *Il Negro* told him the story of the finest fights in a career—his career—that had been interrupted when he was drafted. He taught him to understand his opponent by the way he used his feet. Umbertino went on disfiguring every boxer who dared to challenge him. *Il Negro* told him about Billy Bob Bartelli, also known as "The Wizard of Brooklyn," and Foster "The King" Monroe, a redheaded Scotsman with the finest footwork he'd ever seen. He confided in Umbertino the story of when he fought for the middleweight title and lost.

"What about you, Umbè?"

"What do you mean, what about me, Maestro?"

There was no point in answering him.

The Italian heavyweight title.
The goal had been established.

The first match in the legendary series of twenty-one consecutive knockouts by the boxer-trainer duo of Umbertino and *Il Negro* was in the summer of 1946. The last one came in December 1949. Between those two dates were a series of unofficial fights, all of which ended with the opponent flat on his back on the mat.

They lived together, in the Vucciria, in Piazza Garraffello. They illegally occupied the upper floor of the still-intact wing of a palazzo that had been hit by bombs. They had set up a dignified little apartment there: two bedrooms, a kitchen, a bathroom, and a small terrace where they could bring women. With the prize money from the fights, they managed to get by.

They started talking about whether it would be a good idea to start a boxing gym together.

"There's not a fucking thing in Palermo, what do you say, Maestro?"

Il Negro bought material to construct heavy bags, weightlifting equipment, jump ropes. Umbertino spent his money on women. They never had a disagreement about money. In the world of boxing, more and more, people were talking about them.

"Have you ever been anywhere outside of Palermo, Umberto?"

"Once I went to Cefalù, Maestro."

"Get ready to travel, we're going to Bologna."

"Where's that?"

"In Italy."

"To do what?"

"To knock everyone we meet unconscious."

Il Negro had enrolled him in a tournament.

The climb to the title was under way.

Umbertino didn't keep his newspaper clippings, his plaques, the trophies that proclaimed him the king of Italian heavyweights. He threw everything away the day he bought his boxing gym.

"I never needed tokens of recognition from other people. All I've ever needed to do is lock eyes with anybody who was around back then."

"What happens?"

"They still get out of my way."

When Umbertino came home on one of the last days of December 1949 he found *Il Negro* stinking drunk. He always swore to me that he never knew why that age-old despair resurfaced in his maestro. He wondered about it in the years that followed, but he never could come up with a plausible explanation. On the far side of the kitchen, there was a sizable crack in the wall. *Il Negro* had simply unleashed his fists on the wall. The backs of his hands were covered with blood, all his fingers were torn and scraped. Umbertino crouched down next to him. The smell of alcohol was pungent. They were just two bouts short of the national heavyweight title.

"Maestro, what happened?"

Il Negro held his face between his ravaged hands. He uttered only one short sentence to his pupil.

"Are you training to become a man?"

He didn't bother to wait for the answer.

He rummaged in his pockets and pulled out a scrap of paper.

On it was written: "Have you become the man you dreamed of being? What gives you balance? Is it fame? Strength? Power? Sailing a boat? Drinking chilled wine when the sirocco is blowing? The smell of fried eggplant? Do you have what you want? Do you have a hand that will caress your back when you need it? Then why didn't you pursue this idea of peace? Why haven't you practiced to summon those long afternoons filled with the chirping of crickets and the voices of your children?"

Il Negro vanished from Palermo on the last day of that year, 1949. A dozen people swore that they saw him on the Santa Lucia wharf boarding a ship for Genoa. Umbertino tried for years to find out what had happened to him, without success. *Il Negro* managed to cover his tracks. As he appeared, so he vanished: a flutter of wings and he was gone.

≋

"Your mother is right, and I don't want to hear another word about it."

"But Uncle, you actually left him lying on the pavement."

"The cops were coming, I gave him my handkerchief to stop the blood, and anyway he's your friend."

"He's not my friend."

"You're the one who knows him, now shut up because you're starting to annoy me."

My uncle was driving with a new caution, the risk of more shootouts was ever present. With every car that went by, his eyes busily inspected the landscape. Surveying the field of battle.

"Uncle, I don't want to go to the hospital to see Gerruso."

"What do you think, I'm overjoyed to have to drive you there? The truth is that women should stay at home instead of going to work, the way your mother does. Because she's never home, I have to bear the cross of going with you to the hospital."

"But Uncle, Gerruso is such a loser, they didn't even take him to Mamma's hospital. I don't want to go visit someone who's missing a piece of his finger. That's time I'll lose and never get back."

"What do you know about loss?"

"I'm nine years old, I know things, believe me."

I knew that you lose the things you possess. You lose your string, your patience, your finger bone, the time you waste, the afternoons you spend sitting in traffic, the coins you drop into a pay phone, your pencil sharpener, the buttons off your shirt, the words on the tip of your tongue.

"Davidù, look at how handsome this hand is, look at how big and strong it is. You know what keeps it on the steering wheel? Patience. That's what. And if I lose my patience, you know where this hand will wind up? You understand, angel face? Wait a minute, let's stop here for a minute, this coffee shop makes great espresso."

He double-parked the dark blue Fiat 126, walked into the café, and stepped up to the counter.

"Hey, I'd like a nice hot espresso the way you know how to make 'em, and a glass of sparkling water for my nephew."

A trio of well-dressed gentlemen came into the bar. They were loudly discussing the killing that had taken place three hours earlier in the Sperone district: an ex-convict found dead with a third eye in his forehead. They talked about symbols: if the murdered man has his testicles in his mouth it means he started up some trouble with the wrong woman; feet encased in a block of cement and then a plunge into the sea is the fate reserved for those who pocket the mob's money; a dead man with a fish in his mouth is someone who talked too much. They were about to explore the significance of the corpse dissolved in acid, when the tallest of the three turned to the barman and, in a jocular tone, gave his order.

"*Buon giorno,* could you make us three manly espressos, black, no sugar?"

Umbertino immediately swiveled his head around, staring intently at the trio of new arrivals. Once the discomfort had ripened fully, he deigned to address them.

"You know, maybe I misunderstood, but did you just call me a woman?"

The three citizens were more surprised than baffled.

"Is something bothering you?"

"Ah, so now you decide to pretend like you don't know what I'm talking about?"

"What *are* you talking about?"

Everyone in the café stopped to watch the scene unfold. No one was good-hearted enough to meddle.

My uncle turned to confront the trio, turning his back to the barman. He spoke in a low voice, forcing everyone to turn their ears in his direction.

"So let me get this straight. I'm here in the café, minding my own business with my nephew, drinking an espresso in goddamned peace, when you three come in and accuse me in front of everyone of being a total woman."

"What on earth?"

"Now you're taking back what you just said a minute ago?"

The barman, the cashier, the customers, me: we were all wondering just what Umbertino was driving at. My uncle sensed that the eyes of everyone in the café were on him. There's always a ring, there's always an audience.

The three men were uneasy. Their feet were shuffling and wouldn't stay still.

"Believe me, nobody here would have dared to say . . ."

Umbertino rose up on tiptoes. Maybe it was an involuntary reflex, or perhaps an intentional pose to heighten the drama.

"Oh, no? But when you walk into a café and order 'three manly espressos, black, no sugar,' what are you trying to say, eh?"

"But . . ."

Umbertino luxuriated in that growing doubt, the rising anxiety, the sense of danger that was ripening.

"Ah, now you're acting as if you don't know what I'm talking about. Then let me spell it out for you. For people like you, anyone who drinks their coffee with sugar is a total woman because you three, real macho men, you're citizens who take your coffee bitter, look how strong you are, the flavor nice and pure, and sugar is something strictly for women, so that means that I, who was sitting here drinking my nice hot espresso with sugar, you're telling me in front of my nephew that I'm just a woman."

The customers murmured, considered, and after thinking it over, decided that he was right.

The three new arrivals, demonstrating an impeccable ability to assume a defensive crouch, immediately sensed the sudden change in the wind.

"Listen, I beg your pardon, I certainly meant no offense, I shouldn't have spoken, entirely my fault."

Umbertino's face changed expression. One mask fell away, another fell into place.

"Then it was nothing at all! Everything's been cleared up! Let's all drink another cup of coffee together and we're friends like before! Oh, obviously, your treat."

The trio accepted eagerly. They even thanked him.

We left the café without paying.

"Did you understand?"

"What, Uncle?"

"What do you mean, what? Shit, I taught you a lesson."

"About what?"

"About losing. About how to lose all personal dignity in thirty seconds. It's a good thing that I'm here to explain life to you."

"Uncle, can I ask you a question?"

"Be my guest."

"Since when do you take your espresso with sugar?"

"Coffee with sugar, me? Have you lost your mind? Coffee with sugar is disgusting, you can't drink it, shit, that's a drink for women."

"Then why?"

"I forgot my wallet at home, Davidù, would you believe such a thing? Absurd, isn't it? But listen, why don't you tell me what you think of your time at the gym."

"Uncle, it's only been three days."

"Well, tell me what you're thinking anyway."

The ward where Gerruso had been admitted was disgusting, full of sick people.

"Five minutes, then we'll get out of here in a hurry, because I'm already fed up with this place," said my uncle.

He told me he'd wait for me in the hallway, that just going in turned his stomach. And how could you disagree with him? Gerruso's hospital room, aside from Gerruso, was empty. Even the other patients were avoiding him. Even his relatives. Better that way. I didn't want anyone to know I'd come to visit him.

"Davidù! My friend."

"We ain't friends."

"You came to see me!"

"Don't get any funny ideas, my mother made me come. But listen, did they stitch the piece of finger back on?"

"No."

"Then you're just a stump-finger! Serves you right, you idiot."

"You're right."

"I know I am. Well, I came to see you, I've done my bit, ciao."

"Ciao."

In the hallway, Umbertino was leaning on the wall. His elbow was held high, his feet were crossed, his eyes were staring into the eyes of a chesty nurse.

"Uncle, we can go."

"Davidù, what's your hurry?"

He was telling her a heartbreaking story of friendship and severed fingers, of gunshots and a desire to come see the wounded boy, of a deeply moved uncle and a dark blue Fiat 126 hurtling at dangerous speed through dense traffic in order to bring a beloved nephew to the bedside of an unfortunate friend. Lowering his voice, his lips trembling, he confessed to her—"Oh, by the way, what's your name? Ester?

What a pretty name that is"—that at the sight of all that friendship his sensitive heart had cracked down the middle: "Right here, go ahead, you can touch." He took her hand in his and guided it to that triumph of sculpted musculature that was his torso. Nurse Ester inadvertently let an admiring "Oh" escape her lips.

Because of him, I was stuck in the hospital for another twenty minutes with Gerruso.

"You came back! My friend!"

"Gerruso, you say that again I'll club you to death. We ain't friends."

"Still, you came back!"

"Blame that on my uncle."

"Your uncle is nice to me."

"Sure, he's so worried about you, no doubt."

"Why are you shutting the door?"

"I don't want anyone to see me talking to you, stump-finger. Anyway, I'm not going to talk to you at all."

"I heard that you decked Pullara."

"Who told you that?"

"My cousin Nina."

The swing started to sway back and forth again. The hollow feeling in the pit of my stomach. My head was spinning. My throat was dry.

To regain control, I forced myself to start talking.

"Did you know that they took me to the gym?"

"To do what?"

"To box, worthless piece of crap. I come from a family of boxers: my father, my uncle. But my mother pitched a fit."

"Why?"

"I don't know, she said that I gotta study, that she won't hear of it, that I can't become a boxer, that sort of thing, women's talk."

"And so?"

"And so, first things first, if she got mad at me that's your fault, if you hadn'ta cut off your finger, I wouldn't have had to beat up Pullara, and none of this mess woulda happened."

"That's true."

"I know it."

"Sorry."

"Well, the damage is done."

"I'm really sorry."

"Not as sorry as me. I made a deal with my mother. Really, Umbertino made the deal. I can if I make good grades at school."

"Jesus, that's tough."

"Gerruso, I'm not an idiot like you. I've got all my fingers."

"What does that have to do with it?"

"It matters, it matters. You've lost a part of you, you were already an idiot, now you're more of one."

"But, wait, if I've lost a part of me, I oughtta be less of an idiot, right?"

"No."

"Why not?"

"What did your grandfather do for a living?"

"Traffic cop, same as my dad."

"There, it's obvious that you're completely hopeless. If you'd had a grandfather who was a cook, like mine, you'd understand the intelligence of fingers."

"Would you explain it to me?"

"No."

"Why not?"

"You're an idiot, you wouldn't understand."

"Right."

"Hey, stump-finger, you wanna hear something great?"

"Yes."

"I learned to make fried rice balls: *arancine!*"

"Bravo-o-o."

There wasn't a trace of envy in Gerruso's voice. That was too bad: What's the point of telling someone something if it doesn't make them even a little bit envious?

All the same, I explained my grandpa's lesson to him: before beginning to boil the rice, he had me touch every grain with my fingertips.

"It's the fingers that recognize the quality of the ingredients," he had said.

His hands moved with agility, a caress for every ingredient. Then the boiling, the addition of saffron, meat sauce, and peas, the ball rolled in the breading, then the frying, and finally sheer admiration for the way that out of the incandescent oil there emerged an *arancina a carne*—a little meat orange—beautiful, spherical, appetizing, delicious.

"If you were a friend a mine, I'd have brought you one, Gerruso."

"Thanks, that's nice of you."

Without warning, the door to the room swung open. Umbertino appeared in the doorway. He had the look of someone who expects to enjoy what's about to happen.

"Davidù, see if you can guess who's come to the hospital."

"Pullara."

A quick spark gleamed in the center of his pupils. In the silence that followed, I understood that I'd given the wrong answer, but I also sensed the pride that he felt when he heard me utter that name.

Umbertino did nothing more than step to one side.

Behind him, outside the door, with a bouquet of flowers in one hand, was Nina.

Red hair worn in a braid.

Light-colored dress, ankle-length.

Deep, dark eyes.

White shoes.

Mulberry lips.

And the swing began to sway again.

Behind her, two adults. Nina had both a mother and a father. Gerruso's aunt and uncle weren't as ugly as their nephew, and they had all ten fingers. They went over to him and told him that it was just a matter of minutes, his parents were coming to see him. Nina was with them. She wasn't looking at me.

I leaned against the wall. I felt weak and sick.

Why was Nina over there with Gerruso? He was ugly.

Why wouldn't she come over to the wall with me? I still had all my fingers in one piece.

I couldn't say or do anything.

The wall was all I had left.

Umbertino was already bending over me.

"Hey, everything all right?"

"Uncle, I'm sick."

"Look me in the eyes. I said, look me in the eyes. Now."

His voice was warm. He spoke softly, almost in a whisper.

"You're not sick."

"Oh, yes, I am."

"Davidù, you're just growing up, and what you're discovering is that it's not just your head that decides what and who you like, but your body, above all. Do you want to leave?"

He held out the palm of his hand to me. It was big and welcoming. I felt like crying and I didn't know why.

"Best wishes to everyone, ladies and gentlemen; ciao, Gerruso, take care of yourself; ciao, youngster, you're a sweetheart; ciao, Ester, I'll call you tonight."

I didn't know whether Nina was responding to that farewell; I couldn't bring myself to look in her direction.

And yet I had them, the words.

I had them.

They were the first words that had come to mind.

Nina, I wanted to tell her, look, my hand is clean, my fingers aren't always covered in blood, can I twirl them in your hair until they vanish?

At the door, my uncle stopped.

"Davidù, someone wants to say goodbye to you."

"Gerruso?"

"Lift your head, light of my life."

There was an unfamiliar gentleness in my uncle's voice.

I lifted my head.

Nina was smiling at me and waving goodbye to me.

Then she raised her hand to her mouth and blew me a kiss.

And I died right then and there.

"Davidù, I'm sorry, I didn't understand how much you like her."

In the car, my uncle was patting my head.

I would have fallen to the ground at Nina's feet if my uncle hadn't held me up. My legs had betrayed me. There was a new knot of hardness in my groin.

"It's normal to be ashamed. When you really like somebody, your body does strange things."

"Did it happen to you, too, Uncle?"

"Uh-huh."

"And did it get hard down there, too?"

"Like marble, if I do say so myself."

"So I'm not sick?"

"Since when is feeling the life in your own body a sign of sickness?

There is only one truth and it's a simple one: that girl gets your blood up, with a vengeance."

"Is it always that way when you like someone?"

"Even worse, kid. There are people, poor things, who instead of marble find a deflated balloon."

"I don't understand."

"I knew that we'd get here sooner or later."

"What do you mean by 'here'?"

"The fact that you're turning into a young man."

There were no rough edges to his voice.

He spoke words as soothing as the taste of warm bread.

Words of a father.

He drove slowly, carefully. He listened to me listening. He confided in me, revealing to me fears, anxieties, sorrows, not shying away from the gray areas. He explained to me that when you like a girl, your penis swells up and gets stiff.

"And that's good for when we're in bed with them. Because as soon as you're inside a woman, that's when the fairy tale begins, but that's something—listen to your uncle—that's something you should never tell women, because women are such kissy creatures, it takes the patience of a saint, it's a truth you'll find written in the Gospels: blessed are those who put up with all the kisses of women without complaining before getting down to the real business. And in any case, no, the string doesn't tear off, that's all bullshit. Any other questions? No? Good, now your uncle is going to explain all the best positions for you."

Umbertino was stripping himself bare. He warmed me up, spreading himself over me like a blanket. His memories proliferated along with the explanations. My heart felt lighter, even if a small thorn remained stuck in it and stubbornly refused to be plucked out. It was still there when I got home. My mother wasn't home yet, but this time it was better that way. I stretched out on the bed and shut my eyes. The only thing I could feel was that tiny unexpected thorn. The one person I wanted with me, right then, wasn't there. Nina. I wanted to show her my clean fingers, tell her that as far as I was concerned she had already won, she had both parents, I'd lost my father, so it was two to one, her favor. Also, I wanted my father. My father, whom I'd never met, was the one who should have been consoling me, not my uncle. It was my father who should have explained to me that I wasn't sick, that my penis was standing up in a sign of respect for women, that the swing I felt surging back and forth in my stomach was just my heart dancing. An uncle is an uncle, not a father. But he wasn't there next to me, and neither was Nina. I did what my mother often did: I shut the door to my bedroom and bit my pillow hard to make sure the rest of the world couldn't hear me cry.

It would be five years before I saw Nina again.

For four days Rosario, stripped naked, had been stretched out in the sunlight.

On the first day, all the other grape harvesters chose not to pay any attention, dismissing him as odd.

"He's completely crazy, never says a word to a soul, if he won't work, he'll have to hash it out with the boss, and what the fuck do we care about that."

If he wouldn't work, he wasn't going to get paid, and it was none of their business.

The next day, the same scene; they began to mock him openly.

"Damned lizard."

He ignored them.

On the third day, they progressed to outright insults and abuse, piecing together a mythical saga of his faggotry, but it fell on deaf ears. A stone is indifferent to the words of mankind.

It was on the fourth day of his sun worshipping that Melino Miceli, the row boss, renamed him *La Nèglia*, the worthless thing.

The *nèglia* is something that has no use. Once it has been recognized as devoid of any practical utility, a useless thing just gets in the way, generates confusion; it undermines the very idea of an established order. The larger relationship with the system of things is compromised. To describe something as worthless is an indication of defeat: no potential uses can be found, the interplay of possible combinations—or perhaps we should say: the imagination's ability to create hypotheses—turns out not to be boundless. The thing, in all its infinite piety, sits there, on the mantelpiece, in a cardboard box, or in the garbage, intent on performing the most merciful act imaginable. It serves our ends, allowing us to do anything, allowing us to do to it what we will, never pronouncing judgment on our inadequacy.

But *La Nèglia* cared nothing for details like the harvest, his pay, the insults, being fired.

He'd been drafted.

He was slated to board a troopship, in two days' time.

He was going to war.

Destination: Africa.

How big a place could that be: Africa?

People said that there were no such things as shadows in Africa.

They said that all the savagery in the world was there, lions, snakes, negroes, in Africa.

His friend Nenè would have liked it.

"Come on, *Nèglia*, come drink the first glass with us."

One of the harvesters brought my grandfather a glass full of wine. My grandfather opened his hand to take the glass.

"Look, *La Nèglia* is moving," said one.

"When it's time to drink, even the stones start to move," opined another.

"*Nèglia*, drink it or I'll cut your throat," chimed in Melino Miceli.

In the silence that came in the wake of the threat, the rock decided to prove to the world that it was made of flesh and blood, and therefore capable of motion. It turned its head, it opened its eyes, and it tipped the glass, pouring the wine out onto the dirt.

Melino Miceli decided that the time had come to show why he and no one else was the row boss. Cursing a blue streak, he walked over to Rosario, turned to face him, and without a word of warning raised one arm. Silhouetted against the blue of the sky was a wooden club, gnarled and stout. A shadow fell over my grandfather's face. Even then, he remained motionless.

"Still, this Melino Miceli, he was trouble. But why were you lying out in the sun?"

"What do you think?"

"For the same reason you wouldn't drink."

"Exactly. I was doing what you do every day."

"What?"
"I was training."
"For what?"
"To withstand heat and thirst."

The gnarled dark wooden club was swinging down from above to strike *La Nèglia* when a gleam of light illuminated the September air. The glass tumbler had already been tossed straight up by Rosario's hand. The movement was so fast that none of the grape harvesters even saw it happen. The silence that ensued was dictated more by amazement than by dismay. The glass struck the row boss square in the face, tearing his forehead wide open. Melino Miceli lost his balance and the swinging club, deflected, just grazed my grandfather. On the ground, shards of glass glittered amid drops of blood and scattered grapes. Rosario put on his clothes, walked away from the grape harvest, went back home, and told them that he was being shipped out to Africa.

They set sail from the port of Trapani in mid-September 1942. There were 208 Sicilians. Nearly all the draftees were virtually illiterate, young men more accustomed to building roads than pushing pencils. They were scheduled to come home thirteen months later. They would actually return in the fall of 1945, after the war was over. The ship that brought them back to Sicily sailed from Alexandria, Egypt, and docked in the harbor of Palermo, where the surviving Sicilians debarked.
Two men walked down the gangplank.
One was a peasant.
The other was my grandfather Rosario.
La Nèglia.

The place my family chose to go to the beach was Cape Gallo, the promontory that protects Palermo to the north. A small sandy beach surrounded on all sides by rocky cliffs, excellent for diving and perfect for catching sea urchins. When my mamma was a girl, she collected pretty stones here to take home; my grandfather spent days at a time staring out at the horizon; my grandmother came here to study; and my father trained by running as far as the lighthouse and then all the way back home. All of them had a relationship with the sea that was predicated on silent, complicit contemplation. Not Umbertino. He was first and foremost tactile, and the instant he saw salt water, he dived into it, without stopping to think. Strip down and swim, to the brink of exhaustion, no matter what month it was, no matter the weather.

"Come on, a nice swim never hurt anyone."

"Uncle, it's April."

"Jump in, scaredy-cat. Or should I throw you in myself?"

He rushed into the water with infectious enthusiasm. It was like watching a little kid. He dived and swam excellently well.

"Oh, hey, Davidù, the peace that the sea brings to my soul, not even the finest ass of the finest woman on earth, I swear."

He taught me to swim.

"Swimming is a skill you need, we live on an island, if you want to get away, how you gonna do it? You gonna walk on the water like Whosis?"

And to dive headfirst.

"A manly man has to know how to dive headfirst. If you're a fabulous diver, women feel like covering you in nice warm pajamas of drool."

His instructions were straightforward.

"Watch me closely, my ass is clamped tight, it's like solid steel, that's the one thing you need to think about when you're diving, your body will take care of the rest."

His mountain of muscles described a harmonious curving trajectory in flight. He sliced into the water without splash or spray. During the lessons, he watched me, both from high atop the rocks and from below, at the water's surface, correcting the motion with which I spread my arms, the elastic tension released into my gluteal muscles, the positioning of my hands.

"Keep your fingers nice and straight and your wrists tight and solid; your hand is what tells the water to move aside."

One dive after another, Umbertino was doing his best to impart the technique that he considered the finest on earth: his own. Once I learned it, we began diving together, synchronized. Simultaneous lift-off, identical curve of the arms, spines straight, hurtling like needles into the flesh of the sea. Then we would swim. And that was when our dance truly became impressive. We swam identically. My uncle taught me the swimming style that he believed to be better than any other on the planet: his own. The windmilling arms, the open dorsals to slice through the waves at an angle, the rhythm of the mouth as it opened, took in air, expelled breath, the regular beat of the kicking legs, the foot entering on the diagonal, the position of the fingers. He was shaping my body to his tempo, his rhythms, imparting to the son of his favorite pupil his own syntax of motion.

A lady, seeing us swim together in a race that would inevitably end in my defeat, mistook us for father and son.

"Signora, has anyone told you that your husband and your son swim identically? You can certainly tell that they're father and son."

It was eleven in the morning, there wasn't a cloud in the sky, but my mother's face darkened all the same.

The lady was thunderstruck.

"Saint Rosalia protect us, what on earth did I say wrong?"

My grandmother weighed in and summer sunshine reigned again.

"They really are exactly alike, signora. In fact, you know what they resemble? Two fine gobs of spit."

The lady burst out laughing, my mother shook off her gloom, the topic was forgotten, and the women were the best of friends for the rest of the day.

"It's no accident that my first name is Provvidenza, Davidù. My jokes are always providential. Your grandfather was sitting on his usual bench looking out to sea, your mother was chattering away about what good report cards you brought home, you and your uncle were swimming, and I went back to my crossword puzzles because when it comes to puzzles, I don't ever want you to forget this, I am phenomenally good."

When Umbertino and I emerged from the water, our bodies told in detail how different our histories really were. Umbertino couldn't seem to hold still for an instant, as if, when he was far away from the one place that give him peace, he sensed all the more intensely the dark current that ran through his blood, and so he hopped from one spot on the wave-lapped sand to another, pretending he'd lost his beach towel, and once he'd spotted an appetizing woman, he'd stretch out beside her.

"Please forgive me, signorina, but would you be so kind as to lend me your towel? I'm all alone, penniless, and dripping wet."

In the face of such bold shamelessness, women invariably broke out laughing after a moment's surprise, and gave him a towel to dry off. At this point, the pickup was half done, and we could forget about seeing Umbertino again until it was time to go home.

In contrast, the minute I emerged from the water, I stopped and stood there, drops of water running down my ribs, my eyes contemplating the sea before me, my body motionless in the hot sun. I became my grandfather Rosario.

≡≡≡

When he told me about the bout that preceded the fight for the national championship, Umbertino was lucid and pitiless.

"I didn't feel a thing, Davidù. Not a thing."

In a city that wasn't his, surrounded by people with different, incomprehensible accents, without *Il Negro* in his corner, with all the bookies taking long odds against him, Umbertino held it all in, pressed it down. He didn't say a word to anyone. He didn't let a thing cross his face. He didn't issue a single statement.

"It was like being at the aquarium: water and silence. It was magnificent."

During the weigh-in, he noticed that he'd shed five pounds, 260 against his opponent's 289.

The bout ended with a knockout in the first round.

The day before the bout, Umbertino had had trouble relaxing. He talked to the concierge at his pensione.

"Where is the red-light district in this town?"

The whores were so ugly that he informed one overly pushy pimp: "They ought to be paying me for the sex."

He agreed to accept the pimp's apology after crushing three fingers on his right hand and instructing him to the effect that knives are dangerous playthings, especially when you have someone like him on the wrong end of the hilt. He cadged a pack of cigarettes and smoked half. He thought about *Il Negro*, about the plans they'd hatched together, the betting odds. He felt a surge of anger and accepted it, the way you accept the rain when you have no umbrella. He went back to the gym where he was scheduled to fight the next day, asked who was taking bets, and bet every penny of his savings on himself. The sun was shining brightly out in the street, but without the sea stretching out the sunlight meant nothing. When darkness fell, he went back to his pensione. He slept like a baby.

The match started at four in the afternoon. Umbertino was received with universal indifference while his opponent was greeted with applause and shouts of encouragement. He was a boxer from Milan, twenty-eight years old. He had a record of forty-one victorious fights, he was the odds-on favorite, and he was the current reigning champion of Italy. What was about to happen in the ring was beyond what anyone present could imagine. It was thirty seconds of sheer terror. The instant the referee released the boxing gloves, Umbertino hurled himself against his opponent with every ounce of his strength, forcing him into the corner. That morning, as he looked at himself in the mirror, he had sworn a solemn oath: no marks on his face. He had a goal. He was determined to achieve it. He possessed everything he would need: an icy calm. Not the calm of a surgeon about to operate; a surgeon can always fail. He was the scalpel. The same detachment, the same indifference. The boxer from Milan was hit full-force by a tsunami. A punch to the spleen and the wind was knocked out of him, a hook to the temple and his balance was lost, an uppercut to the stomach to force his body to fight to stay on its feet. And then over again from the beginning, same sequence, spleen temple stomach. After just seven seconds and twelve hits, the Milanese was vomiting gastric juices and blood. Umbertino increased the pace of his punches. Fifteen seconds later, the reigning champion passed out. Umbertino landed an uppercut to the chin, knocking him backward over the ropes and onto the floor outside the ring. The reporters used new metaphors to describe what they'd just seen and admired. One compared my uncle to a cannibal, another to a lion, while yet another dubbed him Umberto Furioso, all of them doing their best to explain the absolute novelty of a boxer who was at once so unrestrained and so fast. Their articles hailed the pioneer of a surprising new form of boxing. An unprecedented mix of speed, power, and agility. One journalist went so far as to employ the adjective *unreal*. Someone else wrote that they had gazed admiringly on a young god.

Yet another wondered whether right then and right there a new chapter was not being written in the history of boxing, and not just in Italy. On one point, all the reporters agreed: my uncle was now a boxer without rival in the whole country.

Franco the Maestro did his best to explain Umbertino's impenetrable approach to boxing. The comparison he made was to the sea: "rain or shine, wind or fine weather, the sea don't give a damn, because the sea is never what's on the surface, the sea is what lies below, what you never get a glimpse of. Young man, your uncle was the most powerful fighter I'd ever seen in my life, until the Paladin bounded onto the stage. How can you hammer the sea with fists? It's bigger, way too big, way too strong. There's water down below with more water underneath it. The sea is sufficient unto itself."

On the day of the championship match, my uncle was the odds-on favorite. His opponent was a trivial flyspeck in comparison. Moreover, the bout was going to be held right in Palermo. Umbertino had sweated blood to get a shot at this fight. The national championship. The goal was within reach.

Negro, why did you leave? If only you'd come back.

But there wasn't going to be any unannounced return, no big surprise. Ships ply the sea and deposit their passengers elsewhere, in other ports, other lands, other languages. *Il Negro* was a dead letter. It was time to turn the page. To continue down the path he had chosen for himself. Looking at himself in the mirror, he swore no oath. He emerged from the locker room and climbed into the ring. A chill descended over the room.

Umbertino chose his words carefully. Even in the endless match against his own memory, my uncle took positions and carried on the fight. We were alone the time he told me about the championship fight. He eliminated the possibility of intrusions, annoyances, other human beings. It was me, him, and his demons. He spoke with perfect stoicism. To remember still caused him enormous pain. Not everyone has a chance to fight for the national heavyweight title. And lose.

What really happened. Understand. Review. Regain mental clarity. And so, one stroke after another, swim and remember.

The movement became increasingly self-aware, the body was moving away from the shore, the tensions clashed in Umbertino's bloodied face.

What happened.

At the end of the tenth and final round of the championship fight, the hall echoed with whistles and catcalls. Disapproval manifests itself best in hysterical and out-of-control reactions. The faces of both boxers were a mess. Blood everywhere. Ten rounds for a total of one fuck of a lot of pain received and inflicted. His opponent had sprawled out on the canvas twice, in the second and fifth rounds. My uncle had never gone down, and yet his face hadn't been so badly battered even in the fight against *Il Negro*. When the referee read out the decision, the sprinkling of applause in the hall failed to drown out the insults. In his own corner, Umbertino had no one with whom to share his defeat. He left the ring without taking off his gloves. He walked down the hall through a rain of jeers and spit, entered the locker room, closed the door behind him, took off his gloves, and started to wreck the place.

What had happened.

First round. The two boxers were sizing each other up. His opponent was slow to block a left hook. My uncle connected twice, the first hook to the cheekbone, the second to the temple.

Second round. An uppercut that emerged from a left feint. His opponent took a punch to the chin. He dropped to the mat, as did his two front teeth. He got back to his feet. He could take a lot of punishment, the information they had on him was checking out. Umbertino kept his distance for the rest of the round. Everything was looking good.

A manager in his corner could have offered some tips. Could have helped him to modify his strategy. That's why you have one, to suggest new ways to attack. To lend a shoulder to lean on. But his corner was empty. *Il Negro* had dumped him, just a few steps short of the summit. He'd have to do it all on his own.

End of the third round. He'd only taken a few shots, just to prove to himself that he was much faster than his opponent.

He gave no interviews. After destroying the locker room, he left dressed in a tracksuit, without even taking a shower. He crossed Palermo at a dead run, bag slung over his shoulder, legs devouring yard after yard, heading for the sea. He yearned to lose himself in a fight, stop thinking entirely, punch to kill. He reached Cape Gallo. That's where he was forced to stop, the road had come to an end. The blood mixed with sweat had turned his face into something nightmarish. On that cloudless night, the glow of moonlight reflected on the surface of the sea only increased his rage. He'd lost the fight. He couldn't seem to get over it. God, what he'd have given to cross paths with any human being at that moment and beat him to death. His prayers were answered. There was a man sitting on a metal bench. A leer dating back to the time of falling bombs sliced Umbertino's face in two. Five eerily silent strides and Umbertino was standing in front of him.

"What's the matter, can't you see the water anymore? Eh? You want me to move? So why don't you try and move me? Eh? What are you doing, you moving instead, you little pussy? Do I disgust you, all scratched up the way I am? What, are you scared? Are you disgusted? Eh?"

His hands were clutching at the air. Come on, answer me rudely, do something, anything, a gesture, a word, anything at all, come on, just let me kill you.

Nothing.

The man sitting on the bench didn't move.

That's not what my uncle was expecting. He wanted to breathe in the man's terror, feed off his fear. He wasn't looking to vent his anger. He wanted to destroy. He cocked his arm to unleash a blow that contained all the might he possessed.

What happened next was something he never could have imagined.

Suddenly both of the man's hands were pressed against his. Of course, they wouldn't have stopped the blow, they weren't a sufficiently solid shield.

That wasn't the point.

Umbertino hadn't seen that attempt at self-defense coming. There were only two people that fast on earth, as far as he knew. And one of them was him. He relaxed the tension in his back. The other was *Il Negro*. That kind of speed couldn't be ignored. It demanded respect. He stared into the man's eyes and recognized that look. It was identical to his own. The look of a survivor.

He felt the sting of the cuts on his face. He was starting to listen to his body again. At the same time, his memory unearthed a scene that he felt certain he'd buried. The first time that *Il Negro* showed him how to work the bag. There are two ways: the first is when the bag is moving away from you, and that's when the punch will be a way of letting off steam, thrown long, your arm opening out wide. The second is when the bag is coming toward you, a punch you throw low, elbows pressed close against your rib cage. Never throw a punch at a bag that's hanging motionless. You have to hit something that's moving, either to knock it off balance or halt its motion. Life is movement, what's immobile is dead. When you hit a motionless bag, all you do is destroy your fingers.

"Oh, hey, so now what?"

The answer took the form of a question, uttered in a faint voice.

"Do you know how to swim?"

Umbertino's mind was beginning to clear.

"I'm a fabulous swimmer."

The man tilted his head forward, in a sign of assent.

Umbertino stripped off his clothes and dived into the sea.

It was March. The water was freezing. Excellent, that would wake his body up and wash away the blood. The salt would disinfect the cuts. Taking a swim had been a good idea. Stroke after stroke, his swimming style changed from raw fury to pure harmony.

Fourth round. Punch and move away, one leap at a time. There was still a long time to go. Too long.

Fifth round. He let fly with a left hook, catching his opponent full in the forehead. The other man dropped to the mat. The referee counted to six. The other man stood up.

He could win whenever he chose.

Umbertino was a furious reed, indifferent to the river's flow.

Sixth round. By this point he was taking punches, and that was about it. A hook to his jaw, countless uppercuts to his abdominals, a right cross that connected with his nose. There was blood on his face again. This was a different fight. Seventh round. My uncle was no longer attacking. He took a long series of punches to his sides. During the eighth round, his left eyebrow was laid open. In the ninth round his upper lip was cut. It didn't matter. It didn't prove a thing. He thought about Giovannella. She wouldn't have been proud of him. Oh well, that's life. When the gong rang ending the tenth round and the match, the audience was worked up into a demonic frenzy.

The referee read the decision. Umbertino had lost the title on points.

But no one had ever explained to him that the higher the goal, the more disastrous the fall. The instant the referee proclaimed his defeat, the roots of the cane plant were cut away, and Umbertino's sanity and tranquillity went drifting downstream.

"I felt . . . no, it wasn't that I felt, no. I was. I was alone. I didn't even have a trainer in my corner or a woman to go home to."

"Did you cry?"

"In my way; I broke everything in sight."

"No, I mean in the sea, when you were swimming."

" . . . "

"Uncle."

"Yes."

As the water streamed over his skin, my uncle's thoughts regained some kind of order. The signs began to illustrate shapes possessed of a meaning all their own. The grand overarching design emerged, crystal clear, necessary. Umbertino reversed course, swimming for shore now, considering what needed to be done from that point forward: open up a fine new boxing gym, there wasn't a fucking thing even close to that in Palermo, the plan would proceed as established, the sea washed away anger and blood. The cuts on his face would heal and scar, the damage to his pride would remain invisible, it was just a matter of training himself to get over defeat, that was all. By the time he emerged from the water, his gaze had regained its razor-sharp edge. The predator had just changed packs. The light of the moon cast his shadow across the rocks. The man sitting on the bench went on staring intently at the sea.

Umbertino sat down beside him, without drying off. He told him everything. Without shyness, without shame. *Il Negro*, the bombs, the prostitutes, the championship fight he lost, the bets, the plan for the boxing gym, Giovannella.

Before getting up, he asked him: "What is it you keep staring at so intently?"

Rosario looked him right in the eye and told him.

Umbertino got up from the bench, got dressed, and picked up his bag.

They parted without another word.

The sun no longer burned their skin. It had penetrated their cores, darkening the color of their flesh.

"We're flesh and sunlight, now," Lieutenant D'Arpa liked to say.

"We look like natives," Melluso would reply.

The night was greeted as a welcome liberation from the heat of the day.

Rosario, lying on his cot, hugged his rib cage, running his fingers up and down the staircase of his ribs. Eyes closed and index finger wide awake, counting them every night. Now he knew that he had twelve ribs on both his right and left side.

For the past month, every goddamned night, there had been air raids. As soon as it became clear that the bombing runs were spaced two hours apart, the bodies of certain soldiers learned to fall asleep after the last roaring sound of an aircraft, only to reawaken with surprising efficiency about twenty minutes before the next raid. But not everyone could manage that trick. Only the lucky ones. Among them, there were no cases of hysteria, no sudden outbursts of rage.

Rosario asked Nicola Randazzo if he would mind letting him count his ribs for him. The other man agreed. Rosario's fingers explored his rib cage. If men have the same number of ribs, then their bodies are equal. It's the mind that must be different.

"Nicola, you have to find a way to get some sleep."

"But what about the bombs?"

"Sleep."

"If I don't?"

"You won't live to see next week."

"Why would you say such a thing?"

If he had been someone who liked to talk, he would have explained that they were at war, that if they wanted to survive they'd have to surpass their own limitations, that the mouth eats rice but dreams of meat, the mind eats nightmares and dreams of eternal rest. But eating a handful of rice is just as necessary as having nightmares: it helps to keep you from dying.

"Eating is how you satisfy your appetite" was all he said.

By the third consecutive week of nightly raids, nearly everyone had become accustomed to the roar of aircraft. There were only three cases of hysteria, of soldiers who couldn't seem to sleep. After a month, the air raids stopped. The shifts of sentry duty were intensified. Double shifts. Watch out for everything, hope to see nothing.

"I don't give a crap what anyone says, tomorrow I'm going to fuck a whore not once but twice, and if she dares to say a word, I'll cut her face."

To heighten the theater of his pledge, Vincenzo Melluso sank the blade of his knife into the embers. When he removed it the blade was as straight as before; it makes no difference to a knife whether it's plunged into coals or into flesh.

The sky above them was so big and full of stars that it really did look as if it were curving around the earth.

"Asshole of a peasant, why don't you tell us exactly what you're going to do to your whore tomorrow?"

Melluso had tossed the question in Randazzo's direction, to see the hot flush explode across his face; Nicola didn't like to talk about women and fucking.

"Randazzo, are you blushing? But why? Is it because you'd rather find a negro hung like a donkey in your tent some night, instead of a whore?"

Melluso had never much liked black guys, even though he'd never seen one back in Palermo. Before enlisting, Melluso was a layabout, he didn't even have a job. He wasted time the way some people waste paper. The war was his first real job.

The silence of Africa surrounded the soldiers, seeping into them like the hot sun.

"No doubt about it, all this silence, a guy could lose his mind, right, Santin?"

Santin was from the continent, from up north near Verona, where they don't have salt water. Santin would talk about the taste of dirt, and tell how his father, Gilberto, before starting any job, pruning, sowing, or watering, would chew some dirt, savoring the taste; sometimes he'd spit it out, other times he'd swallow it. His father never talked much. He'd taught him to listen to nature.

"I happen to like silence."

Santin was big and strong, with the taurine neck and broad hands of someone descended from generations of farmers.

"Oh, hey, you mute, you could take a swim in all this silence."

For the past couple of weeks, Melluso had made a habit of insulting Rosario. "The mute here, the mute there, the mute this, the mute that." And the mute, faithful to his name, made no reply. Melluso threw a rock at him, hitting him on the shoulder. Rosario slowly turned around.

"Look, the mute is looking at me, I'm shitting my pants now," said Melluso. Then he waved a fuck-off in his direction and poured himself a cup of tea.

It was Mino Iallorenzi, the son of a blacksmith and the grandson of a blacksmith and a blacksmith himself in the Acqua Santa quarter of Palermo, who broke the silence.

"Well, all the same, it's just not right that you can only fuck a whore once."

"Then you do the one and only smart thing you can do."

"And what would that be, D'Arpa?"

"Iallorenzi, do I have to teach you everything?"

Lieutenant Francesco D'Arpa was a Fascist fundamentalist. Born in Monreale into a family of large landowners, he had an enviable command of logic. He said that a problem can be defined as such because a solution exists, and since there is always a solution, the problem actually doesn't exist.

"Iallorenzi, give yourself a good hand job, oh, fifteen, twenty minutes before you fuck her, so that practically speaking with the whore it's already the second time, and the second fuck always lasts longer than the first one."

Iallorenzi greeted the suggestion with a smile; he'd give that some serious thought—damn if D'Arpa didn't have a powerful brain.

Carmine Marangola had pulled the tea tin out of the embers and poured himself a glassful.

"What the hell kinda problems are these? Let's not kid around here."

He was from Posillipo. Born into a family of fishermen, he talked about the sea, fish traps, boats, different ways of cutting up tuna, hooks, riptides, currents, shifts in the wind, sails, herbs and spices for cooking fish. He was missing the fourth toe on his right foot. Two years previous, during a December storm at sea, he'd fallen overboard into waters so cold they were icy. He'd managed to clamber back aboard the launch, but he was so absorbed in navigating his craft through waves, tides, and whirlpools that he hadn't had a second to take off his waterlogged shoes. The storm had lasted for three days and the toe had simply rotted away. When he got back to port, they amputated the toe; he'd sunk his teeth into a length of hawser to fight the pain.

"Whores are whores. You, Iallorenzi, are you a whore or are you a man?"

"I'm a man, Marangola, what the hell are you talking about?"

"Then act like a man: you walk in, you fuck her, and you pay your money, in total silence."

"In total silence?"

Francesco D'Arpa had taken the floor again.

"The dick doesn't want to think about things."

And yet there were thoughts, and then some. The fear of catching some nasty disease, the amount of money required to pay for the whore's services, how much time was available for fucking. The last time, a brawl had erupted when a soldier from Rome insisted on staying with the whore until he had a chance to come. There was an unwritten rule, and everyone adhered to it: ten minutes max; if you manage to come, so much the better and everyone's happy, if not, amen, make your peace with it and make room for the next in line. The important thing wasn't finishing, it was getting your dick wet. It's good for morale, according to the higher-ups in the army. The rule was annoying but necessary: the last time there had been a hundred and eight soldiers and only four black whores. Three soldiers had marched into the tent, lifted the Roman from between the whore's thighs, and hauled him away by force. The Roman not only slid into a state of hysteria, he started saying things he shouldn't. He shouted for all to hear that he was the only real man there and that everyone else was a queer who took it up the ass. A couple of vigorous kicks in the mouth restored calm to the situation. A few new gaps in the Roman's teeth served as a salutary reminder to one and all how dangerous it could be to linger in the tent even one second past the prescribed time limit.

Iallorenzi was watching as sparks flew up from the brazier, fluttering and then vanishing, as if the night were swallowing them up.

"Let's at least hope that this time the whores aren't black," said Melluso.

"How do you want yours?"

"White."

"And right you are," chimed in Marangola.

"Of course I'm right, our whores are the best there are."

Rosario couldn't really agree. The first time he'd gone to a whore he was thirteen and he was with his friend Nenè. They'd stolen the money from a Capuchin priest, a total fraud who'd more than deserved the theft. They'd crept into the crypt of the monastery, pried open the offering box, and taken to their heels. They were so eager to lose their virginity that they'd rushed over to the first whore they could find, in an alley behind the Albergo delle Povere, the poorhouse for women.

The whore was fat and missing a front tooth; her legs were covered with bruises.

Nenè was firm: "Rosà, we decided we'd fuck the first one we found, and this is the first one, so let's go."

"Who fucks first?"

"You."

Rosario had walked into the bedroom. The whore had been anything but motherly with him. She'd greeted him with a tired smile, she'd demanded his money, she'd counted it and stowed it in the nightstand drawer, she'd told him to undress, she'd washed his dick in a basin of water, she'd hiked up her skirts, lain down on the bed, and let him mount her, then she'd told him to get up and get dressed, she'd lowered her dress, opened the door, and ushered him out into the hall, then she'd welcomed his friend Nenè into the room, she'd demanded his money, she'd counted it, told him to undress, washed his dick in the same basin with the same water, hiked her skirts, and so yet another virginity ended between her thighs.

Rosario never saw his best friend, Nenè, again after the end of that summer. A landowner in a town near Enna needed laborers, Nenè's family needed cash, and the two friends were separated: Rosario living just outside Palermo, Nenè lost in the island's hinterlands. When Rosario thought about whores, he remembered that first time and what Nenè had said, then and there, as they walked out of that bedroom: "Oh, hey, that whore was so ugly that I wouldn't fuck her again even with your dick." They both burst out laughing so hard that their sides started hurting. On their way home that night, they made up their minds that the very next day they'd get busy trying to pick up two pretty young girls and they'd fuck them even faster than immediately, after all, whatever there was to know about it, they already knew it.

"Because anyway, Rosà, if we've managed to fuck such an ugly whore, two things are clear: first of all, we ain't virgins no more, and second, our dicks just work too damn well."

"No, our whores aren't the best," Rosario replied aloud without deigning to look in Melluso's direction. No one had anything to say about that. When a mute finally speaks, you check the exact weight of every word that comes out of his mouth.

Sitting between Moreno Santin and Nicola Randazzo on the right side of the army truck, Rosario looked out over the infinite expanse of Africa. Marangola was whistling a tune, Melluso was sleeping, Iallorenzi was slapping the mosquitoes that had targeted his legs, and D'Arpa was counting out loud the Africans that they passed along the way.

"Seven, eight, nine. Nine Africans in ten kilometers. For sure, things look different in this Africa, Rosario. You can see that the world is less curved here, you see a tree, you tell yourself, 'I'm going to go over there and get in the shade,' and you walk and you walk and you walk, and the tree is still all the way out there, still in the distance. There are no obstacles, here the eye can take in everything even at great distances."

Nicola Randazzo asked Lieutenant D'Arpa the names of a number of the animals they passed. Sometimes, not even D'Arpa knew the answer.

Iallorenzi was the only one to say out loud what everyone else had been thinking for days.

"Let's hope that today at least there are fewer of us soldiers than last time, and that there are a lot more of the whores."

There were one hundred eighty-one soldiers and three whores.

It would be very late by the time they got a chance to fuck.

There was even an official communiqué announcing that the minutes allotted were being reduced from ten to seven. Disgruntlement was widespread.

"No self-respecting man can hope to come in less than seven minutes, chief."

Melluso suggested the group split up, a few soldiers in each of the three lines.

"That way, afterward, we can report back on the details."

After an hour, one of the lines was eliminated. Something had happened. It never became clear exactly what it was, but a stretcher was carried into the tent and emerged shortly therafter, carrying the whore. She seemed to be sleeping but maybe she'd only fainted. Now there were two lines. Iallorenzi, Marangola, Melluso, and Randazzo in the first line, everyone else in the second. The wait was grueling, they had run out of water, the soldiers put on a show of confidence but deep down they were dying of anxiety. Fear had begun to seep into the crowd, with growing insistency: the fear that when all was said and done, just when anticipation was reaching a crescendo, they might not get their dicks wet after all. They passed the time by putting on a show of nonchalance that was as contrived as it was essential. Amid the most complete indifference, a third line formed: those who had been forced to abandon their efforts midstream had decided to finish off here, in broad daylight, the work they'd been unable to complete in the tent.

Only one fight broke out: a guy from Favara miscalculated and a spurt of sperm wound up on the tip of Santin's shoe.

"Now clean it up."

Before the Favarese had a chance to say a word, his head was already on the ground, clamped between Santin's hands, inches from the sperm-stained tip of Santin's shoe.

"Now lick it off."

A fellow Favarese tried to build a groundswell in his townsman's defense, but he soon realized just how massively uninterested everyone else was in pitching in. Without remorse, he decided to say to hell with it, there were still twelve soldiers in line ahead of him, better to just save his strength for a fine fuck just as the Gospel says.

"Melluso, Randazzo," said Iallorenzi, "listen, Marangola and I have just had a great idea. Seven minutes is less than no time at all. Why don't we go in two at a time? That gives us twice as much time. Marangola and I are going in together, you do the same and you'll get twice as much time, too."

"What if the whore has something to say about it?"

"Randazzo, let me tell you the way the world works: in the first place, she's a whore, in the second place, she's black, and in the third place, I don't give a damn, I'm walking in there, I'm paying my money, and I'm going to fuck her the way I say," Melluso broke in angrily.

Nicola Randazzo looked around and tried to catch Rosario's or D'Arpa's eye in the next line over, but he couldn't attract their attention. They were watching a soldier lick the toe of a shoe.

Nenè often said that he wished he could be a sailor, so that he could touch every corner of the world.

"I trust my hands more than I trust my eyes," he used to say.

They smoked their first cigarette together, at age eight. Rosario won that cigarette in a footrace against Michele, the son of Don Salomone, the pharmacist. Michele had filched a whole pack of cigarettes from his father's bedroom and he boasted about it openly, showing the pack to his friends: look at what fine cigarettes I have; look at how many I have; here, smell them, what a fine odor. Rosario proposed a bet: his glass filled with fishing worms, fresh from the ground, just caught, still alive and squirming, against the pack of cigarettes.

"Race all the way to the church wall, what do you say?"

Rosario was slender, narrow-shouldered, skinny-legged. Michele Salomone, from the full height of his ten years of age, evaluated the offer, sized up his opponent, and calculated accordingly. He'd grind him to dust. Leaning forward, waiting for the starting signal, Michele Salomone looked Rosario in the face and uttered his prediction.

"You know why you can't possibly win? Because you're a *nèglia*."

The first taste of tobacco is harsh and sour; the tongue becomes acquainted with new realms of bitterness, the eyes fill with tears, and the ears echo with coughing. But how good that first cigarette remains in one's memory.

"Rosà, why on earth did you challenge him?"

"I'm faster than you, Nenè."

"That's an eyeful of horseshit."

"You saying you could beat me?"

"Yes."

"Now?"

"Yes."

"And the winner?"

"The winner takes all the cigarettes."

"Fine. From here to there."

"On three?"

"Yes."

They counted together, one two three. They shot off at top speed. They ran, breathless, as fast as they could go, from here to there, pushing past their personal best. Nenè won.

"Okay, then we're in agreement, Marangola."

"Yes, one in front, and one behind."

"Where are you going to be?"

"I can be anywhere, Melluso, as long as I'm a long way from your balls."

Randazzo had decided to move to the other line, he wasn't interested in sharing his whore with another man. It was his fault that Melluso wouldn't be enjoying twice as much time. Melluso swore he'd make him pay for it.

The minutes crept by; it was if they weren't passing at all. The soldiers maintained their positions, standing or on the ground, sweating, flies and mosquitoes everywhere, nothing to drink. This isn't how it should be when someone goes to have a fuck. Santin had asked the other soldiers as they emerged what the whore on his line was like. He received a lapidary, terse, and unanimous response: "The minute you go in, you'll see for yourself."

Randazzo sat down on the ground, his head between his hands:

"D'Arpa, I don't really know if I feel like it, if you want, you can have my time, if that's something that can be done."

"Nicola, stop talking nonsense. You go in before me and you fuck before I do."

"But—"

"No buts, now you shut up and get some rest."

Two hours later, their turn had almost come. There was an enlisted man inside the tent, and after him, Santin was next in line, followed by Rosario, Randazzo, and last of all, D'Arpa. In the other line, Melluso, Iallorenzi, and Marangola still had three people ahead of them. Only a few minutes before the Venetian was due to enter the tent a scream suddenly exploded from the whore. The enlisted man must have tried something bad, fucked up. Santin grabbed the man as he rushed frantically out of the tent, knocked him to the ground, and set on him with a hailstorm of fists.

"You bastard, I can't stand guys who try to hurt my whore."

A few men went in to check on the whore's physical condition. The medical officer restored calm to the ranks by announcing that everything was fine, there had been an unsuccessful attempt at sodomy, nothing serious, next man in line step forward, please.

Then it was Rosario's turn. He found himself standing before a little girl, twelve, maybe thirteen years old. She was black, stretched out on her back on a cot, spread-eagled. By that point, she couldn't even close her legs; she'd held them wide for five hours in a row. On the floor, next to a tin pail, was a sponge to wash off blood and sperm. Rosario stopped looking, dropped his pants, and fucked the whore.

Iallorenzi and Marangola walked in, together with Melluso. They'd decided to go in as a trio, eighteen minutes instead of twenty-one, sacrificing a minute each of their allotted time in exchange for a longer if more crowded stay. "Boys, you'll get in three minutes early." But something went wrong, and Iallorenzi came rushing out and dragged the medical officer back into the tent with him, while what remained of the line was rerouted to the only tent still in service. They answered the medical officer's questions by insisting that it had been an accident, just a prank turned serious, they definitely hadn't meant for it to happen.

They got back to camp three hours after sunset, just in time for the ten o'clock allied bombing raid.

———

"The moon in Africa is bigger than the sun in Palermo, Davidù."

When there was a bombing raid, the airplanes glittered in the moonlight, as if they were made of silver. And above the enemy planes: so many stars that it was was impossible to count them. You could sketch any image you had in your head up there in the firmament: an orange tree, a horse-drawn carriage, Nenè smiling. The starlight was interrupted only when a bomb exploded on the earth in a flash of light.

"What were you thinking about during those air raids?"

"About water."

"About water what?"

"Maybe a bomb—I don't know—might make water pour out of the ground."

"Like a spring?"

"Yeah."

"Did it ever happen?"

"No."

Nicola Randazzo was weeping. Rosario got out of his cot and got into bed beside him, watching him silently. The patience of the open door. Randazzo noticed him, dried his tears, and told him everything. Rosario's silence was free of judgment. When Randazzo was done with his story, he turned over and tried to get to sleep, but that was easier said than done. Nicola went on emitting a faint and broken whimper.

A short time earlier, outside the latrines, Melluso had said to him: "Randazzo, will you come around back with me?"

He'd slammed his face into the wall.

He'd hit him over and over again in the temple with a fist wrapped in a wet washcloth, to make sure he left no marks.

"So you didn't want to go in to see the whore with me."

He slammed his knee into Randazzo's kidneys.

When Randazzo collapsed to the ground, breathless, head spinning, Melluso screwed him from behind.

The orders arrived in the middle of the night, and they brooked no objections. Make preparations to evacuate the encampment, enemy forces had broken through the front. Three minutes after six in the morning, the withdrawal got under way. They set out on foot, shouldering their rucksacks, avoiding the beaten paths, moving out along the rocky wilderness. They were expected to cover forty miles of ground in the shortest time possible, and the temperature in direct sunlight was hovering at just under 120 degrees. Water rations were distributed before they began their march, half a canteen apiece. The line moved forward in silence. The soldiers had learned the importance of economizing on effort, and talking demanded greater salivation, and saliva spelled thirst. By twelve noon, the situation was desperate. Five men had passed out, Iallorenzi had vomited from exhaustion, and Randazzo was losing blood from his asshole. Francesco D'Arpa stopped to help both men. He helped Iallorenzi get back on his feet and he offered his right shoulder to Nicola for support. All around them, in every direction, stretched the desert. Rosario could feel his upper lip cracking from dehydration, but not a drop of blood emerged. Hands held out to shield his eyes, he turned just as Melluso unstoppered his canteen. They crashed into each other. The canteen dropped out of his hands and the water sank into the sand. Melluso hurled himself at Rosario. He managed to land a punch to his ear. D'Arpa pulled them apart.

"Melluso, what the fuck are you doing?"

"He made me drop my water."

Rosario had gotten back to his feet. He was brushing himself clean of sand.

Melluso leveled his forefinger straight at him.

"I'll murder you, you worthless piece of crap."

La Nèglia was back.

Fifteen minutes later, the soldiers were lined up, side by side, hands in the air. The enemy had caught up with them, in trucks, with machine guns. My grandfather's whole division surrendered without a single shot fired.

The line was falling apart. Pushed to the brink by exhaustion or dehydration, prisoners were hitting the ground here and there. The first request to get back on their feet took the form of a kick in the ribs. There was no second request. Those who failed to get up were killed. D'Arpa and Rosario helped Nicola Randazzo to walk, holding him up by the lapels of his uniform. The shivering was getting worse, sunstroke and collapse increasingly likely. After two hours, Santin, the one in the group least accustomed to the fierce lash of harsh sunlight, slammed to the dirt. He fell straight onto the rocks without stopping to teeter on his knees. An enemy officer shouted something, presumably an order to get back on his feet. No answer. A pistol shot confirmed, as if confirmation was needed, that there was no time to waste. The body was left where it had fallen, to be gnawed at by flies and insects. One of the soldiers asked to be allowed to give him a decent burial, none of the rest had the saliva to utter a word. During the march they lost three more comrades. They reached their destination in the middle of the night. An old oasis that had been refitted as a prison camp. There was no water, there were no beds, there were no latrines. An enclosure formed by a wall on one side and barbed-wire fencing on the other three, too tall and too dense for anyone to dream of breaking through. The prisoners were a herd of oxen, but without the luxury of a watering trough. That first night there was an escape attempt, a youngster from Crotone in Calabria, not even twenty. He was immediately caught and tossed back into the prison. For the first time, the guards spoke to the prisoners in Italian. They told them that escape was impossible, and that, moreover, every attempt would be punished by depriving the prisoners of water for two days. That punishment would begin immediately. D'Arpa went over to the young Calabrian and invited him to sit down next to him. Their jailers were trying to get them to turn on one another. No one raised a hand to the boy, no one upbraided him. On the second night, the Calabrian tried to escape again, but he was stopped by four prisoners. Three of them held him motionless, but it was D'Arpa who decked him with a powerful punch to the balls.

"If you try to escape again and they cut off our water for two more days, I will kill you with my own hands."

"Nicola, cup your hands together and do me a favor, don't spill a drop. Then I'll do the same for you."

D'Arpa was having Randazzo help him collect his own urine. If he was saying those words, if he was doing this thing, it wasn't because the sun had driven him mad. It must have a basis in fact. He was someone who'd been to school. Everyone watched the sequence of events carefully: examples help you to survive. When they saw that the lieutenant had urinated into their comrade's hands and then had drunk it without vomiting or fainting, all reluctance vanished. Some of them cupped their hands beneath their genitals and tried peeing into them, but it's already hard to control your flow under normal conditions, forget about trying to do it when you're delirious from thirst. And so for some of them the first gush of pee was lost on the rocks, evaporating in the blink of an eye. Watch, observe, learn: D'Arpa had peed into another man's hands. He couldn't afford to waste a single drop of potable liquid. All they had to do was find a fellow prisoner they could trust, someone who wouldn't try to take their piss and drink it themselves. Rosario peed into D'Arpa's hands, drank half of his urine, looked over at Randazzo, and gestured that he was welcome to finish it off himself. Nicola had a fever, he couldn't even get to his feet. His injured anus had developed an infection. Rosario and D'Arpa lifted him up and set him down next to the wall where there was a tiny patch of shadow, and made him a cushion with their shirts.

After two endless days, the water ration was brought to them. It was going to have to last for three days, the guards informed them. Francesco D'Arpa felt the eyes of the other prisoners focusing on him. The soldiers acknowledged in him, rank aside, sufficient authority to make decisions concerning their survival. When you're on your last legs, you entrust your survival to someone else, hoping that they are strong enough to keep from falling.

D'Arpa considered carefully and spoke: "A handful of water apiece." His throat was on fire. He couldn't believe how painful it had become to emit a sound.

"What if there's some left over?" Iallorenzi asked, under his breath.

There really were too many of them to be able to rely on the honor system, and they were all so terribly thirsty. In that case, it was best to just recognize the state of things and try to hold out by drinking one's own urine.

"Second round for everyone."

The potful of water was carried over to the wall. Without a word, without a quibble, a single line formed up.

For five days, they hadn't had a bite to eat. The enemy was undermining their resistance, systematically undernourishing and dehydrating them. They repeatedly asked for a doctor to examine the prisoners who had collapsed but their jailers ignored them. Seven of them had high fevers and the shakes. Nicola Randazzo was starting to become delirious. He talked about the festival of his village's patron saint and about Gigliola, daughter of Ina, with her long hair and delicate hands. When the doctor finally showed up, he spoke in a foreign tongue and no one could understand a word he said, so he turned and started to leave. Like a flash, Rosario lunged at his left foot and seized it with both hands. He kept his head bowed and his neck bent. The two soldiers who were escorting the doctor started kicking Rosario in the ribs and shoulders but he held tight to the doctor's foot, taking the blows the way an inanimate object might. The medical officer was surprised more than scared. He put an end to the beating with a command. At that exact moment, when the rain of combat boots ceased, without wasting so much as a fraction of a second, Rosario looked up, straight into the eyes of the physician, and threw his arm back to indicate a place along the wall. The doctor decided to go take a look, and that's how Nicola Randazzo was taken to the infirmary and my grandfather was put in solitary confinement.

Solitary confinement meant an iron cube, just outside of the barbed-wire fence, with an air hole just big enough to stick your finger through. Rosario would be spending the next three days in there. Without water, without food. Three days in an oven. The soldiers lacked the strength to object, they'd never be able to shout encouragement to their comrade. Still, there he was, just a few yards away, the other side of the barbed wire. Perhaps a voice would help him. Or maybe it wouldn't. Maybe it would only make his suffering worse. No one could say. It was the first time one of them was being punished in that way.

"He's going to come out nicely roasted," Melluso snickered.

There was no news about Nicola Randazzo.

There was a brawl, one man had tried to drink someone else's piss.

Five men passed out, and no one had the pity or the strength to help them to their feet.

Catching flies in midair to eat was becoming increasingly difficult. Their reflexes were delayed and the flies seemed to move ever faster. There were some who just kept their mouths open in the hope that an insect might happen to fly in. During the day, the thermometer registered a temperature of over 120 degrees. At night, the temperature dropped to 90 degrees or so. Twenty-four hours had passed, and Rosario was still inside that cube.

The next day, a new ration of water was brought in. The line formed up, everyone gulped down the sip of water to which they were entitled, and then something happened. D'Arpa had put a stop to the second round of dipping.

"It's for Rosario," he said, pointing at the water.

"He's dead," Melluso retorted, planting both feet on the ground and facing him down. Then he said, in a threatening voice: "Move, I need to drink."

"No," the lieutenant replied.

Vincenzo Melluso looked around, seeking moral support from the other soldiers, but no one was in the mood to back him up: they were all on D'Arpa's side. He turned his back to the wall and sat down in that tiny fissure of shadow. He stared at the iron box.

"Die, worthless thing."

D'Arpa picked up the pot and carried it over to the shade of the wall. He was going to guard it himself.

That night, another fight. D'Arpa had dropped off into sleep. Melluso kicked him in the head and lunged for the pot of water. The water was warm but it was so wonderful to dip both hands into it. He lifted them to his mouth but never got a chance to drink. D'Arpa was already on top of him.

"This water."

He hit him in the face with a right.

"Belongs."

A left smashed down into his jaw.

"To."

Another right.

"Rosario."

A left, the last punch.

Vincenzo Melluso lay sprawled on the ground, arms thrown wide, legs stretched out. He looked like a Jesus on the cross. His mouth was a bloody mess. The other prisoners might not have understood exactly what happened, but they did know that their lieutenant packed a murderous punch. The pot of water hadn't been overturned, it was still full. D'Arpa turned toward the iron cube and shouted with all the force he could muster.

"Rosà, hold on, as soon as you get out there's water for you."

Everyone turned to look at the cube and under the white moonlight they saw something they never would have believed possible. A skinny finger protruded from the airhole and waggled, up and down; then it was withdrawn, not to be seen again. Rosario was still alive. The water had not been sacrificed in vain. The prisoners sensed such a charge of adrenaline in their bodies that without even thinking about it they all joined together in a primitive shout of jubilation, arms raised and fists clenched. They exulted as if the Italian national team had just scored a goal. They were prisoners but they were still alive. Rosario must and would return to their ranks. His survival had become a reason to hold out.

The third day seemed to stretch on forever. As soon as day dawned, the prisoners started pestering the guards, asking when Rosario would be freed, how much more time until he was let out, come on, he'd been in there three days already. "Twelve hours," they replied. "Ten and a half hours." "Nine hours." The iron cube was the vanishing point, attracting all eyes. Hold on, Rosario, they thought. There were even a few who managed to murmur the words. They would have shouted them but they didn't have enough saliva to emit any sounds.

There were five hours to go now. An officer walked into the prisoners' enclosure. He spoke in his incomprehensible language. He noticed that everyone was looking over at the iron cube. He laughed out loud, and then froze everyone in place by speaking in perfect Italian.

"*Nessuno è mai sopravvissuto all'isolamento.*"

No one has ever survived solitary confinement.

He walked out of the enclosure but stayed close to the barbed wire, watching as the vessels of their hope all sank, one after another.

There were four hours to go. The prisoners' gazes swung from the cube to the pot of water. D'Arpa understood that there had been a shift in the wind. He filled his chest with air and then bellowed out a resounding, hoarse, creaky howl, the air scratching as it rushed past his vocal cords. When he was done emitting that shout, he was in so much pain that he gagged and then vomited blood. Something had broken in his throat. What Francesco D'Arpa had shouted was this: "*Rosà, faccìllo vìdiri ca sì vivo.*" Rosario, show us that you're still alive. No finger protruded from the air hole, there was no movement of any kind. Blind despair descended into the heart of each prisoner.

Dario Tomasello was a peasant from Bronte. He walked toward the pot of water, determined to have a gulp of it. D'Arpa didn't even give him the time to communicate with gestures. A straight punch to the stomach doubled him over. Tomasello fell to his knees and then tumbled over onto his side. Lieutenant D'Arpa assumed a stance in front of the pot of water and glared at his fellow prisoners. The meaning was unmistakable to one and all: they were going to wait for Rosario to emerge from solitary confinement, and they'd better stay quiet or D'Arpa would unleash his fists in order to protect Rosario's water.

Outside the fence, two guards were smoking. Neither of them gave the slightest thought to the prisoner in solitary confinement. By now, they assumed he was a goner. Still no news about Nicola Randazzo.

The soldiers made the rest of the time go by in the only two pursuits that remained to them: surviving and staving off insanity. The heat was surreal. When two guards approached the iron cube to open it, everyone got to their feet and trooped over to the barbed-wire fence.

The padlock was removed with gloves, it was so hot. As soon as the cube was opened, they glimpsed Rosario, hunched in the fetal position. He wasn't moving. An officer arrived and kicked him with his boot. No reaction. The noncommissioned officer addressed the prisoners: "There's no way to survive solitary confinement." He pointed to Rosario. The man had burn marks all over his body: back, arms, and legs. Francesco D'Arpa felt his lips quiver and his eyes well up with tears, but before he even had a chance to wonder how it was that his body still possessed any fluids at all he saw what he saw next and at that instant he lost all self-restraint and dropped to the ground and wept and bawled louder and longer than ever before in his twenty-seven years on this earth. Rosario's inert body was confirming the prisoners' defeat; they'd placed their bets on him and they had lost. The English officer perceived their growing, throbbing despair and, without looking down, he added, in Italian: "*È morto.*" He's dead. And it was at that exact instant that, from that heap of skinny motionless flesh, unhoped-for, unexpected, and blessed, there rose, toward the heavens a finger, supported by an elbow and a wrist: Rosario's forefinger, erect, pointing skyward, in defiance of death and solitary confinement, in defiance of the enemy and in defiance of God. He was still alive and the enemy could go fuck themselves and all the prisoners were hollering, they'd placed their bets on him and he had come in a winner and so had they and D'Arpa was sobbing and the soldiers were hugging one another and the guards were all looking on in admiration at that forefinger, alive and standing at attention.

Rosario's body was brought back inside the barbed wire and laid on a pallet of clothing, in the shade next to the wall. D'Arpa dipped a corner of his shirt sleeve into the water and started dabbing moisture onto Rosario's lips. They were dry, cracked, minuscule. His tongue was tough and leathery, the inside of his throat was covered with sores. There was no hurry. One drop after another. This was the only way to get him to drink.

His forehead was scalding hot, his whole body was on fire.

He had a raging fever.

Francesco D'Arpa covered Rosario with three shirts. He went to the fence and started shouting.

"A doctor, a doctor."

He coughed up blood, but went on shouting.

"A doctor."

This was the first time anyone had survived the iron cube. Even the enemy saw fit to accord him the honor due. When my grandfather was loaded onto the stretcher to be taken to the infirmary, the prisoners saluted the patient's exit by getting to their feet, every last one of them except Melluso.

The luggage was packed and piled right there on the floor between him and Nenè. An insurmountable wall. Just a few more minutes and the story of the two of them would have new and different words. Nenè was going off to work for a boss in a distant land with a difficult name. Those minutes were the last few syllables of their history together. They shook hands forcefully, like grown-ups. Orazio, Nenè's father, tousled Rosario's hair.

"We have to go, right now."

The two friends sealed their separation with the only two words possible.

"Ciao, Nenè."

"Ciao, Rosà."

Few gestures, even fewer words, but everything clear and exact.

Nenè smiled one last time, picked up his suitcase, and trudged off with his father toward the station, disappearing behind the olive trees.

The day before, sitting on the slopes of the mountain of Cape Gallo, they had looked to the future that awaited them, out beyond the horizon line that stretched across the sea. All around them was silence and September. Rosario sat on his friend's left and clamped the bud of an ear of wheat between his lips.

Without looking at him, Nenè confided: "You know what I'd like? I'd like to steal winter's chill."

In silence, Rosario listened to his friend's brief confession. As soon as the flow of words came to an end, the two friends rose to their feet and, side by side, they launched into an agile and vibrant race, their feet biting into the road and their arms carried along by the momentum of their bodies, while their eyes, without warning, wept tears.

Twelve days later, army trucks arrived. The prisoners were loaded onto them. They were being transferred. Francesco D'Arpa wrapped his arms around Rosario again and sat next to him for the entire length of the journey. D'Arpa tried to tell him the whole story, but other soldiers chimed in with other details. They added necessary and unique points of view: their own.

"Why?" my grandfather asked the lieutenant.

"You needed water, more than anyone else."

"Nicola is doing better, they've treated him, he was in the bed next to mine."

"Apart from the infection in his asshole, he's had a better time of it than any of us."

"How come you're so strong?"

"I box."

"Are you a boxer?"

"In my spare time."

"You saved my life, *grazie.*"

"How did you manage to survive in there, Rosà?"

"I remembered."

"What?"

"My friend Nenè, the moments we spent together, his last words."

They saw a long line of elephants and watched as the sky was tinged pink by a passing flock of flamingos. A hyena lying alongside the road and a gnu's carcass enveloped in a cloud of insects. Falling stars and the low trees of the savanna. Two days later, the trucks came to a halt. They'd reached a new prison camp. The trip was over.

"You know what I'd like? I'd like to steal winter's chill, just like that, so that when the sirocco comes, I'd always have a little puff of cool breeze on my skin and in my heart. There are memories, on the other hand, where the only thing I'd want to keep is the few seconds before. The moment before you catch a fish, the moment before you touch a pair of tits, the moment before you taste an orange. Then, if I ever learn to write someday, I'll dream up a whole story of *not*s: the times I didn't leave, I didn't say goodbye to you, I didn't go somewhere far away, I didn't work for a boss, and the day there wasn't a party in the town square, I didn't dance with a woman who was too beautiful to look at, I didn't plant a long, leisurely, flavorful kiss on her lips, and she didn't immediately say to me: Kiss me again, my love. And anyway, I'm faster than you."

"No you're not."

"Yes I am."

"I can crush you whenever I want."

"Race, from here to there."

"Let's go."

And they ran together, away from childhood, side by side, for the last time in their lives.

Nenè won.

◤◤◤

Umbertino had finished running through his thoughts. The March evening breeze began to make itself felt. It was time to put his clothes back on. Rosario, sitting on the bench beside him, had listened in silence, never uttering a word.

"And anyway, to boil the sauce down, this is the way things stand: since there's nothing of the kind in Palermo, I'm going to just go ahead and open a boxing gym of my own."

Even then, my grandfather spoke not a word. The moonlight created a faint glow on his hollowed-out, razor-sharp face. A hawk, that's what he looked like. He looked like a hawk.

"What is it you're looking at?" Umbertino asked him.

Turning his head, Rosario looked my uncle right in the eye. A little shudder swelled his chest, as head and shoulders both rose together, then his shoulder blades sagged again.

"I'm looking back."

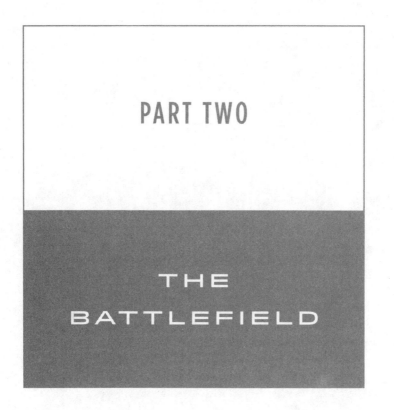

PART TWO

THE
BATTLEFIELD

But after I'm dead, I'd prefer to be reborn as a wild boar."

"You understand that you're a real dumb-ass, don't you, Gerruso?"

"A wild boar is happy."

"How d'ya know?"

"Easy, wild boars don't write."

"You're saying anyone who writes is unhappy?"

"If they weren't, they wouldn't write."

"Well, what would the boar do?"

"He'd go out, under the open sky, and grab all the happiness in the forest for himself. It's like you explained to me, the logic of fair trade."

"You need to stop repeating everything I teach you."

"You're right, sorry."

"Anyway, it's true: everything has a price, not even death comes for free, you have to pay for it with your life."

"That's right, fair trade among animals: they pay for their happiness with the fact that they don't know how to write. They live without thinking about tomorrow; death is like a little wrinkle in their happiness."

"But why exactly a wild boar?"

"It's very tasty with potatoes. But you're not a wild boar, not at all. Yesterday, during your first bout, I was tryna figure out what kind of animal you might be. Wild boar, definitely not. Camel, no. Gekko, no way, not by a long shot."

A gleam appeared in his eyes. Using my nickname, he asked what animal I thought I was like when I was boxing.

I said nothing.

You can't talk underwater.
Fish are mute.

≋

My first fight.

Marcello Brullera, from Catania. Having abandoned his studies after elementary school, he was taken to a gym by his cousin, a respectable amateur who never managed to take the next big step up. He had an unusual physique: extremely tall for his age at fourteen, he was unassailable unless he dropped his guard. His leverage and reach kept everyone at arm's length.

He was my first opponent in the ring.

During the third and final round, one of his punches hit me on my left side, the injured side.

I curled up, biting my mouthguard to keep from closing my eyes.

I was in my corner.

I could feel my heart throbbing in my side.

"This bruise on your side is the size of my hand, kid."

"I can still move all right, Maestro Franco, it doesn't hurt as much as it did yesterday, thanks."

"If you say so . . . in any case, it's just five days until your first fight, youngster, it seems to me that there's already been plenty of nonsense, so listen to me now: no drinking, get to sleep early, and above all, no fucking."

"Yes, but . . ."

"But what? How old are you?"

"Fourteen."

"Sure, at your age you all think with your dicks, kid. Listen to me and learn a great truth: you should never fuck before a fight. But the real life lesson is this: you should never fuck *after* a fight. I'm speaking to you with my heart in my hand, out of hard-won personal experience. When the bout is over, you can't really do a thing, you're so riddled with pain that the best thing to do is renounce any such pursuits. What are you going to do? Break down in tears in the presence of a woman? Heaven forbid! Instead, listen to what I say: after a fight, you need to withdraw to some lonely place and listen to what your body is telling you, you understand? Even if your dick is screaming, ignore it, let it shout. You need to focus on the way you're breathing, whether your ribs are fanning out properly, the way your neck is moving, if your eyes are steady. Most important of all, you need to do memory exercises, make sure everything's operating properly. Do like me, kid, take this fabulous advice that I learned from your uncle: think about all the women you've ever fucked, every last one, the blondes, the brunettes, the raven-haired beauties, the sisters of your best friends, the whores you might have gone to, you have to remember them all. And you have to remember all their names. You have to be straightforward and accurate; some injuries are invisible to the eye, and in fact they come from the punches that you take to the head. So forget about your cock, before and after the fight. Let me have twenty light and agile push-ups on your fists, then jump a little rope with Carlo. And in the ring, the way your first fight turns out is up to you."

"Maestro, can I ask you a question?"

"Be my guest."

"Was my father nervous before his first fight?"

"Who are you talking about? The Paladin? He was never nervous, quite the opposite."

"I'm plenty calm; if anything, it's you and Umbertino who seem nervous."

"Kid, there's an unwritten rule in boxing: you're going to lose your first bout."

"Oh, really?"

"Yes."

"Did you lose?"

"Certainly. And so did the Paladin."

"Maestro, forgive me, but isn't this my opponent's first fight, too?"

"Yes."

"Then it's not like both of us can lose."

"Stop being a smart-ass."

"Like my dad?"

"No, like your uncle. And remember to put a wet towel on your side when you lie down tonight."

Uncle Umbertino, in the front row, was waving his arms for me to move out of the corner. Franco the Maestro was twisting his cap in both hands. My grandfather, standing at the far end of the room, was motionless. Gerruso was crushing a can of Chinotto and shouting my nickname.

Nina wasn't there.

She hadn't come.

Who knows what she was doing, maybe she was looking for a song on the radio or underlining words in a book or drawing a swan on a fogged-up window.

Somewhere else, not here.

I created a narrow opening in front of my face, giving my opponent a glimpse of my forehead.

It was the third round.

Brullera's face lit up.

My first fight was about to come to an end.

Carlo, standing next to Franco the Maestro as my second, was eyeing the alignment of my feet.

"But why did you give that name to this move, Davidù?"

"It's all about diving and whores."

Carlo was like a leaf. He was light; there was always a discrepancy between where the tips of his feet seemed to be and where you knew they were. It didn't even look as if he was lifting off the ground. The only sounds that could be heard were the turning rope and the falling drops of sweat. Knees forward, elbows windmilling, gaze straight ahead.

For years, Carlo was the gym's most powerful fighter. He'd fought twice in national championship bouts. He'd just happened to be matched up with more powerful opponents, that's all. He'd become Maestro Franco's assistant, just as Franco had become Umbertino's assistant. Carlo really loved me. He was the one who knocked me to the canvas when I was nine years old.

"Let's give it another try, I like this move, it's unbeatable," he said with genuine awe.

And again and again, one leap after another, to perfect the movement that had been revealed to me at the beach the summer before.

The footwork of the Buttana Imperiale—of the Imperial Whore.

It started with an offside foot shuffle.

Brullera had just landed a punch to my already battered ribs. Doubled over, I waited for him to continue the attack. He wasted no time. He pulled back his right elbow, cocking his arm to unleash a right cross full in my face, where an opening had appeared. It lasted only a fraction of a second but this movement meant he'd dropped his guard. He was a fourteen-year-old fighting his first match, happy, proud of the way he was boxing, certain he was about to taste victory. For a single fleeting instant, I felt sorry for Brullera. My right fist had already landed square on his chin. It was shoving forward, fiercely. The glove climbed, shattering his septum. He'd only had to give me a single opportunity. Three rounds to glimpse this opening: let him pound my ribs so that I could unleash, with the footwork of the Buttana Imperiale, a single uppercut. A gush of blood poured out of Brullera's mouth. It stained the back of my boxing glove, my forearm, my chest. His mouthguard flew onto the referee's shirt. Brullera fell flat on his back onto the mat.

The referee stopped the fight immediately.

Maestro Franco was clapping.

Carlo was gleeful.

"The Buttana Imperiale! That foot shuffle! You did it! I knew it!"

Gerruso was squealing my last name, waving the can of Chinotto in the air, spraying everyone around him. Whenever someone asked him to calm down, he'd reply: "I know the guy who just won and you don't, and I don't talk to losers like you."

Umbertino climbed into the ring. His eyes were glistening.

"You reminded me of the Paladin, sweetheart."

Then he turned to look at the audience.

"Bow down, assholes."

My grandfather came out onto the square of canvas, too. He took a look at my injured side.

"It's only pain, Grandpa, it'll go away."

He came over to me and, unforeseeable event, he gathered me in his arms, shy man though he was, hugging me despite the fact that all eyes were on him.

I thought about my father.

He would have been proud of me.

My first fight.
KO in the third round.

≡≡≡

"Ciao, Grandma."
"Davidù! You came to see me."
"Eh, sure, if I hadn't you'd be complaining about it from now till the end of the world."
"You idiot."
"Is Grandpa here?"
"He's outside, in the garden, tending to the plants."
"Does he want to give me another one?"
"Most likely."
"Sometimes I look at the cactus that he gave me for my birthday, and I still can't believe that it'll be such a long time until it blooms."
"How many years until it blooms?"
"Thirteen, Grandma. My plant is going to bloom in thirteen years."
"Did you know that your plant is the daughter of the one that his old friend Randazzo gave him?"
"The plant that Grandpa took with him to Germany?"
"Exactly."
"Grandma, can plants be relatives?"
"In my imagination, sure they can. Your grandpa took a sprout from the mother plant, transplanted it, and gave it to you. That plant is the daughter."
"What's that you're holding?"
"Essays my kids wrote."
"Are you correcting them?"
"It's always instructive to see the way my kids manage to abuse the language."
"Just like Gerruso."
"For instance?"
"He dreams up figures of speech, he gets the intransitive verbs all wrong, he systematically ravages the rules, and he always tries to justify his mistakes. For example, he says things are crazy-driving instead of saying that they drive him crazy, and funny movies don't

make him laugh, they're laugh-making. He says it's easier to say things that way."

"He's not all wrong."

"Huh?"

"The point is that if you want to unhinge the language, you have to know what you're doing. Does Gerruso know the language so well that he can afford to abuse it?"

"I doubt it."

"In that case, it's a red and a blue error at the same time, let's not kid around here. If you want to break a rule, first you need to know it the way you know the Hail Mary."

"You like it when someone shatters the language."

"It's a sign that the language is alive and still working. The immediacy indicates the acquisition of a shared code of meaning."

"The construction of a rapid and agile vocabulary."

"Times change and forms of expression follow the things that are happening around us. Once, we all spoke Latin, now we have Italian, and what's more, we speak Palermitan, a fine dialect with deep roots, capable of great speed and strength. But, listen, do you understand why I asked you to come?"

Grandma's voice had faded away. She'd lifted one hand to cover her mouth.

"Go out to the garden and ask your grandpa to come the day after tomorrow."

A piece of advice, an instruction, an indication of a strategy, and, at the same time, something verging on a prayer.

In the little garden behind the house, Grandpa was surrounded by sage and rosemary. His back turned, he raised his left hand, anticipating my greeting. His back was immaculate, his fingers covered with dirt.

"Ciao, Grandpa."

His hands went back to work, uprooting weeds and clover, straightening branches with twine, watering where plants thirsted.

"I wanted to tell you something."

Grandpa's gestures were minimal, orderly, spare. Precision is the product of ceaseless training.

"I wanted to invite you to my first fight. It's the day after tomorrow, at our gym. Would you like to come? It would make me happy if you did."

Grandpa turned away from his plants and faced me. His head tilted slightly to the right, his cheekbones jutting above the hollows of his cheeks. A forward movement of the head confirmed that he'd attend.

"Okay, well, I'm leaving, see you tomorrow."

"Your side?"

"Better, thanks, that is: it hurts, it really hurts a lot, I still have all the marks from the beating I took, just look."

Grandpa turned on the water, carefully cleaned his hands, and, without drying them, placed them, still wet, on both sides of my chest.

"Every man has twelve ribs on each side, did you know that?"

The hands that had raised the Paladin were caressing me.

Grandpa smiled until the water on my skin had dried.

≡≡≡≡≡

Rosario handed the dish to D'Arpa. When jobs had been doled out, he'd wound up in the kitchen with Nicola Randazzo. Francesco D'Arpa and Marangola had been assigned to carpentry, Melluso and Iallorenzi to janitorial work.

My grandfather had certainly been lucky: in the kitchen he was out of the sun, there wasn't a lot of talking, they searched you only on the way in and on the way out, he was reasonably free to move, and he almost never ran into Melluso.

He'd come up with a new recipe for beans and he wanted the lieutenant to be the first to taste it. D'Arpa thanked him, took the plate from his hands, and went on explaining how the National Fascist Party was committed to the fight against the Mafia.

"It's really a competition to see who has the bigger dick. In Sicily, the Mafia can't win, it would be a disaster, and it's the same thing with those corrupt assholes, the Communists, they can't win either."

D'Arpa hated them. When he was a teenager, four Communists had beaten him bloody. His crime was being the son of a large landowner.

"That's why I took up boxing, so I could do a better job of defending myself when the time came."

Once a week, they held tournaments, which included boxing matches, in the prison camp. D'Arpa still didn't feel up to fighting, he was tired, he needed to build up his strength to withstand the blows he knew he'd certainly receive.

"So you've never cooked before, Rosà? Not even back home?"

"No."

"And now you even invent your own dishes. You see, life is funny, and sometimes it leads us to discover talents we never dreamed we had."

He dug his spoon into the food and tasted it.

"Mmm, good, nice work, I like it. When you were a kid, what did you want to be when you grew up?"

Rosario shrugged, he'd never talked about that with his friend Nenè. His one dream was a profession where you talked as little as possible, that much was true.

"I've always known that I'd have to take care of the family land, but when I was a kid, I dreamed of being a merchant: traveling, hearing new languages, seeing the world, having a home port to come back to."

"How is it going in the woodshop?"

"You know, it's not bad at all. Cutting wood, planing it, driving nails, building a chair, learning how to make furniture, how to make a door—not really bad at all."

D'Arpa put his bowl down on the table and started gesticulating.

"You know who I envy? Randazzo. He learned the farmer's life as a child, he knows plants and the exact times for cultivation. Have you seen him use a hoe? He's very precise when he sinks it into the soil. His body is accustomed to certain movements, he's performed them all his life, his hands are familiar with trees, branches, fruit. You need to start from childhood and learn a profession, Rosà. If I'd grown up on a boat, now I'd know the winds, the currents, and how to navigate by the stars; I'd be able to say exactly where to launch the nets based on the intensity of the swell. Instead, I'm stuck overseeing family land. I have to finish a table for the officer who arrived the day before yesterday, see you later back at the barracks."

Rosario stopped to look out over Randazzo's vegetable garden. Every morning, after the general search, Nicola weeded, cleared away stones, and covered the plants to protect them from the lash of the sun's rays. He irrigated them with water filtered through a shirt.

"There's too much salt, and that's bad for the plants," he explained.

His favorite plants were sheltered under the rudimentary roof of a shed made of wooden planks: they were small and green, with tender leaves. Nicola denied himself water to make sure the plants had enough to drink.

"Taking care of plants is like taking care of yourself," he confided to my grandfather, as he showed him just how deep you need to plant onion bulbs. "Plants are honest. If you take care of them, they give you fruit and flowers. They keep you company, they never complain."

A guard warned my grandfather that it was time to get back to work. Rosario picked up D'Arpa's plate and headed back to the kitchen. Halfway there, he dipped his finger in and sampled the new recipe. It was foul-tasting. Far too much salt. He'd forgotten to filter the water. He peeled the potatoes, performing the movement that Nicola had taught him, thumb cocked on the shaft of the knife, the potato turning in the other hand, the peel falling away in a single ribbon.

"Patience has nothing to do with it. You have to be able to read the signs in the dirt, otherwise the rabbit traps will always stand empty."

Mino Iallorenzi had been hunting with his father ever since he was a kid. Wild game, rabbits, hares.

"But the animal that's best of all is also the most dangerous: wild boar. If it's alone, there's a good chance you can catch it, but if they're in a herd, then good luck catching them, they gallop like hell and destroy anything that gets in their way."

"Like tanks."

D'Arpa always managed to find the perfect comparison.

"I'm starving for meat," said Marangola.

How long had it been since they'd tasted any? Months. The prisoners never got to eat animal flesh.

"The cocksuckers that work in the kitchen eat it all for themselves."

Melluso had no doubt about it. Rosario and Nicola were eating meat and not even sharing a bite with their fellow prisoners.

"That's not true, I've never seen a scrap of meat in the kitchen," Randazzo retorted.

"Don't waste time on him," D'Arpa recommended.

Melluso sniffed loudly and spat on the ground.

"If I come into the kitchen to clean up and I see meat, you have to give me some, is that clear?"

Rosario didn't ignore that threat. If it weren't for the fact that they were searched regularly, he would have forced Nicola to carry a knife with him. Melluso was like a weed. His presence ruined the good plants.

Iallorenzi explained a number of hunting techniques—how to lay traps, how to recognize animals by the sounds they made, by their gait.

"The animal has to run to where the hunter wants it. The most important thing in hunting is right there: the trick is to herd them right into the trap."

Marangola interrupted to point out a few differences from the world of fishing. In his experience, the only fish you really hunt are the tuna and the swordfish. Fish with unsuspected power, respected by all fishermen. Sometimes, even harpoons weren't enough. He recalled seeing speared swordfish, harpoons plunged half a yard deep into their flesh, swim away alive; tuna able to drag boats down into the deep.

Iallorenzi piped up with his point of view: "In the sea, blood dissolves, on land it becomes a trail for a hunter to follow. On dry land, a wounded animal has only hours to live."

Randazzo had to agree. He knew animals well. In the countryside where he came from, they raised rabbits, chickens, and pigs. They had guard dogs to watch over the poultry. Nicola knew it: a wounded wild animal was bound to die before long. Hunters will follow a trail of blood to the very end.

"Have you ever slaughtered an animal?" Nicola asked.

The only one to answer in the affirmative was Mino Iallorenzi, who shot back: "Some parts should be eaten while they're still warm."

"That's right, the liver and the brains and the heart and the kidneys and the belly, and you can also collect the blood from the throat while it's still hot, and you can use it to cook black pudding; it's delicious."

If meat had arrived in the camp, Nicola would have known how to fix it.

"What's it like to cut an animal's throat?" D'Arpa asked.

"The smell is powerful, the blood is hot, and you can feel the life ebbing away."

Nicola's father made him cut the throat of his first hog when he was just seven. He'd had to learn to slice through the jugular with a single clean cut in order to keep the beast from suffering: the hog would bleed to death more quickly if the blood was able to gush out all at once. You had to pull the head back high, so that the women could catch the steaming blood in a bucket.

"Every animal has a death that belongs to it."

With chickens, the rule is simple: one hand holds the body, the other twists the neck. The first time, Nicola got it wrong, he twisted with both hands and the hen's head came off in his hand. Terrified, he dropped the hen's body. It was still moving; it managed to run a few yards, until its movements grew gradually more feeble and it petered out and it finally collapsed.

"What's it like for the animals in the countryside where you live?"

"We treat them well."

"Do they live better or worse than us?"

Nicola didn't answer.

The sirens sounded outside the fence, the candles were extinguished, leaving them in darkness, and in no time at all a few people were already snoring, indifferent to the heat, the stench, and the insects.

≈

"No, I swear it's true, she never called, I'm at home all day long, my mother never lets me go out, she says that Palermo is too dangerous now. If you want, I'll call Nina."

"Okay . . . no . . . I don't know . . . I mean, yes, yes, call her, but don't tell her . . ."

"Don't tell her what?"

"Nothing, Gerruso, don't tell her anything, just ask her how she's doing. And whether she'll come see the fight on Sunday. And remind her that it's my first fight. And ask her whether she ever thinks about me, at all. No, better not. Forget what I just said. Just ask her how she's doing. No, scratch that, don't even call her. Listen, let's end this phone call right now, that's probably the best thing to do."

"All right, but I'll hang up first. Ciao, P—"

"Don't you dare use that nickname."

"Why not? It's nice."

"I don't give a damn."

For the past three days I'd been trying to reach Nina. When someone finally answered the phone, it was her mother on the other end of the line.

She wouldn't let me talk to her.

"Don't ever call here again," she said, as an opener.

"She doesn't want to talk to you," she added.

"I never liked you, not one little bit," she concluded.

"So are we saying goodbye?"

"I already said goodbye to you, Gerruso."

"Why are you so grumpy?"

I told him what had happened at the gym, that afternoon.

Maestro Franco wanted to see how fast my hands were.

My left side was in pretty bad shape.

He'd held his palms open flat and waited for mine.

A test of speed.

He shot out his hand three times and grazed me but couldn't land a punch.

Then he lifted my T-shirt to take a look at the bruise.

"Try to get better fast."

"So, can I fight, Maestro?"

Franco crammed his cap down onto his head.

"What do you think, Umbè?"

"Sure, he can get into the ring. Anyway, his opponent, Brullera, the one from Catania, is taller and stronger than him. Carlo, come here, take this twenty thousand lire and go bet it on Brullera to win, he's certain to beat my nephew."

He waited for me to react, but I wouldn't give him the satisfaction. Then my uncle decreed that I was destined to lose even if I'd been in perfect health, since my father had lost his first fight, too. That was when I felt the first drip of hatred for him.

I didn't regret it in the slightest.

"Anyway, Gerruso, you gotta stop calling me on the phone."

"But it wasn't me that called you."

"Then who was it?"

"It was my finger, that's who dialed the number."

"Don't tell me that you use your stump-finger to dial my home number."

"It fits so snug into the holes, just right."

"Listen, I'm tired, I just finished my workout, I still have to go smear some pomade on my side, ciao."

"Do you want me to come over and put it on for you?"

"Are you an idiot?"

"It might be good for you, my hand has a different weight, maybe the stump-finger is miraculous."

"No, really, do you have the slightest idea of how much you disgust me?"

"I couldn't say, how much, ninety-one?"

At the police station, my mother, uncle, and grandfather came to get me. My mother rushed to my side.

"How are you, light of my life? How are you both? What happened?"

It was Gerruso who told the whole story, confirming the version that I had just given the carabinieri. As soon as he came to the story of the beating, he enriched it with a bounty of detail that I'd suppressed in my account.

"Lift your T-shirt, Davidù."

The size of the bruise astonished even the police officers.

"Signora, he didn't tell us a thing."

There would be no charges. The trip to the police station was a formality. Now that our families had arrived, we'd be released. No one told me that what I'd done was wrong. Gerruso's mother came in, too. She shouted the whole time. The first thing she did, instead of asking "Are you all right?" was to slap her son's face, grab him by the ear, and charge out the door. Gerruso threw his arm behind him and waved goodbye, waggling the hand with the stump-finger. Umbertino dropped a coin into the slot of the phone in the corridor of police headquarters and called Franco.

"We have a problem, he was hurt."

I didn't say a word the whole way home.

When we got there, my mother rubbed medicated cream on my side.

"If there was a pomade to put on your heart to make you feel better, my love, I'd put it on immediately, even if it cost me my life."

The bruises on my side would vanish in time. But the wound in-flicted by seeing and losing Nina again wouldn't heal anytime soon.

Gerruso had called me a couple of days earlier.

"This Saturday my cousin Nina is going to the Mediterranean Fair, my aunt asked me to go with her, but I told her I'd only go if my friends came with."

"You don't have any friends."

"Wanna come with me to the fair?"

"I don't know."

"Please?"

"Okay, fine. But your cousin, is she going to the fair all by herself? Or with girlfriends? She wouldn't by chance be planning on bringing that blond friend of hers again, the Imperial Whore?"

"Uh, I don't know, if you want I could ask."

"You could ask? Why would you do that? What the hell do you think I care about Nina?"

I hadn't seen her for two months, since that afternoon at Giusi's party. I hadn't talked to her since the day after the party, when the telephone was heavy in my hand and the click of the receiver brought relief.

Two months ago, Nina and I had nothing more to say to each other, and with the end of words, our relationship, too, had ended in silence.

"Gerruso, how the hell are you dressed?"

On the sidewalk outside the front door of my building, he'd shown up wearing a shiny formal suit: dark slacks and jacket, white shirt, patent leather shoes, a fuchsia tie.

"Why? I look real sharp."

"We're going to a fair, not to a wedding."

"My cousin likes it when I dress up fancy."

"Let's get going before I change my mind."

The Mediterranean Fair was teeming with strollers, cotton candy, young couples, games, colored lights, women shouting, ravenous young men on the make, and sideshow rides blaring amplified music, heavy on the bass.

"I don't believe in miracles."

"But they do happen."

"How can you be so sure?"

"My mother tells me so. And in any case, I always pray to Jesus for the miracle, every night."

"And did He perform the miracle?"

"Not yet."

"So what conclusion do you draw from that fact?"

"That Jesus has a lot on His plate. Even so, though, the miracle I'm asking Jesus for is just a little one."

"What is it?"

"For him to grow back my . . ."

"Your stump-finger?"

"Even just a little piece of the fingernail would be enough for me."

"Gerruso, the fingernails are all growing in your head."

Gerruso stopped in front of the punching ball.

The guys who were trying to rack up points were throwing miserable punches. Everything you could do wrong they were doing, hitting the punching ball with the strength of their arms alone. None of them got the top score.

"How many points can you get with a single punch?"

"I don't know, I've never tried."

"Should we give it a try?"

"Gerruso, I have a fight next week, I don't want to get injured."

"Okay, but you're the strongest."

"That's for sure."

"I'll hit it first, so I can tell you if it hurts."

A small crowd had begun to form around us. They were mocking Gerruso for the way he was dressed. They were snickering and teasing him, and with good reason. I envied them.

"Should I go, Davidù, should I hit it?"

I was about to dip my head forward when the worst thing happened. A kid, fifteen or sixteen years old, started making fun of Gerruso, repeating in a girl's voice: "Should I go, Davidù, should I hit it?"

The match was in just seven days.

I decided to ignore the provocation.

The kid went on, enthusiastically: "Davidù, oh my loooove, I'm going to hit it now."

"Gerruso, come over here, take off your jacket, and give me your handkerchief."

As soon as he took off his jacket, the kids started howling that we were a couple of women.

"Don't give a damn about them; listen to me: the jacket keeps your shoulders from moving freely. Next, stop thinking about your arm, think about the way your foot is pivoting. Give me your healthy hand, I don't even want to look at the hand with the stump-finger."

I wrapped a handkerchief around his knuckles. I arranged it so that it was in the perfect position for him to take the punch.

"Your feet, Gerruso, you need to turn your feet."

I took a look at the score column where the points appeared. Your average customer hits seventy points. If Gerruso got sixty points it would already be something on the order of a miracle. He looked over at me, as if I were his trainer or, even worse, his friend.

Come on, Gerruso, get a move on, let's get this out of the way.

He concentrated, focused on the target, and wound up for the punch.

The kids stopped howling.

Gerruso let fly and delivered the punch with all the power he possessed.

He turned and looked at me with a satisfied expression on his face.

"Did I hit it hard?"

Forty points.

Less than half the max.

Gerruso.

How pathetic can you be?

The kids went wild.

"Faggots! Faggots!"

With his hand still wrapped in the handkerchief, Gerruso went over to them.

"You want to bet that Davidù can make a hundred?"

"Who the hell is Davidù?"

Passersby slowed to a halt. The music died out and the colorful blinking lights stopped winking on and off. The scene staked its claim to a certain solemnity. It was a moment out of a western. Trust Gerruso to ruin everything.

He stretched out his arm and pointed straight at me.

With his stump-finger.

"That's him. Now he'll show you all."

There aren't many sounds that can really wound the ears: a pistol shot, the crack of vertebrae shattering, the scornful roar of a circling crowd. Gerruso, completely ignorant of the way the world works, piled on.

"You want to bet he gets a hundred?"

"How much?"

"Two thousand lire."

"You're on."

Gerruso, two thousand lire is a hell of a lot of money, and if I can't get a hundred and we lose and then we run into Nina, how am I going to treat her to a ride if all of a sudden thanks to you I'm broke?

Nina.

The thought that she might be hidden somewhere watching me caused a radical shift in my approach to the matter.

I walked straight over to the leader of the pack.

"Oh, hey, let's make it five thousand lire. Or are you scared?"

"Okay."

The punching ball had a rough surface, I'd better wrap my knuckles.

"Gerruso, the handkerchief."

A new thought suddenly lunged at me. What if Nina wasn't there? Then this whole production was pointless.

"Gerruso, swear to me that Nina is here."

"But you told me that you didn't care."

"Swear it."

"My aunt told me she was."

"That's not enough."

"I swear it, Nina's here."

No one saw the punch as I let it fly. What came next was a thunderstruck silence while the highest possible score flashed on the display. I hadn't even bothered to wrap my hand.

While we were hunting for Nina in the jungle of the fair, suddenly the most breathtaking ride of all appeared before us in all its majesty: the pirate ship.

Why are we fatally attracted by extreme amusement park rides, the ones that create vacuums and drive up our blood pressure, the ones that, unless you hold on for dear life, are sure to throw you to your death?

What is this determination to test the outer limits of what the body can withstand? What creates this need for the adrenaline charge that surges into every last inch of our flesh?

At the gym, once a month, we were put through a circuit of somersaults and tumbling: five forward somersaults, five backward somersaults, five side tumbles, to the left and then to the right, and then we had to leap immediately to our feet. Walls, floor, and ceiling spun dizzyingly, depriving us of the comfortable certainty of a handhold or footfall. Some of the boxers tried to set their feet right and regain their balance but they would inevitably and helplessly lose control, tumble to the floor. Others managed to stay erect on trembling legs, eyes darting in search of support while their mouths filled with churning gastric juices. It was the best simulation that could be created in a training session of the feeling that you have when you take a punch to the temple— except for the pain. The minute we managed to get our bodies back into a vertical position, we were supposed to throw as many punches as we could as fast as we could, straight ahead, in every direction, trying to strike every inch of space available.

"But how did you ever come up with this exercise, Franco?"

"I happened to be at the tavern and Peppuccio was there, drunker than usual. He had a bottle of beer in one hand, he slipped and fell to the floor, all on his own, but then he did something I'd never seen before: he leaped back upright in a flash and, with the bottle in hand, started waving it all over the place, as if he were brandishing a sword, ready to cut anyone who came within reach."

"Attacking as defense. And that's why you teach them this feeling."

"There's more, Umbè. I want to teach you to think with your body. If the mind is too fucked up, the body has to know how to do the right thing at the right time."

Gerruso asked me what I was thinking.

"Punches thrown at the empty air."

"Like at your own shadow?"

"More or less."

"But that's pointless, you'll never hit the shadow, but he'll catch you off guard, striking a chill into your heart, like a ghost."

"Gerruso, what are you talking about?"

"Ghosts. They exist. My mother told me so. Sometimes her aunt Concetta, the one who died of a broken heart, appears to her in her dreams. My mother invokes her protection for the family, plus power-balls and bonus balls."

"Have you ever won?"

"No."

"Even your dead relatives are Gerrusos. Come on, let's ride the pirate ship, as long as you promise to shut up, okay?"

Everyone on the pirate ship was shouting: women, men, grown-ups, and Gerruso. I was the only one who didn't open my mouth. I was watching the crowd, hurtling closer, hurtling away. Nina, where are you?

"Let's climb up to the highest place on the ride, Gerruso."

The best vantage point for a view of the broadest slice of the world. My hands firmly gripped the steel bar in front of me. The pirate ship gathered speed. It rose into the air and the earth below dropped into the distance; it hurtled downward and a shiver ran up my spine. The ride went on creating turbulent air pockets, indifferent to the startled cries of the passengers. I had to respect its point of view. The pirate ship would have made a fine boxer.

Right at the exact opposite end of the pirate ship, facing us, perched a noisy clutch of girls. There were seven of them: seven identical hand-bags and seven indistinguishable hairstyles. The one directly across from Gerruso was pretty scrumptious. A red ribbon atop her head. A colorful bead necklace traced a thin line between neck and chest, a point that I decided to stare at in order to ward off unexpected bouts of nausea. The girl's hands were intertwined with the hands of her girl-friends. They were all screaming, every last one of them. Before the pirate ship started moving, all the passengers had started pointing at Gerruso in his jacket and tie. Gerruso looked back with laughing eyes and waved with his stump-finger hand. Like his holiness the pope, only dressed in men's clothing. The ride operator interrupted the am-putee's benediction and the pirate ship started moving. Once it had begun to build up a head of speed, all inhibitions fell away and the screaming began in earnest. Everyone was shrieking but me. If Nina was watching me, I'd have earned plenty of points. I tore my eyes away from the chest of the scrumptious girl to take a look and see whether she was down there watching me. But my sense of equilibrium was knocked off-kilter just then, the sort of thing that happens when, in a moment of distraction, your foot lands right on a hollow spot in the ground and for an instant everything—world, body, mind—is pushed off balance. It lasted no more than the blink of an eye, it was an impression more than anything else. But it was more than sufficient. My body experienced an immediate urge to throw a punch. I lashed out at the air right in front of me with as many jabs and straights as possible. I wasn't merely learning the rote grammar of a new form of movement. My hands had let go of the steel bar. I was acquiring frameworks of autonomous thought. My fingers had already clenched tight. My flesh was thinking and acting toward a specific objective, the first and most urgent directive that I'd been taught since the age of nine: survival. My right hand shot forward, only to resume its cocked position as I let my left fly, and by then the right was back again with an uppercut.

I loosed three punches into the empty air, over an infinitesimal arc of time.

Without even realizing it.

I was thinking with my body.

Unfortunately, I wasn't the only one.

Gerruso, too, was thinking with his body. He started vomiting. Without warning. Without sounding the alarm. He vomited, straight ahead, no care for where it would land. He vomited voluminously, showering the unfortunate girl sitting right across from him with puke. Face, bead necklace, red ribbon: all defiled by Gerruso's geyser of vomit. A person would want to soak in bleach for a whole year. It was the onset of such a wide-scale slaughter that it could have held its head high among even biblical sacrifices and been foully unashamed. The girl, hit directly by Gerruso's vomit, reacted the only way she knew how: by throwing up in turn, and with no more consideration for her fellow passengers. No presence of mind to throw up into her own lap. Her face was transformed into an unsightly grimace as she sprayed vomit over everything and everyone. The pirate ship, blithely indifferent to this gastric inferno, increased its rhythm and its velocity. There came into being, in midair above the vessel, a colorful galaxy of vomit. Every time we hurtled down, new astronauts ventured into that celestial realm and, eager to pitch in, added a little something of their own. The screaming had died out. Everyone was busy vomiting. The democratic nature of amusement park rides. My hands, balled into fists, protected my face. I kept my guard high, my eyes wide open, my torso tensed, ready at any instant to dodge. The first voices floated up from beneath: tiny acidic meteors had rained down on the strolling pedestrians below. Down there, too, the plague of vomiting began to spread. Gerruso's face was split down the middle by his tie. His shirt looked worse than a tablecloth after an Easter Monday feast. On my left, a skinny boy was vomiting between his legs. In a paroxysm of sisterhood and solidarity, the once-attractive young woman's friends were now vomiting onto one another.

I was in the last row on the pirate ship. My back was covered. In my path, two planets of vomit. I still had everything under control.

The ship plummeted, its descent newly impetuous. I threw a combination right cross paired with an aggressive left-handed uppercut, and once I'd passed, those two planets no longer existed, shattered into countless fragments that splattered down onto the crowd. I weaved my way through with a simple shimmy of the hips, right, left, and then right again. Down below, they were begging the operators to stop the ride. I threw four more punches, each of them executed to perfection. Every time I swung through, new worlds of vomit scattered below. My face was still clean. I was ready for my first bout. I was almost sorry when a compression of air as loud as it was sudden brought the pirate ship to a definitive halt. The ride operators helped us out, assuring us in their Slavic accents that someone had already hurried over to the phone booth to call an ambulance. Many of the riders were incapable of standing up straight. They hit the ground without even extending their hands to break their fall. Gerruso looked like a rag, but deep in the back of his eyes glittered a fierce light of happiness that defied his tears.

"Jesus, Davidù, my mother's going to murder me."

He vomited one last time, then his face lifted. He was smiling. He cleaned the vomit off his face with his fuchsia tie. As soon as he felt certain he was done vomiting, he came over to me, took both my hands, and, with his filthy necktie, started cleaning them off.

In that exact instant, in the silence born of the passing of an unmitigated disaster, Nina appeared. She came straight toward us at a run. Her hair tossing free, loose, the way I like it. She stopped in front of Gerruso.

"What happened? Are you okay?"

She turned her back to me, absorbed in that conversation between cousins, from which I was excluded.

Gerruso, come on, get her to turn around, I understand that if I want to make peace I have to apologize to her for what happened at her girlfriend Giusi's party, please, see if you can get her to turn around, if you do, I'll give you permission to come to my first fight, oh, come on.

"Nina, Davidù is here, my best friend, did you say hello to him?"

An icy shiver ran through my body. Gerruso, are you and I communicating telepathically now? But what if you infect my thoughts? And anyway, you and I aren't friends, I refuse to break bread with you at the table of friendship.

Gerruso's question imposed a silence that contained everything imaginable, except for stasis. It was a ragged-edged silence. It expanded and spread, farther and farther, second by second.

Come on, Nina, turn around and let's clear things up, I'm ready to admit that it was my fault with Giusi, all I need is for you to turn around, Nina, here I am, just take one look at me, there aren't any splatters of vomit on my face.

Instead, the inconceivable happened.

There hove into view an enormous, ridiculously tall guy, heavy footsteps, buzz-cut hair, plain white T-shirt, a motorcycle helmet under his arm. This guy was, at the very least, nineteen. He was accompanied by three other bikers, each with his own helmet cradled under an arm. He came over: no introductions, no questions, no clue as to the importance of the moment. He shattered the solemnity of the silence that Nina and I had achieved and, ignoring me, with a voice devoid of all charm, said simply: "Babe, let's go."

And he laid his hairy paw down, swallowing up Nina's delicate little hand.

Not only did she not recoil, pulling her fingers away from that bestial touch, she actually flashed the enormously tall adult a smile.

And so, just inches from the objective, as I was closing in on the finish line, virtually about to attain my goal, I, too, was seized with the urge to retch.

And yet just two months ago, we would have come here to this fair together, you and I, Nina. You would have been sitting next to me on the pirate ship, not Gerruso, there wouldn't have been any vomiting, no hairy-handed boyfriend. Because just two months ago, Nina, you and I were together. Then there was that damned party at your girl-friend Giusi's house. And I made the mistake of telling the truth. And you got mad at me. And an abyss opened between us, separating us.

Two months.

And now you had a new boyfriend.

You hadn't wasted any time, had you, Nina?

Is that why you weren't turning around?

Because you didn't want me to catch a glimpse of the shame on your face?

What was this? Now that we'd broken up, had you lost your bold recklessness?

Were you no longer able to look me in the eye?

Then Nina turned.

And she leveled her gaze straight at my eyes.

"Ciao."

Her voice didn't belong to the present. It came from two months ago. We had just finished having a fight on the phone and, after a lengthy silence, she had told me "Ciao." More a surrender to exhaustion than to defeat. No words of love to fill the void that stretched between us.

Over time I'd eventually learn how, in communications between human beings, meaning travels very short distances in the vehicles of words. In sex, for example, bodies speak louder and more eloquently: grimaces, arousal, taste, moans, and sweat. Or when a relationship comes to an end. There are few experiences that tell the story more eloquently than the silence between two people who have just broken up. And yet it is only when the break is certain that at last two people are able to listen to each other, in a silence that is pure because it is absolute. And they understand that the abyss constituted by the other has never truly been explored.

And yet it wasn't that long ago, Nina, that there was no gulf between us, no edge of the cliff. There was me and there was you and there was the red wrapping paper around Giusi's birthday present.

"Fifteen is an age that really matters," you were saying.

"That's true, you only turn fifteen once in your life."

"You dope."

Between the two of us there still existed, in that moment before the disaster, a familiar and reassuring silence. It's nice to be close to someone without necessarily having to speak. And so there followed a series of actions to all appearances innocuous: ringing the buzzer at the gate of the enormous villa, walking through the garden, entering the building climbing the steps past tapestries and paintings, wondering inwardly how much money, how much heaven-sent cash Giusi's family must have. Then the door to their lavish apartment swung open to admit us and we were simultaneously greeted by the light of the afternoon and Giusi's fifteenth birthday party. And then, teetering on those heels that even a wading bird would have mocked, sheathed in that ill-fitting black tube dress that squeezed her in all the wrong places, her face coated with a thick layer of makeup meant to conceal her acne, immersed in a sickly sweet hurricane of expensive perfume, a pair of chandeliers hanging from her ears and two irregular picture frames in place of eyes, Giusi made her appearance.

She was squealing.

And you, Nina, told me under your breath: "Try to behave."

Was I coarse? Yes, unquestionably.

Was I a hypocrite? No, this, too, was unquestionable.

Giusi was homely.

Was continuing the charade like everyone else the right thing to do? Why, because she's wealthy and therefore immune to the laws of aesthetics? But the day that she wanders out of the garden of her estate and steps into the real world, do you have any idea of how badly she's going to be hurt? Someone like her, Nina, is trotting blithely toward sheer mayhem. Might as well get her used to the beatings now. Your body starts to get used to them, and eventually it practically can't feel a thing.

And that's why, after Giusi gave you a hug, and she asked me, "How do I look?" I, Nina, gave her the answer that I gave her.

I wasn't proud of what I'd done, by any stretch of the imagination. But you were standing in front of her, you were standing at my side. Another category entirely. Was it conceivable that she didn't see the difference? Could she be so blind? In that triangle, neither you nor I was the wrong side, Nina.

I couldn't lie to her.

"You may have on an expensive dress, ostentatious earrings; your hair may be teased into the latest style; you may be rich and you may be able to afford it, but loveliness, Giusi, loveliness: that's something priceless and its not available for purchase in any store anywhere."

You shoved me away, taking Giusi's side and pointing to me, denouncing me as "the usual asshole who doesn't understand shit about the world." And the door slamming behind me and me trudging home and the telephone not ringing for countless hours of torment and then it rang and it was you and it was impossible to talk because of the shouting, me a little and you a lot, and words starting to be inadequate, sentences falling apart, silence claiming more and more territory, and, while I clutched at the telephone to keep from plunging into the abyss, at the other end of the line, your voice as you said: "Ciao." And in the silence of abandonment, continental drift in the air between us.

Two months ago.

And now, who was this holding your hand?

Was this the shame that you were trying to conceal from my eyes?

As if by telepathy, Nina turned to look at Gerruso, as if in response to my question. Nina was able to read my thoughts. Is that why she said, "Try to behave"? What was that, a warning?

"This is Raul."

Raul?

What the fuck kind of name is Raul?

She introduced Gerruso to Raul's three friends, and the situation only got worse.

Igor, Loris, and Mattias.

They came over to me and extended their right hands, still cradling their helmets in their left. Their hands, however, were denied that pleasure. I refused to shake hands with them. I had no idea who they were; they had the advantage in terms of age, weight, and height, but they wouldn't get the honor of a handshake from me.

In a bubble of rapidly swelling discomfort, surrounded by the pungent scent of vomit that continued to emanate from our clothing, it was Gerruso who spoke first.

"His name is Davide, it is, and he has a normal name, he does, and he's a friend of mine, he is."

Nina, the only person there who could have or should have said something, chose not to utter a word.

Raul spoke.

"Let's get out of here."

"No."

Gerruso's voice was so annoying that it immediately had everyone on edge.

"Little boy, what the fuck right do you have to stick your nose into my business?"

"Raul, don't you dare disrespect my cousin."

"Nice cousin you have, he's all covered in vomit. And who is this other one? His boyfriend? You never told me that this guy and your cousin were married."

Bravo, Raul, excellent work. You were doing it all with your own hands, and I couldn't have improved on a single detail.

"Fucking faggot, if you don't have the nerve to go on the rides, then you'd better stay home and suck your husband's dick, understood?"

"Cut it out, Raul!"

"No, first these two bed wetters need to apologize to me."

"What for?"

"They're irritating me. Come on, little shits, say you're sorry."

"Raul, I told you to stop it."

Nina's voice was determined, firm, unbroken.

Raul's friends formed a wall of solidarity with His Miserableness. They eyed me with scorn.

To make matters even more complicated, Gerruso piped up.

"Okay, if that's how you want to be about it, sorry, ciao, you can go ahead and leave."

Now that he'd been given an apology, Raul evidently swelled with self-importance.

"Now you ask forgiveness, too, pitiful jerk."

That parenthesis of silence, that physical stasis could have gone on forever. I was younger, smaller, lighter. There were four of them. My eyes weighed options, considered possibilities. My body stood motionless. In my head, there was a single, unavoidable thought: my first match was in seven days. I couldn't afford the luxury of doing something stupid. But no sound would issue from my mouth; I wouldn't apologize, and everything would remain exactly as it was, suspended, indeterminate, devoid of pain and sorrow. Nothing would happen, I'd climb into the ring without lacerations and contusions, the side of my body healthy and undamaged. If only you, Raul, hadn't ruined everything by using words so deeply offensive that only blood could wash away the insult.

"Son of a bitch."

After so much—too much—time, a ferocious calm swept over me again.

I'd been missing that.

There was nothing else I needed.

Nina, I know you can hear me now, that's the way it is between the two of us, I think and you understand, so I'm begging you, don't try to get between us, go, run away and take Gerruso with you, I know you can hear me, Nina, I'm begging you, go fast and far, do it for me.

Nina placed herself between me and Raul.

Her back remained straight and her hand was steady as she delivered a straight-armed slap.

"Don't you dare!" she said.

Slapped in public, his pride ground to pieces, Raul decided to react. He wound up to return the slap. Nina stood there, motionless, firm and ready for combat. I was too far away to do a thing, the slap was bound to hit her face. It would have been the death of me.

It would have taken a miracle.

And a miracle took place.

Between Nina and the open palm of Raul's hand, Gerruso's face suddenly appeared. Diving arms-first, ass muscles clenched, he intercepted the straight-armed slap with his cheek. The resounding smack was deafening.

What if Raul had hit Nina?

My back turned into a triangular fin, the world turned into the sea, and my hands became teeth.

Raul didn't even have time to understand what was happening. My fist had already cut his breath short. The good thing about having a low center of gravity: you can slam your fists into the other guy's balls. A sharp vertical uppercut connected with his jaw, shutting his mouth for him. Raul fell to his knees. He was still practically as tall as me upright.

Nina, why in the world did you get such a tall boyfriend?

A sheet of flame spread over my shoulder blades. Someone had hit me with a motorcycle helmet. I had the bout in just a week. There were too many of them. I didn't stand a chance. I threw in the towel, raising both arms in a gesture of surrender, while Raul collapsed to the pavement, both hands clutching at his groin. He was moaning softly.

Gerruso, flat on the sidewalk, was rubbing his flame-red cheek.

Nina's eyes were focused on me.

Nina.

You hadn't looked at me that way since before that time Giusi came walking toward us both, the time you whispered to me: "Try to behave."

And now I see that look again.

Is this how you want me?

In a never-ending battle?

They lunged at me. Igor, Loris, and Mattias. Bigger, taller, stronger. Nina was there, flight wasn't an option. So the only thing to do was submit, hoping that it would be over as soon as possible, somebody was bound to intervene. I curled up like a porcupine, wrapping my forearms protectively around my head. A boot caught me on my right shin, a motorcycle helmet hit me square on my left shoulder, knocking me over. Amen, that's how it goes, everything comes with a price, you always have to sacrifice something. The motorcyclists weren't doing Nina any harm. All weighed and balanced, it was an acceptable exchange. A myriad of kicks, delivered boot-heel first, rained down on the left side of my body. The curse of the first bout, I decided, I'm bound to lose by forfeit. Suddenly I heard a shout. Unexpectedly, there was a pause in the beatdown. Gerruso had lunged at Loris. And right behind him came Nina.

Gerruso, you're an asshole. If anything happens to Nina, I'll kill you with these hands of mine.

A crowd stood watching, people covered their mouths with their hands, keeping a cautious distance.

I needed to move fast. Do the greatest amount of damage in the shortest possible time.

Nina, please, don't get hurt.

I'm coming.

A sharp jerk of my abdominal muscles and I was back on my feet. I blocked a helmet with my right forearm and with a sharp hook I shattered Mattias's eyebrow.

Nina.

Igor was trying to shake her off his back by reaching around behind him. A sudden lunge forward and my fist shattered his septum. He deflated, toppling to one side in a puddle of blood and mucus. Nina was watching me. She was breathing hard. Just wait, Nina, just wait. The shark fish isn't done yet.

Gerruso.

He was still clinging to Loris. Oh no, Gerruso, no, biting's no good, only little kids bite. The motorcyclist let out a yell. My fist ground into his stomach, depriving him of voice and breath.

"Gerruso, that's enough biting."

It was only then, once everything was over and the risk had vanished, that the passersby decided that common courtesy demanded they notice us.

They were sure to ask questions and erect barriers.

I had little, very little time.

"Nina."

Her eyes were puffy from crying.

"I'm sorry about Giusi. I was wrong to say what I said to her. I was mean to her."

She was seething.

"You just don't get it."

"What don't I get, Nina?"

Her hands were shaking.

"It wasn't her you were mean to."

"No?"

Her eyes were blinking back tears.

"You were mean to me. You were supposed to lie to her, and you were supposed to do it for me. You should have been nice to her for my sake. Instead, you're so staggeringly selfish that you don't even realize it. And I'd even asked you."

Try to behave.

That wasn't a command.

It was a plea.

Strangers arrived. Now they were eager to find out how I felt.

Little, very little time for one last, desperate attack.

"Will you come to see my first fight this Sunday?"

Her eyes could no longer stand it, and they burst into tears.

A crowd of people created an abyss that separated us.

She disappeared.

The carabinieri arrived, took me and Gerruso, and carted us away.

Nina and I hadn't seen each other in two months.

There's really not a lot you can do about it.

The first match is always a losing proposition.

Franco returned to the gym after a series of uphill sprints, bandaged his hands, put on his gloves, and started going a few rounds with his sparring partners. He threw punches with an unfamiliar violence, once, twice, three times. He thought Livia liked him, he thought she really liked him a lot, but it turned out he got it wrong and the slut had let that shithead Pino the mechanic feel her up. He was so furious that he instinctively changed the established sequence, came this close to hitting his sparring partner in the face. This close. All Umbertino did to avoid the punch was take a small leap backward. Then he took steps accordingly. He laid Franco flat with a one-two punch to the face that the boxer never even saw Umbertino wind up. From the canvas, while the flowing blood outlined the contours of a new face, he heard: "Dickhead, keep your guard up." He felt like laughing but he couldn't quite: his maestro had just broken his nose. He retched and then, for the first time in his life, vomited blood. He dragged himself into the bathroom, filled a basin with water, plunged his face into it, and cleaned himself up. Half an hour later, he was stretched out on the dressing room's wooden bench, ice wrapped in a towel pressed on his nose, Umbertino's complaints in his ears.

"Hey now, that cost me two lire worth of ice, Franco, you're bleeding me dry."

Another trainee showed up, Ugo Moscato, twenty-six years old, from the Noce quarter.

"So what about the match in ten days?"

"What about what?"

"Am I going to fight, Maestro?"

"What are the odds on you?"

"Pretty low, I'm the odds-on favorite."

"Then no. Franco's going to fight instead of you."

"The little kid?"

"Yes."

"But he has a broken nose."

"And what do you think, that I'd send one of my boxers to fight without a broken nose?"

"Maestro, had you already made up your mind?"

"You just mind your own fucking business. And anyway, in ten days or so Franco's nose will be all better. Go tell Half-a-Kilo that we're introducing a brand-new boxer, age fifteen. Make it very clear to him that this is going to be his first fight."

"All right. So do we bet on Franco to win?"

"Moscato, I've always told you that you're a good kid but you don't understand a single fucking thing about life. We're betting against Franco. This is his first match. It's a sure loss."

"Whatever you say, Maestro."

"That's right, Moscato, whatever I say, and now get the fuck out of my hair. Franco, how's your nose? It hurts? Don't worry, the scent of pussy, you'll still be able to smell it."

He'd learned it from the Americans toward the end of 1943. The prize was a chocolate bar or a stick of gum or a cigarette. "*Fight! Fight!*" the soldier would urge them on, and the kids would whale away at each other with their fists. The last kid standing was the winner of whatever was put up as the prize.

In Piazza Zisa, right before his eyes, there was a brawl that pitted a dozen street kids against one another, scattershot, disorderly. They were fighting because someone had said something about someone else's mother, and because streetfights are fun, and because there's nothing better to do in Palermo; ten years later, and the city was still in ruins, the perfect place to fight to your heart's content. After a few minutes, he decided to intervene. He waded into the fracas, quieting it down with his mere presence. The kids, with quick reflexes, immediately assumed a defensive stance, sensing the danger that this giant brought with him. Instead, a welcome surprise: the enormous man pulled a pack of chewing gum out of his trouser pocket.

"These are the best sticks of gum in the world, they're American. You want them?"

The kids bowed their heads.

"All right then, *fàit.*"

At first they looked at him curiously, and then with a shade of doubt dimming their expressions, and finally with the look of those who truly fail to understand.

"*Fàit,*" he said again, but still no one moved.

Finally, a curly-haired kid worked up the courage.

"What's that mean?"

"That you've got to murderize each other, one on one, but just fists, no kicking and no biting. Whoever wins takes the whole pack."

He stood there for an hour watching the kids murderize each other.

Three days later, he walked across Piazza Zisa again. Some of the kids recognized him, and left off torturing a lizard to come running over.

"You have a stick of gum?"

He walked on, paying them no more mind than you'd give a swarm of flies. One kid stood in his path, brow furrowed and flinty-eyed.

"Give me a stick of gum."

"How old are you?"

"Ten. I want a stick of gum."

"Get the fuck out of my way."

"First the stick of gum."

The giant pulled his hands out of his pockets, displaying his palms to the kid. With a glance, he invited the kid to lay his hands over his own. The kid obeyed and waited for further instructions on how to win the stick of gum.

"If you dodge the slap, I'll give you a stick of gum, okay?"

"Yes."

The kid caught a slap full in the face so hard that his eyes welled up with tears. He'd expected a slap on the back of his hand, but that's not what he got. Bastard. He glared at him with hatred. He tried to keep back the tears but he failed. The giant, gazing at him calmly, said: "Dickhead, keep your guard up." Then he added, seriously: "Ah, a piece of advice that will be useful in life: never bust my balls again as long as you live." He was no giant. He was a beast. He went on his way.

On the kid's right cheek the flaming five-fingered brand continued to burn. His friends called his name but he ignored them. One of them walked over to him and took him by the hand.

"Franco, come on, let's go home, it's late."

Franco didn't move. He just kept repeating under his breath, "I'll kill him," until the Beast's broad shoulders vanished beyond the rubble to the left of the Zisa castle.

He was returning home at a dead run with a brand-new cap on his head, a gift from his maestro.

"In just a week you have your first match, Franco, and since you have just a few hairs left now and before long you're bound to be completely bald, at least this cap will keep you from having to worry about pneumonia."

Franco was so happy that he hadn't been able to find the words to thank him. Running through his head was a relentless stream of triumphant pictures: he'd be victorious, Maestro Umberto would be proud of him, Livia would dump Pino the mechanic and from now on he'd be the one taking her out for strolls along the Mondello wharf.

In Piazza Ingastona, an unexpected encounter: two men, taller, stronger, and older than him.

"Hey, you," they called to him—a challenge.

Franco understood immediately that it would be pointless to try to say anything.

"Give me your money and your hat," commanded the taller of the two.

In a week he'd fight his first bout. He had to keep calm and react like a grown-up, worthy of his fifteen years.

"No."

As soon as the criminal reached his hands out toward him, Franco's feet went into action, pushing him backward. He threw a left cross at the first man's face, then a hook that bent the other man in half at the stomach. Both of them fell to the ground; neither was able to get to his feet. Franco examined his hands. Not a mark. He clapped his cap firmly on his head and resumed his run homeward.

As he was punching away, he had remembered the words that Maestro Umberto had spoken to him that very afternoon, during the lower-abdominal training session.

"On paper, there are laws, like if it rains you're going to get wet. Bullshit. You make your own laws. If it rains, you grab someone's nice umbrella and to hell with getting wet. There's always going to be a time when you'll have to start throwing punches without stopping to think about whether your opponent is bigger than you. In real life, you're never fighting someone who weighs the same as you. So, *p'una mano*, on the one hand, when in doubt, do as the Gospel says: throw punches first, ask questions later."

He was excited and scared at the same time. Fear produces adrenaline but the razor-sharp knife in his pocket helped to calm him down. A large, broad blade, it was a *liccasapùni*, a "soap licker," so called because in the old days it was used to smooth soap. Modern times had transformed its function; now it was used to lay out on a slab bastards who acted highhanded with kids. The Beast. He'd waited for him every single day for three endless weeks, right there, where the most powerful slap in history had left its firebrand on his cheek for six days running. The Beast. He'd pay for what he'd done. When the Beast finally reappeared, crossing Piazza Zisa, he followed him, without letting himself be seen. That was how he discovered the Beast's lair: behind a roller shutter that concealed a door through which Christians entered and exited: once outside, they'd invariably take to their heels and vanish. The plan that he had devised was infallible. He'd wait for the Beast to be alone, and then he'd enter his lair, slamming the door loudly behind him. A bold and reckless entrance. He'd brandish his soap licker. He'd show no pity whatsoever. He'd stab him just as the Gospel says. Then he'd deliver an open-handed slap right to his face. Last of all, to do things by the book, he'd spit no fewer than three sticks of gum right in his face. Perfect.

The minutes had passed, and no one had come out. He felt he was ready to make his move.

As he'd calculated, he began chewing three sticks of gum simultaneously. It had cost him a world of trouble to procure three sticks from his wealthy friends, the ones who could afford to buy gum themselves. For the first stick, he'd had to capture no fewer than twelve lizards, alive and with their tails still on: it was difficult, he'd spent a whole afternoon on it, the damned tails always seemed to come off. For the second, he'd had to beat a certain Pasquale Mistretta silly: that was easy. For the third, he'd had to catch a live fly in a glass. The lawyer's son wanted to pull the wings off a live insect: really hard, it had taken him two whole days.

Franco felt important and invincible. He couldn't lose. He drew a nice deep breath, started walking, and entered the den of the Beast, bent on obtaining satisfaction. Without hesitating he threw open the door and damn, the last thing he expected, there was the Beast sitting in a chair, easy and comfortable, legs stretched out and both hands crossed behind his head.

"Oh hey, how long did it take you? I've been sitting here waiting forever."

Franco's unforgettable entrance had been ruined. He decided to raise the stakes. Clenching his teeth, he glared at the Beast, looking him straight in the eye the way grown-ups do before beating each other to a pulp. To augment that fearsome effect, he swallowed fiercely right in his face, with conviction. Forgetting he had three sticks of gum in his mouth. He gulped them down whole, all but drowning himself on dry land. He bent over, coughing helplessly. This wasn't the way it was supposed to be, this wasn't the scenario as he'd imagined it. The scene was supposed to be one of tears and abject fear and the Beast shrunk to a whining puppy, a helpless little beastie he could kick freely without fear of consequences. Instead, there the Beast sat, mocking him at his ease. He had to regain control. With one last powerful burst of coughing Franco finally managed to propel the chewing gum down into his stomach. He dabbed at his eyes with his right forefinger to see whether they had filled with tears: his credibility would be fatally undermined if it looked as though he'd been crying. His eyes seemed to be gratifyingly dry. He was a tough customer, a citizen of the Zisa. Pride in his native quarter set him back on his feet. Now he could pro-claim the reason he was there, thus stirring abject terror in the heart of the Beast. With a tone of contempt that outdid even the scorn that dripped from his father's voice whenever he talked about the cops, he said: "I'm going to kill you." And there he stood, glowering, his head tilted forward, his mouth curled in a sulky sneer. He felt like a warrior. His pose conveyed strength and self-respect. It was all working out just as he'd imagined. So it came as a bitter disappointment when one last, unexpected scorpion sting of coughing spoiled his fine dramatic pose, forcing him to bend over double again. Damned chewing gum, those bastards gave me defective gum, the minute I catch up with them back at Piazza Zisa I'll slit their throats, one by one. Once he managed to stand upright again, gaze elevated and body erect, he saw to his genuine astonishment that the chair was empty. He looked around and saw the Beast standing close beside him. How had the Beast managed that? The man was enormous and Franco hadn't heard a thing. He couldn't let himself be intimidated. He still had the soap licker in his pocket.

"Sure, you're going to kill me. Of course you are! Maybe someday, but not today. Do you want me to tell you why?"

He walked over to the heavy bag. In the presence of the kid's ten-year-old eyes, he slaughtered it bare-handed. Franco felt a chill. The Beast's arms were so fast that it was impossible to fully glimpse their movement, he just heard one punch sink into the heavy bag, followed by another and then yet another.

My great-uncle, the Beast, walked back over to Franco. Was this the right moment to stab him? The plan didn't seem as foolproof as it had at first. There was even the concrete possibility that the knife would just snap off at the handle; the Beast looked as if he were carved out of marble. Still, Franco didn't retreat, he stayed there and didn't take to his heels. It was a point of pride with him.

It almost came as a relief when Umbertino finally spoke.

He pointed to the heavy bag.

"If you want, I'll teach you."

"Yes."

"Yes, my ass, if you want me to teach you, first you have to dodge the slap."

"You're on."

Face-to-face, Franco's child's hands in Umbertino's grown-up hands. The first slap caught him on the back of his left hand. Hard. Franco hadn't even moved his hand, instinct had made him dodge a slap to the face, not the hand. My uncle waited for the pain to be felt in its entirety.

"You wanna keep going or do you wanna to go home and cry?"

"I wanna keep going."

For twenty days in a row, every day, for an hour each day, he pounded Franco's hands, shattering capillaries and veins and still beating away at them, pitiless, and as soon as Franco started to react properly and move his hands in time, he pulled a change-up and landed a serious smack to his face, with an ample and resounding report.

"Dickhead, keep your guard up."

And the torture would start all over again.

"But why, Maestro?"

"My hands were slow, Davidù, and do you know why?"

"No."

"My eyes were slow."

Suddenly his face lit up with a brilliant idea.

"Kid, here's what let's do, let's make a bet: if you manage to bring me a live fly inside this glass, then tomorrow you can go to the fair."

"Is that the truth, Signor Maestro?"

"The truth."

"Can I go get it now?"

The maestro burst out laughing. He held his belly with one hand and clapped his cap down onto his head with the other. He looked like a roughly sketched picture of joy.

"You want to go get it now? But you have the whole day tomorrow to try to get permission to go on the rides."

"Can I go into your office?"

"Be my guest."

I walked in, I picked up a glass, I headed for the locker room, and I reemerged less than a minute later. Inside the glass was a live fly.

"But . . . but . . . but how'd you do it?"

"I put a little chunk of bread in the bottom of the glass."

"And the fly went right in."

"Yes."

The maestro looked first at the fly and then at me. He caressed my head with his stout hands.

"You're just like your father."

I smiled at him even though I didn't understand.

"But why are you so intent on going to the fair? Don't lie to me, kid."

"Nothing, Maestro, it's just that there's a girl . . ."

"Women, I knew it. I was wrong, youngster: you're not just like your father, you're the spitting image of your uncle Umberto."

"So why did you want to see all three of us together?"

Franco didn't answer. The sun was so high over Piazza Zisa and the dead silence at three in the afternoon was so fine, why ruin with words the ineffable moment preceding a wholesale slaughter? The lawyer's son, the doctor's son, and the professor's son seemed to differ: when asked a question, they felt, one ought to reply. Their patience exhausted, they exchanged a knowing glance and turned to leave.

"Your chewing gum," Franco said in a grave voice.

"What about our chewing gum?"

His hands no longer hurt. The Beast had stopped hitting him ten days ago or so. Now he just made him run and jump, nothing more.

"Your gum was defective."

And he felt like using his hands.

The three looked at one another in astonishment, and then burst into laughter, the kind that crescendos, where you have to hold your belly from the pain of the abdominal contractions. They couldn't possibly know that they were about to experience one of those memorable afternoons, an afternoon they'd never forget, when they'd buckle under a clubbing the likes of which they'd never received before, a clubbing they'd always been spared because of the fear their fathers struck into the hearts of one and all.

Franco decided to follow the Beast's advice.

After all, now the Beast was his maestro.

"Let's go, assholes, come on."

He spread his arms wide, offering up his solar plexus, embracing for the first time with eyes wide open the anticipation of a fight.

He felt free and happy.

≋

My grandfather witnessed his second boxing match at Passau, in Germany. In the neon-lit hall, the audience was smoking and guzzling beer. The boxers wore professional gloves and shoes, the referee wore a white shirt and black slacks. In Africa it had been different. When my grandfather saw the first fight of his life, Lieutenant D'Arpa was barehanded, he wore ragged shoes, and there was no referee: he and the other boxer were expected to murderize each other at will, until one of them either was flat on his back on the canvas or else gave up.

In Germany, Rosario sipped a beer as he watched the boxers. Under his arm he held the wood he had bought to build a rocking horse. His son had just turned one. He hadn't seen his son since leaving for Germany. The two boxers rarely dodged and both landed most of their punches. Rosario couldn't bring himself to cheer. He was a stranger to both sides.

Two days before his departure for Germany, Rosario had gone to see Nicola Randazzo in the countryside where he lived, just outside of Palermo.

"I swear I'll be back."

"When?"

My grandfather didn't answer.

Nicola said that he'd stay there, he'd go on taking care of the plants in the countryside, he'd never stop plunging his hands into the dirt, and, when things stopped going the way they ought to, amen, he'd just remember the happy times. He hadn't read books in his life. All he knew was the meaning of his own work, which all lay there, summed up in the process of watching a sown field. He felt sure in the knowledge that, not today, and not tomorrow, but in a while, if cared for and cultivated, the plants would bloom and bear fruit. And then at nightfall: unlacing his shoes, washing his hands, sitting in his good chair, and pouring himself a glass of wine to savor slowly.

He leaned over and picked up a cactus. It was so small that the pot fit into the palm of his hand.

"This is a gift. It will bloom for you in twenty-two years. It's strong, it's like you, it needs nothing, not even water, just a sip every three weeks in the summer, and, if you take care of it, there you are."

Twenty-two years for a blossom.

It forced you to look beyond the natural horizon presented by daily events.

Rosario caressed it.

The thorns of the cactus didn't prick him.

After the boxing match was over, D'Arpa had no interest in sleeping. Stretched out on his cot, a wet bandage covering his left eye, he talked about how a car works: one pedal accelerates, the other pedal brakes. About how film takes an impression from light and becomes a photograph. About the rivers Kemonia and Papyretus, which were buried by the Arabs and now run beneath Palermo.

"You have to learn to read and write, Rosà, it's important. No, listen, as soon as we get back home, I'll teach you myself and you can pay me back by fixing me a few of your finest treats."

All of the Italian prisoners, except for Melluso, went to see him, as if in a religious procession. Just a few hours earlier, he'd beaten a German boxer, a prisoner just like them. The Italians hailed that victory as a collective personal triumph. They'd come to pay him the proper tribute. A short chat, a quick farewell, the dignified silence of those who express their thanks with their mere presence. Sports had succeeded in bringing together people who spoke a variety of dialects, cementing the idea of the group.

"And after all, let's face it, Rosà. Ours is the comradeship that slaves feel for one another; you saw for yourself that they congratulated the German, too, didn't you? Beating another prisoner isn't the same as beating a guard. Still, victory is important for its own sake, it helps to create a sense of belonging. Just like playing games—I'm playing on this one's side, you're rooting for that one. Games teach you how important it is to take a position and stick to it."

"You need to know how to pick sides, too."

"Certainly. But there's only one way to learn that: by losing."

In Germany, my grandfather worked for forty-four days as a mason, for sixteen days as a stevedore at the fruit and vegetable market, after which he was put to the test in a fake-Italian restaurant and hired the same day. The restaurant belonged to a Calabrian who had emigrated to Passau before the war. It seated fifty-nine. The vegetables were no good. The meat was no good. The flour for the pasta dough was no good. The pay, though, was good. Rosario stayed on there, working as a cook, for thirteen months. He did what he was told, head bowed, working in silence. It was pretty much the way it had been in Africa. The diners ate anything. Once, he'd made a change to one of the dishes on the menu, improving it. He'd been subjected to an offensive tongue-lashing by the owner, a dressing-down that he accepted without so much as blinking an eye. The Calabrian didn't like new things. He owned a long black four-door German automobile. When he drove down to Italy on vacation, everyone else was forced to sit down and shut up as they mutely admired his big black car, admitting that he had become a success.

There were two of them working in the kitchen. The other cook came from Brescia, a city in northern Italy. His name was Paolo Terenghi but he said to call him Pol, the Italian spelling of the American pronunciation, like an Italian movie star. You couldn't understand a thing this northern Italian said, his pronunciation was cavernous and he spat out well-masticated but completely unfamiliar words and phrases. For the most part, the two men communicated through gestures, to their immense mutual satisfaction. Pol was an expert at processing and stuffing vegetables. Rosario imitated him, studying the way he cut them and transformed them with heat. These were months of silent lessons. Pol was broad-chested and had a prominent pot belly. He guzzled beer and braised the meat. They worked morning, noon, and night, six days out of seven. On his day off, Rosario spent the morning walking around this chilly Germany, then he'd go back to his rented room and carve wood. His friend Nenè wouldn't have liked it, this gloomy country. When Rosario was weary, he'd gaze at the cactus he'd brought with him from Sicily: if anything, the thorns stood out more sharply, but the plant expressed no opinion, it didn't seem to mind the weather. Then my grandfather would resume his work: the rocking horse he was carving for my father was taking shape. He was not going to come home empty-handed.

It happened a week before the inferno. A chisel was missing from the carpentry shop. All the prisoners were called to report. Either somebody produced that chisel or they'd all be punished: a whole night on their feet until the tool was turned in.

The ones who had access to the carpentry shop were D'Arpa and Marangola, who worked there, and Melluso and Iallorenzi, on their daily janitorial shifts. All of them denied stealing the chisel, and all the other prisoners claimed to know nothing about it. The guards were especially irritated by this solidarity, and they threatened brutal repercussions.

Melluso broke ranks and took a step forward.

"What do I get if I tell you?"

"*You get to stay alive.*"

Guards and inmates, one and all, bore the marks of war on their faces, wrinkles and creases. The faces were drawn: masks of weariness, every day a little wearier of this constant contest for survival. The eyes of victims and executioners were equally dead.

"Too bad, I don't know a thing."

Melluso stepped back into line.

A hasty, angry search began. When nothing turned up, the search turned increasingly violent. Searching was hard work. Sweat streamed. The chisel was found in Iallorenzi's duffel bag.

He fell to his knees, swearing he knew nothing about it, it wasn't his fault, someone had framed him.

The guards were unyielding. Despite Mino Iallorenzi's protestations, he was hauled off by main force. As they dragged him out of the dormitory, he wept, swearing he was innocent. It reminded Nicola of the squeals of a hog being taken to have its throat cut.

That was the last time they ever saw him.

"And you know what the absurd thing was, Davidù?"

Nicola Randazzo didn't look at me. His eyes were fixed on the full glass of wine that his hands still hadn't raised to his lips.

"The one who stole the chisel really was Iallorenzi after all, D'Arpa told me so. Iallorenzi had made a bet with Melluso, just to do something different for a change. He was planning to take it back to the carpentry shop the following day. Melluso knew all about it, but he never turned informant, honor to his name. If you're a slave, the hatred you feel for your jailer is greater than anything you can feel for a fellow prisoner. People hate those above them and beneath them, never those on the same level."

"What happened to Iallorenzi?"

"A prisoner's life was worth less than a chisel."

Everyone was punished. Outside the barracks, everyone standing, no way to sit down or move away to defecate or urinate. They spent the night in the throes of bodily cramps and the stench of organic fluids released more out of exhaustion than any real need. At dawn, they were wrecks, dehydrated, filthy, demoralized, and with another day of work awaiting them. Still, they stubbornly survived. They were plants in the desert. They challenged a rainless sky with the insolence of their very existence.

Rosario decided to turn his back on Germany during a lunch shift. For the second time since he'd started working there, he decided to try something a little different on his own, a Sicilian dish, *pasta alla trapanese*: raw tomatoes with garlic, toasted almonds, and a drizzle of olive oil. It was the south in all the fullness of its elementary flavors. A customer demanded that the tomato sauce be cooked. The boss strode into the kitchen.

"What's this crap?"

Rosario went straight up to the customer in the dining room.

"Is there some problem?"

"Raw tomatoes on pasta is slop you'd only feed to pigs."

The man talked like Santin, he must have been a Venetian emigrant.

"That's the way this dish is made, if you don't like it order something else."

The Calabrian flew into a rage on the spot.

"How dare you speak that way? You better beg the customer's forgiveness and get straight back into the kitchen, immediately, and cook the sauce just as the Gospel says."

"No. That's the way this dish is made."

"As far as I'm concerned, you can get out of here and go back to the street where I found you, you goddamned good-for-nothing no-account Sicilian."

Rosario looked at him without moving a single muscle in his face. The Calabrian couldn't meet his gaze and dropped his eyes, looking at the floor. Only then did my grandfather take off his apron, fold it, lay it over the back of a chair, walk to the cash register, take out the pay he had coming, slide the cash drawer shut, walk into the kitchen, put on his winter jacket, walk back through the dining room, and leave the restaurant. Pol came running out of the kitchen after him, in search of an explanation.

"Pol, I'm sorry."

"What do you mean?"

"I've finished the rocking horse. I'm going home."

The next day, Pol quit, too. They took the train back together. Pol got off in Milan and took the next train for Brescia. Rosario rode the length of the Italian boot, all the way to the toe, such a long trip that it felt as if the train would never get there. After fifteen months spent working in Germany, he had a little money in his pocket to feed and clothe his family, a suitcase full of heavy winter clothing, a cactus, and a wooden rocking horse.

———

After we were done eating, Grandma started doing the dishes.

"We waited for him on Track Three at the main station. Me, your father, and Randazzo, who had come to help us with the luggage. It had taken your grandfather more than fifty hours to get back home from Germany. It had been more than a year since the last time we'd seen him. The minute he stepped off the train, I started waving my arms in the air."

"How did Grandpa look?"

"Skinny."

"That's not what I mean, Grandma."

"Tired, after fifty hours on a train."

"Come on, Grandma."

"I understand what you want me to tell you."

"Exactly. Did he kiss you?"

"No."

"I don't believe you."

"Listen, when he came home—"

Her voice cracked, like a sheet of paper tearing. Her eyes were focused steadily on the bottom of the sink, as her left hand twisted the faucet shut.

"Grandma, are you all right?"

"It had been such a long time since we'd seen each other. Fifteen months is a long, long time. I'd written him so many letters. He sent back three. He wrote in block print, it was still so hard for him to write."

"What did he write you?"

"His impressions of Passau: the snow is white and when the sun shines it's blinding, on Sundays after Mass they eat a white *würstel*, I learned how to make baked rabbit with apples. That sort of thing."

"Watercolors."

"That's right."

"So what else? What happened when he got off the train?"

Grandma's forefinger started tracing small circles in the suds of the dish soap. With every circle, the finger sank a little deeper into the suds. When it touched a plate, the sound of the contact was muffled by the depth of the rinse water.

"Your father burst into tears. He hadn't recognized him. He couldn't remember. I felt myself die inside."

"And Grandpa?"

"Then he took a step back, set suitcase and cactus both down on the pavement, and put the present in front of the kid."

"And Papà?"

"He grabbed at the present, always a little prince."

"And Grandpa?"

"A smile on his face, but still keeping his distance."

The finger had stopped, by now the regular circular movement had made it possible to see beneath the suds. There were dishes. They were white. We'd always known it, we'd just forgotten.

"We were in the train station, there were so many people all around us. You know what your grandfather's like, never says a word, never does a thing in public, and when I say nothing I mean nothing, likewise mute when it comes to displays of affection, you know. But instead, right there on the platform, your grandfather took my face between his hands."

"He kissed you!"

"No."

"Like fun, he didn't! He kissed you! In public! In front of everyone! Jesus, girl stuff."

"Listen, stupid: first of all, displaying one's emotions isn't just something girls do. And if you really want to know, he didn't kiss me."

"I don't believe it."

"The kid started crying again."

"He did?"

"Maybe because he saw my face in Rosario's hands, what do I know. Your grandpa took his hands off me immediately. Then he noticed his friend and they shook hands."

"Didn't they hug?"

"He didn't hug me, so you think he hugged Randazzo?"

"Oh, come on, what does that have to do with it, you're a girl."

"What do you use for brains? Anyway, in the end, Randazzo came home with us, right here, and he insisted on carrying the suitcase himself. You know what the first thing your grandpa did was?"

"He kissed you."

"No. He planted the cactus."

"And my father?"

"He was playing on his rocking horse."

"Even then, he was already the Paladin."

"Right."

In the train station, Provvidenza held my father, still in swaddling clothes, in her arms. The child observed everything, immersed in an attentive silence. The train would cross the sea and steam the length of the mainland until it reached distant Germany. Rosario thought of his friend Nenè.

"It always rains in Germany, Rosà. When it's cold you could freeze to death, wear your pajamas under your pants. And one piece of advice: you'd do better never to pee outdoors, because if your dick freezes it'll snap off and you could be left dickless for the rest of your life."

That's what Nenè would have said.

The thought made him smile.

There was so much talk about this Germany where there's a job for everyone.

People said that finding a position was easier, there wasn't all the Mafia you have down here, in that Germany up there.

One way or another, he'd make ends meet.

He always got by, that was for sure.

But it was the ones he was leaving behind in Palermo who filled his heart with sorrow. His wife and his son. He wouldn't be there, whatever might happen, a sudden thunderstorm, the onset of the sirocco, the kid's first steps.

Standing on the platform by the tracks, caught in a mass of strangers, Rosario was about to say goodbye to his own life, once again.

"I'll write you, Rosario, always. You, if you can find time, you write me, too, my love?"

My grandfather had a suitcase full of the warmest clothing he'd been able to afford, a train ticket in his pocket, and a cactus in a burlap sack. Provvidenza blinked back her tears but it was obvious that she wouldn't be able to hold out for long. The moment of departure had arrived. The conductor bawled out the final boarding call. Rosario set down his suitcase and the burlap bag.

"Put your arms around me."

"There are people."

"I know that."

They embraced for all the world to see, and in that moment their bodies forged a contact that would be this hot and despairing only once more in all their lives.

⸺

Maestro Franco, too, emigrated to Germany.

"It was after I had a falling-out with your uncle, in the aftermath of the match with D'Angelo, the half-Marchigiano, half-Neapolitan boxer."

Once they'd won the regionals, they tried for the nationals. It seemed like Franco had a decent shot at the title. In the first few fights, excellent boxing: not much pain suffered, plenty of pain inflicted. Then he ran up against Roberto D'Angelo, who was, simply put, a better boxer than him. After the fight, in the locker room, Franco and Umbertino had a knock-down, drag-out argument. Bitter words flew on both sides. Franco insisted that the tactics had been defective, while Umbertino shouted that that was bullshit, the strategy had been perfect and Franco simply hadn't been up to the task of implementing it, thereby making a mockery of Umbertino's work and his good name.

The rift was left unmended. Franco quit the boxing gym and left Palermo. He was barely twenty. He started boxing for a living. He turned professional. Was there a purse? Then he signed up for the bout. He manipulated his own physique to hopscotch from one category to another. And so it went, as he punched his way up the peninsula and finally made his way to Germany. There he fought five matches, but it was the last two that he recounted with the greatest delight. Determined to win a purse worth a heap of deutsch marks, he started fighting as a heavyweight. It was his next-to-last fight on foreign soil. To bulk up to the minimum required weight for the heavyweight bout, he ate bread and cheese, six times a day, for twenty days running. He needed to put on fifteen kilos. The opponent was a squat, rocky Spaniard. It was a violent fight, but Franco's agility stood up well against the Iberian's sheer power. Umbertino's teachings had come in handy, and then some. It was a draw. They split the prize money and headed off, each in his own direction.

In Heidelberg the purse was smaller, fewer deutsch marks, because it was for a lower-ranked category, the one Franco really belonged in. He'd need to lose fifteen kilos in twenty days. He went to the sauna and he worked out fully dressed: two undershirts, two shirts, two pairs of pants. Sweating, shedding fluids, drinking no water. If he wanted to get the money that even a loss would entitle him to, he needed to come to his weigh-in with his body in proper condition. As long as he could stay on his feet long enough to fight, well, after that who cared? At night he bought a peach. He'd stick a straw into it. Whatever he could suck out of it was his dinner.

"I only had one round in my legs. Just one. Then I was bound to fall to the mat all by myself. There was only one way I was going to earn all that money for myself: win in the first round."

And sure enough: KO. TKO, to be exact, in two minutes and thirty-seven seconds. He cut the challenger's eyebrow, making it impossible for the match to go on. Every time he talked about it, Franco would add some new detail or other. A painful punch, a weave and a feint that a choreographer could have turned into a ballet, the footwork of his attack so blindingly fast that the referee never even saw it. On the strength of his formidable photographic memory, Franco mixed an increasingly minute array of details into the broth of his story. The color of his opponent's shoes, the roots of his hair, the way his nostrils flared when he inhaled. But the way the story ended never varied: "If only Livia had been there to watch, but no such luck." It had been his moment of glory. What followed was a string of defeats that made clear the time had come for him to go home. All he needed now was a job in Palermo so he could start a family.

"The truth is that there are times when hard knocks in the head can be good for you."

From the train station he went directly to the gym, with his suitcase still in his hand.

Umbertino was tormenting his students, as usual.

"*Buon giorno*, Maestro."

"You're dead to me."

"I've come back."

"I'm thrilled."

Franco swallowed all the pride he had left.

"Maestro, please forgive me, I was wrong, I apologize, take me back to work with you."

"You, as far as I'm concerned, can go dick around somewhere else, anywhere you want. Get out of here."

"No."

With two quick leaps, Umbertino was standing before him.

"Give me a single reason, Franco, just one reason, why I shouldn't club you to death, right here and right now, in front of everyone."

"You're training people wrong, Maestro."

He'd gotten it off his chest: the burden he'd been carrying for so long. The fact that he'd lost at the national championships was partly his maestro's fault, too.

Umbertino ended class, tossed all the boxers out of the gym, gave Franco a pair of boxing gloves, and climbed into the ring with him.

Umbertino stood there bare-handed.

"Can I tell you something first, Maestro?"

Franco decided he had no choice but to play all the cards he held. He talked about the hook-uppercut combination. He broke down the dynamics of the punch: the way the arm rose vertically until the punch landed, the thrust of the legs, and, especially, the twisting torque of the opposing foot. Umbertino never taught this move because he'd never noticed it: his body executed it naturally, unconsciously. Franco showed him new offensive and defensive patterns and moves. He described training methods he'd learned elsewhere: differentiated abdominal workout sessions, jumping in place with a tennis ball clamped between the feet, weights and sprinting circuits. All of them exercises that *Il Negro* would have liked.

"You have one round to convince me, Franco, just one round."

But it wasn't true. Umbertino had already made up his mind. Franco's movements were more cunning, self-aware, in-depth, and thought through. He'd noticed it immediately, the minute Franco had walked through the gym's front door. Umbertino broke three of his ribs just to teach him a lesson. He wasn't going to let someone abandon him just like that, overnight, without making sure he paid the consequences.

Franco started working as his deputy. After two months, Umbertino gave him permission to address him with the informal *tu*. Franco was gifted; he had an exceptional eye. He focused on details that my uncle had never really noticed. He'd lost at the nationals for one simple reason: Franco wasn't Umbertino and the bout had been planned according to my uncle's natural rhythms. In his pilgrimage north the entire length of Italy and into Germany, Franco had developed a profound and refined understanding of boxing. He noticed details and worked to fit them into a larger framework until their underlying logic made sense to him and, what's more, he was capable of explaining them to others. Between Umbertino and Franco, Franco was the one with a vocation for teaching.

≡≡≡

My mother was seventeen years old when she was orphaned. My maternal grandparents, whom I never met, died one after the other in the span of just one year. These things happen.

"So I moved to your house, that is to say, my sister's house, your grandmother's house, your mother's mother's house, Jesus, I'm getting mixed up with all these family ties. Your mother was solid as a rock. She managed to finish school and her nursing course and got a job immediately."

In the hospital everyone said that she had a boundless talent for veins, no one could touch my mother when it came to giving injections. Whenever she had to give a kid a shot, the first thing she did was show him the syringe, reassuring him all the while.

"It's nothing, take it from me."

Then she'd turn him around and swab one butt cheek with disinfectant.

"Would you like it better if I give you the shot on the other side?"

While she was swabbing the other butt cheek with a cotton ball soaked in alcohol, she did the injection on the part she'd already disinfected.

"All done."

The little kids, incredulous, would stare wide-eyed, swearing they'd never felt a thing. She'd fooled me a bunch of times with that trick.

"Uncle, were you still living in the gym then?"

"Sure, it was handy, home and office in the same place. It was more affordable."

My mother was the only family relation he had left. To be able to spend time with her, he shut down the gym for a few weeks.

"I had the boxers move my things. It was easy: Who wants to try out a new training exercise? Fuck, people will swallow anything."

It was June. To make my mother happy my great-uncle took her to stay on her favorite stretch of beach, at the Addaura.

"It was a sandy beach, typical woman's choice, Jesus, what a pathetic place."

When they got there, they found the beach covered with rubble. Someone had built a house a hundred yards up the beach in violation of zoning ordinances. The debris left over from the construction had been dumped all over the place.

"If there's one thing the Mafia lacks, and it's what will eventually prove its undoing, it's an appreciation for beauty."

That place was truly beautiful. It was sandy, that much is true, so there wasn't even a rock to dive off, but it had a quiet charm all its own. But now it had been reduced to little more than a dump.

Without a word, my mother knelt down and picked up a couple of rocks.

"Let's go home."

The next morning, she asked my uncle to take her back to the same beach. This time, she took off her skirt and blouse, leaving just the swimsuit she wore beneath. She dived into the water for a quick swim, emerged from the water, and gathered up her clothing and two more rocks. The whole summer went by like that, a dive in the water and two rocks carried away, in a truly long-term clean-up project.

"Did she manage to clean up the whole beach?"

"She did not. My boxers? Half a day and the beach was a pearl again."

"When did they clean it up?"

"In October."

"But the summer was already over!"

"Your mother needed to do that work."

As soon as she finished school and signed up for the nursing course, Umbertino rented an apartment a couple of blocks away from our house, so she could have the privacy she needed.

"After I'd gotten used to living in a normal apartment, I hated to go back to living in the gym. Your mother was capable of living her own life, and after all, Davidù, the Paladin always seemed to be around. At least, if they were going to do things together, they could do them at their leisure, on the bed, instead of having to scurry around who knows where, all uncomfortable in the open air."

Umbertino never took the place of my mother's father.

That wasn't his job.

He just made sure she lacked for nothing.

One day, before I started boxing, I was playing with an ivory cross, a relic of my mother's father. I was tossing it from one hand to the other. My mother ordered me to put it down this instant; it was fragile and could easily break. I still didn't understand the emotional importance people place on objects, how we entrust our entire lives to them. Ignoring her warning, I went on playing with it. I ventured one especially daring trick and missed the catch. The cross fell to the floor and broke. My mother leaped out of her chair, both cheeks bright red. She began slapping herself in the face, teeth clenched, right hand, left hand, one smack after another. I just stood there, watching her.

Umbertino demanded that the reception for my parents' wedding be held in his boxing gym, and so it was.

"With the money you save, you can take a trip to somewhere far-off and fantastic, like maybe Rome."

One evening, a week before the wedding, he summoned all the boxers from the various training sessions.

"The Paladin is getting married, let's get busy."

The boxers repainted the walls, cleaned the greasy floors, brought in potted flowers, found a band, and unleashed their mothers. In the gym there was a bounty of food, all homemade, and enough wine to float a damned boat; Randazzo alone had brought twelve barrels.

Umbertino was already drunk the day before the wedding party, his own Zina was getting married to the Paladin, red wine was in order, authentic and genuine.

"I wore a gorgeous suit with a killer tie, yellow and purple. You'd have thought I was the groom, to judge by how fabulous I looked. Still, the most beautiful one there was your mother."

He walked her to the altar.

For the first time in his life, he felt unsteady on his legs.

Franco brought Livia as an officially invited guest: they weren't a married couple yet, but they were living together and engaged.

"Already Livia was busting his balls as if they'd been husband and wife for thirty years now. She never shut up. Franco showed up in church dressed to the nines himself, extremely elegant, all the right things.

We'd both had suits custom-made by a tailor, Pisciotta by name, the father of one of our boxers: he gave us a considerable discount, we were a couple of fashion plates. Livia, on the other hand, was impossible to look at, she came wearing an all-pink outfit, damn, she looked like a Jordan almond."

Once the ceremony was over, on the church steps, with doves flying skyward and handfuls of rice showering over the heads of the newlyweds, my mother tossed her bouquet into the air.

Livia, determined to catch it, leaped vehemently.

Standing next to her, with both feet on the long hem of her pink gown, was Franco.

"Livia was left bare-assed, completely exposed: Franco's shoes had split her dress down the middle."

Livia started furiously beating him over the head with the bouquet: she wanted to run away, disappear, vanish from the face of the earth.

She was mortified to the point of tears.

Franco, motionless, was taking a bouquet beating over the head and doing nothing to stop it. Zina went over to Livia and hugged her tight, while Provvidenza, who had picked up the skirt from the floor where it was still pinned by Franco's foot, used it to cover her behind. Livia was shaking with fury. It would have been less painful to just die on the spot. My mother took her face and framed it in her hands, telling her that the party would be much less fun without her: "Please, hurry home, change your clothes, and come back to the boxing gym."

Livia didn't know how to refuse her. Franco offered to see her home so she could change clothes. Her response was terse and categorical.

"I hate you, I never want to see you again."

A fantastically long banquet table had been set up in the gym. There was so much food that, instead of running out, it seemed to multiply.

"It was like a miracle, I felt as if I'd wandered into the Gospels."

The musicians played, took a break, had something to drink, and went on playing.

Randazzo's wine went down like water and wafted up into the head like fire.

"We were all blind drunk, fuck, it was an epic party."

Livia still wasn't back.

Franco, with a gnawing sense of guilt, had hurled himself body and soul into the gobbling and the guzzling, stuffing himself without restraint: bread, pasta, meat, fish, wine. He ate and he drank, he drank and he ate without stopping.

Umbertino tossed out a challenge.

"Whoever can fit the most whole cannoli into their mouth wins!"

The first few attempts were clumsy: the wafer broke, the ricotta gushed out everywhere, and there was still no hyperbolic exploit that could be recounted to future audiences, the teller swearing up and down that this really happened. The first true point of no return was reached by Randazzo, who succeeded in cramming four whole cannoli into his mouth. A spontaneous and heartfelt round of applause rang out. Umbertino glowered. That the winner of this competition should be on the groom's side of the family was something that he simply could not accept. He stood up, loosened his belt, took a mighty breath, and unhinged his mouth to its maximum capacity. Then he crammed in six whole cannoli. A roar filled the gym, fists pounded the table, feet drummed on the floor: pass me more wine, I've got a thirst in me.

"In that moment of my own personal and entirely well deserved triumph, Franco felt the entire wave of frustration that had been building up over the course of that day break over him. He grabbed the cannoli tray, opened his mouth wide, and one, two, three, four, five, six, seven, and eight! He crammed eight whole cannoli into his mouth at once. His mouth turned into a tunnel of cannoli."

Umbertino leaped to his feet, holding up both hands, eight fingers extended. Everyone shouted their approval. The cheers and applause were thunderous and joyous. The guests sounded like the crowd at a championship match. Umbertino was placated, Franco was one of his own people, a guest from the bride's side of the family, and the party went on magnificently well.

In that exact moment of jubilation, the door swung open and in walked Livia. She'd changed clothes, hairdo, and makeup, all designed to match the color of her new dress, which was green.

"She looked like an olive."

When Franco saw her, he hurried straight over to make his apologies. He took her by the hand and tried to pour out the entire store of words of contrition that he'd been ruminating over the whole time she'd been gone, words of regret, pleas of forgiveness. Words of peace.

"Livia," he began, completely unmindful of the eight cannoli that were crammed into his mouth. He projected a stream of ricotta, flake pastry, and candied fruit onto Livia and her new dress. After a dumbfounded silence, the other wedding guests burst into a wave of convulsive laughter. Livia gazed down at the disaster that was her outfit, contemplated the fact that once again it was Franco who had caused it, and as the roar of laughter washed over her, found herself for the second time that day the object of ridicule before the exact same group of people; she felt her eyes welling up with tears and, her heart devoured by shame, she teetered on the brink of a fit of hysteria. Something unexpected stopped her from toppling over: my father had taken her by the hand. He placed himself as a shield protecting her from the laughter. He called out for the band to strike up a tune and led her into the ring, where he proceeded to dance with her as long as it took for some semblance of serenity to return to her pupils and her cheeks.

They danced very badly.

"Livia was tense as a wire and covered with shame and the Paladin was stinking drunk. Fuck, it was a memorable party."

≡≡≡

I'd happened to run into her on the street.

Five years after I'd last seen her, that time at the hospital.

She'd recognized me.

She was walking with three girlfriends.

"How are you?"

I felt like telling her that I felt fine now that I was looking at her, that I was bubbling over with happiness, but I couldn't seem to string together a sentence, couldn't seem to organize my thoughts. I wanted to know all about her, what are you doing, where are you living, what are you studying, do you ever think about me? My throat was parched, the world had started to seesaw. I said nothing.

"Well, all right, I'd better get going."

And sure enough, she left. But after taking just three steps, Nina turned around.

"It was nice to see you again, Davidù."

She remembered my name! I had only one card left to play. I strangled my pride, picked up the receiver, and made a phone call.

"Listen, no beating around the bush: I'm takin' you to the beach."

"..."

"No, that doesn't mean we're friends, I'm only taking you to the beach on one condition: you have to bring your cousin with you."

"..."

"What do you mean, your cousin who? Your girl cousin. Damn, Gerruso, I hate you, and anyway how many girl cousins you got?"

"..."

"Really? Twelve?"

"..."

"And what do they look like?"

"..."

"For real?"

"..."

"How about that."

"..."

"Well, okay, we can talk about that later. Right now, I was talking about your cousin Nina."

"..."

"That's the one."

"..."

"Tell her to come to the beach with us."

"..."

"Call her on the phone."

"..."

"Yes, you can tell her that I'll be coming, too. In fact: you have to tell her."

"..."

"Yes, if she comes, you can, too."

"..."

"No, I'm not taking you to the beach without her."

"..."

"I don't like people to see you standing next to me."

"..."

"No, absolutely out of the question."

"..."

"You wouldn't know how."

"..."

"Wait a minute, are you blackmailing me, Gerruso?"

" . . . "

"What do you mean: yes, you are?"

" . . . "

"All right, all right, I'll teach you how to dive headfirst."

" . . . "

"Wait a second, Gerruso, one last thing."

" . . . "

"Call her right now."

"This is the kind of date that I especially like the sound of: the seventh of September, the ninth of November, that kind of date."

"I understand."

"No, you don't understand a thing, you never understand a goddamn thing."

"No, this time I get it . . . Thirty-seven."

"Give me an example."

"You like . . . thirty-eight!"

"Stop counting."

"You like . . . the twenty-seventh of December!"

"Gerruso."

"Did I guess right?"

"You have no idea how much I detest you."

"But what did I get wrong? The twenty-seventh of December is a wonderful date."

"It doesn't have anything to do with what I was talking about! The seventh of September, don't you get it? Seven and seven! The eighth of October, eight and eight, the ninth of November, and—"

"That's Nina's birthday: the twenty-seventh of December."

"Really?"

"Yes. Thirty-nine!"

"Gerruso, stop counting the whores."

"Forty! But how many whores are there?"

"Lots."

"And why on earth?"

"Because there's a lot of need for love out there."

"I like Mondello better than Cape Gallo, there's sand."

"There, I knew it, you're a weakling. Girls like sand, a real man likes rocks and cliffs. When are you ever going to grow up?"

"Soon, if you'll teach me."

"Why would I want to teach you?"

"We're friends, Davidù."

"Gerruso, we're not friends. Do you understand that?"

"Yes."

"Repeat it back to me."

"We're not friends . . . Forty-one!"

"Gerruso. What's wrong? Why are you looking at me that way?"

"Nina."

"What does Nina have to do with anything?"

"Do you like her?"

"Who? What? What did you tell her on the telephone, Gerruso? Tell me every word of that phone call, down to the very last detail! Now! What did you tell her? That I like her? Did she tell you? Does Nina like me? What did she tell you? Did you invite her to Cape Gallo, full stop, end of story, the way I told you, or did you decide to do your own thing, like always? What did you say to each other? Does she like me? Christ, Gerruso, answer me!"

"What I did is what you told me to do."

"Are you sure?"

"Yes."

"Are you sure as sure can be?"

I was dancing around on the tips of my toes, finding out just how hard it can be to keep your balance on a moving bus.

"No."

"No? What do you mean, no? No?"

"No."

"Gerruso. What. The fuck. Did. You say. To Nina."

"I invited her to the beach and . . . Forty-two!"

"Stop counting whores and answer me."

"I asked her to bring a friend as long as I was going to be there and so were you, just so you wouldn't feel neglected, since Nina is my cousin and she likes me, so maybe she'll wind up spending all her time with me, so I asked her if she could bring a girlfriend for you, just so you wouldn't get bored, that's all."

The light filtered through the splayed intertwining tree branches outside the bus windows, spreading a chiaroscuro pattern across Gerruso's face.

"And why didn't you say a word about that to me?"

"I wanted it to be a surprise."

"Nina's coming, right?"

"Yes."

"You're sure?"

"Yes."

"How can you be so sure?"

"She's my cousin, she loves me, but why do you care so much about her?"

"About who? Her? Are you kidding? I don't even remember what she looks like."

"You promised that you'd teach me to dive headfirst."

"Gerruso, it's not an easy thing to do."

"You promised. Forty-three!"

After counting twelve more prostitutes along the way, we reached the end of the bus line at 9:15 a.m. We were supposed to meet up at 11:00.

"And now what are we going to do?"

"Whatever you want, so long as you shut your mouth."

"What are you going to do?"

"I'm going to shut my mouth and look at the sea."

"What do you see?"

"Water."

"Can I tell you something?"

"No."

"Too bad, because last night—"

"Gerruso, what part of 'no' is so hard for you to understand?"

"When Nina gets here can I talk?"

"Only if it's strictly necessary."

"Thanks."

"You're welcome."

"Because I just wanted to tell you . . ."

"Is it all that urgent?"

"No, maybe not . . ."

"Then shut up until Nina shows."

"Okay, I can do that."

"Just be a good boy and pipe down."

"Because I had a dream about you."

"Who did?"

"I did."

"When?"

"Last night."

"You did?"

"Yes."

"About me?"

"About you."

Why do we pay such close attention to someone who says that they had a dream about us?

Why this slavish devotion to the world of dreams, when they aren't our own?

"I was working as a salt harvester, and there was a strip of salt in the sea, hard and white."

"And where was I?"

"You were walking on the strip, but that was afterward."

"So what happened before?"

"I was harvesting the salt by hand, it was all getting stuck between my fingers, then you showed up and you took off your boxing gloves, they were black. Inside your glove was a note on a sheet of paper. It was a poem. You'd written it."

"A poem?"

"Yes."

"Written by me?"

"Yes."

"Fuck, what a stupid dream."

"Yeah, I know."

"What was this poem like?"

"Beautiful."

"Hunh."

"I'm telling the truth, in fact I jotted it down the minute I woke up, I wrote it on a sheet of paper with a pen, in blue ink. It's nice. It's about swallows."

"I like swallows."

"Should I read it to you?"

"You brought it with you?"

"Yes."

"All right, let's hear it."

"Poem: 'I've seen the swallow, it goes and ungoes, in the distance, it turns on the wind, once, again, and yet again again, a flutter of the wings and another of the eyelashes, in the overturned meaning of life.'"

"It's full of mistakes."

"Yeah, I know."

"You even get things wrong in your dreams."

"Anyway, the dream went on, you went into the water and you were walking on the strip of salt. You were very handsome."

"Gerruso, wait a sec, tell me the truth, swear to me that you're telling the truth."

"I swear."

"Are you gay?"

"No, why?"

"Are you coming on to me?"

"No, why?"

"The dream, the poem, me, you."

"I don't understand."

"And when would you ever understand."

"If you explained it to me."

"No, I'm not going to explain anything to you."

"Would you like me better if I were gay?"

"Have you lost your mind? Gerruso, let's drop this once and for all."

"Okay."

"No, I have a better idea, just shut up entirely."

"All right."

"No, wait a sec, what about the dream? Was there more?"

"Yes."

"The part with me in it, I mean."

"Yes."

"Then go ahead, I give you permission."

"Thank you. You were looking out at the horizon and you were doing something stupid."

"What?"

"You were throwing punches into thin air, right in front of you."

"That's not a stupid thing to do, it's what I do every day as part of my training. What next?"

"My dream kept going but you weren't in it anymore."

"So that's the end of my part?"

"Yes."

"Was your cousin Nina in the rest of your dream?"

"No."

"Then from this minute forward, shut your mouth and let me look at the water in goddamned peace."

"Fuck, they've pulled a fast one on us. I knew this would happen, Gerruso, you're a disaster."

"She told me she was coming, and if she told me she was coming, then she's coming."

"Sure, of course, she'll never show up."

"They're women."

"What is that supposed to mean?"

"Doesn't your uncle always say that women are late for everything except for the exact second when it's time to bust your balls?"

"Gerruso, you need once and for all to get over this bad habit of talking about me or any of my family."

"Sorry."

"Fuck, already half an hour late, five more minutes and I'm going to leave."

"No, that's it, I'm leaving."

"Where are you going?"

"What the fuck business is that of yours?"

"Maybe you wanted me to come along."

"The last person I ever want to see again in my life is you."

"Don't worry, they're coming."

"Look, the only reason I'm still here is to tell her to go fuck herself the second she steps off that bus. It's obvious that she's your cousin. Your whole family is screwed up: it's in your blood."

"Look, a bus."

"She won't get off this time either."

"You want to bet?"

"Sure. If she doesn't get off this time, I'll smack you on the shoulder every day of your life, you worthless stump-finger."

"But if I win, you have to stop calling me stump-finger . . . at least for the rest of the day . . . agreed?"

Nina and her girlfriend stepped off the bus, hand in hand. In the midday Palermo sun, Nina's hello rang out clear as a bell. Gerruso ran to meet her. Nina loosed her fingers from her friend's and gave him a hug. They stood there, stationary in the roundabout where the bus line ended. They would come say hello to me, sooner or later. If only we didn't have this friend of Nina's underfoot.

"Who's he?" she asked, pointing in my direction.

I disliked her already.

"Davidù," Nina replied.

It would have been perfect. A dream come true. I'd come up with a foolproof plan. But Gerruso, as usual, had screwed everything up by doing things without being asked, telling Nina to bring along an extra friend. Nina—she was the only one that mattered. But now, here was her girlfriend, skinny and blond, and once she had been informed of my name, all she could think to say was: "So why doesn't he come over and introduce himself?"

And dislike ripened into hatred.

She regarded me coolly as I walked over.

I said hello, extending my hand to her.

"Pleased to meet you, I'm Davide."

The blonde left my hand dangling in midair.

"He's shorter than you, Nina."

I wanted her dead, but only after a long period of horrible suffering.

Eliana Dumas. Blonde. Skinny. Fourteen. The Buttana Imperiale. The Imperial Whore, in person.

We got to the second inlet and I still hadn't succeeded in squeezing in a word edgewise with Nina. The whole way, the blonde complained about the fact that the sun was yellow, that June was hot, that it was a long way to walk. Once we spread out our beach towels, Nina exclaimed: "It's nice here." Maybe even then, during that first personal interaction, I should have understood how easy it was for Nina to read my mind, gathering the loose yarn of my thoughts and knitting them back together, when my anguish was darkest and I could no longer see.

Inopportune as ever, Gerruso butted in.

"Nina, do you know how to dive?"

She shrugged her shoulders, forming a tiny dimple at the base of her neck. I was starting to feel weak again. Gerruso referred the question to the most unlikable fourteen-year-old girl on the face of the earth.

"Diving is stupid."

In my head, I cursed her and her family a thousand different ways, but it was only when the Dumas added "And anyone who dives is soft in the head" that my body acted of its own accord and broke into a run, launching into a breathtaking dive headfirst into the waves. Blondie, take a look at this, watch and learn. In midair, I experienced the beauty of a sharp knife slicing. The challenge between me and the Buttana Imperiale had begun. Of course, checking the seabed before taking a dive is usually considered wise. In the length of the coastline, there was one—just one—stretch of shoals, and I was about to hit it square on with my head. Twisting to my right with tremendous torque, I just managed to graze the shoals with my left side. Blood poured and it stung like a bastard, but that cut was nothing compared with the laceration of my pride. I swam angrily. I could feel my heart pumping in my ribs. My self-respect was kicking, lashing out, shattered.

When I got out of the water, it was Gerruso who noticed the cut.

"You're bleeding."

The Dumas remained poker-faced.

"I told you, you can get hurt diving."

It was Nina who tossed the monkey wrench into the works: "I like diving."

Then Nina started talking about her father, Emerico, and her mother, Lia, Gerruso's mother's sister.

"Ah, so Gerruso isn't your last name?"

"No."

Her father worked at the Fiat plant in Termini Imerese. Her mother ran a stationery shop. Like me, she had no brothers or sisters. I told her so. Gerruso pointed out that I was basically an orphan, that my father was dead. That unexpected twist stirred the blonde from her indolent torpor.

"So how did you manage?"

"Manage how? Manage who? Manage what?"

"Without a father."

"We just managed."

"Just managed how?"

"We just lived, day by day."

"Without a man in the house?"

"Oh, if that's what you're asking, we always had plenty of men in our house."

"Oh, you did?"

"Yes."

"Like who?"

"Like Uncle Umbertino."

"Who's that?"

"My mother's cousin."

"Her cousin or . . ."

"Or what?"

"Nina, when are we leaving? I'm starting to get bored."

Without a word to a soul, Nina stood up, dived into the water like a nail piercing the waves, and swam off toward the horizon. She got lots of her moves wrong. An instant later, I was in flight, heading away from the only rocks breaking the surface. With vigorous strokes, I caught up to Nina. When I was near her, with Sicily as a backdrop and the sea spreading out as far as the eye could see, I no longer felt so shy and ashamed. I was even able to speak to her.

"Ciao."

She smiled at me.

Nina, you have such big eyes, capable of watching over me even from afar. That's what I wanted to say to her. Instead the words tumbled out before I had a chance to weigh them.

"When you dive, you get your liftoff wrong. And when you swim, the way you move your left arm is wrong. And you're all uncoordinated when you kick. And you turn your head in both directions to breathe. And the way you hold your hands, actually, is wrong, too."

My heart stood still in my chest.

What. The fuck. Was I. Saying.

Nina's eyes had opened wide.

There was astonishment in every syllable she uttered.

"Do I really make all those mistakes?"

I no longer trusted my own mouth. I answered the way my grandpa did, by dipping my head forward. Nina's eyes got bigger still, and truly, it was no contest, she was much more beautiful than the Sicily that lay off in the distance.

"And you noticed all those things just by watching me for a couple of seconds?"

I nodded my head again.

"My cousin told me that you're a boxer. Aren't you too young to be a real boxer? I thought you couldn't start boxing until you turned eighteen. How old were you when you started boxing?"

For an instant, everything came back to me, crystal clear.

The gunshot, the hurtling shards of exploding glass, Gerruso passed out on the pavement without the end of his finger, Pullara raving out of his mind, my uncle running, and Nina standing motionless, fearless.

"Nine."

"It was that same day?"

"Yes."

"The man who came to the piazza and then brought you to the hospital, is that your uncle Umbertino?"

"Yes."

"He's nice, he called me 'honey.'"

"Yes."

"Well, so will you teach me?"

"Teach you what?"

"To swim the right way."

The surface of the sea was smooth. In that velvety water, I felt safe and protected.

"Look, the movement doesn't start from your arm, it starts from the center of your body, like that, you see? You have to concentrate on your pelvis, Nina . . . Why are you laughing? Did I say something stupid?"

"That's the first time you've ever called me Nina."

And she pushed off. And I saw her, as she swam along getting every single movement completely wrong, for what she really was.

Perfect.

Stretched out on their beach towels, Gerruso and the blonde were arguing animatedly.

"No, I know I'm not wrong. It's something you can say: 'laugh-making movie.'"

"No, you definitely can't say that. You don't even know basic grammar."

"Yes, you can. It's something you can say. Like, it's Latin or something."

"And what do you know about Latin?"

"*He* knows Latin."

I felt all eyes on me. They expected an answer. But I wasn't even dry yet, I could hardly be expected to speak. I tilted my head and, showing the palms of my hands, rocked my head back and forth, yes, that's right, nothing to be done about it, I know Latin.

"I don't believe it," said the Dumas, stung to the quick.

"How come you know Latin?" Nina asked me. Not an ounce of doubt in her voice, she was sincerely curious. I couldn't believe that it could be so simple to release me from my paralysis. I answered in a low voice, to keep her girlfriend from hearing me.

"*M'u 'nzignò mia nonna.*"

That's how it came out, in dialect: my grandma taught me.

I spoke from my blood.

"In Italian, anyway, that's not something you can say," the Dumas said to hammer home the point.

Gerruso was genuinely surprised.

"Something you can't say? What do you mean: 'Not something you can say'? I just said it! And I say lots of other things just like it: tear-jerking movie, fear-making movie, yawn-making movie. You can say it, and how."

"You're just ignorant. But how on earth could he know Latin?"

"His grandma."

It was Nina who provided that answer.

"Ah, is she a schoolteacher? My mother is a teacher. In fact I know all five declensions, and the verb *sum*."

Gerruso glanced over at me with a mist of terror clouding his eyes. I reassured him with a nod of the head. I knew how to conjugate the verb *sum*, in all tenses and all moods. My grandmother truly is a very, very, very persistent woman.

"Ah, then my mother and your grandma are colleagues. Where does she teach?"

"At Tomaselli."

"Tomaselli? What's that? A new high school? A humanities magnet school? Is it in town? Where is it? I've never heard of it."

"It's an elementary school."

"An elementary school?"

"That's right, why?"

"They're teaching Latin in elementary school these days?"

"No."

"Well?"

"She majored in classics."

"And now she's stuck teaching elementary school."

"What do you mean, 'she's stuck teaching'?"

"If she'd been more successful in her career, now she'd be at the classical high school, like my mother. Instead, there she is, stuck teaching kids who barely know how to read and write, so maybe she just didn't know Latin and Greek all that well."

"Eliana."

Nina's voice was stern without being harsh.

"Don't be rude."

The Dumas ignored her, or pretended not to have heard.

"So that's why," she went on, pointing at Gerruso, "he ran through that whole speech on teachers' salaries."

Gerruso suddenly flushed red as a beet.

The speech about teachers' pay.

That was my personal ax to grind.

It had been the topic of the essay portion of the final exams for ninth grade, three weeks ago. Gerruso wanted to know how I'd done on the exam. Fine, I replied, and no, I didn't give a damn about his exam, and what had his topic been anyway? On the importance of friendship? What kind of essay is that? Fifth grade, back in elementary school?

Then a shiver ran down my spine.

"You didn't mention me in your essay, did you?"

His silence was more explicit than any full confession could have been. My name was there, in Gerruso's essay, and it would be preserved in the archives of the Italian school system until the last echoing trump of time, and anyone who happened to read it was bound to get the tragically mistaken idea that he and I were friends. I was about to shout into the phone when Gerruso asked me what my essay was about. "You don't even deserve a reply," I huffed indignantly. Still, he persisted, and in the end I gave in. I explained that I had structured my essay around the inequity of teachers' salaries. The underlying theme had been developed during a Sunday luncheon at my home. Over a portion of roast suckling kid, my uncle and I both insisted that elementary school teachers deserved higher salaries than the teachers in middle school or high school.

"Because they do their work at the beginning of the educational process," my grandma summed up.

"You need to straighten trees when they're still little," Umbertino chimed in, in confirmation.

We were in full agreement, we knew that your legs, not your arms, were the foundation upon which you climbed into the ring.

Gerruso had taken my theory and used it as a pretext for an argument with the Dumas. I was torn between two impulses: to lose my temper or else tender my congratulations. Using an idea of mine was tantamount to acknowledging its excellence. Nonetheless, the truth remained: any idea, even the finest one, was once and for all discredited in the worst way imaginable as soon as it had been mouthed by Gerruso. He was a stump-finger even in his thinking.

The obnoxious blonde was about to blather on with some unspeakable new drivel when Nina intervened, firmly.

"Let's all go swimming, right now."

She got everything all wrong again: the lift of her feet, the curve of her spine, and the position of her neck. Nonetheless, there was a certain grace to her movement that made it unique and unrepeatable. Nina had a grammar of motion that was all her own. Certainly, it could stand some polishing, but to eliminate it would be unforgivable.

Gerruso went next. It was a horrible sight. He managed to get a *cannonball* wrong. He made only a tiny splash, plus he rope-burned the inside of his arms because he forgot to angle his elbows into the water.

The evil blonde was about to kick off her dive.

I beat her to it.

An angel's flight, my body in the shape of a cross, arms spread like a swallow's wings, fists clenched, hands cleanly aligned, fingers spread

out straight at the end of the dive, to open a passage into the water so
the body could make its rapid diagonal entrance.

"Who ever taught you to dive like that?"

Nina's eyes were glistening.

"My uncle."

We might be poor, but we were talented.

"Ooh, now it's Eliana's turn, watch her, Davidù."

The only reason I turned to look was that Nina asked me to, otherwise I'd never have taken my eyes off hers, for anything in the world.

And what I saw made me feel sick.

The Dumas lifted off into her dive with precision and balance, ex-
ecuting a perfect and well-calibrated vertical takeoff, snapping into her
descent with elegant rapidity, and broke the surface of the sea without
so much as a splash. She had executed a stylish and technically flawless
jackknife. She rose to the surface and began to swim away. She had
utter mastery of an impeccable technique.

"She's a swimmer. She won the regional championship in back-
stroke and low-board diving."

She was a far more estimable foe than I had given her credit for. I
knew before we ever left the bus stop that she was going to try to take
me down. But it only became clear that she actually had the weapons
to hurt me the instant I felt the full impact and beauty of her athletic
prowess.

If I ever needed anything to make me even more emotionally un-
stable, I could always rely on Gerruso.

"Will you teach me to dive?"

"Now?"

"Yes."

"Climb up on that rock, I'll come over and join you."

Nina watched him in amazement, then her eyes turned back to
mine. Her gaze was filled with understanding: I could hardly have
blamed you if you'd told him no.

But I'd made a promise.

"Are you really going to teach him?"

"Yes. At least now, your friend isn't around to see."

"Don't talk like that. Eliana has a unique personality, but she's a
good friend. And, in her way, she's really quite modest."

"Her? Modest?"

"Yes. Take diving, for instance: she's a champion diver, but she doesn't go around talking about it, in fact, she's always dismissive of any of the fields she excels in."

"Are there lots of them?"

"At school, for example, she's the first in her class, and next year she'll be attending the classical high school."

The competition was on.

And I had no intention of losing.

"Me, too."

"Maybe you'll be in the same class."

"I'd rather enroll in the nautical high school."

As she spoke, Nina kept moving to stay afloat. The sun kept sketching different arrays of shadow on her face.

"I'm going to enroll in the school for languages, I like to travel," she said.

"Traveling's great."

"Have you traveled lots?"

"Some."

"Have you been to Rome?"

"No."

"Venice?"

"No."

"Milan?"

"No."

"So where *have* you been?"

"Lots of places."

"Like where?"

"The Libertas in Milazzo, the Invicta in Catania, the Pugnace in Donnalucata, the Forza e Costanza in Barcellona Pozzo di Gotto, and the Virtus in Sciacca."

"Haven't you ever left Sicily?"

"No."

"But you've traveled lots?"

"I think I have. Haven't I? Am I wrong?"

Nina burst into a luminous smile that I was incapable of fully comprehending. But there she was, smiling at me, and there was nothing else I cared about.

"What are all those names you mentioned?"

"Gyms."

"Boxing gyms?"

"Yes."

"So you want to be a boxer?"

"My father was a boxer."

"Was he good?"

"He was the best."

"Do you want to be just like your father?"

"I don't know, I never knew him. What do you want to be?"

"I'd like to be a translator, that's a job I'd enjoy. Eliana wants to be a musician, she studies cello."

My heart stopped. The Dumas played an instrument. She exercised her fingers on a musical instrument. Light-fingered, hands capable of delicacy. Fingers that generate sounds.

"She lives in a big apartment on Via Libertà."

So she was filthy rich, too.

"It's a beautiful apartment, you'd like it, it's on two stories. She has a great big bedroom with paintings on the wall. What's your apartment like?"

I couldn't hope to win. I might possibly fight to a draw, emerge with an honorable mention.

"My family isn't rich, Nina, but my mamma keeps our apartment clean and my uncle comes to have Sunday dinner with us, my grandpa keeps a little garden that he calls a truck garden, and my grandma taught me to read and write when I was four."

And with a jackknife thrust I plunged, simultaneously, into the cold salt seawater and the dark depths of shame. I swam without stopping for breath and I reached the rocks. The scrape along my ribs was no longer bleeding, it was just a slightly brighter red than the surrounding skin. I took a deep gulp of air and I focused on my next sure losing bet: Gerruso. As if I needed anything to heighten the tension, the virtuoso cellist made her unwelcome return.

"Gerruso, trust me, do what I tell you."

In the water, Nina was telling the Dumas that I was about to teach Gerruso how to dive headfirst.

"Who is? That guy's going to teach your cousin how to dive? He'll never be able to do it."

The gauntlet had been thrown down.

"Gerruso, it isn't hard, you can do it."

"Are you telling the truth, Davidù?"

Gerruso had to be treated with care, like a plant, not brutally attacked the way he deeply deserved.

"Yes, I'm telling the truth. Just do what I tell you. Think of your butt cheeks, Gerruso. Think of them and nothing else. Clench them tight and throw your arms straight out in front of you, like this, up at an angle, like Superman."

Gerruso tried out the move three times running. He was awkward, but it was technically correct.

"Will you show me a dive?"

"Certainly. Watch closely, because you, under my instruction, are going to dive exactly like I do."

I lifted off with a good, high, long jump.

Look at me, blondie, I've got the legs of a boxer.

The water absorbed me, not a trace of foam on the surface to testify to my passage.

Nina broke into enthusiastic applause.

The Dumas: "Okay, not bad."

Then the unthinkable happened.

As if he'd fallen into a mystical frenzy, Gerruso shouted from the rocks.

"Not bad?"

"Competent," the Dumas decreed.

Gerruso's eyes opened wide.

"What does that mean?"

"That it was a properly performed dive," I reassured him.

"Competent," the Buttana Imperiale said again.

"I just explained what that means: a perfectly executed dive."

"Oh, I forgot, they teach you how to use a dictionary in elementary school."

On her back, the blonde swam away with ample strokes, her arms windmilling easily: Jesus, once again every move she made was the epitome of gracefulness and precision.

Gerruso was furious.

"You need to cut that out right now."

His voice was rising to a keening pitch.

Nina and I were both surprised by that outburst of rage.

The Dumas, on the other hand, was completely indifferent to anything Gerruso might have said.

"Do you hear me? I'm talking to you! You need to cut it out."

Nina and I exchanged a look of bafflement.

"You need to cut it out, don't you dare say it again, because Davidù is a poet."

And, for the whole world to see, he pointed at me, afloat in the salt water.

With his stump-finger.

At that moment, Gerruso somehow seemed different. As if, with that head-on attack, he had begun a process of transformation before our very eyes, under the bright sun at two in the afternoon, on an outcropping of rock at Cape Gallo.

After thirteen years of loserdom, perhaps Gerruso was actually approaching the distant shore of decency.

To bloom at the age of thirteen.

All around me, every detail was sharply carved: Nina's hair, red, tucked behind her ears. Her mouth, open in surprise. Gerruso's arms, raised skyward. The stump-finger pointing at me. Shattering that light-showered moment, the voice of the Buttana Imperiale. She was laughing raucously, repeating one single word over and over.

"Poet."

Unexpectedly, Nina, too, began to laugh, throwing her head back. Her hair floated out around her in the salt water, like a flower opening its petals at dawn. And, without any logical reason, Gerruso burst into laughter as well. In that chain of contagious laughter, I was the only one left unamused. They were all laughing at me.

"All right, then, if he's a poet, he'll teach you a perfect dive, a dive in rhyming couplets."

The Dumas's eyes were like the barrel of a rifle.

Nina asked if I really was capable of teaching her cousin to dive headfirst. The cards of the final standoff were on the table now. Any future I could hope for with Nina was going to stand or fall on that dive.

I looked at Gerruso and I saw a cactus. As I watched him, I cherished the all-too-slender hope that perhaps that flower, in defiance of all reasonable logic, would choose to reveal itself to the world on that very day, for the first time, after thirteen worthless years.

"Gerruso, stop laughing and listen to me. Clench your ass and swing your wrists, like that, a little slower. Then sink down, bending your knees slightly, throw your arms up fast, take off hard with your feet, and your body will do the rest. Come on, let me have a nice, strong, competent dive and we won't say another word about it."

"Do you trust me?"

The coin had been flipped and was spinning in midair.

"Yes, Gerruso, I trust you. You're going to do an amazing dive."

The Dumas looked at me and me alone, with the eyes of a cannibal. Nina was watching, open-mouthed.

Gerruso shook his wrists, in front of and behind him. He curved his back and bent his knees.

Come on, Gerruso, come on.

His wrists shot out fast ahead of him, then his knees straightened, his feet lifted into the air, his body leaped up, his torso straightened, and there was flight.

Unfold, blossom, right now.

Please.

For an instant, the sun was darkened by his body. He flew horizontal over the miseries of the world, eyes wide open lest he miss even a second. He seemed happy, a cactus in the heat of the desert.

Would you believe that he's about to . . .

But no. He belly flopped. A fat and violent belly flop. A disturbing and dolorous sound rang out into that June day in Palermo. Gerruso had forgotten about curving his body in midair. He landed wide open, hands arms belly legs and face. He hovered, floating, on the surface of the water for a few brief instants and then sank slowly out of sight, like a leaf on a lake. As soon as he bobbed back to the surface, we saw blood streaming from his nose.

"I dived beautifully, right?"

I swam in silence over to where he was. Draping his arm around my neck, I ferried him back to shore.

"Did you see that, Nina? I learned to dive headfirst, Davidù is an excellent teacher, he's a poet from head to toe."

We stretched him out flat on his back.

The front of his body was fiery red, as if he'd been scorched.

"Why don't you rest here for a second, that's right."

Eliana was speaking into Nina's ear. I'd placed my bet on Gerruso. I deserved defeat based on that fact alone. The Dumas launched one last, painful whiplash with her angry eyes, turned her back, and prepared to dive.

And I saw something I never would have believed possible.

As she performed the same movement that I had tried to teach Gerruso, she offset the alignment of her feet. It was an imperceptible shift, but her right foot was just a little farther back than her left. She put her weight on the tips of her toes, and then she pushed off. Her legs described the same arc as a butterfly.

A movement of the legs that was unpredictable, impeccable, lethal.

More powerful than mine.

The Buttana Imperiale's footwork.

"What are you thinking?" Nina asked.

"Her feet are magnificent."

"How's my cousin?"

"He took a tremendous belly flop, but he'll recover, eventually, the pain goes and ungoes, let's just let him get a little rest."

"Come with me."

"Who?"

"You."

"Me?"

"Yes."

"Where?"

"Over there."

We sat down on the rocks, our feet dangling in the water.

"I'm happy we spent this day at the beach together."

"You are? Really?"

"I was happy when my cousin called me the other day."

"Oh!"

"Let's do this: since the invitation to go to the beach came from you in the first place, because I know that it came from you in the first place, now you can ask me for anything you want and I'll give it to you."

Embarrassment burst across my face in a blush so intense that I was forced to lower my eyes. I watched her foot paddling at the surface of the water.

"Well?"

I clutched feverishly at that image.

"I-want-a-lace-from-your-shoe."

"Then let it be a lace."

She walked away, leaving me all alone on the wave-tossed rocks of Cape Gallo, in a motionless undertow. I was a *nèglia*, incapable even of shipwreck. Shame roasted my flesh. I was dying. Leave me here, forget about me. Waves, swallow me up, cast me against the rocks, let's be done with it. I didn't die, but that was only because Nina came back and sat down beside me.

"Here."

"Who? What?"

"The shoelace, isn't this what you said you wanted?"

She dived into the sea and from the water she tied her shoelace around my left ankle, carefully, patiently.

"There, that ought to stay tied."

"I'll always be able to wear something of yours," I murmured, without thinking.

"Exactly," she concurred, sitting back down next to me.

I chewed on the inside of my lip. I'd worn sandals to the beach that day. If she asked me for a shoelace in return, I was screwed. Oh, why does life have to be so hard?

"Well, then, what will you give me?"

"Me?"

"Yes, you."

"Me, give you?"

"Yes."

"I'm wearing sandals, Nina, damn, I feel like a fool, me with no laces to offer."

"I want my gift."

"Now?"

"Yes."

"What?"

"Kiss me. On the lips. Now."

And before I knew it, I was in her mouth.

It was a long, passionate kiss, a kiss straight out of the movies.

From where he was standing on the rocks, Gerruso cheered.

"What a beautiful kiss, you're a real poet!"

The surface of the sea was smooth, the Dumas was far away, I switched off my mind and luxuriated in the sound of the water rising up over the rocks, breaking into spray, surging into the seaweed, and then washing away, in an endless return.

"What are you thinking, Davidù?"

It's surprising how insistently women ask men what they're thinking. The answer, most of the time, is simple, as elementary as the very nature of men: nothing. Often, we're just looking at a patch on the wall. Sometimes, our minds are absorbed by a spectacular electric guitar solo. There's never any logical process of thought. Even more astonishing is the fact that men feel obliged to provide an answer somehow bespeaking depth and insight, in order to accentuate our mysterious allure.

I wanted to give a fine, concrete answer, but instead I asked a question.

"So does this mean we're dating?"

Either I'd lost my mind or else this was how genius manifests itself: unfiltered, uncalculating.

"What do you think?"

Again with this unhealthy obsession about what I think? Nina, I'm a man, we do a lot less—and when I say a lot less I really mean *a lot less*—thinking than you women seem to believe. Men, do you have a picture of them? We spend hours and hours watching men in shorts chasing a ball, boasting relentlessly to our friends, doing push-ups on our fists. Men, Nina. What kind of thinking do you really expect to uncover beneath these activities? Already it verges on the miraculous that we're able to walk and whistle at the same time without tripping and falling every three steps.

Nina raised the stakes.

"Tell me one good reason why we should be dating."

I already had my hands full trying not to die right then and there, so once again I answered without thinking.

"I have a cactus that won't blossom for another thirteen years, it would be nice to watch that flower bloom together."

She didn't use words.

She replied in the best way possible.

Another open-mouthed kiss, wet and intense, a kiss involving both our tongues, eyes shut, shivers running down our backs. When we broke away, our foreheads were still close together.

"That's nice—'Poet'—I like it."

"Cut it out."

"I'm telling the truth, I like it. Don't boxers have fighting names?"

"Yes."

"Your father?"

"The Paladin."

"Nice."

"Right."

"I like 'The Poet.'"

"You mean that?"

"Yes. From now on, to me you're 'The Poet,' I've made up my mind. It suits you; it's perfect."

"But Gerruso's the one who said it!"

"So what?"

"No, nothing, okay."

I looked out over the sea. I reflected on recent events in my life: I had a shoelace tied around my ankle, a nickname to flaunt in the ring, and a girlfriend with whom I could ride the bus back to Palermo. If she had chosen to ask me just then what I was thinking about, I would have had a formidable answer. But Nina, womanly in every thing and in every way, didn't ask again.

═══

What happened beforehand, my mother had told me many times. As if she were trying to let me know, subconsciously, that she was calm now, that she could talk about it, "Davidù, you see my eyes? They're no longer filled with tears, light of my life."

That day, she'd woken up early, as usual. She'd gone to work, at the hospital. In the ward where she worked, it had been an untroubled day. On her way home, she'd bought some mullet fillets at the Ballarò market. She was planning to cook the fish for dinner, according to one of Grandpa's recipes: first a marinade of orange marmalade, then a breading with bread crumbs, almonds, and pistachios, then just a few minutes in the oven. It was a warm September. She was wearing a white T-shirt that was becoming a little tight around the belly. She was starting to show. She got home about five. In the dining room, a magazine caught her eye. There was an article about chess. It told the story of one of the generals in Napoleon's army, a first-class strategist. Before every battle, he followed a remarkable ritual: he would take on the winner of a chess tournament that was scrupulously kept open to the army's entire rank and file. The champion was welcomed to the general's quarters as a guest and the two men would play. It sometimes happened that the challenger was so skillful a player that he was able to force the general to come up with new plans of attack. Still, the general was unbeatable. The article focused on one peculiar wrinkle: a number of moves before checkmate, informing his opponent that the game was over, the supreme officer would seize his opponent's king. In response to the challenger's understandable objections, he would describe the moves he'd make and the inevitable countermoves, culminating in the final outcome. After that, with a single impetuous move, the general would overturn the chessboard, knocking it to the floor. When asked the reason, the general responded: "To leave my adversaries no trace of the paths that allowed me to defeat them."

My mother wasn't crazy about chess, but there was something about that story that made an impression on her. She laid down the magazine and picked up her knitting needles and ball of wool. She started knitting and purling. She felt thirsty, went into the kitchen, poured herself a glass of water, and walked back into the dining room to drink it. Sitting was beginning to calm her down. It was just as she set the glass on the table that the front door swung open and Umbertino appeared.

September 9, 1973, at four in the afternoon: it was still a beautiful day out.

In the gym, Umbertino was explaining a combination to the boxers: forward left cross, leap backward, right cross. He performed that double punch masterfully: speed, precision, and timing that left everyone open-mouthed. He had a renewed energy in his body. This was the one time that he believed the gym had a shot at the national title—deep down, he felt sure of it.

Shortly after four in the afternoon, Franco burst into the gym, his face contorted, his cap gripped in his hand.

Umbertino immediately understood that a tremendous truth was about to be revealed. He hurried over to him and propped him up by the shoulders.

Franco started sobbing.

"The Paladin's dead."

Umbertino hugged him to his chest.

"Get out of here," he shouted at the boxers.

They all left.

As soon as they were alone, Umbertino pushed Franco away from him and wrecked everything in sight, bare-handed.

His voice was pitch black.

It came out of somewhere not of this world, this life.

"What happened?"

Franco was unable to speak. He lifted his hands and they were both covered with deep bite marks. He mimed the act of accelerating.

Motorcycle.

The Paladin had been killed in a motorcycle accident.

"Where?"

Franco couldn't seem to emit a single sound.

"Franco, look me in the eyes. Where."

Franco lifted his head and glimpsed that gaze straight out of hell.

"Tunnel," he managed to yelp.

The tunnel.

The highway.

"Franco."

His voice was a snarl.

"Does Zina know?"

Umbertino's hands were ripped and torn from sharp fragments of wood, glass, cement. There was blood everywhere.

Franco shook his head, pointing to himself with his right hand.

He was the only one who knew. No one else.

Umbertino walked into the locker room and came back with a pack of cigarettes. He lit two and handed one to Franco.

"Smoke."

It wasn't an invitation.

He took a long drag on his cigarette and surveyed the wall that he'd destroyed with his bare fists.

He was going to have to deliver the news himself.

He went out the door without a word, running as hard as he could.

When she saw him outside the door, Provvidenza took fright. He was dripping with blood and sweat.

"Umberto, what happened?"

"Where's Rosario?"

"*Che succirìu?*"

She repeated the question in dialect.

"*What happened?*"

Grandpa appeared from the garden. He still had a hoe in his hand. Umbertino put his hand on Provvidenza's shoulder, but he looked my grandfather straight in the eye.

"The Paladin was killed in a motorcycle accident."

My grandmother started darting her gaze around, from the eyes of one man to the eyes of the other, but the two men formed a closed circuit; in fact, only Umbertino even noticed that the hoe had dropped from Rosario's hands—all of a sudden all strength had fled his body. Provvidenza started wandering aimlessly around the room, sensing the looming catastrophe that was about to rain down on her. She made one last attempt at rational thought.

"Does Zina know?"

"Not yet, I'm going now."

At the front door on his way out, all Umbertino could get out was: "I'm sorry." There was still silence when he left, but just a few seconds later there rose from behind the door the wail of a mother who had just lost her son.

My mother lost her balance and staggered into the table, knocking over the glass of water. She fell, and both she and the glass shattered into a thousand pieces. Over the years, shards of glass continued to emerge, having stubbornly outlasted all previous cleanings, as if they had been hiding or had somehow crept away into deeper recesses, and then: out pops another one, a reminder of that moment in the past, the mayhem it had inflicted, and the way that day by day she had been struggling to get past it ever since.

But the instant when the news broke—that was the time of crashing to the floor.

My mother didn't give way to grief with a scream. Instead she began ripping out her hair and scratching her face. Silently.

"She'd slowed down. There were two forces battling each other furiously inside her. One was the urge to go crazy and unleash sheer mayhem, destroying everything within reach."

"What was the other, Uncle?"

"The other was you. She was pregnant. And her head, her instincts, or the Lord knows what all else, kept her from exploding."

Umbertino got a good grip on both her hands and hugged her close.

"We'll survive this, too. I swear it."

My mother was a wounded wild animal. She lunged at Umbertino's shoulder and sank her teeth into his flesh, drawing blood. Perfect, Zinù, take it out on me, bite, scratch, I'm here for you, free your heart from all this darkness. His flesh was pierced by my mother's teeth and nails. His eyes rested, motionless, on the photo of the wedding. He'd been there, he'd attended that ceremony, dressed in a fabulous suit. It had been a long time since he'd worn that suit. His gaze was starting to turn peaceful, just like his voice. The hunting season was beginning again. The predator was back.

"I've got everything under control, kid."

It would take tough training, necessary to keep her from going under. My uncle moved in with us for the second time. He watched over my mother every day and every night, for as long as he deemed necessary, watching to see how, over time and with constant love, all of the tiles of her personal mosaic were reassembling themselves, making it possible for her to survive this period of mourning. Umbertino knew. He'd been through it himself. He'd emerged in one piece. You can survive anything, as long as you fall in love again. And when he understood, once he was certain that my mother had fallen in love again, only then did he return home, leaving Zina's heart ready and able to fill and overflow with the joy of her new beloved. Me.

He left the bedroom when Provvidenza, crushed by grief and sorrow, finally managed to get to sleep. Rosario hadn't yet shed a single tear. He wasn't in a state of denial. What he felt was confusion of the most intense kind. He needed to distill the blow, drink it down in tiny gulps before he could face up to it. It wasn't a matter of accepting the news, it was a question of when he'd start fighting to keep from sinking under the weight of the thing. He walked as far as the kitchen, shuffling his feet. His ankle knocked against the hoe. It was lying there where he'd dropped it. He bent over to pick it up and, in that moment, it all became clear to him: his son had been killed in a motorcycle crash and now he'd never see him again.

He picked up the hoe, opened the French door leading out to the garden, and pulled it half-closed behind him. He turned to the left, where his mint plant grew. With sharp, short, well-placed blows he hacked away at the roots, then bent over and dug his hands into the dirt, lifting the plant out whole. He laid it on the gravel. He inserted the hoe between the wisteria and the wall and, with precision, cut off the crucial branches. The wisteria came down on its own. One by one, he plucked all the lemons from the tree. He felt exactly the way he had that morning of the bombing raid on the prisoner of war camp in Africa: alive, but with no reason to go on living. He uprooted the basil, sage, and rosemary plants. With a pair of clippers he snipped off all the rosebuds. He laid them on the stones the way, years before, in Africa, he had set down the remains of human bodies. He tore the ivy and the jasmine vines away from the wall. He was about to cut all the leaves off the magnolia when he stopped, frozen to the spot by what he'd just seen.

The cactus.

A bud had sprouted.

Twenty-two years had gone by.

He'd been to Germany, he'd come back to Palermo, he'd raised a family, he'd lost a son.

And the plant had kept its promise.

It wasn't strictly speaking a flower, it was a bud, but it had sprouted, there it was. Rosario knelt down. He picked up the plant with both hands, loosened the ties of resistance within himself, and his eyes rediscovered the ability to weep, sobbing inconsolably, a lament that never seemed to end, from Africa to Palermo.

※

On the way back from the beach, the minute the bus entered Parco della Favorita, Nina rose from her seat next to the Dumas and came over to sit down next to me. Gerruso had taken a seat in the back of the bus. He was still counting whores.

"What are you thinking about, Davidù?"

Leave it to her to pick the exact time I wasn't thinking a thing. To answer "nothing" would have sounded wrong, it would make Nina think I was empty. I replied with a question. Only after uttering the words did I consider the implications.

"Why did you kiss me?"

I did my best to weigh every option mentally. One incontrovertible fact was clear: in the battle between me and the Dumas, I was the one who had lost, from every possible angle. I hadn't taught Gerruso to dive, and that bitch—this was especially galling—dived better than me. So why had Nina spent time sitting with me on the rocks, why had she even kissed me? I couldn't figure it out. And so her answer swept over me like a Copernican revolution. That whole day long I'd thought of Nina as a battlefield. A trophy to be won and to show off to the world. Once I heard her answer, it became clear to me just how wrong I'd been. I was mortified, more deeply than ever before in my life.

"It's up to me who I kiss and who I don't, who I date and who I don't. Right then, I wanted to be with you because I felt like letting you kiss me, we kissed, I liked it, so why not do it again? You want to know why I felt like kissing you? Because of the way you behaved. You were nice to my cousin, you took care of him. You inspire trust, you're ready to commit yourself to lost causes, devoting your whole self to make sure they win, in defiance of logic and common sense. Plus, your eyes are green and beautiful. Hey, you're blushing, Davidù."

"I know that."

"You're handsome."

She laid her head on my shoulder.

"My poet."

Her hands were delicate. I felt like stroking her hair, but I considered how inadequate my fingers were to the task. I was thirteen years old and I already had the hands of a boxer. I turned to look out the window. Parco della Favorita alternated light and shade under the wild inlay of branches crowning the road we were traveling.

"What are you looking at, Davidù?"

Her voice was soft, she was trying to establish a tone of intimacy. That effort deserved respect and consideration. I answered in the sincerest way I knew how.

"The future."

"And what do you want from the future?"

I laid my hand, with its cargo of calluses from hours enclosed in boxing gloves, on the window of the bus. Nina's fingers were caressing my chest. I closed my eyes and surrendered to her touch.

"To win the title."

PART THREE

WELCOME BACK, FEROCITY

The front door of the gymnasium swung open with its usual weary creak.

Umbertino turned to stone.

Rosario and a blue-eyed child had just walked in.

Franco went over to them.

"*Buon giorno*, I'm the maestro's assistant: Something I can do?"

My grandfather laid his hand on my father's head.

"Is this your son? What's his name?"

"Francesco."

"How old is he?"

"Twelve."

My father looked around at the gym: the ring set up on the right, the blankets stacked up against the wall, the punching bags hanging from the ceiling, the tennis balls in the corners, the boxers' bodies leaping, bending, hitting.

"Papà, is this boxing?"

My grandfather replied by nodding his head forward. Then he held out his hand to my uncle.

"Rosario. It's a pleasure."

"Umberto. The pleasure's mine. It's been a while."

"Yes. Teach him to box."

"After everything I told you, you're coming to me?"

"Yes."

"Why?"

"When you say you're going to do something, you do it."

Umbertino remembered how fast those hands had been. The kid was his son. Everybody should get a chance to show what they can do.

"Franco, trade some smacks with this kid."

Initiation by mayhem. My father placed his hands against Franco's, palm to palm. His hands were slender, tapered fingers, not the hands of a boxer.

"Ready? Let's go."

Franco let loose and failed to land a solid smack.

Seven times out of seven.

"Well?" asked Rosario.

"Taking lessons here isn't free of charge."

"Money is no problem."

"Every day except Sundays, two hours a day, bring him in at two or four or six. One month, on probation, paid, then I decide whether to keep him on. Now, if you want, you can stay and watch what we do in here."

Rosario took a seat. He hadn't watched boxing since Germany. His son, sitting on a bench next to the ring, was moving his legs back and forth, like a young king curiously surveying what would someday become his domain.

"We all have guardian angels, even me, even you, even the victims of Mafia shootings, though I have to say that their guardian angels aren't anything to brag about, since they don't even know how to deflect bullets."

"I don't believe in all that stuff."

"That's all right, the important thing is whether the angel believes in you, that's how it works. My guardian angel believes in me fervently. His name is Caterino Gerruso."

"With a last name?"

"Sure, he's my guardian angel. I think about Caterino Gerruso at night when I can't sleep because I've got thoughts in my head."

"What kind of thoughts?"

"When you used to punch me in the belly, when you used to throw eggs at me, when you call me 'idiot' at school, thoughts like that, day-to-day stuff. Where are your uncle and Maestro Franco?"

"Out signing some papers, they'll be back soon."

"Are locker rooms always so shabby?"

"It's spartan, not shabby."

A wooden bench, a coatrack, a shower, a Turkish bath, a sink with a piece of green hose in place of the faucet. Bare and functional, designed for use. No frills. Gewgaws are pointless when you're about to climb into the ring and trade brutal punches.

"There's not even a Coke machine."

"We never drink before a bout."

"Jesus, but what are you: boxers or priests? You're turning all man-of-the-cloth on me here. Anyway, come on, today we're really going to take the regional title, right?"

"We?"

In two years, 1988 and 1989, I climbed into the ring sixteen times. I won every last match, seven by knockout.

People talked about me with growing interest.

I was a finalist for the regionals.

My opponent was Gaetano Licata, seventeen, from Villabate, a left-hander, known as 'U Ziccùso, literally, the Tick-ridden One.

He bumped me with his right shoulder, spoiling for trouble, as I was walking toward the scales for the weigh-in.

"Who the hell are you, anyway? What am I supposed to think of you?"

I looked straight past him.

Grandpa was sipping an espresso.

Umbertino was standing with his back to the wall, smoking, lost in thought, on edge the way he was before every finals bout. The minute he walked into the locker room, all it took was a jerk of his head to shoo Gerruso out.

"Poet, I'm going to go take a seat in the hall next to your grandpa. Watch me while you fight, I'll always bring you luck."

Maestro Franco saw him out, shut the door, and then came back to talk to me.

"Kid, fight the same way you did in the last bout, no more, no less. Fight clean, fight fast, and don't overdo it, keep your distance and land your punches, score points and maintain your position."

He started unrolling bandages.

Umbertino, sitting on the bench, was smoking in silence.

"Anyway, kid, the important thing is to have a woman by your side, the only problem is that women are too much, it's as if they're stealing the beatings they take from you, it's enough to make you lose your mind."

The only time the maestro wrapped the boxers' hands was before a fight. He knew every callus, every curve, every line. He performed quiet movements, with old-fashioned devotion. The bandage was white and smelled freshly laundered.

"You can't imagine how many times I've practiced on my wife, Livia, every night, for a year and more. Livia has slender hands. With your uncle's hands, it's a whole different thing, you'd need a bedsheet, wouldn't you, Umbè?"

The silence of the desert. He was smoking, lost in his thoughts. He wasn't checking the bandages, he wasn't talking about tactics, he wasn't wishing anyone the best.

The first two years, my father climbed into the ring only a few times, just enough to rid him of his fear of being hit and to allow his body to learn the dimensions of the battlefield. He was the only kid in the gym, but he, too, was subjected to *Il Negro*'s stern teaching methods: running and jumping, abdominals, knee bends, and push-ups, building up and dodging sequences.

He was fast, well mannered, and a good student at school.

A couple of times a week, they played at slap-fighting.

Umbertino never managed to slap him in the face.

He and Franco worked harder to train my father than they ever had before. They took turns as his sparring partners; they went home with him, running alongside him; they corrected imperfections in his movements, suppressing the instinct to curse every saint on the cross; they inquired after his studies; and, at Christmas, they bought him a pair of expensive black gloves.

"There, when you snap off your opponents' horns with these things, we'll be able to see all the blood they lose."

When he fought his first match, Umbertino and Franco knew that he'd lose. But it was during that match that they understood why the young man had captured their imagination. During that first unsuccessful fight, my father was one soldier against an enemy of thousands, but he remained calm and composed and elegant. A knight in battle, unspattered with mud.

"A paladin."

He lost on points, two rounds to one, and he gained a nickname.

My grandparents loved his new nickname.

So did my mother, the day they met; in fact, a little too much so.

"Are you waiting for someone?"

"This gym belongs to my uncle."

"Are you going in?"

"No, thank you, I'd rather stay outside."

"I understand what you mean, it's not a pretty sight. If you're in a hurry, I'd be glad to call him for you."

"No, really."

"Anyway, training's over, Maestro Umberto is about to come out."

"You call him Maestro?"

"What else would we call him?"

"Are you a boxer, too?"

"Yes."

"What's your name?"

"Francesco."

"Pleased to meet you, I'm Zina. You don't look like a boxer . . . Francesco, did you say?"

"Yes, why?"

"My uncle only calls you by your nicknames: 'u Mosca, 'u Tirabusciò, 'u Panza Lenta, 'u Morto 'nta l'uovo—the Fly, the Corkscrew, the Slack Belly, and the Dead Man in the Egg. Do you have one, too?"

"Yes."

Umbertino appeared unusually confused. He started by saying "What are you doing here?" but he didn't even give my mother the time to answer before pouring out a list of urgent errands that had to be taken care of right now, in fact sooner than that, groceries to be purchased, people to go see, chores to be completed at home, right now, absolutely, it's really more important than you can imagine, only you can save me.

He took two steps and then stopped short.

"Zina, forgive me, I forgot something in the gym, you head home and get started on the things I asked you to do, wait for me there, I'll catch up with you in a minute, now get going, go go go."

The instant Zina turned to go, my uncle leaped backward and planted himself square in front of the Paladin.

"Don't you move from this spot."

Zina had reached the corner.

Her smile gleamed.

She waved goodbye to them both.

The minute she turned the corner, Umbertino started dancing on the tips of his toes.

"Paladin, I don't know what the hell is in the air these days, all this Communist garbage, free love and easy flesh and so on, so just to be perfectly clear let me tell you in the words of the Gospels: if you so much as touch my Zina even in your thoughts, I'll slit your throat, you understand? Now get the hell out of my sight because right now I already hate you."

Franco lowered the roller blinds in front of the gym, snapped the padlock shut, and caught up with Umbertino.

"Holy shit of a world of shit."

"What's the matter, Umbè?"

"Zina."

"What?"

"It's done, finished."

"What the fuck are you saying? Zina? How old is she anyway?"

"Seventeen."

"But she's still just a girl."

"Exactly."

"Now who the hell dared to try something with her? Do we know him?"

"Yes."

"Tell me who he is and I'll shoot out of here like greased lightning and bust his headlights."

"The Paladin."

"No."

"Yes."

"The Paladin."

"None other."

"With Zina."

"Right."

"But when did they meet?"

"Just now."

"Just now?"

"Five minutes ago."

"And you're sure that . . . ?"

"I'd be willing to bet half a yard of hard prick."

"So this is serious."

"This year is starting badly, very badly."

"Zina and the Paladin, ridiculous. I can't believe it. Even though, actually, now that I think about it for a minute, if you have no objection."

"No, on the contrary, I do object, Franco."

"Where's Zina?"

"At home, waiting for me."

"Are you going to see her now?"

"First let's make a stop at the tavern."

Along the way, they discussed the upcoming mission. The following week, there was going to be a bout, and one of their boxers, Michele Lo Quarto, aka "Ciaca," would be taking on a fighter from the mainland.

"Umbè, did you have a girl in mind?"

"Either Moira or Nenzi."

"Who's Nenzi?"

"Nenzi, Nunziatella, the one who talks all arrogant, with the foreign accent."

"Who? Oh, you mean 'Nancy, the Americana'?"

"None other."

"This would be her first mission."

"I know."

"The Americana, sure, I like it, she could be perfect."

Umbertino didn't think through the reasoning behind that suggestion. He lacked his usual drive in planning a new mission. He seemed hollowed out. He ruminated over a single thought. The conclusion he came to over and over remained the same: there was nothing to be done about it. Before long, Zina and the Paladin would be married. My mother was growing up and he had no way of stopping her. He couldn't set his mind at ease. He got stinking drunk the way *Il Negro* used to do.

In the locker room the questions that Franco asked him fell systematically into a pool of silence. My uncle was lost in thought. For him, the finals always had the taste of loss and defeat.

"When the Paladin won the regionals, youngster, he was fifteen years old, just like you are now. KO in the third round. But it was obvious that he'd win from the outset. There's no logical explanation for it, it was just something you could sense in the air, a hunch. But from that instant on, you know how it's going to turn out, and that's all there is to it. It happened at the weigh-in: the Paladin stepped onto the scale and it was obvious to everyone that he was going to win. We knew it, period. Of course, he did fight a legendary last round, didn't he, Umbè?"

Once again, Franco ran headfirst into that wall of silence.

Umbertino ran a hand through his hair, lit yet another cigarette, and walked out the door, closing it behind him without a word of farewell.

"He's on edge."

"I know it, Maestro."

"Your fingers, how do they feel?"

"They're wrapped perfectly, thanks."

"It was easy, your hands are as slender as Livia's. Don't pay your uncle any mind, he's always restless before the finals. He was uneasy whenever the Paladin fought, too. Unless your uncle is completely in control of the situation, he goes through all the miseries in hell. Today, for example, not even a mission to occupy his thoughts."

"Is there no mission because I'm fighting?"

"That's not the only reason. The missions have been abolished for the finals. Your uncle and I care about fair play, we don't kid around. And then there's one more thing."

"What's that?"

"Your opponent is a minor."

Cigarette ash was flying everywhere inside the dark blue Fiat 126. Umbertino was at the wheel, the driver's seat shoved all the way back, his elbow sticking out the window. Franco was hunched over, scanning the notes he'd taken. Umbertino let him study as he spoke to the female passenger sitting in the back.

"Still, from what you know, there's no chance at all?"

"Are you asking me if he's gay?"

"Yes."

In the rearview mirror Umbertino saw a cigarette being lit between a pair of buttery lips.

"He isn't gay."

"Not even a little bit? I don't know, like, gay every thirteenth of the month?"

Franco snickered.

"Shit, gay on the installment plan."

Salvo Gurgone of Messina, the "Bull of the Strait," was no faggot. He presented a serious problem, because he truly was a formidable boxer. He was planning to challenge the Paladin, who had roughly a hundred fewer bouts under his belt.

"Franco, you know what we're dealing with here, right?"

"We've got the Paladin matched up with the Monk."

"Hell, that's right."

"Hell, amen."

The mission had been specially planned out. They'd even brought Lazzara along with them. She wasn't like the other girls. She was truly, heart-stoppingly beautiful. Dark-skinned, with long black hair that nipped at the fleshy curves of her lips, giving her a tormented look that would kindle protective feelings in even the flintiest heart. Her eyes, in contrast, were insolent and vivacious. Lazzara was one step up from sensuality. She was a queen in the realm of conquest.

"Lazzara," Umbertino was telling her, "if a priest sees you, his robe'll turn triangular: head, feet, and hard-on."

They walked into the Palestra La Trionfale, a boxing gym in Noto, they took their seats, they watched the fight. As expected, Salvo Gurgone, the "Bull of the Strait," won. As the prizes were being awarded, Lazzara undid a button on her blouse. Immediately, an unexpected, intense hormonal tempest was unleashed. Every man in the room was going gaga over that impossibly sensual woman. All but one: Gurgone, the "Bull of the Strait."

"So you're absolutely positive?"

"Yes."

"How can you be so sure?"

"I just know."

But Umbertino knew, too. Gurgone wasn't gay. He was a monk.

Franco was studying his notes. He had to find a crack, an error, something he could leverage.

Lazzara remained silent. She was resentful. She hadn't expected Umbertino to ask her to take part in another mission; of course, he'd paid her the way he did every goddamn time: it was just that she hadn't expected it, that's all. She was waiting anxiously for the moment when she'd see the waters off Palermo at the foot of the mountains ahead of her. It was late and she was hungry.

Franco had shown excellent skills as a trainer. When he decided he needed to be able to take notes on his ideas and impressions, the better to plan out fighting strategies, he enrolled in night school and got his junior high equivalency. He was twenty-six years old. Umbertino felt such respect for that decision that he paid for Franco's textbooks out of his own pocket.

Franco possessed a special talent for reading boxers, glimpsing their potential and their shortcomings. In the first half of the seventies, one of the many boxers he and Umbertino trained was Bruno Salatino, an eager young man who was, however, a mediocre fighter at best. He was slated to fight a certain Hernandez, an Argentine boxer who'd been working the circuit in Italy for the past couple of years. The two trainers traveled all the way to Naples to study the South American, boarding the ferry on a Friday night. Franco vomited the whole way; Umbertino brazenly tried to bed a woman from Enna but came up empty-handed. They landed, went to see the fight, understood in thirty seconds that their boy Salatino was done for, ate three puff pastries apiece, caught the boat back to Sicily, Franco vomited, Umbertino managed to bed an attractive blonde from northern Italy, they landed, and the two of them trooped off to the port café to drink a nice hot bitter espresso.

"So we're going to bet against Salatino?"

"It seems like the only sensible thing we can do; this match is a washout. Salatino is worthless as a boxer; at least this way he'll get a little experience and we, who are neither fools nor dickheads, can bet against him to pick up a little money on the side."

"Yes . . . well, I don't . . . yes . . . that is . . . oh, well."

"Franco, what's wrong?"

"First off, the odds on Hernandez winning are going to be very low."

"True enough."

"Second off, in spite of everything, Salatino is still one of our boxers."

"He's nobody and nothing blended together."

"That's not what I was saying."

"Then what?"

"That's our name out on the ring. I sincerely dislike the idea of our name losing. You can imagine how little I give a damn about Salatino, but for our name to be seen as losing: that's something that's tough to swallow."

"Go on."

"Umbè, this Hernandez is really good, he's a good defensive boxer, and he's fast. There's only one way to win the match and clean up on the bets, and that's to make sure . . . how to put this . . . that Hernandez shows up for the fight dead tired."

Those words flashed straight through to my uncle's brain.

"Dead tired!" he shouted.

He started dancing around on the tips of his toes, loosening up his arms in a series of straight-ahead air punches.

"Tell me everything you know about Hernandez."

Franco told him every detail he'd stored up in his mind: the way he moved, his most successful punches, the color of his shorts and his shoes, his perfectly beardless face. The harder he tried to reconstruct Hernandez's personal tastes, the brighter the flame burned in Umbertino's eyes.

He remembered that he had long black hair, slicked back with brilliantine.

"So he likes to get all fancied up. Fine, fine."

A tattoo on his left forearm, a woman, maybe the Virgin Mary, framed by knife blades. A small scar on his left cheek and four larger scars on his dorsal muscles.

"So he likes fighting in the street. Good, good."

He'd taken note of the way that, after winning a bout with a terrifying right cross to his opponent's face, the minute the referee counted ten, Hernandez climbed onto the ropes and raised both arms.

Umbertino finished his sentence for him.

"And undressed with his eyes every single woman in the audience."

"Yes."

"Magnificent."

"What are you thinking?"

"All hail pussy, praise be to a fine piece of ass."

"Amen."

"So, Franco, now you understand clearly that we're going to bet as much money as we can on Hernandez to lose and Salatino to win?"

Franco couldn't believe his ears.

"Are you saying you know how to make sure Hernandez shows up for the fight dead tired?"

"Better. I know how to make sure he shows up ground to a pulp."

Franco was beside himself with glee.

"How? How? It's the one thing I can't figure out."

The predator smiled with knowing ferocity.

"*La Porca.*"

Franco exploded into a howl of joy and embraced my uncle in a transport of genuine jubilation.

This was how the missions came to be.

"*La Porca.*"

A pair of rock-solid tits. An ass that, in its fullness and pliancy, was a triumph of the life force itself. And her mouth, dripping with lipstick, prominent, fleshy, a living invitation to sin. When she swung her hips down the street, men went home with sprained necks. While it is true that she was not exactly a classical beauty, it is equally undeniable that she could lay fair and unquestioned claim, without any possible challenger, to the top ranking when it came to sheer carnality. She sprayed a fine mist of sex. She winked broadly at any man who crossed her path, she leered double entendres, she took pleasure in the greedy looks that clung to the slopes and curves of her body. She fed her vanity with the continuous, unconcealable chain of consternation that followed in her wake. Heads of households went head over heels for her. Between her legs, months of hard-won savings were abandoned. Her cleavage was strewn with the wreckage of mortgages. Promises of matrimony lay shattered on her lips.

"You took one look at her and the only thing you could think of to do was fall to your knees and beg her to let you take just one bite, anywhere, ass tits thighs arm, it was all excellent heaven-sent flesh. She was *La Porca*, youngster. She won thirteen fights for us. Pure hot flame. You took just one look at her and your eyes were scorched."

It was thanks to *La Porca* that they discovered how there is always a hidden crack, in even the most elaborate of strategies, capable of ruining everything.

One afternoon the door of the gym swung open and the boxers all turned to look, attracted by something inexplicable but irresistible. Even the sound of the door opening wasn't the usual creaking. Something unique was about to happen. First of all, in that sweat-drenched air, the scent of a pungent perfume could be detected. Then—headscarf, sunglasses, lips smeared with lipstick—*La Porca* made her appearance. A skintight black dress, bare legs, high heels. At her throat, a necklace with a tiny fish pendant, swimming blissfully through the softest sea of flesh. Every pair of eyes in the room was on her. *La Porca* headed straight for Umbertino, stopped right in front of him, lifted her left foot, swayed her ass voluptuously, and thrust her tongue deep into my uncle's mouth.

Everyone in the gym was holding their breath.

The general level of envy for Umbertino had just shot up to historic highs.

And, in fact, he was the one who broke the silence.

"Oh, hey, let's get out of here because, with the possible exception of Franco, it stinks of faggots."

La Porca followed him. Ten footsteps, ten clicks of her high heels on the floor, ten nails driven into the hearts of all those present. *La Porca*, an absolute thoroughbred, managed to meet the gaze of every last boxer in the room, only to discard them all, leaving each alone, abandoned to the squalor of his solitary drudgery. The door closed behind her. The boxers were baffled. In the ring, they'd taken punches—some of them lots and lots of punches—but they'd never been this dazed, so stunned: it was a foreign experience. They weren't ready for that massive charge of sheer sexuality.

Confounding expectations, Umbertino suddenly came back in. It was Maestro Franco, however, who took the floor. He unleashed upon the still dumbfounded boxers a very serious tongue-lashing.

"You no-good lazy bums, get over here, in line, and right now. What is it exactly we're doing in here, kids? We're boxing. And if someone feels like fucking up, is this the place to fuck up?"

The boxers were stunned, uncomfortable, intimidated.

Franco came to a halt in front of a guy from Trabia, a baker.

"Answer me."

"No, Maestro, this is not the place to fuck up."

"Exactly. Not the place to fuck up. So now, who wants to explain to me why you're all such complete and total fuckups? Will somebody answer me? Is this any way to behave?"

The one who finally spoke up was Gulì, a well-behaved young man, the son of a seamstress who'd been widowed at a tender age. Her husband was killed when a bridge he was working on collapsed: caught in the rubble, he was brutally crushed. Gulì was a middleweight, a kid who could really take a punch, not much of a fighter but a first-rate sparring partner: there was no need to make believe when you were sparring with Gulì, you really could lay into him with all your might. He always got back up again. His nickname was "Old Faithful."

"Maestro, I can't figure out exactly what you're saying we did that was so wrong."

Franco snarled.

"Ah, you can't figure it out, Old Faithful? There isn't one of you who understands? No? Fine: then every one of you, strip naked, right now."

The boxers were more generally disconcerted than dubious.

"Men, didn't you hear what I just said? Strip off your clothes, immediately: no, even faster than that."

Old Faithful was the first to comply. He was a guy who truly had no fear of pain. He'd already stripped off his T-shirt. It was only in that instant that Umbertino decided to turn up the heat.

"Oh, hey, Porca, come on in."

The uncontrollable flame of their yearning to see her again, just once more, only once, rose high. They wanted to glimpse her and all her luscious flesh, just begging to be bitten. And through the door came *La Porca*: a cigarette in her mouth, a slit skirt open to the crotch, the blessed holy fish between her breasts.

"No question, that woman won a bunch of fights for us. It was something incredible to behold, you could hear everyone's heart pounding away, thu-thump, thu-thump, thu-thump. Kid, it was like a tom-tom concert."

"And then?"

"And then your uncle Umbertino spoke again."

"Strip down, boys. Strip down now or I swear I'll lose my temper for real this time, and I'll have every damned right."

T-shirts, shoes, shorts, socks, underwear: every last article of clothing flew off.

Between the legs of all the boxers, there reigned one general, tyrannical erection.

"Look at that, Franco, it looks like there's going to be an explosion, heh heh, look at that, they've all snapped to attention, *brava* Porca, it worked just the way we hoped, heh heh, you really are the best . . . What's that you say? There's one who . . . ?"

Palazzolo.

Fuck: always was a weird one, Palazzolo.

Umbertino rushed over to him with all the motherly concern you might feel for a baby bird that's taken a tumble out of the nest. He cradled Palazzolo's head in his hands.

"Are you sick?"

"No."

"You really aren't sick?"

"Really."

Umbertino slowly moved his fingers over his student's temples, almost caressing him. Palazzolo felt the heat of an ominous calm.

"Palazzolo, my boy, look me in the eyes, I'm your one and only maestro, you need to confide in me completely, so answer me truthfully, and before you say a word, swear that you're not lying to me."

"I swear it, Maestro."

"On the head of your mother."

"I swear it on my mother's head, Maestro."

"Are you a homo?"

"No."

"Are you sure?"

"Yes."

"You're not a homo?"

"I swear it on my mother, Maestro."

"Fuck."

Umbertino's fingers were motionless on Palazzolo's temples. Now the only movement was in his voice. The hurricane seethed in every syllable.

"All right now, Palazzolo, do you want to explain what the fuck this all means? How can it be that the twenty-five of them have hard-ons while you have a complete famine between your legs? Can you explain it to me? Because if you're not sick and you're not a homo, then I must be losing my mind."

Palazzolo had nowhere to turn. He was naked, he was clearly the only one who wasn't aroused, and his head was imprisoned in Umbertino's viselike grip. He knew he was lost in any case, so he decided to play the card of the truth, the whole truth, and nothing but the truth.

"Maestro, I have a fight in two weeks. You're the one who told me not to fuck up, so ever since you gave me that order, I just stopped thinking about women, that's all."

"Slow down, Palazzolo, hold on. Take it easy. Whoa there. Let's start over from the beginning. Are you telling me that, instead of getting a hard-on like any mentally sound citizen, you actually manage to prevent a boner?"

"Yes."

"Are you also capable of getting a hard-on at will?"

"No. But keeping it limp at will, that I can do. You ordered me to do it."

Umbertino let go of the boxer's head. In silence, with an indecipherable expression on his face, he took a couple of steps in Franco's direction but then, a sudden interruption in his train of thought, and Palazzolo's head was cradled in his hands again.

"Palazzolo, give me an honest answer: this friend of mine, this woman, this fine piece of ass, wouldn't you happily slide a foot and a half of hard cock into her?"

"Maestro, no, not today."

"Why not?"

"You ordered me not to. I have a fight in two weeks."

"So, what you're telling me is that, after the fight . . ."

"After the fight, no disrespect intended, I'd fuck your friend in a heartbeat."

"You like her?"

"Once again, no disrespect intended, she's insanely sexy—*è troppo porca*."

Umbertino slowly let go of his head and raised the forefinger and middle finger of his right hand.

"Two things, boys. First point: none of you better dream for so much as a split second of laying a finger on my girlfriend here. Is that clear, or are you all having your ears rebuilt?"

"We understand perfectly, Maestro."

"Second point: Franco, we have a problem."

Franco had taken a seat on the wooden bench. He nodded that he was ready to hear the news.

"There's a factor we forgot to include in the equation. There's a whole third group, aside from the two well-known categories we considered: boxers horny for women and, on the other hand, those poor bastards, the homos."

"Which is?"

Umbertino pointed to Palazzolo, the bug in the system.

"The monks."

"Fuck, it's true."

How could they have failed to foresee this? There are those who are less susceptible to the temptations of the flesh. The existence of a figure like the Monk clearly undermined the future success of the missions. Umbertino felt a bottomless spring of sadness welling up within him. There are boxers in this world who are insensible to the charms of a first-class slice of prime veal cutlet. Suddenly the world looked deeply wrong and unjust to him.

Franco got up from the bench, jamming his cap onto his head.

"Go ahead and get dressed, boys."

"But take your time," added *La Porca*, as she leaned comfortably against the door, biting her lower lip.

From the way a boxer stood in the ring, from the way he walked down the street, Umbertino and Franco found topics of discussion. They reasoned and they excluded, they argued and they approved, they pondered endlessly to figure out a personality profile, to divine the inclinations, the type of dish that might most appeal from the many on offer at the giddy buffet of sex.

Hernandez was the first mission. He was a high-strung, wiry, loose-limbed braggart, and Umbertino reckoned he was the sort of man who'd be willing to cut off his arm in exchange for a fiery night of passion with a bounteous Junoesque odalisque who radiated sex from every square inch of her flesh. Hernandez was part *Indio* and dark-skinned, so a big blonde was in order. The law that opposites attract was sure to make fantasies multiply. Hernandez was a swaggerer who feared nothing, so the right woman would be one whom every other man was bound to undress with his eyes—provocative, fleshy, pneumatic: *more.* Hernandez would take pleasure from the feeling that every other man on earth must envy him. First, a throbbing erection of the ego, and then she'd take care of the rest. She'd lightly brush his elbow with one hand—"Want to buy me a whiskey, handsome?"—and laugh helplessly at anything he said, look him right in the eye, unblinking, for a few split seconds, no more, while her hand—"Oh, silly me"—rested lightly on his chest, caressing it languidly—"What do you say we drink another, champion?"—and she'd laugh and laugh until her forehead was pressed against his neck. At this point you can see the inexorable physics of attraction kick into gear: he's bound to brush his hand over her hair while she unleashes the sucker punch that's bound to lead to a total KO, rubbing her tits against his chest; then, biting her lips while the spark between the man's legs builds into a roaring fire, she'll lean over and pour gasoline onto the flames, whispering into his ear: "I'm getting wet."

"Can I count on you?"

"You can bet your goddamned balls."

"Bravo, Porca, you're the best."

"And you're nothing but the usual piece of shit, Umbertino."

"Though I'm handsome and you like me."

"True enough."

"So you know exactly what to do."

"Don't worry, if I see the slightest sign of slumber, I'll give him a blow job that the whole city of Palermo will be able to feel."

"Like I said, you're the best."

"Speaking of which."

"Tell me."

"Payment in advance."

"You don't trust me?"

"No."

"You really are a whore, Porca."
"The best there is, honey."

Hernandez lost against the mediocre Salatino in the second round. His trainer threw in the towel. The sporting news reported that the Argentine boxer didn't seem himself, someone wondered openly whether he might not have some strange disease, he was emaciated, there were long, unmistakable scratch marks on his arms and on his back, and from the first round on he seemed dazed, as if he'd just barely survived a battle.

The mission had scored its first glorious victory.

The boxers came and went, the years rolled by, and their ability to understand various human types and their preferences improved.

Angelo Morello, a heavyweight from Avellino, trained by his brother Marzio, who was a vainglorious loser. The choice fell on Pina, also known as *'A Trimmutùra*, "The Trimotor," because of her skill at handling several men simultaneously. *'A Trimmutùra* demanded double the usual and she was worth every penny. She proved to be exactly what everyone had called her for years, a tireless sex machine, capable of dashing the Morello brothers' fleeting hopes for victory on a filthy mattress in Via Firenze.

TKO in the third round.

Morgantini from Perugia, a mid-heavyweight. His tastes were a bit of a mystery. They unleashed a blonde, a redhead, and a brunette, pinwheeling around him. He eyed them all but it was no good, nothing, not so much as a spark. What proved providential was Franco's eagle eye: he discovered that for a fraction of a second Morgantini had glommed on to a young girl who was all skin and bones.

"What if Morgantini likes his girls with no meat on them?"

He fell into the bony arms of Santa, also known as "The Spike," after less than a half hour of friendly banter.

KO in the fourth round.

Luca Paolantonio, featherweight.

"It's like I called it, Franco, trust me."

"But how could you possibly know?"

"I've been around."

Paolantonio lost on points after spending the night with a bottle of gin and Anna and Cira, together.

"How could you tell that he liked a three-way?"

"If your last name has two first names in it, it's as if you've been branded. There's no mistaking it."

Cesare Galluzzo, the "Wonder Man of Misilmeri." A heavyweight, a crude man, an inflexible father and husband. Umbertino poured some money into Mariana, a Brazilian whore on her way from Palermo to the mainland, an exotic type, fit and strong, who knew how to move her ass. The inflexible Galluzzo barely had time to see her walk by him: five minutes later he was fucking her in a hotel room for rent by the hour.

"Mariana danced the samba on the head of his cock for seven hours without stopping, kid."

And the "Wonder Man of Misilmeri" went down by a knockout in the second round.

Gaetano Bruno of Rome, "The Adonis." A middleweight, as tall as he was skinny. An observant Roman Catholic, he collapsed at the feet of Rosalia Maggio, also known as *La Chiàgni e Fotti*, or "Miss Weep and Screw." She fainted right before him, and he came to her aid. *La Chiàgni e Fotti* began recounting a story of being orphaned and beaten and humiliated and raped and a need for warmth and what lovely eyes you have. As she got to her feet, she wound up on her knees at the exact height of his cock.

"The Adonis" was defeated on points, two rounds to one.

"All things considered, Franco, we're helping to create jobs. First of all, we give work to the women we know and like. Second of all, thanks to us, the bookies get more work, too. And most of all, let's not forget, our name gains renown. It's not our fault if those guys start to think with their dicks the minute an unbelievable piece of ass presents itself before their all-too-willing eyes. They do it all to themselves. If I'm cold, that's no reason for me to leap headfirst into the fire."

They fine-tuned their deductive technique by practicing on passersby they spotted on the street. They developed an experimental method and they came to appreciate the importance of statistics.

A well-dressed, well-groomed man is attracted by a slightly ugly, brazen woman, a woman who ignores her own shabby and unkempt appearance and still wants to be the boss when it comes to matters of the mattress. An elegant man enjoys his state of superiority, beforehand. But once he's naked and stripped of the shield of his clothing, he wants a woman to run the show.

Students are more catch-as-catch-can; in fact, every opportunity for sex is greeted like so much manna from heaven.

The taciturn type likes women who don't talk, and if he runs into a woman who's an expert at working with her mouth, the easiest of victories is mathematically guaranteed.

For those who spend most of their time out of the house, away from the family, the ideal thing is a nice big woman all tits and ass, plenty of reassuring flesh that you can even sleep on if you like.

In the section of hooks and lures, among the numerous different female typologies, each of them with their own ineluctable qualities, there was a mysterious niche. Here you found those exceedingly rare females that Umbertino had dubbed "the killer fems." Everyone liked them, without exception. Sparks flying, fires breaking out in all directions. A "killer fem" walked by, desire bloomed, and then vanished.

Lazzara was one of them.

Her real name was Meri. She was born in Palermo in May 1945. Her grandmother was a whore, her mother was a whore who had her at age fifteen, and now she was a whore. Her father, apparently, was an American soldier, a guy who might talk but no one could understand a thing he said. Her mother died of tetanus in 1951. Meri was raised by the other whores. They made sure she lacked for nothing. Her "aunts" went hungry to make sure there was bread on the table for her: Zia Gnazia, Zia Santuzza, and Zia Miriam. They brushed her hair and taught her to do needlepoint. Every May they'd wash her with rose petals. She never felt lonely as a child. When she was twelve, she first noticed that men left a trail of drool behind her when she walked by. At fourteen, she was already the highest-earning whore in Ballarò.

Meri handed over a part of her earnings to her two surviving aunts, Zia Gnazia and Zia Santuzza; in fact, she supported them. Her poor Zia Miriam had made the mistake, one November evening, of welcoming the wrong kind of person into her bed—he'd seemed shy, instead he was a wild animal. Miriam's body was so badly bruised that she hadn't even survived until Christmas. The man, the animal, was never arrested.

She met Umbertino one February morning.

"Hey."

"Oh, hey."

"What are you doing?"

"Minding my own fucking business."

"I wouldn't mind minding your own fucking business myself."

Lazzara was gorgeous, a dolorous beauty. An orchid: the same precious quality, the same apparent fragility.

It was my uncle who gave her that name.

"Why did you decide to call her Lazzara?"

"Because she could bring even a dead man's cock back to life."

"What do you think of me?"

"That you're beautiful."

"That's what everyone tells me."

"No, everyone tells you you're sexy, which is a totally different thing."

"Say it again."

"*Bìedda sì*, Lazzara."

"Would you stop calling me that? My name is Meri."

"To everyone else, sure. But I'm not everyone else and to me you're Lazzara. After all, if you happen to be in a room full of women and they're all named Meri and I show up and I need you in a hurry and I call your name, 'Meri,' it'll turn out badly, every woman in the room will turn around, and what a disaster *that* will be. How much simpler: 'Lazzara,' and no one turns around but you."

"Ah, so that's the reason."

"Yes."

"Say it again."

"Lazzara."

"Not like that, you idiot, come on."

"You."

" . . . "

"Are."

" . . . "

"Very."

" . . . "

"Lazzara."

She lunged at him, trying to hit him, to land a blow. He was so huge that a fist was bound to hit some part of its target, she reasoned. But that's not how it worked. Umbertino's big, rough hands, however delicate and kind they might be with her—hands that would never so much as scratch her, she felt sure—blocked her every time she attacked. And so she gave up and gave in, listening to him, doing her best to believe him, until her strength was consumed, until she was in pain, because he had his arms around her and his eyes were dark.

"Biedda sì, Lazzara."

For a moment, she felt happy.

"How long have we known each other? Two years?"

"Four."

"Fuck, time flies, doesn't it?"

"Still, every so often . . . I don't know . . . what do you think if . . ."

"Lazzara, are you asking whether we could be a couple?"

And there it is, the moment in which the truth emerges and everything is ruined. Every last little thing.

"No no no, I wasn't asking you that, not at all, it's just that . . ."

"What?"

"No, it's nothing."

"What's nothing?"

"Listen, beat it, you can't stay here right now, I've got work to do."

"Right now?"

"Yes."

"This very instant?"

"Yes."

"But didn't you tell me that you'd taken the whole day off?"

"You can't stay here right now, you have to leave."

"If you say so."

"Ah, Umberto, on your way out, just leave the usual five hundred lire by the front door."

Only after those broad shoulders left the apartment did Lazzara get out of bed and hurry to the front door, take the five hundred lire, and impulsively kiss them. That made her feel stupid and vulnerable, and if there was one thing she couldn't be it was weak, because weak women wound up like Miriam.

The flame that consumed the money glittered intensely, the evidence that he had been there vanished quickly, all that remained behind was the smoke, stunning the mind a little longer.

Only once the smell of the smoke was gone did Umbertino slide away down the stairs. He ran into no one on his way out.

The Paladin fought the Monk, Salvo Gurgone of Messina, in January 1971. The fight started at 5:00 p.m. and ended after a minute and thirty-seven seconds, with a KO. The Paladin was much more powerful and lethal than Umbertino and Franco could ever have imagined. He was a magnificent boxer.

"Seventy-one fights, seventy victories. The numbers don't lie."

"When did you understand just how good my father was?"

"From his very first fight, the only one he ever lost. You know the story: the Paladin fought with a broken left thumb. He had hit the heavy bag just wrong during a training session, the kind of thing that happens. Umberto and I expected him to withdraw but instead the Paladin insisted on climbing into the ring. We expected it to be a bloodbath but he fought the match almost to a standstill, and even won one round on points, boxing with just one hand, attacking and defending himself with that same fist. Kid, the Paladin was a constant surprise. With every match, he pushed the limit, the envelope. He would have taken the national title, as sure as death and taxes put together. He had all the credentials he needed. A boxer achieves the important victories on his own: that is, your uncle and I could carry him as far as possible, but then there's that stretch of road that each individual boxer has to cover on his own two feet. The Paladin could travel that road with his eyes closed. That's why we try to understand a boxer's psychology. Do you remember when your uncle made you nervous right before your first bout by reminding you that none other than the Paladin himself had lost his own first fight? He did it on purpose."

"Were you in cahoots?"

"We just needed to understand what kind of head you had on your shoulders, kid. If you want to get the most out of a boxer, you have to know the right way to get him worked up. Do you have to get him angry at the world, or is it enough to tell him: 'You're the best there is'? A trainer has to be able to understand if a boxer has that extra something that will make him overcome exhaustion and bewilderment."

"How can you tell?"

"Only in the ring can you see whether a boxer merely has talent or if he's actually born to box. Strength has nothing to do with it. Legs, balls, and brains, those are the three things that make a boxer. Now, you may be able to train a boxer's legs and balls, but the brains, the strength of his nerves, the ability to keep his wits about him when he's being overwhelmed, all those qualities are something an individual either has or he doesn't. You're just feeling your way forward. Every boxer is a world unto himself, a singular experiment."

"Was my father an experiment?"

"No. The Paladin was a lesson, for everyone. He saw things before anyone else could, as if he lived apart from the stream of time, as if the world slowed down for him and he could anticipate all of its movements. It was a thing of beauty to see him fight. Watching him, I understood that I had been a mediocre boxer, I lacked that light, that extra something that was so unmistakable in the Paladin, or in Umberto. And now we're going to fight this regional final, kid. Let's see what you're really made of."

Franco walked beside me. Carlo, already in the corner, was folding and arranging the towels. Grandpa and Umbertino, sitting in the crowd, were silent. Gerruso, clapping and whistling, had launched into a running commentary, live and on the spot.

"Here's the Poet, ladies and gentlemen, he may not be tall but he throws a murderous punch, observe him, get to know him, learn to respect him."

The buzz in the room died down, the crowd had started to listen to what he was saying.

"He's the Poet and no one stands a chance against him, hair slicked back and beautiful boxing gloves, glittering and black."

Gaetano Licata, 'U Ziccùso, the Tick-ridden One, came in.

"I already hate him for his nickname, he has black boxing gloves, too, but it's a different kind of black, dull and flat, a miserable shade of black, the Poet's boxing gloves are better than his, the Poet may be shorter, but he's better-looking."

An old man with a white mustache and a red sweater, hair greased back, leaped to his feet.

"What the hell is this? A beauty contest? What's your friend anyway, a boxer or a woman?"

Everyone laughed. Spectators. Judges. Gaetano Licata. The referee. Gerruso. Not Umbertino. He was smoking and looking elsewhere.

"The Poet is already in the ring, now the Tick-ridden One from Villabate is climbing in, which means that a small-town bumpkin is going up against a fighter from Palermo, the capital of Sicily. No contest. The regional title has practically already been snatched away. Bow down, you hicks, I feel absolutely no pity for you, in fact, I feel nothing but boredom."

Gaetano Licata's hair, dark brown like his eyes, was buzz-cut. His lips were moving over his mouthguard. His neck was undulating as he loosened his muscles. When the referee called him into the center of the ring, he looked at me with disgust.

"Well? You still haven't answered me: What the fuck are you?"

During the first round, my father kept a constant distance between himself and his opponent. Uncle Umbertino and Franco compared him to a wasp, almost impossible to catch and capable of delivering a tremendous sting. In the first two minutes, he staged a wild, exhausting dance routine, a continuous whirling activity that only amplified expectations. The Paladin didn't lunge into an attack, but he also prevented his opponent from landing any solid punches. In that spinning vortex of inexhaustible movement, his gaze was level and calm. A gardener faced with a tangled welter of overgrown plants. A boxer's temperament has nothing to do with the fury of his assault. It lies in the wisdom with which he waits, the way he sizes up his opponent, the distance created and eliminated by his own strong will. Chaos is a telltale sign of anxiety, nothing more. During the study phase, boxers aren't testing the other guy, they're testing themselves. Are my blows going to hit the mark? Am I capable of deflecting the counterattack? How much will this hurt? Imagining the possibility of a garden in which weeds and thorns flourish triumphant. Two minutes of merry-go-round. Then my father's hands plunged into the tumult.

———

"My God, ladies and gentlemen, an absurd one-two punch to the face, damn, that's got to hurt, that cracker hardly saw the wind-up, two total haymakers in the face, tremendous pain, the Poet takes a step back, the peasant seems to have recovered, they're still circling each other in the ring, the peasant lunges to the attack, the Poet takes one tremendous leap sideways, he's trying to pin him down, but how can he do it? The first round is over, ladies and gentlemen, go Poet! Bust that shitkicker's ass in two."

One of Gaetano Licata's fans leaped to his feet.

"Little boy, why don't you call your sister a shitkicker?"

"Why, what'll you do if I don't? Flunk me in geography?"

Five people intervened and made them both sit down.

One of them commented: "These guys from Palermo are all the same, they get all worked up for no reason."

Grandpa didn't move.

Neither did Umbertino.

"Second round, ladies, gentlemen, and ignorant shitkickers! 'U Ziccùso, the Tick-ridden One, can't figure out what's going on here at all. There, now they're hugging, the referee breaks them up, but don't you find it disgusting to see a couple of boxers rubbing up on each other? Revolting, they're both streaming sweat, look out! Damn, a punch to the chin, the peasant took it straight, nice work, Poet, here's the counterattack, smooth, and smooth again, this is a one-sided match, you hicks, so shut up and suck on that."

In the second round of the regional finals, my father hit his opponent once and once only, winning the round with that single point. He was stripping down the logic of boxing, reducing it to its essential elements. Attack only when you're certain you'll hit the bull's-eye. Elegance attained through subtraction. Umbertino and Franco watched the Paladin in action, then turned to look at each other. On each other's faces, they read astonishment even more clearly than satisfaction.

In our corner, Carlo was swabbing the sweat off my face with a towel. In the opposing corner, Gaetano Licata was pointing at me with his right glove. Before putting his mouthguard back in, he swore to me that the kidding around was over and that he was going to slaughter me in no time flat in this last round of the match. Out in the arena, Gerruso went on with his running patter of insults.

"I told you to shut up, worthless idiot," one of Licata's fans retorted angrily. He crumpled a sheet of newspaper and threw it straight at Gerruso, who, slow as boredom, couldn't even dodge it. The peasant, pleased with his shot, warned Gerruso to shut up or he'd kick his tongue and teeth right down his throat.

"You're just a bunch of hicks, incapable of appreciating true poetry."

'U Ziccùso's fan was foaming with rage.

"Fuck, now I'm going to kill you."

It took seven men to hold him back.

Gerruso wouldn't let up: "Do you really think I'm scared of some small-town redneck?"

By now, theirs were the only voices that could be heard. Everyone else was watching them, except for Umbertino, who was lost in contemplation of a past that he thought was gone forever. The redneck, unable to get through the wall of bodies, settled for wounding Gerruso indirectly. He started lobbing insults at me: "Poet: a mushroom-shaped dick of a poet! Why don't you scribble a little verse on my asshole! The poetry of your deflated balls!"

Gerruso leveled his stump-finger straight at him.

"Don't you dare! Leave him alone!"

Licata's man, as rabid as a stray dog, first cursed the Virgin Mary, then threw a punch at his seat, and finally went back to egging his boxer on.

"Come on, Gaetano, break this pussy ass in half."

Then he pointed at me.

"You're going to spit blood, who the hell do you think you are?"

He flashed his middle finger at me.

Umbertino, in his seat, had lit yet another cigarette.

The third round began.

Rosario had gotten to his feet.

He'd sharpened his gaze and clenched his teeth.

The wasp buzzed here and there, the bull tried to gore it with its horns and failed. It seemed like the same old script. Instead, suddenly, a plot twist: feigning a lunging attack, the Paladin, no the Poet, advanced half a yard, arching his body forward.

The cigarette fell out of Umbertino's fingers.

The opponent was cornered.

And finally, the fury had been unleashed.

A hail of punches rained down, one two three four five six.

His opponent tried to escape that maelstrom, but when his elbows left his sides, a new series of punches tanned his hide, seven, eight, nine, ten times, faster and harder than before.

He tried to throw a right hook to put an end to the punishment he was taking.

Unsuccessfully.

He took an uppercut to the cheekbone and felt his legs give way under him.

He needed to prop his elbows up on the ropes to keep from falling.

Franco watched, open-mouthed.

Umbertino had lunged from his seat to ringside.

Identical in both timing and method, he was watching the same style of attack with which the Paladin, all those years ago, had triumphed at the regionals.

In that moment it suddenly became clear to them just how much they'd missed my father.

Gaetano Licata's knees folded and gave way.

He lifted his right hand from the ropes to create a little extra distance, but his arm failed to respond as quickly as he expected.

It was slow, heavy.

His fans had fallen silent.

Their boxer was a broken thing.

Do you want to know who I am?

Unlimbering my shoulder, I let fly with a left cross in midair.

I'm the Poet.

My fist smashed straight into his face.

The mouthguard flew out of his mouth.

How do you like my poetry now?

Gaetano Licata started to tip over to one side.

No, not like that.

The shark fish isn't done with you yet.

Another hook straight to the temple.

A punch so urgent that it never even took the form of thought.

He collapsed, the way a wall collapses.

Welcome back, ferocity.

I'd been missing you.

The only voices in the hall were the referee, counting to ten, and Gerruso's singsong: "Redneck cocksuckers, redneck cocksuckers!"

≡≡≡

Melluso's scream cut through the muggy afternoon heat.

It came from the carpentry shop.

Rosario asked the soldiers standing guard permission to go to the latrine; when they consented, he left the kitchen. Once he was out of their sight, he set off at a run to see what had happened. He found Melluso laid out on the ground, both hands clutching his mouth. He was spitting blood. D'Arpa was fine. He had both fists still clenched.

"He was stealing a hammer, and he planned to hide it in one of our beds. He wanted to get us punished."

Melluso wiped the blood from his mouth with the back of his hand.

"I'll kill you," he promised.

He spat blood and saliva and left the carpentry shop.

"Rosà," said D'Arpa.

"I know," was the reply.

Nicola had to be warned.

They'd have to watch their backs from now on.

What had happened to Iallorenzi intensified the fear and paranoia. The climate had become intolerable for everyone. The guards lost all sense of proportion. Searches of prisoners became much more frequent. In an atmosphere of continual tension, punishments increased in severity. Domenico Musso was thrown into solitary confinement because he tripped and dropped a pile of mess tins. Alessio Panechiaro lost three days of water rations: it was because his shoelaces were untied during a surprise inspection of the barracks. Ernesto Corabbio was killed while attempting to escape. He'd reached the end of his rope: he hadn't slept in two days and was in a state of delirium. Breaking ranks during morning assembly for roll call, he clambered over the metal gate and ran headlong into the desert wastes, followed by conflicting voices, some shouting to run faster, others imploring him to turn back immediately. A rifle shot finished him off.

Everyone's nerves were in tatters.

Every day, another collapse.

One night, a rifle shot rang out.

The soldier who shot Corabbio had killed himself.

Every night, in two-hour shifts, one of the three of them—D'Arpa, my grandfather, or Randazzo—stood watch over his friends.

Melluso walked into the kitchen.

His pupils were like needles.

"I want meat."

Nicola spread both arms helplessly.

"Can't you see that, in here, we don't even have the idea of meat?"

"You've hidden it from me, you and that worthless thing."

Rosario had already stopped peeling potatoes.

"I want meat. Where the hell is the meat?"

Melluso crushed mosquitoes on his forearms with violent slaps.

As soon as he killed one, he'd pick it up, holding it between his fingertips.

"Isn't this meat? Isn't it meat? Every fly liver is a piece of nourishing meat."

He'd lick it away, swallowing without chewing.

"I want meat."

His eyes roamed in search of signs, hints, colors of meat.

"He's not well," Nicola told my grandfather.

Without warning, Melluso lunged at Randazzo, seizing him by the throat. Nicola fell to his knees. Melluso was throttling him with both hands.

"Meat, I want meat."

Rosario tried to pry open the fingers clutching Nicola's throat, but Melluso refused to let go. My grandfather sank forefinger and middle finger into his left eye. With a scream, Melluso yielded. Rosario shoved him aside and bent over Nicola, who was coughing. The guards arrived. They asked what had happened.

"He must have fainted from the heat."

Randazzo and Melluso both confirmed that version of the story.

Melluso went away, the soldiers left the kitchen, and Rosario looked at the blade of his knife, without resuming his potato-peeling.

"He's delirious," said Randazzo.

"From today on, you're not even going to take a piss by yourself," my grandfather replied.

Lucio La Mantia from Enna had made a deck of cards out of forty aloe leaves, carefully carving the four suits using the thorn of a cactus. It took him twelve days. A *scopa* tournament began. Marangola was unbeatable.

"In Naples, we learn the suits of the cards even before we learn the numbers."

He knew all the games: *briscola*, *rubamazzetto*, *tivìtti*, *tressette*.

During the course of a single game, he could remember every hand that had been played. He possessed a memory forged by sheer dint of practice.

"On the boat, if the weather is good, we spend a few hours playing cards, the night passes and we listen to the sea."

The card games were watched by most of the prisoners.

Marangola played against a guy from Potenza for his shoes, and won.

"Can I keep these shoes with your stuff?"

D'Arpa said yes. After the boxing victory, everyone loved him. No one would have dreamed of trying to steal anything of his.

Marangola went over to D'Arpa's cot, lifted the blanket from the floor to slide the shoes underneath, and gave a desperate shout. A scorpion had stung him right on the thumb.

"What was it?"

"A scorpion."

"Everyone get away," D'Arpa ordered, trying to figure out where the scorpion had scuttled away to. Rosario had taken off at a dead run. "Where are you going?" shouted Nicola, but my grandfather was already out of earshot. He crossed the camp, ignoring the shouted "halt" of the guard, burst into the kitchen, went straight to the cutting board, seized the largest knife, burst through the barrier of soldiers, and continued running, indifferent to the shouted orders to stop, there was no time, he had to go faster and faster still, taking good aim and firing at his back was in any case a process that required time, however little. He managed to get back to the barracks without a shot being fired, at the exact instant that D'Arpa was crushing the scorpion with the heel of his combat boot.

"Nicola, here."

Randazzo saw Rosario handing him the knife but at first he didn't understand. The guards rushed in shouting, rifles leveled, safeties off, but the minute they saw Marangola's body convulsing on the floor, they understood.

"Go ahead, cut."

Rosario's voice was firm.

This was the only chance they had of saving Marangola's life.

"The thumb?" Nicola asked.

"The hand," D'Arpa replied.

"It's useless, whatever you cut," Melluso snickered.

Rosario and D'Arpa held the arm tight. Three others immobilized Marangola.

"Go ahead."

Nicola felt Marangola's wrist with his thumb. He held the knife straight up and down and pushed it into the flesh, driving it down with the weight of his body. Butchering a pig was harder than this, he thought. Two sharp blows and the hand was severed.

The soldiers escorted them to the infirmary, then to see the officers. Rosario was not punished for having taken the knife, Nicola was not punished for having used it. The urgency and necessity of their actions were recognized.

The doctor stopped Marangola's hemorrhaging by cauterizing the wound, but it was too late, the scorpion's venom was already circulating in his bloodstream.

Marangola died a little before noon.

≡

We drove back to Palermo crammed into Franco's Fiat Ritmo.

Umbertino drove.

The car radio was turned off after the news anchor reported yet another Mafia bloodbath in the city.

"Bad signs," said Franco.

"It's going to rain blood," Umbertino said, continuing his thought.

"And soon," my grandfather concluded.

Gerruso forced us to make a pit stop: "I'm practically wetting my pants."

We stopped at a café. Umbertino ordered an *arancina a carne*, a fried rice ball filled with ragout, and invited me to step outside with him. Spread out before us, beyond the fields of prickly pear, was the sea.

"This is the worst *arancina* I've ever tasted."

"Then why are you eating it?"

"Did you see the barista? Too damn sexy."

"What a surprise."

"Davidù, beauty should be celebrated when and where you find it. Speaking of which, it's only right for me to tell you: you fought fabulous, kid. There were times in the bout when you were exactly like the Paladin, you know that?"

"Maestro Franco told me the same thing."

"It was just stunning, you were the spitting image of your father. That said, though . . ."

He popped into his mouth the last bit of *arancina* and lit a cigarette while still chewing.

"But Davidù, what happened there at the end? You had the fight in your pocket. 'U Ziccùso was about to hit the mat. What were you thinking? Why did you give him that last punch to the head?"

"Wouldn't my father have done it?"

"*He* wouldn't have. *I* would've."

Umbertino took a long, deep drag, then blew out smoke for a good twelve seconds.

"The Paladin," he said, putting an end to that hard-won silence.

"Better than *Il Negro*?"

His cigarette, clenched between forefinger and middle finger, had burned down to the end.

"That would have been a beautiful match."

He confided that, a couple of years before my father married my mother, he and my father had been alone in the gym. My uncle had even sent Franco away.

"I just wanted to verify one thing, all by myself."

"Did the two of you fight?"

"That wasn't the point but, anyway, yes, we fought."

The Paladin was tired and all he wanted to do was drop by and say hello to his girlfriend. If it were any other girl, Umbertino would have said something sarcastic and cutting, but this was Zina, and if he heard of anyone failing to show her the proper respect, he'd have clubbed him right out of this world and into eternity.

They climbed into the ring, both wearing boxing gloves.

"You have one round, Paladin, just one round to land a punch to my face."

He had a longer reach than the Paladin, he could hold him at a distance with his left, and his footwork was still formidable.

"Still, he managed to hit me, on the chin. No one, from the times of *Il Negro* . . . no, from the time I lost the finals, no one had laid a fist on my face. It was by no means a knockout punch, let's be clear about that. Still, it was exactly what I'd asked him to do: hit me in the face. It took him less than a minute to do it, too. That day I told him: You're going to win the national title. There weren't any other boxers like the Paladin, there was just no one like him, period. Enough said."

That punch was worthy of *Il Negro*, so different from the ones taken in the championship loss.

"I remember every last one of them. Every last one. They still burn."

"Was that your darkest moment?"

"That, and the times when Giovannella and the Paladin died. Only then it was them who died, and I couldn't do anything about it. The night of the championship fight, on the other hand, I died, and it was all my fault."

My uncle narrowed his eyes, laying both hands on my shoulders.

His fingers pressed into my flesh.

"But you, Davidù."

There was no longer a hurricane in his eyes.

Gerruso walked out of the bar. He was drinking a Chinotto with a straw. He was telling Franco about the filth that littered the street where he lived: garbage bags, syringes, refrigerators, rats. He'd seen a purse-snatching, right outside his front door. The mugger knocked the old woman to the cement, and she'd hit her head.

"A geyser of blood was pouring out of her forehead. The motorcycle was roaring away down the street like it was a motocross event. Insane."

I went back in, ordered a mulberry granita, and sat down next to my grandfather.

"Grandpa, I've won the regionals. But now there's the national title fight, and our family's never won that."

"Then you'll have to be even faster than you are now."

"Like my father."

"Faster still."

"Like you?"

"Even faster than me."

"And who's faster than you?"

"My friend Nenè."

Gerruso sat down between us.

"Let's hope we don't get in a car crash on the way back, because if you die, Poet, Jesus, the national title curse, that really would be just too much bad luck for one family."

≡≡≡

The same way she vanished, she reappeared.

Two years without seeing her.

Ever since that afternoon at the fair.

I'd kissed three of my classmates: Eva, Annalisa, and Silvia.

Especially Eva.

She was a really good kisser.

Annalisa was a year older than me and she had a really remarkable pair of tits.

Silvia was bright and funny.

We got to know each other, we dated, we sniffed around each other, we got to like each other, we fell for each other.

But none of them was Nina.

Enough said.

I ran into her in Via Notarbartolo, at the corner of Via Libertà.

I was sixteen years old.

I was going into the Cinema Fiamma, and she was coming out.

"Nina."

"Ciao."

And once again, separating the two of us, the Great Wall of China.

"You're by yourself."

"Yes, I am."

"I'm with . . ."

"I can see who you're with."

There she was, as proud and arrogant as she was two summers ago.

Eliana Dumas.

The Buttana Imperiale.

She had her arm cradled snugly around Nina's waist.

She hadn't changed a bit.

She asked with feigned interest what I was doing there, she'd never thought of me as someone who liked that kind of movie. By the way, who had I come with? Oh, I was alone? Eh, there's so much loneliness in the world. Was I still boxing? I was? Then I must have flunked out of school. I hadn't? She guessed my high school must be much easier than hers. When was my next bout? On the twenty-first of January, here in Palermo? Where? What was my opponent's name? Fabio Rizzo? Well, he was certain to beat me, and whatever happened, she'd be rooting for him. They'd spent enough time with me, it was really time for them to go. She had to say that it hadn't been much of a pleasure. Ciao.

"Nina, will you come?" I asked, but in such a faint voice that even I couldn't hear it.

A city is a labyrinth. Arteries that turn into piazzas, alleys that dovetail at diagonal angles. The thoroughfares you take every day, and the streets you've never even seen. A city conceals people, encounters missed by an instant because someone stopped to tie a shoelace or turned distractedly into the wrong street. The strategies of the labyrinth are incomprehensible to the human soul.

Two years without seeing you.

You'd grown up, Nina.

Your hair was longer.

Your breasts were bigger.

Your posture was even more elegant than before.

Your awareness of your own allure had increased.

Mulberry lips and deep, dark eyes.

Nina didn't come to the bout against Fabio Rizzo on January 21.

Gerruso did.

He argued with everyone.

As usual, he shouted out: "Poet."

By now, that's what everyone on the boxing circuit called me. They called me by the nickname that Gerruso had given me. Nina liked it.

Nina never came to the fights.

After the fight, after the shower in the locker room, outside of the gym, I found myself in *her* presence: legs straddling a Piaggio Sì, black helmet under her arm and purse draped over her thighs: the Dumas.

"Is Nina here?"

"No."

"What are you doing here?"

"I just happened to be in the neighborhood."

"Of all the places in the world, you had to come here?"

"Yes."

"Of all days, the day I'm having my fight?"

"Coincidence."

"Of course, how could I forget, I told you, outside the movie house."

"Life is full of odd coincidences."

"Where's Nina?"

"I don't know, I'm not her mother. Did you lose?"

"Do you give a damn either way?"

"Less than zero. I don't go to see these brute animal spectacles."

"Ah, true, you play the cello."

"Who told you that?"

"Nina."

"And you remembered it."

"I remember everything that Nina tells me."

"Remembering's not the same as understanding."

"Where is she?"

"Forget about her, she doesn't want you, she's seeing someone else."

"That's crap."

Just then, Gerruso appeared.

"Your bag is heavy, it took me a while, here you go. Ciao, Eliana."

"You see that I came? Now I have to go, ciao. And ciao to you, too, boxer."

She stood up on the pedals, pushed down with her feet, arching her back as she turned over the scooter's engine, and she angled away with a roar.

"Gerruso, did you invite her?"

"Sure, but I never thought she'd actually come."

"What made you do it?"

"Nina called me."

"Nina calls you?"

"Well, not me, she calls my mother."

"And why on earth would she call your mother?"

"I don't know, to say hello to her and put my aunt on the line, that kind of thing, girl stuff."

"Well, so?"

"I told her about the match, and did she want to come see you fight? Eliana was at her house and she put her on the line and I said hi and I invited her to come, too, if she wanted, that's all."

"Gerruso, we hate the Dumas."

" . . . "

"Gerruso."

" . . . "

"Fuck, I can't believe it: you like the blonde."

"No."

"Gerruso, look me in the eyes and tell me the truth."

"I'm not in love with her."

"Gerruso."

"Maybe just a little."

"You're a complete Judas."

"I know, sorry."

"Sorry, my ass. I'm never speaking to you again."

"Can I ask you something?"

"No."

He asked me anyway. The following Saturday the Buttana Imperiale was going to hold her recital at the conservatory. Would I go with him? I told him yes, without the slightest hesitation. Nina was sure to be there.

The boxing gloves had fallen to the locker-room floor. I hadn't picked them up. The exhaustion that follows a fight had swept over me all at once.

"Will you get them for me?"

"Only if you answer me."

"Enough, I'm tired of questions about angels, they don't exist."

"If you won't answer my question, I won't pick up the gloves."

"Gerruso, are you blackmailing me?"

"Yes. Now, who's stronger, men or angels?"

"Men. You can snap a human being in two, but not an angel."

"So that means the angel is stronger, doesn't it?"

"Strength is something that can be broken but doesn't break."

I had my eyes closed. I was listening to the expansion of my ribs, the way they stretched and then contracted. I was feeling no pain.

"Who teaches you these things?"

"My grandma. And boxing."

"Then can I learn to box, too?"

"No."

"The only reason I'd do it is to learn these thoughts."

"You'd take too many punches to the head, you wouldn't be able to think a thing after a while, you're slow."

"Too bad, if I were an angel the punches wouldn't have connected with me at all. Fists hurt, let me tell you. So do slaps. And kicks. But what hurts most is spitting. And you know something about that."

Fabio Rizzo.

The fight that had just ended.

"Until the spit, the match looked like a merry-go-round. You kept whirling around."

"We weren't whirling, he was chasing after me."

"Were you running away?"

"No."

"Still, the minute he spat in your face, you really lost your temper."

"No, I didn't. I was totally calm."

"Calm? But you practically beat him to a pulp! You were in a frenzy!"

When boxers face off, there's usually one who's more proactive and goes on the attack, while the other tries to avoid the confrontation, at least at first. Most of the time, all that's going on is you're seeing which of the two is the better fighter. The more aggressive boxer wants to lead the fight, and is determined to charge into the fray from the outset. Unless something fucked-up is going on, he's likely to be the last man left standing. It may happen, though it's rare, that the boxer who's keeping his distance is simply dragging out the clash. He's toying with the other one, like a cat with a mouse. He knows he can snap his adversary when and as he pleases. All he needs to do is drop his mask and attack. It's just a matter of time. Sooner or later, the shark fish always reveals his basic nature.

Nina didn't come to the recital at the conservatory.

"Gerruso, it was a terrible idea to come, let's get out of here."

The musicians made their entrance. The Dumas was wearing a floor-length black velvet dress. Her blond hair hung loose, draped over her shoulders. She took her seat, exchanged glances with the other musicians, and they began to play.

The fingers of her left hand pressed down on the strings with graceful energy—unthinkable distances were surveyed and conquered. The wrist of her right hand paced the movement of the bow while her feet, solidly planted, pushed down through the tips of her toes.

Her eyes were closed.

Once the recital was over, she handed her instrument to her mother. She shook hands with a small army of people, dispensing smiles freely.

"Gerruso, let's go."

"Aren't we going to say hello to her?"

"No."

Gerruso started waving his hands, leaping from foot to foot, his shirt half tucked, half untucked, hanging out of his pants. The Dumas waved to us to wait for her, but it took her twelve minutes to join us.

"I didn't think I'd see you here."

"I just came with Gerruso, *'un fare màle pensate*—don't get the wrong idea."

"Oh, a poet speaking in dialect, I can feel shivers running up and down my spine."

"Hold on to that, it's the one sign that you may actually be a human being."

"Did you enjoy the concert?"

"You want the truth?"

"Of course."

"Yes."

"Good, we're even."

"We're even how?"

The blonde came over to me.

All ten of her cello-playing fingertips were splayed upon my chest. Her head was next to mine. Her mouth was pressed against my ear. There was no hesitation in her voice.

"I like you, boxer."

Mouth, hair, and fingers all pulled away.

Walking backward, she flashed me a quick smile.

"I told you, we're one to one."

She turned on her heel and walked away.

Gerruso laid the hand with the stump-finger on my right shoulder.

"Poet, will you help me to make her my girlfriend?"

As soon as he bought the space that would become his boxing gym, the cellar of a newly erected building near the juvenile detention center, Umbertino walked every inch of Palermo in search of students. He talked to anyone who would listen, flatly indifferent as to whether they possessed the physical prerequisites for success in the world of boxing. Umbertino needed money, and so he had to recruit students. The real estate purchase, as expected, had cleaned him out. A month after inaugurating the space, he still hadn't managed to recruit a single student. He had no income, no way of surviving the coming month. He needed to get the word out. He went from one construction site to another, he combed the bars on Via Libertà, he went to the stadium, out to Mondello, to the Ballarò, Capo, Scàro, and Vuccirìa markets, and even down to the port, until he finally understood that the problem wasn't one of explaining the benefits of going to the gym. What was essential was getting the word out that a boxing gym even existed in Palermo. Establishing its existence in the imagination of the populace. Then, of course, the first lesson would be free, let them understand that he could help them to sculpt their body to a state of such flawless perfection that women would be lining up to lick the sweat off their chests. He needed hubbub and clamor. After his defeat at the finals, he swore to himself he'd never fight again in an official bout of any kind. Now he started fighting in clandestine bouts, eager to show with his own body just what a person could become, with the proper training. But the successful tip of his strategic wedge was his use of the

two most effective channels for getting the word out to men and sway-
ing them in his favor: priests and whores.

"Listen to me, Father, and listen good, let's not waste each other's
time. For every individual who comes to my boxing gym from your
parish, I'll make sure that you receive, every Sunday, from that person,
an offering that will make you want to come here and kiss my hands,
Father. And so, every time you say Mass, in the homily I want you to
counsel the faithful to come to my gym. You can come up with your
own reason why: you're good with words after all, you're a priest. Why
should they come to the gym? What? How can you even ask? To form
an awe-inspiring army of the faithful, with all these Communists out
there it's just getting worse every day. I'm a proper Christian myself, you
can count on that. I know all the religion there is, from A to Z. There's
Jesus, Son of Joseph and Mary. His word is the Gospel truth. Thou shalt
not kill, thou shalt not steal, thou shalt not bear false witness, ten things
just like that, Moses-style. Then, there's the miracles: the loaves and the
fishes, the lepers, and then that spectacular one, the water into wine.
But the raging multitude choose Barabbas and Baby Jesus dies on the
cross, you'd think that was Amen, but no: three days later He's up again,
risen and on fire, He walks on water, doves fly, and roosters crow."

"There were a bunch of eager men, Davidù, piling in here, every last
one of them saying: I'm here in the name of Rosa 'La Ciùri Ciùri,'
Carmelina also known as 'Bedda Matri' sent me, I heard about you
from Piera 'La Spagnola.' This was how it worked: when a young man
went to see a whore, first my girlfriends went to work on him, caressing him and complimenting him, 'Oh you're so handsome and oh
you're so strong,' then they'd start to plant the first seeds of doubt,
'Certainly, of course, if you were to take up boxing,' then they'd let their
voices trail away, they'd drop the subject, they'd screw for a while, then
they'd pick up where they'd left off, 'No, it's just that one of my clients
is a boxer and, well, I guess I can tell you, you're a friend: he fucks me
so well sometimes I don't even make him pay; I like you so much, if
you want I'll tell you where the boxing gym is, it belongs to a guy I
know, mention my name and he'll give you a discount.'"
    "So did you give them a discount?"

"Don't be ridiculous. If someone came in mentioning the name of some woman I knew, I'd make sure they paid quite a bit more and I'd give my girlfriends a commission."

"A percentage."

"Business is business."

"Did you always pay them?"

"In the early days, I did. After a certain point, they refused to take the money. Poor Gina was beaten to death by a lawyer, a filthy pig who thought he was untouchable."

"And they called you. So what happened to the lawyer?"

"What do I know, he moved to another city, he left town, he went to the mainland, the continent, far from Palermo."

"Far away."

"Out of sight, out of mind, as they say."

"Uncle, what about a payoff? Did the Mafia ever demand a payoff?"

"Davidù, do you know what keeps the Mafia going? 'U scànto, sheer fear, the fact that four thugs can just come by and kick your teeth down your throat and no one will come to your aid."

"So nobody ever came to shake you down?"

"Even if they'd come in here with a team of fifteen, they would have taken such a beating that they wouldn't even have had the breath to yell 'enough.' That's something the mafiosi know all too well. People who make a living with fear are the first to know when it's time for them to be afraid."

The adrenaline of victory had begun to subside. None of my bones was causing me any pain. I had no bruises on my chest. All that lingered from the fight I'd just experienced was the taste of the mouthguard on my tongue, the scrapes and bruises on my knuckles, and the blood on my fingernails.

No delicate vibrato-inducing, piano-playing fingers on my neck.

The water in the shower was steaming hot. I insistently scrubbed my face. I could still feel the spit on my cheeks and forehead. The second round had come to an end. I'd walked over to Fabio Rizzo to greet him, touch gloves, and go back to my corner. He dropped his mouthguard into his right glove and spat in my face. The saliva sprayed over me before I had a chance to raise my guard, to retreat into a protective crouch. My arms hung at my sides. The referee led him away, giving him a formal warning. Umbertino was invoking a string of saints. Carlo dried off my face while the Maestro commanded me to remain calm. Gerruso spat in Fabio Rizzo's direction but, seething with rage, he failed to coordinate mouth and saliva properly and the spit dribbled down his chest. Grandpa sat there, seraphic, arms folded over his chest, legs crossed, his eyes on the boxing ring.

A gang of five good-for-nothings had started picking on my father after school.

"He was on edge, Davidù. He said that he didn't know why they'd decided to pick on him, but he hadn't reacted to their bullying."

He was fourteen. For the past two years, he'd been going to my uncle's gym. He was fit, not skinny. His shirt concealed shoulders that were much broader than they looked. He had slender hands and long fingers. He'd enrolled in the science high school. My grandparents were proud of how well he was doing.

"Of course he was on edge, Grandma, there were five of them against the one of him, plus the fact that they'd insulted you by calling you a . . . well, you know what they said, it's a serious insult, you can't let people get away with talking about your mother like that."

"They were just kids."

"They were hood rats. At least when you beat someone up, you're teaching them some manners. There are some people that words are just wasted on."

"Words are always useful, the important thing is to use them with precision. When a message fails to get through, it's because the vocabulary of your interlocutor does not include the words in question."

"Grandma, don't mistake bad manners for a small vocabulary."

"Getting into a brawl with a bunch of kids over an insult was pointless, that time."

The next day, the same scene: the five punks showed up outside the school and shoved my father around, insisting my grandmother was a whore and my grandfather was a faggot. My father managed to elude their grasp and run home.

"Better to avoid a fight."

My grandmother's advice seemed reasonable. Rosario wasn't in Palermo, he was finishing out the season working in the kitchen of a hotel outside Messina, and he wouldn't be home for another couple of weeks. The following day, the little thugs took things even further. They took my father's books out of his bag and pissed on them.

"Oh, how I missed your grandfather then. I didn't know which way to turn. Maybe I had chosen the wrong strategy, I was confused."

My father had erected a wall between himself and the rest of the world. He had shrouded himself in an impenetrable silence. With death in her heart, Grandma sat down beside him and took his hands in hers. His hands resembled Rosario's.

"Francesco, if it happens again, this time you should fight back. Never let anyone take advantage of your good nature."

My father looked her in the eye. The blue of his irises was still, like the horizon on the sea.

"Mamma, there's five of them and they're all bigger than me."

Grandma caressed his temples.

"Well, you'll just have to make sure you hit them harder."

Four months after the championship defeat, Umbertino returned to boxing in an underground fight. Right away, he decided he didn't like the guys who were taking the bets. They talked too much. They were arrogant and quick to anger. Where money's involved, people need to stay calm and keep cool.

The Guadagna gym had nothing: no ring, no ropes, not even any chairs for the audience. It wasn't a proper fight. It was going to be a bloodbath. The rules were simple: last man standing is the winner. There was the semblance of a referee. After all, they had to have someone who could count to ten.

"I hopped around for a whole minute without landing a single punch worthy of the name, would you believe it? I'd never been face-to-face with an opponent for that long without going on the attack."

"You were out of practice."

"Hell I was. I was waiting."

"For what?"

"I'd missed it, Davidù. The eyes of the audience, the back-and-forth of the bout, feinting to avoid punches, understanding just how far I could push things. I'd really missed it, more than I'd realized. I wanted to make it last as long as I could."

His uppercut was intercepted by his opponent's forearm, but that didn't do much to help him. Umbertino penetrated that shield of flesh and bone, unleashing hooks and crosses, avoiding the head but shattering the man's entire torso.

All it took was a single attack.

"I was back."

It wasn't true. He wasn't back. He'd never left. Six months after it opened, the gym had twenty-six paying students. Umbertino fought only three more clandestine boxing matches. No one wanted to take him on after that.

As soon as he came back home, my grandfather was told about the brawl that had taken place outside the school.

"I told him myself, he couldn't keep taking the abuse."

"Leave us alone."

Grandma went into the kitchen and pressed her ear against the closed door. On the surface of the wood she could feel the beating of her own heart.

My father told his father about the insults, the shoves, the pissed-on books. When they'd grabbed him to strip him and steal his clothes, he'd laid all five of them out with a fast round of punches.

When he was done with his story, a lengthy silence ensued, interrupted only by the sound of chair legs scraping on the floor. Rosario had risen to his feet.

"You did wrong, Francesco."

Grandma felt a wave of shame wash over her.

Her son must have felt the same sensation.

"Papà, what was I supposed to do? Let them strip me naked?"

"No, you weren't wrong to fight back. You were just wrong to use your fists."

Grandma felt the tears welling up in her eyes.

"You're a boxer, you know how to use your fists better than they do. You should never take advantage of your superiority, and if you do, you're just a piece of shit."

Grandma began crying, her hand covering her mouth to keep from being heard.

"They had come to an understanding: if your father ran into them again, this time he wouldn't use his fists. It happened again a few days later. He was as good as his word."

Only one of the crew wanted to get his own back for the last time, the one who'd gotten off the easiest, evidently. My father ignored the words—"cuckold and cop lover"—launched in his direction by a voice dripping with mockery; he refused to hand over his bag, he wouldn't step off the sidewalk. The other guy, frustrated by my father's unflustered response, spat right in his face. My father took the gob of spit, wiped it off with the back of his hand, and walked off without so much as a blink of the eye. No one ever bothered him again.

At home, Grandpa was in the dining room, alone with his son.

"In Africa, my friend explained to me that a great general isn't the one who wins the battle, but the one who wins the war without having to fight at all. You shouldn't be afraid of people, but of what you can do to them. Never forget that. You're a seed taking root in the earth, that's what you are."

Through the half-open kitchen door, Grandma saw him caress his son's cheek.

When Fabio Rizzo spat, he betrayed tension, rage, and base hooliganism.

I took it the way you take the sirocco in November.

These things happen.

"If you were an angel, it would have passed right through you."

"If I were an angel, I couldn't have beat him to a pulp."

At the start of the third round, Fabio Rizzo got to work immediately. His left fist grazed my temple. At the same time, my hook, totally unimpeded, caught him square in the cheekbone. He lunged at me, his whole body sprawling in dead weight, the mass of it a shield preventing me from continuing my attack. The shock of the next hook I threw was absorbed by his arm. My right fist, however, managed to land against his chin. It was a hard blow. Fabio Rizzo bent forward from the waist. A one-two punch straight to his face drove him back onto the ropes. He crossed his arms over his head, but his legs were giving way beneath him. He staggered to one side, took three steps, shattered on his right flank.

He dropped to the floor like a broken toy.

The referee counted to ten.

I was ready for the national title fights.

I went into the locker room, I took a shower, I left Gerruso to carry my bag, I walked out into the open air, and I ran into the Dumas.

≡≡≡

"What are you doing here?"

"I was just passing by."

"Sure, another coincidence."

"Funny, isn't it? You still in your tracksuit? We dress better at the conservatory."

"I train here."

"Every day?"

"Yes."

"And you fight here, too?"

"Only when it's my gym that's hosting the bout."

"Will you come to another one of my recitals?"

"Never underestimate divine providence."

"Do you want a ride?"

"No."

"Why not?"

"I don't trust women on scooters."

"Then you can drive."

"No."

"Do you know how to ride a scooter?"

"I'm confident I'm a fabulous driver."

"Show me."

"No, you show me."

"Then get on."

"I just live around the corner."

"I'll take you home later, first there's something I want to show you."

"All right, let's go, as long as it's not on the other side of the world."

"So what was it you wanted to show me?"

"Are you really such a dope or are you doing it on purpose?"

"I don't understand."

"Come over here and shut up for a minute."

Lips, tongue, saliva.

A stolen kiss.

She pulled away from my mouth.

An amazing kiss.

"I like you because you went to the movies all alone. And because the other day you came to my concert. And because you have pretty eyes."

My eyes.

The same compliment that Nina paid me.

She kissed me again.

Our tongues intertwined.

"Toward the middle of the fifties, I think in '55 or '56. White skirt, bare arms, slender neck. A spicy morsel."

Her name was Chiara.

He'd nicknamed her "Libera." Freedom.

"She belonged to no one, she was her own girl, that one."

The oval shape of her face, the glint in her eyes, the way she wrinkled her nose.

"She had a powerful effect on me."

She looked like Giovannella.

She was studying to be a lawyer. She came from the upper crust of Palermo.

"We didn't have anything in common, the two of us."

"Then how did you wind up together?"

"Davidù, did you just suddenly go stone blind? Take a look at what a fine, handsome man your uncle is now, and try to picture me thirty years ago: I was God's own gift."

Libera wore a headband: she was twenty-one and carried a gift-wrapped tray of pastries.

"What are they?"

"St. Joseph's Day cream puffs: *Sfinci di San Giuseppe*."

"Are they for me?"

"Why, we haven't even been introduced."

"Introduced? What, like a thermometer?"

She replied that she was in no mood for jokes, she was in a hurry, she was expected at Sunday dinner, and she really had to go. Still, she showed no sign of leaving.

"Oh, hey, she stood up her whole family and we took a walk to see the ruined church at Spasimo."

My uncle ate the entire tray of pastries. As soon as he finished, she told him that she had to get going. He asked her to stay a little longer, and she politely but firmly declined. That evening her future husband's parents would be coming to town from Ganci.

"You're getting married?"

"In two months. Aren't you going to congratulate me?"

"No. So now you're leaving? Without even giving me a kiss?"

"You had the chance to choose between me and the *sfinci* and you picked the pastries."

He waited a whole week for her, on the very spot where he first met her, and he finally laid eyes on her the following Sunday, at the same time, with the same tray, the same bold twenty-one-year-old girl.

"Cream puffs again?"

"Genovese pastries."

"I like Genovese pastries even better than I like *sfinci*."

"So no kisses for you this time either?"

They spent a month together.

A week before her wedding, Libera asked him why he'd never returned to professional boxing.

Umbertino took a long pause before loosing his answer on the world.

"Everything has a price."

"Love has no price."

"Sure it does, you pay for it with your life."

Libera got married. Their affair came to an end the same way it started: without any parting words, without the regret of broken promises.

She really looked a lot like Giovannella.

"You had feelings for her."

"I was in love with her."

"Really."

"I've been with plenty of women, and you know it, but some of them, for the time I was with them, I was truly in love. And Libera is one of those women."

"Then why did it end between you?"

"Are you kidding? It never even got started."

"If she had wanted, she could have decided not to get married."

"It's not that simple."

"Explain."

"Being in love and being happy aren't the same thing, and often they have nothing to do with each other."

The wall thermometer read 109 degrees. Grandma, in her dressing gown, stood up, moving the chair without a sound. She mopped her forehead with her handkerchief.

"Have you seen my pack of cigarettes?"

"You're holding it in your hand."

She lit one, took a drag, and set it down on the ashtray.

"Did you hear the shooting?"

"Yes, I was in class, and they were shooting right outside our window."

"I don't like it, I don't like it a bit."

"Palermo?"

"There's the same whiff of poverty in the air I remember from when I was a girl. But back then the world was at war, whereas now everyone pretends nothing is happening, while brother murders brother all over the city. The Mafia has unleashed a bloodbath inside individual families."

"Weren't you all killing each other during the war?"

"Not like this."

She stubbed out her cigarette and started loading the Moka Express coffeepot.

"Everything all right at school?"

"Yes. I'm top of the class in Latin."

"So you see that teaching you Latin served a purpose?"

"Sure, it ruined three whole summers."

"You dope."

She put the coffeepot on the flame and sat back down.

"Come on, tell me something about yourself. Do you have a girl-friend?"

"Grandma!"

"You're seeing a girl, aren't you?"

"Grandma!"

"I know, I know, I wasn't trying to pry into your business."

"Sure, of course you weren't."

"No, really, it was just a test. There's no two ways about it: you're the spitting image."

"I'm as close-mouthed as Grandpa?"

"Not at all. Rosario isn't close-mouthed, he's just quiet, but he talks. You talk all the time, maybe you even talk too much, and you hide behind that wall of words. You're the spitting image of your father, he held his cards close to the vest, he never gave anything away."

"Is that wrong?"

"It's unique. Do you have a friend you can talk to?"

"Yes."

"And do you confide in him?"

"Yes."

"What do you tell him?"

"Things."

"What about with your uncle? And with your grandpa?"

"I talk to them, too."

"And do you tell them things? I'm not talking about the things you say to fill the silence, Davidù. Confiding in someone, establishing a relationship means sharing the weight of the day, every day, for as long as it lasts. Do you ever talk about yourself with someone else, about the things you really feel, your joys and your sorrows? Do you know what struck me in particular about your father's nickname? That it fit him perfectly. Perfectly. He really was a paladin, but not because of the way he fought—what would I ever have been able to understand about that? It was perfect because of the armor he wore around himself, the perennial suit of chain mail that he placed between himself and the rest of the world. He never took it off. Of course his opponents couldn't understand his moves. He was completely inscrutable. In the ring and in his life. Now drink your coffee before it gets cold, coffee's just disgusting cold."

"So the championship fight is really going to be held in Palermo?"

"Yes."

"Absurd."

"Not really."

"But it's the same exact thing that happened to your uncle! Now don't tell me that you're going to lose, too, and then wind up opening a boxing gym of your own, just like he did?"

"Thanks for the vote of confidence, Gerruso."

"You're welcome. But don't you ever get tired of it?"

"Of what?"

"Training, running, waking up super-early and breaking off your dreams midway through the second half, only being able to eat certain things, push-ups, pull-ups. I eat as much as I want, I get lots of sleep, and my dreams never involve sweating."

The idea of not wanting to wake up already on your feet, outside it's raining and before you know it both shoes are already laced, fifteen push-ups, *fio, fis, factus sum, fieri*, and home is already far back in the distance, hook uppercut feint, *tollo, tollis, sustuli, sublatum, tollere*, cross feint cross again, every day until the minute you collapse into bed, until the next time the alarm goes off, at 5:30 in the morning.

"It's what I know."

"And you've never skipped a session?"

"Rarely."

"And when you did, did you tell them why you hadn't shown up, or did you tell them a little white lie?"

"First of all: if I skip a training session, there's always a perfectly valid reason, and in any case I'm training for the nationals and so no, I never skip a session. Second: What's a white lie?"

"They taught us about it at catechism. A white lie is what you say to keep from hurting a person's feelings. Sister Emilia explained it to us at catechism. She was nice, she always told me how handsome I was."

"White lie."

"Really?"

"Gerruso, what do you think? The nun was telling you that to buck you up."

"And it worked, actually. Do you know any stories about lying?"

I told him a story about the truth.

Once upon a time, a king was born with donkey ears. The only person who knew the truth was the doctor. The queen mother had died in childbirth. The doctor gave the following order: for the rest of his life, the king was to wear a headcovering that would conceal his ears. It was vital to his own health and the future of his kingdom. Far better to keep the truth quiet. The doctor, crushed by the weight of the secret he kept, abandoned the court and the kingdom. He fled overseas and fetched up in distant lands, living among people who ate bread without salt. There he dug a hole in the ground and whispered into it: "The king has donkey ears." At last, he felt freed of his burden. He covered the hole with dirt and that was the end of his part in this story. That field was sown with crops. A single tree grew in the field, broad and strong. Its wood was perfect for carving flutes. Word spread everywhere about the mellifluous tone of the flutes made from the wood of that one tree. News made its way to court. A concert was scheduled, the finest flutist in the kingdom would play the finest flute made from the wood of that tree. The populace gathered around their king to listen to the wonderful sound. The flutist picked up his flute, lifted it to his lips, and blew into it. The flute sang out: "The king has donkey ears."

"Are you telling me that little white lies are eventually revealed by the flute of time? Like the white lie Sister Emilia told me?"

"Would you rather she had told you that you were ugly?"

"I'd rather she'd told me the truth, for her to say that in her opinion I'm very handsome, maybe I just happen to make an especially good impression on nuns, what do I know? Anyway, can I tell you something about truth?"

"If you absolutely have to."

"I made a fool of myself today."

"With who?"

"Eliana."

He'd gone to meet her when school let out, with a flower in his hand. The Dumas came over to him, trailing an entourage of girlfriends behind her. She'd asked who the flower was for and acted dumbstruck when Gerruso gave it to her. Then she burst out laughing. She hadn't taken it. She hadn't thanked him. She'd asked about me.

Gerruso had told her that I was winning all my fights, that I was aiming for a shot at the national title, that I was getting good grades in school.

Amid a chorus of snickers from her girlfriends, she interrupted him, saying that she'd just remembered she had to be somewhere, and turned to go without another word. Then she stopped short, turned around, and shot him a glance: "Give the boxer a kiss from me," she said, and left him standing there, forlorn in the middle of the street, with a flower in his hand.

"Do you have any idea why Eliana would have sent you a kiss?"

"No."

"If you did know, would you tell me?"

"Yes."

"Is that a white lie?"

"No."

D'Arpa had lowered his voice.

"All right then, we agree?"

"Yes, we won't say a thing to Nicola."

They both thought the same thing: it was Vincenzo Melluso who had hidden the scorpion in D'Arpa's blanket.

He was getting worse every day.

He'd clobbered La Mantia from behind with a rock. If four guys hadn't pulled him off, he'd have crushed La Mantia's skull. Melluso had accused him of being a card cheat, La Mantia must have marked the cards, that's why he always beat him.

"Randazzo thinks Melluso is delirious because he's sick," said D'Arpa.

"Nicola is a good man, and Melluso is a bad seed," Rosario replied.

"If we lose our ability to feel pity, we'll be just like him."

Rosario said nothing.

"All the same, we're going to do what we decided to do," D'Arpa concluded. He was well aware of the risks he was running, but the concrete threat that Melluso constituted made extreme measures necessary. The piece of wood that he'd slipped into his shoe was stiff and sharp. He'd have to use it like a nail and strike deep. Before going out, thinking of the danger involved, that he might be searched by the guards, he hesitated a moment. If he was caught, he'd be exposing Rosario and Nicola even further: Melluso would understand and he'd take revenge, that much was clear. D'Arpa weighed his options and decided to act as they'd agreed. He headed for the exit; the guards, crossing their rifles, ordered him to halt.

"*Boxer,*" they called him.

His victories had made him popular.

They told him to empty his pockets.

D'Arpa complied.

"*The jacket.*"

D'Arpa stood there bare-chested.

"*The shoes.*"

D'Arpa bent over slowly and began working on the knot, but instead of untying it he only knotted it tighter.

"*Help me,*" he asked the soldiers, pointing to the knot to show that it wouldn't come undone.

They gave him a look of irritation, then they waved him through, saying he was free to go without removing his shoes. D'Arpa walked toward the soldiers and, his hands held high, mimed a pair of uppercuts, one for each soldier. The guards broke into laughter and saluted him. D'Arpa found Rosario and the two of them asked Randazzo to accompany them to the latrine.

"If Melluso tries something at night, use this to defend yourself."

"Where did you find it?"

"Don't worry about that. Just make sure you keep it well hidden, and within easy reach."

"But what about you?"

"Just worry about hiding the stick, don't worry about us."

Nicola went back to the barracks alone, weighed down with unasked questions.

It was Rosario who first recognized the potential for confusion.

"He wouldn't know how to use it."

"I know that."

But they hadn't done it for him. Knowing that he had some small weapon with which to defend himself was really just a way to put their own minds at ease.

They stopped for a few minutes and looked up at the sky.

The light of the stars spread out in all directions.

"The African sky is beautiful," said D'Arpa, laying one hand on my grandfather's shoulder.

"It's endless."

They went back to the barracks.

They agreed to take turns standing guard to prevent Melluso from attacking them by night, and they said goodbye with a handshake, for the last time in their lives.

That piece of wood was never used.

The following day, the inferno descended on the prisoner-of-war camp.

≡≡≡

Adolescence passed: studying schoolbooks, training at the gym, dating one girl or another in a city that was becoming ever more filthy and violent.

Antonio Provenzani from Lecce, aka *"Fritto Misto"* (Mixed Fish Fry) for his great skill at shifting styles in a single bout. TKO in the second round.

Marco Dambrosio from Formia, *"Il Polpo"* (The Octopus): he'd glue himself to his opponent, only to slither away suddenly. A win on points, 7 to 0.

Mimmo Alba from Genoa, a boxer who could take punishment, as mangy as he was rocky. He didn't get in a lot of punches, but when he did, they hurt. He was nicknamed *"Beneficenza,"* like a charity ball. I won on points, 5 to 1.

Michelle, an English girl, seventeen, on a school field trip, encountered on my morning run as she was returning to the hotel after a night out carousing with her female classmates. Serious French-kissing and heavy petting, that same evening. No sex, we were both virgins. I called her "Mabbèl."

Duccio Tessori from Lucca, called *"Il Ladro"* (The Thief) for the speed with which he could dismantle his opponent's defense. Victorious on points, three rounds to zip.

Luisa, the cousin of a girl someone else introduced me to at some birthday party or other. Sixteen years old, a curly head of hair, a piercing voice, wet wet kisses. I nicknamed her *"Mulinello"* (Whirlpool).

Mizio Dal Collo, from Popiglio, a section of Piteglio, in the province of Pistoia. *"Lo Spaccaossa"* (The Bone-Breaker). Won on points, 15 to 6.

Damiano Palano from Mantua, also known as *"Tradimento"* (Betrayal). KO in the second round.

Alessandro Coscia, a left-hander from Pozzolo Formigaro in the province of Alessandria, *"La Locomotiva Piemontese"* (The Piedmont Locomotive). Victorious on points, 7 to 4.

Letizia, eighteen years of pure insolence, rechristened *"La Flautista"* (The Flutist). And her girlfriend Teresa, *"Occhio Bello"* (Bright Eyes), going on eighteen, and going on real sex.

Mauro Genovese from Trapani, the boxer without a nickname. I won on points, two rounds to one.

Massimiliano Biffi from Rho, *"Il Bauscia."* His nickname indicated that he was an arrogant Milanese. KO in the first round.

I never lost.

I was just one fight away from the national title, just one fight away, when, after fifty years, the bombs came back to Palermo.

The city had once again been plunged into war.

Maestro Franco gave us the news in the gym.

"They planted a bomb on the highway. The Mafia, a terrorist attack, a lot of innocent people were killed."

Umbertino was indignant: "And now, just because the Mafia has decided to run roughshod over everything, I'm supposed to interrupt my training sessions?"

Still, something really had been broken. Before war belonged in survivors' stories, in memories handed down on Sunday afternoons after lunch. The damage that could still be seen in the center of the city reminded us that, yes, there had been a war, it had been destructive, but then it had ended. The explosion of a bomb, on the other hand, brought war back to the present day. It was a point of no return, completely different from mere gunshots. It was no longer possible to pretend nothing was happening. Everyday life was overturned, as was the city itself, subject to martial law.

The first result of that increasingly tense atmosphere was an even more defensive crouch. Changing the route you followed because of a sudden hunch, mistrusting unfamiliar faces, feeling a stab of anxiety at the sight of a car you'd never seen before parked outside your apartment building. Police sirens wailed everywhere, at all hours of the day and night. No one had the heart to say it, but everyone expected new attacks. It took only a month and a half for that unspoken prophecy to be borne out. Another bomb exploded, and yet the people of Palermo did not flee. The one sure thing in that war was this: to survive unharmed was in and of itself something praiseworthy.

Gerruso called me the night the first bomb went off.

"Are we going to run away?"

"We're not running."

"By 'we' do you mean yourself and your family?"

"Not just us."

"Am I included in that 'we'?"

"Yes."

"Jesus, Poet, I almost feel like saying thank you to those bombs if you consider me part of 'us.'"

"Don't get carried away, Gerruso."

"So we're not running away."

"No."

After all, where were we supposed to go? We had school to finish and a title bout to fight, a hot meal on the table at the end of the day, and a face I hoped to see again, someday. There was a whole lifetime ahead of me, between one bomb and another.

My mother's sorrow knew no bounds.

"This isn't the world I wanted to bring you up in."

Maestro Franco wanted to know the exact route I was taking for my morning run. He studied it meticulously.

"It looks safe, I don't think any prosecutors live anywhere nearby."

Umbertino and Rosario reacted as they'd been taught to growing up. They maintained their routines, continuing straight down their usual paths. Grandpa limited himself to saying that he'd been wondering for a long time now when this would happen.

"For how long?"

"For at least ten years now."

Umbertino confirmed his analysis: "Only the blind or the liars would have told you it was going to end any other way. Palermo has always been a powder keg, fucking miserable shithole of a city."

Their eyes, after growing up with death, were sharper, more practiced at reading the tea leaves of disaster.

Gerruso confessed to me that a thought had been tormenting him.

"Poet, let's just hope that a bomb doesn't go off right near you, if you died that way, damn, the finals would really prove to be bad luck for your family. But maybe nothing'll happen and you'll just lose the championship bout anyway, go figure."

I tried calling Nina.

I went downstairs, out into the street, I didn't want my mother to overhear that phone call.

That phone booth was a small space.

Standing there, with the receiver in one hand, the coin inserted in the slot, the line ringing free, my head resting against the pay phone. It smelled of metal.

I would ask Nina how she was, whether the Mafia's attack, the one that had resulted in the death of the judge and his police escort, had made her cry the way it had my female classmates. Whether she'd take a different route to school now, and whether her parents would let her go out at night: my mother let me, in part because my uncle insisted that, especially in a situation like this, you had to go on living. Changing your habits meant bowing to the Mafia's power and he wouldn't bow down even before Muhammad Ali, the greatest boxer of them all.

Then I'd tell her that I wasn't upset, because boxing helps you to keep a steady keel: you see, Nina, boxing is more than just throwing and taking punches, the sweet science is a discipline that demands respect and sacrifice, in fact—would you ever believe it, Nina?—the boxer who wins is never the one with the strongest arms, it's the one who's fastest, in body and mind, because he possesses a richer vocabulary of movement.

Then I'd astonish her with the news that, yes, Nina, I have just one bout to go, one more victory and the title that had always eluded my family's grasp would finally be ours, isn't that wonderful?

Last of all, I had to address our last conversation, the phone call I'd made from that same phone booth a few weeks earlier just before the fight with Mauro Genovese, the boxer without a nickname. I'd reiterate that in my opinion making a full confession had been the right thing to do, maybe I'd picked the wrong time to do it, but it was ethically correct, Nina, you have to rid yourself of dead weight if you want to unleash your strength in battle, useless ballast only slows you down, far better the implacable hardness of honesty.

It would be yet another of the countless lies I'd tell her, with love and squalor.

I held tight to the receiver for a good fifteen minutes.

It rang and rang.

Nina didn't answer.

≡≡≡≡

When the phone rang, it was dark out. It wasn't a normal sound. It was a worried ring. Objects, if you listen to them carefully, will tell you what's about to happen. They reek of emotion.

I leaped out of bed. The next day, I was scheduled to fight the championship bout for the national title. My body was poised for combat. I ran down the hall, grabbed the receiver, listened without answering, ended the call by pressing two fingers down on the little white knobs on the cradle.

My mother was up, too. She watched me from her bedroom door, tying her dressing gown sash at the waist.

My left hand was still gripping the receiver.

"Mamma, something's happened."

My grandpa told me that the day that all hell broke loose in Africa, there were no particular foreshadowings. He'd always described that day in precise detail. When something unforgettable happens and you come out of it alive, you think back methodically to the moments preceding it, as if they constituted a map on which you could read a premonition of the impending disaster.

"There was no sign of what was coming."

My grandfather had peeled the potatoes and put the pot on the stove. Melluso was nowhere to be seen. The animals, especially the guard dogs, were untroubled, there were no cases of insubordination from the prisoners, no particular abuses had been committed by the guards; in the kitchen everything was in its place.

Rosario turned off the flame, poured out the coffee, and handed a demitasse to Nicola Randazzo.

"Let's enjoy this fine cup of espresso," he said, breaking his habitual silence.

And then all hell broke loose.

"Are you all right?"

"I'm fine, Mamma, don't worry about me."

"Are you ready for the fight tomorrow? Are you nervous?"

"No."

"Are you sure?"

"Yes, I'll stay here, you go check the hospital."

"Give me a kiss."

After kissing both my cheeks, my mother took my hands and kissed the back of each of them.

"You'll see, everything will turn out okay, now you go try to get some rest, my love."

She blew me one last kiss and I got out of the car.

The street was deserted. No one ever went out at night anymore in Palermo.

The front door stood ajar, the light was on. Scattered across the floor were broken plates, shattered glasses, silverware, dollops of food sprayed in all directions, and, off to one side, a small bloodstain.

Nothing had been touched.

"Gerruso, tell me what happened."

He was stroking the wall with his stump-finger.

They'd just finished dinner: *brociolone* with meat sauce and peas.

His mother had stood up to clear away the dishes.

She had stacked the plates and was heading into the kitchen when she fell to the floor, without warning.

She'd never come to.

The ambulance had arrived, his father had gone to the hospital, and he'd stayed behind at home.

"I didn't know who else to call, I'm sorry."

"Don't you have any relatives?"

"The only phone number I could think of was yours."

"Don't you know that tomorrow is the championship fight?"

"I'd forgotten."

"Well, the damage is done."

"Sorry."

"Amen."

"Thanks for coming."

"It's fine, don't mention it again."

"She collapsed like a . . . like a . . ."

"Gerruso, don't think about it, my mother's gone to the hospital, everything's going to turn out okay, she knows all the doctors."

"First she was . . . and then she . . ."

"Come on, cut it out."

"She was standing there and then . . ."

"I get it, she fainted."

"No, no, no, she didn't faint. She collapsed like a . . ."

"Like a boxer?"

"No, like a dam collapsing."

"You've never seen a dam collapse."

"No, but I've seen my mother collapse."

The stump-finger continued to slide over the wall, covering it inch by inch, with a painter's tender care. In that room, Gerruso's world bore the stigmata of destruction.

Except for me, he had no one with whom to share the anguish of the present.

"Do you want me to call Nina? She's your cousin, should I call her?"

He seemed not to have heard me, or else he was unwilling to reply. He kept on tracing imaginary figures on the wall.

"Well? Should I call her?"

"No."

"Why not?"

"Because she never wants to see you again."

"Don't worry about me. When you like, if you want, we can always call her, I know the number by heart."

Gerruso had stopped moving his stump-finger, it was motionless on the wall, at nose height.

His voice was a fragile thread, about to snap.

"Will you tell me what I should do? You tell me what to do and I'll do it."

"Me? What?"

"You know what I should do."

"Why?"

"You've already collapsed once."

Trapani, second round of the fight against Mauro Genovese, the boxer without a nickname. He landed a hook square to my temple. Gerruso was there. I hit the canvas. My eyes were closed and I could taste blood in my mouth. Except for the time that Carlo hit me when I was nine, I'd never fallen to the canvas before. Never.

"What are you thinking?"

"My father never once hit the canvas. And neither did my uncle."

"But you did, eh? Still, you got back up."

"Yeah."

"Teach me how to get back up."

When the hook caught me in the temple, the second round had just started. Everything turned white, soundless, silent. The red flavor of blood. The immediate sensation of effort, fatigue. The urge to vomit.

"So if I get to my feet I'm like the mulberry bush underneath my window that survived the fire and is covered with leaves again."

Nails were crucifying my pride, there was an unfamiliar and inconsolable despair in my heart.

"Leaves fall, Gerruso."

The weight of guilt never fades. It comes back when you least expect it, a shard puncturing your bare foot. It always cuts you.

"But the tree is still standing."

"Three."

The referee was counting, holding Mauro Genovese off at a distance. He looked toward my corner.

"Four."

I could smell the sweat inside my nose.

I was biting my mouthguard to keep from retching.

"Five."

A buzzing in my ears.

Why get back up? Why take more punches?

"Six."

Better to stay on the floor, just four more numbers and it's all over, right?

On "Seven" I was up on my knees.

At "Eight" I was back on my feet.

At "Nine" I had regained my fighting stance, guard up.

I nodded my head at the referee.

I was ready to fight to the death again.

It was the sound of a blast that tore open the curtains of the disaster. There was an enemy air raid under way. Explosions went off in quick succession. The airplanes must have been flying so low that they darkened the sky. Randazzo was about to run when he saw Rosario sitting motionless, a cup of coffee in his hand, with no intention of going anywhere.

Grandpa swore to me that, really, there'd been no hunch, no voice inspiring that decision.

"Right then and there, the most important thing was to drink my coffee, even if that was the last thing I ever did in my life."

Randazzo was agitated.

"Let's go to the infirmary, that's never been bombed."

Rosario shook his head and took another sip of his coffee.

Nicola, oddly, calmed down.

"Rosà, come on, we don't have much time."

"That's not true."

"No?"

"No. We have all the time that's left."

Every damn time that Nicola Randazzo told that story, he would emphasize that exchange.

He took another sip of his own coffee.

Explosions all around them. He thought of the countryside back home, he felt an overwhelming desire to prune his apple tree and graft a branch onto the almond tree. There was just one more sip, the last sip that would reveal the grounds that had sunk to the bottom: that was when he heard the loudest noise he'd ever heard in his life. It tore away all hearing in his left ear, stripped him of his other senses. When he regained consciousness, he was in hell.

"Sometimes I think back on stories and tell them over to myself."

"Which stories?"

"The ones you tell me."

"Why my stories?"

"No one else tells me any. Do you know a story about getting up?"

"No."

"If you did know one, would you tell it to me?"

"Who knows, I don't know, maybe I would."

"Will you tell me another one? Any story you like."

I told him the story of this old guy, a mystic, a saint. He lived on a donkey's back, facing back to front. Why do you always sit the wrong way around? people would ask him. The future is in the hands of God, the ascetic replied, all I care about is knowing where I come from.

"And then what happened?"

"That's all."

"This is a story about looking."

"Yes."

"And also about riding."

"Yes."

"And also about asking and answering. Still, in the story I'd like to have been the donkey. If God appeared, I'd be the first to see Him."

He felt pain in his back, so he was still alive. He tried moving his fingers and toes. He could feel all twenty of them, so they were still attached. He opened his eyes and found himself crushed into the ground. The pantry's wooden cabinet had fallen over onto his back. Without all that much effort, he managed to lift it off his body. The cabinet was riddled with shrapnel. The wood had shielded him and had saved his life.

Rosario.

The thought of Rosario shook him awake like a whip crack. He started to let his gaze wander. Under a layer of ashes, he glimpsed Rosario's leg. He'd been pinned to the floor by the table and other pieces of furniture. He hurled everything aside: plates, sheet metal, boards. Rosario wasn't moving. Nicola Randazzo bent over him and began imploring God, the Madonna, Saint Rosalia—I pray to you all, save this friend of mine. With a cough, my grandfather opened his eyes. Nicola immediately asked him how he felt. Rosario tried to answer but no sounds came out of his mouth. Nicola felt infinite pity for his friend.

"You understand, Davidù, I was convinced that your grandfather couldn't speak, but it wasn't him, it was me, I was the one who was permanently deaf in my left ear. He was speaking, I didn't hear a thing, and I thought: poor guy.

Randazzo paused. He'd revisited those few moments, the despairing silence into which he and Rosario emerged to try to understand what had happened. They saw flames, smoke, and ashes. Practically nothing was still standing. The kitchen was the only place that had been left intact. It was the only structure visible.

"Saved by a cup of coffee, can you imagine? That's the way it is in war, completely senseless."

They went out in search of survivors' voices. Nicola Randazzo saw an arm sticking out of the rubble where once there had been latrines. He and Rosario worked to push aside heavy beams, mounds of dirt, and rocks, but there was nothing attached to the arm. Randazzo started crying.

My vision was blurred, but I could feel my legs, my feet, my fingers inside the gloves. Earn a little time, keep my guard up, keep my distance. As soon as the referee signaled that the fight was back on, Mauro Genovese lunged at me. I leaped backward, a fish under attack by a bigger fish. Open my guard, let him hit me in the head again, collapse, and stop worrying about things. A weave to the left, a feint to the right, another leap backward. Just one punch, and it would all be over. A shift in direction, backward again, less and less room in the ring to escape. I feinted backward again, but my feet leaped forward.

"That's it," Umbertino yelled from the seats.

I furiously punched the air in front of me. Trying to win back a little room. Small, fast jabs, syllables of movement. Writing new words to put an end to my anguish.

"Ciao, boxer."

"Ciao, blondie."

"There's no point looking around, she's not here."

"I wasn't looking for her."

"But you're wandering around the party like a damned soul in hell."

"I was looking for the bathroom."

"Aren't you going to ask me how I'm doing?"

"It's been a while."

"Just a couple of years. I was expecting a phone call."

"You could have made that call yourself. Are you still playing the cello?"

"Yes, I'm still playing the cello and yes, you're still good at changing the subject."

"What subject am I changing?"

"We haven't spoken since then, two years ago now, evidently neither of us cared all that much. What are you doing here?"

"I was invited."

"How do you know Eva?"

"Do you want the nice version or the nasty one?"

"Spare me the nasty one."

"She's an old classmate."

"Are you still in school? You haven't been expelled yet?"

"No."

"Held back a year?"

"Never."

"Teachers these days just aren't what they used to be."

"That's the damn truth, but the best teachers still seem to be in the elementary schools."

"Let's drop it. What about the nasty version?"

"Already changed your mind?"

"I was hoping it might be less boring than the first one."

"Eva and I used to date, and we made out a lot."

"And she invited you to her party?"

"We stayed good friends."

"Did you fuck her?"

"No, it was all years ago."

"Years ago? Before me or after me? Or at the same time? Or do you not fuck because you're still a virgin?"

"I don't talk about stuff like that."

"You're talking about it right now."

"I answered a question, out of courtesy and honesty."

"You? Honest? Please."

"I am honest."

"No, you're not."

"No, I'm not?"

"No. And that's why you've always fascinated me."

"I don't understand."

"Nobody's asking you to understand. By the way, are you still boxing?"

"Of course."

"And do you lose often?"

"Always, I always lose."

"When's your next fight?"

"In a couple of weeks: my opponent's called Mauro Genovese and he's—"

"Boxer, do you think that I actually care about your world in the slightest? Too much sweat. Listen, though, are you allowed to drink?"

"Sure, in moderation."

"God, you're boring."

The smoke made it impossible to see more than a couple of yards. The buzzing in his ears had subsided, and was now almost gone. Rosario was certain that he'd heard voices. Someone was still alive, somewhere under the rubble. He leaned over his friend and tried to help him up, but Randazzo was a limp rag, shattered by the pain. He took his old friend's head in his hands.

"Come on, Nicola, get up."

Randazzo started shaking his head.

"I can't hear you, Rosà, I can't hear you anymore, I'm deaf."

Rosario stilled his friend's face and pushed his own forehead closer until it was almost touching Nicola's. When Nicola stopped shaking, he let go of his face. Rosario was alive only because Randazzo had seen him. His eyes were necessary.

Rosario held out his hand to him.

Come on, Nicola.

We need to keep looking.

Your eyes are needed.

We have to find D'Arpa.

Rosario's hand was steady.

It wasn't shaking.

Nicola took the hand and got to his feet.

"Where should we start?"

Rosario pointed to the carpentry shop. It no longer existed.

They started walking around it, slowly, careful not to miss a thing, a shoe, a moan, any sign of life, ready to destroy their fingernails, their fingers, their hands in order to find their friend. Rosario heard a moan, Nicola saw a movement in the rubble, they lunged at the collapsing heap and pulled away detritus, stones, and dirt at frantic speed.

Gerruso was wearing a pair of dark brown pajamas with a little breast pocket over his heart where his name was written in bold.

"Did you mother embroider that?"

"Yes."

"It looks very nice. Gerruso, what are you thinking?"

"Is there something I can do for my mother?"

"Yes."

"What?"

"Let's clean everything up."

"Will that help? Is it useful?"

"You know how you win a fight?"

"No."

"One punch at a time."

"Are you teaching me how to get back up?"

"Yes."

"Then wait a second."

He went into the kitchen and came back wearing a white apron and a pair of pink rubber dishwashing gloves.

"This is what my mother always wears when she cleans house."

I took care of the dining room while Gerruso washed dishes in the kitchen. He told me about the mulberry tree he could see from his window. He'd named it Sergio.

"The names with an *r* in them are the strongest ones, they snarl."

"Sure, like Gerruso."

"No, it's true, your uncle's named Umbertino and your grandfather's Rosario, both names with an *r* in them."

"I don't like it when you talk about my family."

"You say that because you don't have an *r* in your name, even your father had one."

"I don't like this subject, quit talking about it."

A swing was hanging from Sergio, with a wooden seat and iron chains. Gerruso spent whole afternoons standing on it, though without swinging, because his mother didn't want him to.

"She said it would make me sweat and that sweating is bad for you."

He looked out on the world from a new height. He'd learned every crack and every graffito on the wall across the way by heart. His favorite: "Men: without a skirt and a wig, what kind of women are you?" His mother would lean out the window and call him for dinner. That was his moment of greatest happiness. As he got down, his feet were bound to make the swing move. It lasted only a second, but it was a kind of enchantment: the world turned into an amusement park ride, and the swing became the vehicle of wonder, but none of it would have been possible without Sergio the mulberry tree.

"I like the mulberry tree, it's where my swing hangs and it has dark, soft fruit on its branches that get your fingers and your T-shirt filthy, which mothers scold you for but the stain is there to stay, evidence of the happiness you experienced."

Sergio was struck by a bolt of lightning. The branch with the swing caught fire. The leaves became butterflies of fire in the night. The firemen came, with hoses and sirens. He helped to put out the fire by pouring water from the balcony.

"I used the glass I keep my toothbrush in, it's deep and yellow."

The next morning, the mulberry tree looked like an old man who had just been released from the hospital after a lengthy illness. No replacement swing was hung up. The mulberry tree was still there, under his window.

"Poet, I've washed all the forks, where should I put them?"

"Leave them by the sink."

I was searching for shards that had eluded the broom; it's the kind of thing that happens whenever anything shatters, glass shards ready to surface in the future, bringing the anguish of the past into the present.

"My mother never leaves forks by the sink."

"Then dry them and put them where you keep the other forks."

The way the shards were scattered, they told the story of a vertical plunge, they diagrammed the fall of what might as well have been a single body of crockery. The dishes must have fallen from Signora Gerruso's hands in a single instant. Her strength must have fled her all at once.

"Poet."

"Stop calling me that."

"What does it feel like when you fall to the ground? Does it hurt?"

"You were there."

"I was afraid that you were dead."

"The moment you hit the mat isn't really the moment you collapse, that's just the end. The fall, Gerruso, the real one, begins earlier, at the top."

I found a broken piece of plate under the leg of a chair. I threw it into the bag with the rest of the shards.

"This party is boring me, boxer, I'm going home, what are you going to do?"

"Are you here on your scooter?"

"Yes."

"You can't drive, you're drunk."

"No, you're drunk."

"I'm not drunk."

"Ah, of course not—the picture of propriety."

"I have a fight in just—"

"I don't care."

"Why don't you ask someone to come pick you up?"

"My folks are away, there's no one home."

"So?"

"So, why don't you take me home?"

The dining room seemed to be spic and span. I'd picked up all the food, swept the floor, cleaned with a wet rag, and carefully picked over every corner of the room in search of mutinous shards. I asked for and received permission from Gerruso to make a phone call, yes, I know it's late, thanks, why don't you just worry about washing the dishes.

"Uncle?"

"I was wondering when you were going to make up your mind to call."

"No, it's just that here—"

"Calm down, your mother told me all about it. You did the right thing. But now see if you can't get at least six hours of sleep, all right? Davidù, buck up, tomorrow we're going to knock all of Italy to its knees. The worst is over."

We went into Gerruso's bedroom.

I asked him to give me a blanket, and I put him to bed.

"Now lie there, calm and quiet, and let's get some sleep."

I lay down on the sofa and turned off the light.

Not even a drop of sleep.

"You have a nice home, blondie; it's big."

"My family has impeccable taste in interior decoration, come on, let me show you my bedroom."

"Well, actually, I . . ."

"I said come on."

Her cello-playing hand intertwined with my punch-throwing hand.

Our chests brushed against each other.

"It's been a while since the last time: two years," she said with a smile.

A lock of blond hair lodged on her upper lip.

"Right."

I brushed it away with my forefinger.

She took my finger and gripped it in her hand.

"So . . . where were we?"

Gerruso had fallen into a rocklike sleep. He was snoring without an exact, cadenced rhythm. Just a rattling gasp every once in a while. A nervous sleep. He kicked. He moaned.

I mentally reviewed the plans of attack I'd agreed on with Maestro Franco for the final bout, the precise way to dodge a left cross and attack, the exit feint to the right, the double punch with a hook. Not even a hint of sleep.

My fall had begun long before I dropped my guard, before the second round began, before I climbed into the ring to fight Mauro Genovese. My feet had buckled the day before when, in the phone booth downstairs from my house, the coin slipped into the slot, the number was dialed, and the voice that I hoped wouldn't answer, did.

"Yes?"

"Nina."

"It's been forever since you last called me."

"I have something to tell you."

But it was in the ring that things went wrong.

———

He jerked awake, startled by his own snoring.

"Did you call me?"

"No."

"Is the sofa comfortable? Should I sleep on it?"

"No, don't worry."

"Do you want to get in the bed with me?"

"Gerruso, have you lost your mind?"

"How come you aren't asleep? Tomorrow's your title fight."

"You're snoring like a pig."

"Really? I snore?"

"Yes, and loud."

"Can I ask you a question?"

"Just one, then we get some sleep."

"Does it hurt when you fall down?"

"Right then and there, no, it doesn't hurt. You're too confused to feel the pain, you've just taken a punch to the head, everything is foggy. Afterward, though, it all comes to you."

"It always comes to you?"

"Yes."

"You're sure?"

"Yes."

"Absolutely sure?"

"Gerruso, we said just one question."

"Do you think I got the fall wrong?"

"Every time you fall it's an error of equilibrium."

"And how do you get back on your feet?"

"With your legs. It's not just a matter of will, it has something to do with the character of your body."

"I saw you when you fell: you were all twisted, you were flying to one side, like when you dive, your arms were straight out in front of you, it reminded me of being at the beach together. Did you know that you were about to dive into the canvas?"

After the bout, Maestro Franco left me alone in the locker room with my uncle. He understood that this wasn't about boxing: this was a family affair, this was something personal. The sweet science had nothing to do with this. Umbertino held my head in his left hand. He was turning it this way and that and observing my eyes. He snapped his fingers three times, far from my line of sight. It was a trick he'd learned from *Il Negro*. He was checking the reflexes of my pupils.

"Your head's fine. You've got a good hard head, just like mine. But now I want you to explain to me why."

Umbertino knew.

I'd been knocked to the mat because I'd intentionally let my opponent hit me.

Tongue on tongue, the taste of her lips, the hand that unbuttons, caresses, squeezes, finding ourselves naked, stretched out on the bed together.

"You want to do it?"

"Yes."

"Do you know how?"

"Yes."

"Are you a virgin, boxer?"

"No."

And I found myself inside a woman, for the first time in my life. The penetration took place in silence, slowly, with restrained gestures. At first, my curiosity was greater than any pleasure I might have felt or given. What if I don't like it? What if she doesn't like it? What if the string on my cock breaks?

My survival instinct put a halt to the multiplying questions. I adopted Umbertino's advice, excellent for every occasion life presents you with: "When in doubt, throw a punch."

I entrusted myself to the rhythm that my hips chose to establish. My thrusts simultaneously increased in depth and self-awareness. The first uncontrollable moans made themselves heard. Sweat glistened, lubricating the motion of body over body. Hands became more eager and willing to clutch and grasp. Teeth sank into flesh, tongues explored.

It was sweet, hot, and wet.

While I was coming for the first time, naked, panting, inside the blonde, her taste in my mouth, I thought of Nina.

The ceiling above us was white, the bedroom door was closed. Her bedroom was as big as my whole house.

"Was this the first time for you, too, boxer?"

"I told you it wasn't. Wait a minute, what do you mean 'for you, too'?"

"I don't know if I should believe you: if you ask me, you were a virgin just like me."

"What is 'just like me' supposed to mean?"

"It means that I, at Eva's party, was still a virgin."

"You? What?"

"Look, I even bled a little, to tell the truth, I expected more. Remind me to put the sheets in the washer."

I hadn't noticed a thing.

"What are you doing, boxer?"

"Sorry, I've got to get home."

"Is your mommy worried about you?"

When I bent over to give her a kiss, the Dumas rolled over on her side.

"None of that lovey-dovey stuff."

I went home at a run, taking it easy: small, measured pumping strides.

Out on the street: police, soldiers, and roadblocks.

My uncle sucked on his cigarette in silence. I was expecting him to curse all the saints, to dismiss me as immature, to accuse me of having failed to respect the work that he and Franco had put in. I was waiting for the moment when he compared me with my father, in a merciless critique to which I would inevitably succumb in mortification. Instead, his words headed in an entirely different direction.

"So now you've finally fucked a girl. That's all good and blessed news. But that's not the point: What do you really want, Davidù? Nina? The blonde? To be alone and whine about how much you're suffering?"

"I don't know, Uncle. Maybe it's because the two of them are good friends, but I'm confused, I only know that I felt like I was dying and little by little I found myself no longer caring, that's all I know."

"Son, it doesn't matter what you do or don't know, it only matters what you want. You can't claim property rights on other human beings. If you're with a girl, then you have a pact. If you're not with her, then everyone's free to do what they want. Wounds of the flesh: needle and thread and the bleeding is over. Wounds of the soul, on the other hand, are fountains of blood. You just have to figure out what you really want."

"What if I can't figure it out? What do I do then?"

"The same thing you did today. Get to your feet and throw some punches. It's only once you accept the idea that you've fallen down that you can get back on your feet. When you hit the ground, you're always starting over again from the lowest point. Still, Davidù, a piece of advice, with my hand on my heart: if you really want to hold on to Nina, never—and I mean never, understood?—say a word about having been with her best friend."

A volcanic blush exploded across my face. My uncle leaped to his feet. His calves hurled the chair backward, and it clattered against the wall ten feet behind him.

"Have you lost your mind? You told her? When?"

"Yesterday, I called her from the phone booth."

"Fuck, you're no nephew of mine! And we're supposed to have the same blood flowing in our veins? Haven't I taught you a thing? If you're not capable of holding in the weight of something you've done, then you might as well hole up in your bedroom, lock yourself in, and throw the keys off the balcony. You told her? Why on earth would you tell her?"

Hit head-on by a higher intuition, he froze to the spot. A second later, he was bent over me, speaking in a low voice, his gaze level.

"So that's the way things are, you let him hit you because you felt guilty, not because of the fucking, but because you told her and that made her feel so bad."

He picked up the chair from the floor.

"You wanted to hurt yourself, destroy yourself."

He set it down on all four legs.

"But you got back up."

He sat down, laying his hands flat on his knees.

"And you won."

He resumed staring at me.

"After you got back up, you fought differently."

His voice was dark.

"Like my father?"

Eyes unmoving.

"No, like me."

He stood up and came over to me with the chair.

"The way your father boxed was happy, filled with freedom. The way you boxed today, there was none of that. And you know that already. You need to stop hating yourself, Davidù. It's easy to feel sorry for yourself. A sense of guilt is just one more excuse for tears of self-pity. What do you want to become? A crybaby who's always complaining or a man who stands up straight? Remember this always, there are only two words that mean anything in love: *hurt me*."

He slipped a hand into his pocket, pulled out two cigarettes, lit them both, and handed me one.

"After you win a match, what you need is a nice cigarette."

We smoked in silence, looking each other in the eye the whole time.

Maestro Franco came in. He asked me how I felt, when I was born, the exact street addresses of my home and the gym, his own wife's name, and what my uncle's favorite proverb was. When he was finally convinced that I was capable of thinking and understanding, he tousled my hair with his rough hand.

"Kid, what we learned today is that, even when you have all the reasons in the world to let someone hit you, fists always hurt like hell. And the lesson is that it's far better to punch than be punched. It's a good thing that, aside from the fall, you were the only one to score points, especially in the third round. Don't worry, kid, it won't be long now before they're all sucking our dicks. Tomorrow we'll analyze today's bout carefully. But right now, go take a shower, you smell like a goat."

The person they extracted from the rubble of the carpentry shop wasn't D'Arpa. It was another prisoner. Both his legs were shattered. He said that when the bombing started, he'd been alone in the carpentry shop, he had no idea where the boxer was, what he needed was a doctor and some morphine.

The carpentry shop, the camp hospital, the dining hall, the munitions dump, the infirmary, the firing range, the fence, the barracks, the machine shop.

There was nothing left.

Everything was burning.

The heat was intolerable.

Eyes were watering from the smoke and dust.

Rosario and Nicola were wandering in search of their friend.

They asked everyone they met: "Have you seen D'Arpa?"

Whenever they heard someone calling for help, they started digging.

The two of them had pulled twenty-one people out of the rubble, and five of them were still alive.

No one could give them any useful information.

As the minutes clicked past, as if in some blessed belated harvest, survivors started coming out of the woodwork, some of them unhurt, most of them wounded.

"Have you seen D'Arpa?"

Some had no idea who he was, others hadn't seen him, and a few swore that they'd seen him run for cover at the camp hospital. Rosario and Nicola headed there. There were three soldiers moving rocks. Some of the rocks were covered with blood. There must have been a number of poor souls underneath. Everyone dug together, with total disregard for rank, hauling beams and rubble aside, recovering lifeless bodies, some of them naked, others still in uniform. The twelfth dead body they pulled out of the rubble was D'Arpa's. His fists were still clenched, his mouth was filled with dust, his eyes were wide open, and there were cuts and wounds all over his body. Rosario gently lifted him over his shoulder and set off. Randazzo followed him. The others let them go without a word and went back to digging through the wreckage. My grandfather walked out the front gate. He was going to bury Lieutenant D'Arpa outside the fence, in soil slightly freer than the dirt inside a prisoner-of-war camp. Nicola managed to find two pieces of wood with which to dig a grave. With hard work and determination, they managed to make a hole; they eased their friend's dead body into it and then covered it back up. They stamped down the dirt vigorously and covered it with a blanket of stones meant to protect that particular burial site. Nicola constructed a rudimentary cross with wooden sticks and metal wire and he planted it between the stones. Rosario touched the cross and then sat down beside it, cradling his forehead in his hands. At last, he managed to cry, weeping in silence, a profound lament, as long and deep as the war itself.

"I just remembered that I fell down once myself."

"Gerruso, this one last story and then that's it, we've got to get some sleep."

"It was at my first communion."

"You fell in church?"

"I was dressed in a white tunic, from head to foot, I was a sight to behold, my mother made it for me out of her wedding dress. We didn't have enough money to buy a new one. She'd left it a little too long for me, so when I went up to take my first communion, my shoe got caught in the hem and I went head over heels onto the floor."

"You see that you've fallen down, too? Then what happened?"

"I just lay there."

"You didn't get back up?"

"I burst out laughing and everyone around me started laughing with me, the other kids, the nuns, my father, my mother, the priest, everyone. That's why I thought that falling was a good thing, the church had become a house of happiness. After you fell, were you happy?"

Something had clicked into place inside me. I was moving forward instead of running away. I was moving my hands with a speed I'd never possessed before. I was attacking, and I meant to hurt someone.

Nina's voice on the telephone.

I couldn't silence the sound of it.

"No, Gerruso, I wasn't happy."

My gloves were shooting out, returning, then punching again. No time to waste on repetition. Right, left, another right. The blank sheet of the ring was being filled with my words and my words alone.

Mauro Genovese was incapable of bringing home any attack.

The match ended with a victory, on points, for me. Two rounds to one.

"Aside from the fall, it was your best fight yet, Poet."

I was raging.

While I was fighting, I thought of Nina crying at the other end of the phone line.

"I know."

I'd never been so powerful.

The ringing of the home phone interrupted our dialogue.

"Will you answer that? Please."

The telephone sat on a low circular mahogany table in the living room. Before I could place the receiver against my ear and hear my mother's voice on the other end of the line, the glitter of a shard of glass in the middle of the room caught my eye.

There's no amount of cleaning you can do.

The shards always show up later.

"No, Mamma, no, don't worry, I'll tell him."

Gerruso was bouncing on the tips of his toes.

"Was that your mother?"

"Yes."

Pupils dilated, arms hanging limp at his sides, fingers in constant movement.

"Is there news about my mamma? How is she?"

In his dark brown pajamas, he looked younger than his eighteen years.

I laid a hand on his shoulder.

"I'm sorry."

His head kept moving back and forth, as if he were nodding to himself as he accepted the enormity of what had happened. Without warning, he rushed into the kitchen, donned his white apron and his pink gloves, picked up the dishes, put them in the sink, turned on the water, and squirted in dish soap.

His voice was a broken thread.

"Maybe I just didn't get them clean enough."

The road to hell is paved with shards of glass and crockery.

You have to walk on it barefoot.

I picked up the phone and dialed the number.

"Hello?"

"Nina."

"What do you want now?"

"Something happened."

Nicola had waited for the weeping to end. The cross, in the moonlight, cast a serene shadow over the stones of the grave.

"You know what, Rosario? I could tell you that it's useless to sit there talking to the dead, that it would be more useful to go back to the camp and help dig. But that's not what I think, you have every right to do what you feel, especially now that D'Arpa is dead."

"Francesco."

"Sorry, what did you say?"

"His name is Francesco."

Nicola's right forefinger started tracing lines in the dirt. He performed the movements with concentration, his eyes attentive, his brow furrowed. His mouth uttered the sounds that his finger was sketching, for the whole length of the line. Once he had written the word out, he checked it and checked it again. As soon as he was persuaded that it was written correctly, he called Rosario over.

"Is that right?"

My grandfather looked at him with defeated eyes.

"I don't know how to read, Nicola."

"Don't worry, it must be right."

And, pointing down, he told my grandfather the word that he had written in the dirt: FRANCESCO.

Then he found a sharp rock, pulled away the rocks at the foot of the cross, uprooted it, and patiently began to carve into the wood, copying the name in front of him.

"It's right for us to add the name, you were right. The way I imagine the angels, they can read all languages."

He was concentrating. He couldn't make a mistake on his friend's headstone.

"Do you like ants, Rosà? When I was a kid, in the country where I grew up, I'd spend whole afternoons watching ants climb up the olive tree. Always in line, always one behind the other. Once I crushed an ant, just to see what would happen, maybe they'll leave it there, an obstacle, or else they'll steer clear of it and change their path. Instead, I barely had time to kill it before its fellow ants had picked it up, thrown it over their shoulders, and were carrying it along, climbing their way up the bark to their den high up in the tree."

"To eat it."

"Does that matter? We eat our memories, come to that."

He reread the name three times in a row, running his finger over the letter that corresponded to the sound he was uttering. Then, after replacing the stones, he again planted the cross.

"The ant that I killed was carried off as if in a procession, it looked like the cart of Saint Rosalia at the Festino. Since then, I've always done my best to avoid killing ants. It would be nice to carry the graves of those we love with us wherever we go. Ants are so strong that they can. We have to find a different way of doing it."

Rosario's eyes were a paler hue than usual, crying had washed away any and all filters. But the breath in his throat was calm again.

My grandfather had risen to his feet.

Nicola understood that he was ready.

"I'll wait for you there," he said, and walked over to the place he had indicated, leaving him alone to say his final farewell.

My mother told Gerruso's father that he ought to let him come to the bout, it would distract him to see me fight. It would make him feel better.

"Unless . . ."

She suddenly blushed. Truth is a scurvy plant, irritating, bristling with thorns.

"I understand, Mamma, I understand."

I respected the fact that she hadn't said it.

I was two years younger than my opponent.

The odds being given were against me.

The national finals had become a curse for my family.

A couple of hours before the weigh-in, Gerruso left the sports arena with my uncle.

"Did he take you somewhere to eat?"

"No."

"Will you tell me where you went?"

"I can't, it's a secret."

"You have a secret with my uncle?"

"Yes."

"He's my uncle, not yours, come on, tell me where you went."

"Secret," he said, pointing with both hands toward his trouser pocket.

"What do you have in there?"

In answer, Gerruso let loose a profound, extended yawn.

"Are you tired?"

"A little."

"Try to get some rest."

From the moment he'd been given the news of his mamma's death, he hadn't been able to shut his eyes. Umbertino had driven over to pick us up, not twenty minutes after my mother's phone call. He'd taken us to my house. Gerruso said that he wasn't sleepy and he spent the whole night in the living room with Umbertino, watching horse racing on TV.

I slept like a rock.

"If I was a woman, by now I'da already made up a well-rested face."

"Eh?"

"You know how women always put on makeup? There. Maybe I coulda used makeup to paint a fresh face."

"There's no makeup that erases exhaustion."

"Oh, yes, there is. Women have different makeup for every occasion. My mamma used to get made up every Sunday, for Mass: she painted her cheeks, she put on her hairspray, and she went off to church. I've seen Nina do her face, put on her lipstick, pencil in the eyebrows on her forehead, stuff like that. Hairspray, now, she never used that. Nina always used to put on makeup when she was going to see you."

"Really?"

"Yes. Women are strange creatures, did you know that? They're crazy."

"Goddamned truth."

"If you watch them when they're putting on makeup, they get all upset, 'What are you looking at?' 'Go on, get out of here!' they'll scream. But then, in the middle of traffic, in a crowd, they decide they have the wrong makeup on, they'll pull open their purse, pull out a tiny hand mirror, they always have one with them, and they paint their faces, super-fast, in front of everyone. Did you ever think about it?"

"To tell the truth, no, I hadn't."

"There you see, my thoughts are growing up; now that my mother's dead, I must be more mature."

My opponent in the fight for the national title was called Renzo Ceresa. He was Sardinian, twenty-one years old, and nicknamed "*Bentu Maìstu*," after the mistral wind that blows out of the northwest, unexpected gusts that cut to the bone, chilling.

"Poet, what are you thinking about?"

"About when a fight begins."

The hall filling up, the referee calling the boxers into the ring, the bell sounding, the clock starting to run.

The last chapter of a much longer story.

"Do you ever miss your father?"

"Yes."

"But you never even knew him. I knew my mother. I have lots of memories of her, you only have words. Was he a good boxer?"

"That's what they say. I miss never having seen one of his fights."

"What I miss is my mother when she would take my temperature when I had a fever. She never yelled at me when I was sick. She'd come to my bed with a bowl of stew with potatoes and put a pillow behind my back. She'd put the thermometer under my armpit, it was always cold and it tickled me and made me laugh. When she checked it she'd hold it between her hands as if it contained life itself. You're such an expert on missing people and things, can you tell me if I'll miss her lots?"

"You'll always miss her."

"Sorrow-making things."

"Right."

"Poet, how can you miss something you've never seen?"

"My father?"

"No, not him. One of his fights. You know your father from words, to you he's not something about seeing. But I knew my mother in a lot of different ways, we lived together, she always had me underfoot. You know that I can't think about my apartment without her inside it? I try, but it's no good, she's always there in my thoughts. It's like when I think about my hand, in my head I have all my fingers intact, I'm not a stump-finger in my thoughts. But you, on the other hand, are completely a stump-finger in your memory. You don't have any memories of your father's voice, of the way he moved, of the times he took you in his arms. He never scolded you. You don't even know what he smelled like. I know my mother's smell: she smells like hairspray."

"I can't be a stump-finger in my memory, Gerruso. I never had a father. There was never any finger to cut off."

"Then you're a no-finger! I win, I win, I still have a little piece of my finger."

"It's not a contest."

"But did you ever meet your father?"

"He died before I was born."

"That's not what I meant. You, Poet, you know your father in words. Do you ever meet him in the words you use?"

He yawned a powerful and liberating yawn, eyes closed, mouth gaping wide.

In the last few months, the training sessions were brutal.

"Come on, how can you be slow? You lazy good-for-nothing, step it up, let's get faster, faster still, again."

Everything was much angrier and more intense. To keep my level of concentration high, I practiced reciting names and dates for my tests at school. The amount of time I spent working out in the ring increased: sparring matches extended from three to four minutes in length. In the "dishing out punishment" sessions, in which I was supposed to attack and nothing else, the sparring partner who was defending himself from my attacks was Carlo. The goal was to score as many points as possible, calibrating my speed and strength. In the "taking punishment" sessions, the point was to limit the damage inflicted: feint, weave, keep your distance. These were apocalyptic four-minute sessions: the sparring partner changed, now it was Umbertino's turn. To spend four minutes in the ring with my uncle was an unforgettable experience: 265 pounds hurtling down on you all at once. He'd throw a punch and, while my body was shifting to avoid it, here came another before I knew a thing. It was an avalanche, a landslide you couldn't escape. What you had to do was lunge into that whirlwind, move through the openings where they presented themselves, fighting the water from within. I'd look into his eyes to guess what moves he was about to make. Deep in the center of his pupils, an intense flame glowed. After the training sessions with *Il Negro*, after sparring with the Paladin, my uncle was dancing again. He was no longer alone with his demons. All other activity in the gym came to a halt. A respectful silence reigned. The other boxers knew they'd never get to that level. Meaning my level and Umbertino's, of course. Watching the four-minute training session reminded Maestro Franco of when the Paladin was in the ring, responding blow for blow with the elegance of a man who feared nothing. The blood shed in training blossomed into the finest of buds. This wasn't boxing. It was fury turned into dance.

From inside the locker room you could hear the buzz of conversation in the hall and the drone of helicopters overhead.

"So here we are."

"Yes, Maestro."

"We're almost there."

He was wrapping my hands at a much slower pace than usual, as if that act were the last stretch of calm sea before we plunged into stormy waters.

"Kid."

"I'm not worried, Maestro, I'm fine."

"That's better, good, perfect, bravo, kid."

He was bending at the waist. An old lily buffeted by the autumn winds. He was rubbing his hands together.

"I've waited a lifetime for this moment. With the Paladin I missed it by a hair."

The door was closed, the locker room had no windows, and yet for Franco the wind was gusting even more vehemently, shaking him more and more.

"Now that I'm here, now that we're about to climb into the ring, I'm not as on edge as I would have expected. I don't have a hole in the pit of my stomach. And you know why I'm cool and collected? Because I just turn my thoughts to my wife, Livia."

"But don't the two of you fight all the time?"

"What does that have to do with it? We fight because Livia has a poisonous personality. There are Sundays when we don't say two words to each other. After lunch, she watches her ladies' shows on TV, I listen to *All the Soccer, Minute by Minute* to see if I've hit the jackpot in the Sisal soccer pools, so in practical terms we don't see each other again until dinner. Still, just knowing that she's sitting in the other room calms me down. You know what I like? Afternoons in the country roasting meat, your uncle telling stories about women, Livia complaining about the heat, and the cicadas all around us."

Now the oscillation had infected his feet, too. They rose and fell and rose again. When his eyes met mine, his body slowed down without stopping. His eyes were still in love.

"My Livia is beautiful, isn't she?"

His lips arched into a smile.

I was being good as gold.

I wasn't getting a thing wrong.

I had managed to conceal my anguish even from him.

———

As soon as we walked out of the locker room, the noise of the audience swelled to an enormous roar. In the ring, an announcer spoke our names and weights into the microphone. Gerruso, in the second row, was shrieking my nickname. He had dark circles under his eyes and the euphoria that normally precedes a collapse. Sitting next to him were Grandpa and Uncle Umbertino.

Maestro Franco and Carlo were sticking close to me.

I was dancing on the balls of my feet, the movement that, according to Grandma, was the true secret of how to walk on water.

"You should never set your feet down truly flat; that way, since there is no weight, you don't sink in. The trick is to be really fast."

My gloves were pounding the empty air, tiny jabs at nothing just to limber up my arms, extend my elbows, fire up the shock troops.

The three judges and the boxing federation's physician were all introduced.

"Poet!"

A young photographer at the edge of the ring caught my eye. He asked me to strike a pose for the traditional photograph. I stood there, motionless, gloves at my sides, in the position I used to let the warm sun dry me off. He asked me again to pose, gloves high, with a fierce expression, like a warrior. Even then I didn't stir an inch. Fed up, he took the picture and moved on to my opponent.

The announcer informed the crowd that I was wearing black shorts and black gloves, Renzo Ceresa white shorts and red gloves. He asked for a minute of silence to honor the victims of the recent Mafia attacks. As the audience got to its feet, silence fell like snow settling over the landscape.

Nina.

The death of Gerruso's mother.

The bombs.

The Dumas.

Things weren't right, not at all.

It had never even occurred to me that I might lose.

The important things never seemed to occur to me.

The voices began rooting again, shouting out names and nicknames, insults and prophecies. Gerruso was arguing with two men in the row behind him. He pointed at me with his stump-finger, repeatedly. Grandpa and Umbertino, sitting next to him, were a pair of sphinxes.

The referee summoned me and Ceresa over. He didn't want to see any blows below the belt, he wanted to see a nice clean fight, and if either opponent hit the canvas, we were to wait for a sign from him before resuming the fight. He wished us good luck, had us touch gloves, and sent us to our corners, where our trainers awaited us.

Carlo was giving me a neck rub.

Maestro Franco was rinsing my mouthguard.

Was this what I wanted?

To dive into the raging sea in the middle of a tempest?

I focused on the center of the ring and waited for the beginning of the end.

"Ciao, blondie."

"Ciao, boxer."

"Listen, I only have one coin, so I'll get right to the point: I just got off the phone with Nina, and I told her that the two of us—"

"Have you lost your mind?"

"What?"

"What did you tell her? No, look, I don't care what you said, I'm speechless."

"Huh?"

"What do you think, that you're the only boy in the world? That you sign an agreement of exclusivity the minute you have a few private moments with someone?"

"I don't understand."

"I went to bed with you because I felt like it, and you felt like it, too. Period. Stop. End of story. And instead you and your usual gift for tragedy, what do you do? My God, your sense of guilt. Try to grow up, Davide, the world doesn't revolve around you."

"What are you talking about?"

"You don't give a fuck about me or Nina."

"Horseshit."

"Horseshit? But you just destroyed our relationship."

"How can you say that? You and Nina are friends, while you and I—"

"So what? First of all, you two haven't been a couple for a long, long time."

"But we were a couple."

"When I was twelve I remember giving Giuseppe Guagliardo some great French kisses, and now? I don't get upset when he forgets to send me a Christmas card. It's over, I'm done with it, I don't expect anything from the past."

"Is Nina part of your past?"

"You're part of my past."

"She needed to know."

"Needed to know? How dare you? The relationship between me and Nina is a relationship between me and Nina, and it has nothing to do with you."

"You're a hypocrite."

"You're a child, Davide, you can't see past the tip of your own dick, and by the way, let me tell you that you're hardly unusual in this world we live in. You're a pathetic egotist. You devour other people. Nina was right to break up with you."

"You're nothing but a miserable bitch."

"Oh, go fuck yourself, you and your childish judgments."

In the deafening din of the sports arena, one voice reached my ears: the most squawking, croaking voice of them all. Gerruso was out of control, and the people in the row behind him had made bets on *Bentu Maìstu*, the Sardinian, the odds-on favorite.

"No matter what you claim to know about things, I'm in the second row, I'm ahead of you guys in life."

"Listen, kid, you want to cut it out?"

"You guys count for nothing, you know that, right? You're sitting behind me, your seats are poverty-stricken compared to mine."

The photographers' flashes lit up the air at ragged intervals. Carlo was massaging my legs, while Maestro Franco dried the mouthguard with a handkerchief. In the opposite corner, Ceresa was flanked by his trainer and his second. His face betrayed no emotion. The referee signaled for everyone else to leave the ring. The square of canvas emptied out. The roar from the audience gradually subsided and turned into a murmur. There were those who had one eye on the ring and the other on their watches. Some were ready to applaud, fingers extended, forearms tense. Others were still standing up, and had to be asked to take their seats. A few were checking their betting slips, over and over again, as if they might be written in disappearing ink or, even worse, might suddenly reveal the name of the wrong boxer. Here and there, people crushed out cigarettes with the heels of their shoes. Someone was taking a sip from a can of beer. There were those who emitted piercing whistles and those who nervously tugged at their hair. Gerruso slipped his hand into his pocket, pulled out a sheet of paper folded in four, kissed it, crossed himself, and prayed to Caterino Gerruso to make the miracle happen.

One last glance around the hall.

She wasn't there.

She hadn't come.

I knew it.

I'd always known it.

It was just to get a confirmation of her absence.

I never even heard the sound of the bell.

The championship fight had begun.

Ceresa had moved to the center of the ring before me.

The wind was gusting, hard and fast.

I went straight at him with my guard down.

My chest bared before the fray.

A simple and inconsolable anguish in my heart.

"Hello?"

"Nina."

"It's been a lifetime since you called me."

"I have something to tell you."

"What?"

"I called you a few days ago to find out if you were okay, after the bomb."

"I wasn't in Palermo. But I'm fine."

I was holding the coins in my right hand, ready to slip them into the slot when the beep announced I was out of credit.

"I went to a party."

Putting all the coins into the slot would have meant a carefree phone call: no worries about how much time is wasted, talking about nothing in particular just for the pleasure of sharing something, putting together phrases just to hear the sound of your voice.

"Did you have a good time?"

Slipping in one coin at a time was the triumph of the provisional: breaking time down into units of measurement.

"I saw the blonde there."

Plant the seed.

"Who is the blonde?"

The silence before the words was the kind that comes before a catastrophe.

"Eliana."

On the other end of the line, Siberia.

The phone booth became uncomfortable, inhospitable, drained of oxygen.

"Well?"

To begin a slow death.

"I drove her home, on her scooter."

Knowing full well that it would come to an end, sooner or later.

"Then what happened?"

The words weighed heavy in my mouth, they were sharp-edged, my tongue trembled and the cuts were continuous, one after another. I thought that saying the words would lighten my burden.

The beep didn't mark the end of my credit, but the beginning of the battle. I inserted another coin and the mayhem continued.

"We kissed."

Her reply was an absence of words that turned into weeping.

His guard up, his eyes calm, Renzo Ceresa waited.

Shouts of "Kill him!" poured down on us from the four corners of the auditorium.

As I bobbed and weaved my way around the ring, keeping my distance from *Bentu Maìstu*, I could feel each instant flow by.

As soon as they touched the ground, my feet sent me somewhere else.

I tried out a couple of punches, Ceresa came back with a left cross.

They were feints, neither of us was fighting for real.

"I'm sorry, Nina."

We were savoring the last few moments that come before the slaughter, when the hands are still firmly gripping the harpoon and the fish is swimming free in the water.

Both my gloves were held low.
They were pinwheeling in circles in front of my stomach.
I was holding no defensive position.

"Were you already at her house?"

Ceresa let go with a sudden, rapid right cross.
The glove came hurtling toward my face.
It was red, like a mouth.

"Yes, Nina."

I dodged it, pulling my neck back at the last moment.

"Were her parents home?"

The Sardinian's right uppercut had already been released.
It crashed into my abdominals.
The northwest wind was suddenly gusting.

"No."

I lunged at Ceresa and wrapped my arms around him to stop him
from attacking.

"Were you alone?"

The referee came over and separated us.

"Yes."

The preliminary phase of feeling each other out was over.

"Why are you telling me this?"

Ceresa resumed his charge.
I avoided his right fist by leaping backward, and the instant I touched
down, I let loose with my left.

Once the harpoon has penetrated the flesh, the struggle has become inexorable.

"I miss you, Nina."

Umbertino hadn't felt his body so present since the brawl in Piazza delle Sette Fate. He could sense every scrap of flesh, like when he was making love with Giovannella. It was just three days to his finals match. He could sense life flowing in his fists.

He walked out into the street after spending a few minutes in *Il Negro*'s bedroom. He had no illusions of any kind. His maestro wouldn't be coming back. At the finals, he'd have no one in his corner.

Outside, the sky was leaden gray but it showed no intention of raining. The sky just made sure the sun couldn't get through, nothing more: no cleansing rain fell on Palermo. It was the early fifties and the city still stank the way it had during the war; Palermo was filthy and there was no work. One power was emerging, gaining strength: the Mafia. The territory was under its control, and loyalty was spreading. The air was torn now and again by a scream or a shout. A theft, a brawl, a stabbing, a settling of accounts. There was a growing demand for violence.

In the ruins of the Magione, Umbertino watched a priest distribute rye bread to a line of starving citizens. A father holding his son by the hand came up and received his ration. The man and boy left the line with the bread. The son held out his hand for his share of the bread, but the father gave him nothing. The father ate all the bread himself, in two bites. The son dropped his hand without objection.

There was no time to waste.

It was time to act, to look to the future, to make a decision.

He headed for Vicolo Marotta, to see a whore he knew.

Fucking did nothing to tame his black thoughts.

It was still quite a few hours to the finals. Gerruso was baffled, confused. He oscillated between moments of disillusionment and blinding bursts of enthusiasm. He refused to listen to suggestions that he get some rest; still his eyelids were drooping all by themselves.

"Gerruso, your pupils are singing a song of sleep."

"I don't hear a thing."

"It's just a figure of speech. Your eyes look wrecked, try to get some shut-eye."

"But you have your weigh-in any minute."

"If you're asleep, I'll wake you up."

"You promise?"

"Yes."

"Will you tell me a story? That'd help me get to sleep."

"Gerruso, I understand that your mother just died, but now you're starting to take advantage."

"Come on."

I told him a story that my grandmother taught me.

A king had to decide which of his two sons should be the heir to the throne: his successor would defend lands and populace. He decreed that his two sons, in turn, would go down into the courtyard, where they would find a tiger awaiting them. The survivor would be next in line for the throne. The elder son was given to anger, and feared by one and all because of his great strength. The younger son was meek and mild, widely beloved for his kindness. He was the first to go down into the courtyard. The tiger lay down and curled up at his feet. Then it was the older son's turn. A single glare from him was enough to make the tiger quake in terror. The older son's power, the father said, is enormous. All the tiger had to do was take one look at him, and it understood it was done for. But it was the younger son's power that left the father breathless. The tiger was willing to die for him. And so it was that the younger son inherited the kingdom.

"What happened to the older brother?"

"That's the end of the story."

"Too bad, I liked the older brother best."

"Because the best way to rule is with force?"

"No, just the opposite, I like someone who has the strength to disappear from a story."

"Grandma maintains that it's a work of art to get into a story. To get out of it is a masterpiece."

His eyes had finally closed, his hands lay motionless on his belly, crossed as if in prayer. His stump-finger created a void in the pattern of fingernails.

"The people who get lost in stories, Poet, they're the ones I like, and when they come back by surprise, when you least expect them, for me, that's a real celebration. It would have been nice if Nina and Eliana could be here with us, right? I don't love her though, or maybe just a little: I really like her a lot. Too bad they had a fight."

Gerruso knew that they were no longer friends. Nina had told him herself, the night before, when I'd passed her to him on the phone: "Mamma collapsed, Nina, the way a dam collapses. Yes, he's here with me, Papà is still in the hospital. Not so good, Nina, my thoughts are bothering me. Listen, will you tell your friend Eliana that my mamma is dead? You had a fight? Too bad, no, it's just that maybe she could have come to the funeral."

The depth of the circles under his eyes told, better than words could ever do, of the anguish that tormented him.

"Poet, Nina loved you once but now she never wants to see you again, and now she doesn't even have her girlfriend anymore, can't the three of you make up?"

"It's not that simple."

When does a fight begin?

"When I was a little kid, there was a little girl, Barbarella, just beautiful, she had pouty lips and a head full of curls. I said to her: 'Barbarella, I love you.' She asked me: 'Just like grown-ups?' And I said: 'No, I *really* love you.' There. That's how it ought to be."

"Gerruso, come on, get some sleep."

"It's too bad that Nina and Eliana argued. Poet, do you know what it was about?"

Is there a transitional moment, a shift that can be seen as a beginning?

"No."

"If you did know, you would tell me?"

Something that marks the beginning of a new chapter?

"Yes."

"It's a good thing you're here."

His head slumped forward and he started to snore.

Two minutes later, they called me for my weigh-in and I left without waking him up.

Bentu Maìstu was punched square in the face by my left glove.

The audience reacted dramatically.

With a right hook, I creamed his face again.

Maestro Franco, just outside the ropes of the ring, was crushing Carlo's arm with one hand.

Renzo Ceresa had taken both punches without so much as blinking.

His legs were solid, his eyes level, his arms front and center.

We hopped, face to face, feinting and weaving with each step, in a race to see who was faster at dodging attacks that were never launched.

Gerruso commented on my weaves and feints and Grandpa nodded. Even Umbertino had abandoned his posture of immobility. He was echoing movements with his whole body, the punch that he'd have thrown, the feint he would have pulled, a leap forward, a weave to the left. Syllables of movement that failed to become words. A smile lit up his face when we both executed the same attack: the hook that forced Ceresa to raise his guard, even as a sharp cross-hook combination had already been unleashed. My hand completed the movement for Umbertino, smashing into the Sardinian's chin.

Umbertino spread all ten fingers wide in a sign of jubilation.

Ceresa had doubled over.

In my training, a month before the bout, there was a change in the "dishing out punishment" exercise. The point had become to turn every punch into a double punch. A right hook followed by a right hook, a left cross followed by another left cross. Throw the same punch twice, every time.

There was also a change in the four minutes of "taking punishment."

Umbertino had asked Carlo to climb into the ring.

"What's the matter, Uncle, are you tired already?"

"Pipe down, dummy. Carletto, put on your gloves."

"What are you doing, throwing in the towel?"

"You don't understand a thing."

He'd just doubled the number of punches thrown in this exercise, too.

"Go for his sides, Carletto. My nephew's face is all for me."

A myriad of punches rained down on me from all directions.

I was bobbing and weaving to keep from collapsing.

I was in a state of peace.

Every now and then, my sense of guilt vanished.

I unleashed eight left-handed crosses on Ceresa, one after the other, in a double punch that expanded exponentially.

Umbertino echoed my movements from where he was sitting and grinned.

Five out of the eight punches hit their mark.

Ceresa took the punches and remained on his feet.

His legs never stumbled.

I landed one to his temple.

Bentu Maìstu remained perfectly solid on his feet.

The smile faded from my uncle's lips.

There was still a whole minute left before the end of the round.

Umbertino went to the appointment in his good suit. He'd even dabbed himself with a few drops of cologne. He showed up early. When the owner of the cellar space arrived, he apologized to Umbertino for making him wait and offered to treat him to a coffee at the nearby bar.

"I'm not here to drink, here, take your money, now hand over the keys."

When he got home, he laid the keys on the kitchen table, took off his suit, and looked at his bedroom with the awareness that comes to you when you're about to leave a place. Now he had a gym to build.

He tucked the newspaper clippings, the plaques, and the trophies into a cardboard box.

He walked into *Il Negro*'s bedroom.

It was exactly the way his maestro had left it.

He hadn't touched a thing.

"Oh, hey, I did it, I bought the space. Now I'm going to start a fine boxing gym of my own. I'm going to live there."

He closed the bedroom door behind him, put on a tracksuit, picked up the box, walked downstairs, and tossed his past onto the rubble of Vuccirìa.

He bought everything he'd need to clean and set about preparing the cellar space. After washing the floor, he turned to whitewashing the walls. He built wooden benches with an assortment of boards. He hung a heavy bag from the ceiling. He planted four iron bars in the ground and covered them with blankets, stretching ropes from one pole to another. Once he'd constructed his ring, he didn't have the heart to step into it. He swore an oath that he'd never fight in an official bout again as long as he lived. He'd made his decision before the title fight. Now all he needed to do was follow that oath to its logical conclusion.

Gerruso split his attention between the match and his ongoing duel with the row of seats behind him.

"What's the matter, having trouble getting a good view?"

"Sit down, little boy."

"I'll sit down if and when I please: you're sitting behind me, that's your problem."

"Sit down and calm down, your boxer has nowhere to go."

My opponent looked fit and well rested.

Gerruso couldn't get over it.

"What kind of locals are you, if you're rooting for the other guy?"

"Locals who're betting on the winner."

"Locals who are going to take it up the ass."

"Kid, you're going too far!"

"You have no right to tell me I'm going too far, you mean less than nothing to me, you're even sitting behind me, so shut your mouth and show me the proper respect."

The other guy leaped to his feet, but his friend sitting next to him held him back.

"Can't you see he's a dickhead idiot? Let's just watch the Sardinian, he's making a comeback."

Gerruso parroted the phrase, mocking him, managing to make an enemy of him as well.

"Kid, you need to cut it out."

"What are you going to do if I don't, sell your house so you can afford a seat in the row ahead of me?"

Ceresa regained possession of the center of the ring and began his attack. I leaped to the right to avoid an uppercut but he was remarkably fast, a whirlwind, and his hook slammed into my chest, shoving me half a yard backward.

An "oh" of astonishment rose from the crowd.

I raised my guard, lifting my gloves in front of my chest. Ceresa lunged and I weaved, forced into continuous movement.

Bentu Maìstu persisted, relentlessly. It was almost as if the guy never got tired. It was only in the last few seconds of the round that his attacks subsided slightly in intensity and I was able to catch my breath. We ended the round in a standoff, cautiously reducing our risks, breathing deeply. Not a minute too soon.

In the corner, Carlo was massaging my arms.

"My eyes, clean up my eyes."

Carlo's hand stopped massaging.

"My eyes are tired."

He took the sponge and ran it over my face, slowly, with care.

Maestro Franco had taken his cap off his head.

He was clutching it in his hands.

"He's not as tired as I am, Maestro."

He said nothing.

The guys sitting in the third row had started to needle Gerruso with insults.

"Now watch the Sardinian tear your friend a new asshole."

Gerruso leaped to his feet to block their view, but the two guys' four hands thrust him vehemently back into his seat. After a silence that lasted a few seconds too long, Gerruso resumed shouting my nickname, without a glance behind him. His voice was altered; he sounded more like someone yelling as they fell.

Umbertino hadn't noticed a thing.

But my grandpa had turned to stare at the pair of friends with his usual indecipherable gaze.

They were at Randazzo's home in the countryside. Provvidenza was talking to Nicola's wife, Gigliola, while the two old friends, their husbands, were talking about aromatic plants. My father was five years old and in a hurry to discover the world. He walked into the rabbit hutch. He'd figured out that if he wanted to pet a rabbit he had to move slowly, a calm but continuous gesture, until he could feel the soft fur on his fingertips. After that, he decided he wanted to feel the textures of the rooster's comb, but the rooster was fast, it kept outrunning him, and in the henhouse the chickens were screeching and pooping out eggs.

My grandmother kept calling him back, but Randazzo reassured her.

"Don't worry, he's just playing."

Rosario's son was as dear to Randazzo as if he were his own. The boy thought of him as his uncle, and called him "Zio Nicola," something that filled him with pride. For that reason, when he heard the boy scream he rushed to his side, blindingly fast, almost as fast as Rosario. The little one had been bitten by the dog. The child had tried to touch his tongue and the dog, Filippo, had sunk his fangs into him.

"Davidù, I felt like I was dying," Randazzo told me, "'Filippo,' I yelled at the dog, 'what are you doing?' As soon as Filippo heard my voice, he immediately lowered his ears. He'd always been a good dog, I couldn't get over the fact that he'd turned on the child."

Randazzo was trembling with fury. He picked up his stick and strode angrily toward the dog.

"Stop."

Rosario stepped between Randazzo and the dog. He took the stick. His son's hands had only the faintest of bite marks, no blood, his fingers all moved properly: he was sobbing out of fear more than anything else. Rosario handed the stick to my father.

"You do it."

My father ran both hands over the knotted surface of the stick. The dog Filippo, sitting obedient, whined in terror.

"Or else, forgive."

My father stared at his father. Rosario was seraphic, his gaze never wavered. Francesco leaned the stick against the wall, bent over the dog Filippo, and petted him. Calm returned to the scene. Francesco spent the rest of the afternoon throwing sticks that the dog Filippo retrieved for him. Rosario and Nicola watered the vines and their wives gathered blackberries. They ate shelled beans and drank Zibibbo wine: the grown-ups a whole glass, my father just two fingers.

An instant after the sound of the bell marking the beginning of the second round, *Bentu Maìstu* was in the center of the ring. His legs still possessed agility and power. My offside position forced me to keep moving around him, continuously, like a moth around the flame.

I landed a double left punch right in his face.

He absorbed the blow without showing any ill effects.

He could take some punishment.

Just like the boxer who beat Umbertino in the finals.

I tried everything on him: uppercuts, hooks, and crosses, but Ceresa retaliated every time, punch for punch.

The crowd was braying.

Gerruso was begging me to take care.

The Sardinian was clearly gaining the upper hand.

The northwest wind had started to gust again.

He attacked from all directions.

I lunged at him, wrapping my arms around him, trying to halt his fury.

He was inexhaustible.

Maestro Franco was holding his breath.

Umbertino was biting his lips.

Grandpa was sitting bolt upright, rigid in his seat.

Gerruso was screaming "Poet," but by now there was a shadow of gloom in his voice.

The referee separated us.

In the morning, on our way to the sports arena, Gerruso counted aloud all the roadblocks we passed. There were twelve of them.

In the auditorium, I showed him where he'd be sitting.

"That way, you'll be next to my uncle and my grandpa. Gerruso, what's wrong?"

"Nothing, I was just thinking of something about my mother."

His voice had once again become little more than a faint wisp of wind, feeble and frightened.

"Tomorrow, when we take my mother's coffin to the cemetery, do you think the police might stop us at a roadblock and open the coffin?"

"How on earth do you come up with these things?"

"By observing Palermo."

"Why don't you get a little sleep?"

"After you've weighed in."

"It'll be a little while longer."

"I'll tough it out. We're strong in my family. Even if I have to admit: my mother broke, truth be told."

"Gerruso, come on, stop thinking about it."

"But life, it's all just one long story about breaking: when you're born, the water breaks. And as people grow, sooner or later they break, just like toys. My mother's heart broke. Sometimes it works differently, and people are interrupted, like your father, who was perfectly fine inside, but who broke when he ran up against the outside world, it wasn't his time yet, have you ever thought about that?"

"Yes."

"Sometimes, though, the toy is so well made that it lasts all the way to the end, to where it was supposed to go."

"Like my uncle."

"Actually, I was thinking of your grandfather."

"Gerruso, come on, get some rest now."

"You know what, Poet? We ought to speak in colors. We'd save ourselves so many words if you could tell everything you need to know from the color. All you'd need to know would be the color of all the feelings."

"That's not a bad idea."

"It's colorful, right? Anyway, Poet, don't worry, I'm here with you."

"But in the ring I'll be the one taking all the punches."

"Not really."

"What do you mean?"

"Your body takes all the punches in the flesh, but we take the invisible punches to the soul. Let's just hope that Caterino Gerruso remembers to keep his dukes up, because invisible punches land square on your heart and they hurt just as bad as the other kind."

Umbertino was alone in the locker room.

Soon, he'd be climbing into the ring for the finals.

Il Negro wouldn't be there to watch him fight.

He tried out a series of jabs to warm up his arms, he stretched his back, grabbed the jump rope and jumped rope for a while.

He'd always liked warming up before a fight.

The silence that comes before a battle.

It reminded him of what it was like to swim in the sea, far from everyone else, with no one there to take part in that intimacy.

Igniting his body.

Ready to inflict mayhem right from the start.

This would be the last time he did it.

He had to avoid mistakes.

He threw a series of violent, very fast punches.

He could sense every muscle, every tendon, every inch of skin.

He was at the height of his strength and there was desperation in his eyes.

He opened the door, slipped on his gloves, left the locker room, and strode off to lose his championship bout.

Nina continued to weep.

Her breathing was labored.

She sniffed.

And still she went on talking to me from the other end of the line.

"Go on."

The receiver was as heavy as a boulder.

I had three coins in my hand.

They were enough for what I had to say.

"Nina."

She did her best to cry quietly, trying to keep from drowning out my voice.

"Tell me what I need to know."

When the beep indicating I was out of credit sounded, it was followed by the click of a coin I'd just inserted into the slot.

"I'm sorry."

The sobbing came more frequently.

I still had two coins in my hand.

Bitter words flew.

"Kid, you don't know shit about boxing."

"I'm in front of you and I understand before you even get a chance, piece-of-shit traitors."

"The show's over, you idiot, take your seat."

Neither Umbertino nor Grandpa turned around to offer Gerruso moral support. They were focusing on the ring.

The referee signaled for us to resume the fight and Ceresa returned to the center of the canvas, as if it belonged to him by right.

He wasn't as tired as I was.

He lunged at me, pushing me into the corner.

The northwest wind was capable of slashing my face.

I raised my guard to protect my face, leaving my abdominals, my elbows, and my ribs unprotected.

"Tell me what happened next."

Forcing my calves to leap, I escaped that maelstrom of punches—jabbing and hooking randomly as I went.

"After the kiss?"

My opponent never seemed to fall.

"Yes."

I needed to move quicker, as quick as I could.

He was outflanking me.

I had to retake the initiative or I was fucked.

"You want to know if the blonde and I . . ."

None of my attacks were succeeding.

All of my attempts were proving to be failures.

I couldn't seem to score a single point.

"Yes."

When did breathing become so labored?

When had giving an answer become so degrading?

When did mortification wound more deeply than the act itself?

"What do you want to know?"

Nina had no fear.

She uttered the words I had been unable to pronounce.

The question had been spoken.

The whole time I was giving her my answer, I kept my eyes shut.

I welcomed with relief the beep announcing that the call was about to come to an end.

"That was the last coin, Nina."

She didn't answer.
    She just cried, nothing more.
    That was the end of our phone call.
    I looked at my reflection in the glass of the phone booth.
    It wasn't over yet.
    I inserted the coin that remained in my hand and I called the blonde.

Nicola Randazzo didn't understand how it was possible. Rosario had been digging for hours, without rest. He was just a walking skeleton, but still.
    There were so many people missing. They must still be trapped under the rubble. Only when someone was certain that they'd found a living person did they call out to the others for help. It was vital to husband what strength remained, focusing only on survivors for the moment. There would be plenty of time to extract the dead later.
    From the minute Rosario had left D'Arpa's grave, he hadn't stopped working for a second. He went on moving rubble, wooden beams, body parts. Nicola couldn't keep up with him.
    "I can't keep it up, Rosario."
    "Lie down here, so I can find you later."
    It was still at least two hours till sunset, but Nicola curled up all the same, next to the kitchen wall, where my grandfather had directed him. Exhausted, he fell asleep right away.
    Dust and smoke had made the air unbreathable.
    Every now and then, someone passed out.
    Everyone was starting to run out of strength.
    "We were Christs of mercy."
    The following day, the Allied troops would arrive.
    "Grandpa, who else knows that all this happened?"
    They would take care of everyone, even the prisoners.
    "No one."

Eight months later, when the war was over, they'd repatriate them all.

"Not even Nicola?"

There was still two hours of light to dig by, before darkness fell over everything.

"No one knows what I'm about to tell you, but you."

The moaning was faint, like the sound of a hair being plucked, but Rosario had heard it.

On that spot, a few hours ago, the barracks had stood.

The sound of the lament guided my grandfather's fingers. His hands needed to move the rubble preventing the extraction of the survivor, and only that rubble, in order to prevent new collapses.

By digging and clearing, Rosario had carved out a channel through the debris. He made his way in, picked up a piece of stone, a handful of dirt, a length of wood, then he emerged, discarded what he was carrying, and went back in. Sometimes he'd remove something that caused so much dust to fall that it forced him out of the tunnel so he could catch his breath. The air outside, smoke-filled though it was, was still better than the dust-saturated air down there.

The voice went on moaning. There was just one more obstacle in his way: the canvas of a military cot. Rosario armed himself with a sharp shard and cut through it.

He reached out a hand and touched a face.

"He . . . elp me."

It didn't matter that the dust made it hard to see.

"He . . . elp . . . me."

My grandfather's fingers recognized him immediately.

Melluso.

The voice was faint.

From the head down, the body was completely crushed.

Melluso couldn't move.

Rosario pulled his hand back.

"He . . . el . . . me."

The syllables were breaking up, more and more. Something was pressing down on Melluso with growing intensity, or perhaps it was just that his body was breaking.

"H . . . he . . . l . . ."

Rosario didn't reach out his arm, he didn't turn around, he didn't say a thing.

"He . . . he . . . lp."

He stood there.

After a few minutes, some of the dust in the tunnel cleared away.

Melluso's pupils dilated.

He'd recognized him.

"M . . . mu-u-ute . . . ma . . . n . . . h . . . h . . . he-elp me . . ."

He coughed.

He had no more saliva.

His eyes were full of dirt.

His face was covered with blood and bruises.

"He . . . el . . . elp."

He was breathing through his mouth, between moans and coughing fits, but the moaning, the breathing, and the coughing were all fading in intensity.

Rosario looked at him.

The only thing disrupting his total paralysis was the blinking of his eyelashes.

"He . . . he . . ."

A tear welled up in Melluso's eye, but it lacked the strength to fall.

His lips started to tremble.

Once more, he tried to beg for help, but he was no longer able even to make a sound.

He tried once more and once again his mouth failed.

Only then did Rosario move.

Melluso's eyes widened still further.

He'd started to move away.

Melluso tried to cry out, but his pupils remained mute.

A rain of dust fell where shortly before the dying daylight was filtering through.

My grandfather had emerged from the hole.

The sun had almost set.

All around, people went on digging while others did their best to comfort the wounded.

Rosario went over to Nicola.

He found him still sleeping.

He lay down by his side, his head resting on Nicola's shoulder.
He closed his eyes, the darkness came, and he collapsed into it.

Gerruso, wracked by a continuous tremor, couldn't tear his eyes away from the ring.
Umbertino had folded his arms across his chest.
Grandpa had laid his hands on his legs.
No one was saying a word.
It was in the ring that the battle was raging.
Ceresa resumed his charge and, tumbling over me like an avalanche, crushed me into the corner once again.
There was no other way out now.

"You want to know if the blonde and I . . ."

An army of fists.
One right behind the other.
Pounding me with furious might.

"Yes."

What had I expected, when I dialed that number?
Nina had always been a person of fierce pride.
Nina was afraid of nothing.
She was ready to endure the last plunge of the sword, head held high.

"What do you want to know?"

I belted myself to Ceresa, wrapping both my gloves around his neck, pulling him toward me.
I had to cling to him.
If he got a shot at my head, it would all be over.

"Did you fuck?"

The fists pounded into my ribs.
They hit me twenty times.

———

I wish I could have been there, in front of her, could have stripped away the safety of distance.

Let her slap me, spit on me, scratch my face.

Anything would have been better than that silence, as heavy as cowardice.

"No."

Is this what losing is?

"Swear to me."

This inability to act in the face of the inevitable?

"There was nothing but a kiss."

I could no longer breathe.

My eyes filled with tears.

My legs were about to give out.

For Gerruso it was like reliving the beatdown at the fair.

He stood up and started to scream, raising his hands to his head.

Grandpa reached over to reassure him, but it was pointless.

Umbertino had sunk into his seat.

"Swear to me you didn't fuck her."

Why had I called her?

Why had I told her?

What need was there for all this every time?

"I swear it."

My arms shoved him away.

My back was in flames, but I'd started breathing again.

Ceresa hurtled back onto me.

He never gave up.

I pushed him away with my elbows, he came back, then I moved him aside with both gloves.

When the wind is cutting sharp, never step directly into the brunt of it.

Bentu Maìstu kept coming back to me, I kept pushing him away.

Again and again. For the entire length of that round.

When the bell signaled the end of the second round, I was shattered but still standing.

A slap of the fin and I veered back to my corner.

Umbertino no longer had anything to prove.

In five rounds, he'd knocked his opponent to the canvas twice, without ever overreaching.

Now the important thing was to avoid falling at all costs.

No one would ever deck him: ever.

By the ninth round, his face had been through the stations of the cross: split lip, lacerated eyebrow, blood everywhere. His opponent might have been slower than him, but he was still a very nimble boxer. Every single time, my uncle had to repress his instinct to jump out of the way.

He'd spent the whole morning sprawled out on his bed, fully dressed. There was a mosquito on the ceiling. It takes an absurd force of will to risk your life every time you set out to suck some blood, he mused. The mosquito alternated statuesque immobility with off-kilter zigzags. Its last flight concluded right on the back of his hand. He could have killed the insect whenever he chose, smashing it with a slap or capturing it in his fist. He was faster than it could ever hope to be. Still, he let it drink his blood, respectful of the mosquito's defiance of danger. Then he killed it, clutching it in his closed fist. There was no work in Palermo and money was in short supply. He'd never wind up like that mosquito. He reached into his pocket and extracted the bookie's receipt. If it paid out, he'd clean up on that bet. It called for him to lose on points. He'd bet all his savings against himself. He laid the receipt on the nightstand, lit a cigarette, clasped his hands behind his head, and looked at the ceiling, planning his future.

Maestro Franco talked while Carlo massaged my calves.

"How do you feel?"

"He didn't break me, Maestro, he couldn't do it."

"Tell me the saying from the Gospels that your uncle always quotes, right now, hurry."

"He who strikes first does the most damage."

"You're a tough one, kid. Your head is still working. Do you still have a pair of legs on you?"

"I think so."

"Aim for the head, kid, he's not moving the way he was."

"No?"

"No."

The guys in the third row were making fun of Gerruso.

"What's the matter? Aren't you shouting 'Poet' anymore? Teach us about life, kid. 'Poet,' sure, why not?"

Gerruso couldn't take it anymore. He lunged at the bigger of the two but my grandfather snatched him back by the belt, catching him in midair.

"What the fuck do you want?" snarled the guy in the third row.

"I'll murder you when and how I please," the guy continued.

"Son of a bitch," he concluded.

Gerruso stood there, openmouthed. Suddenly, the tension in his body slackened, like an old bedsheet. He'd given up resisting it. He'd finally crashed face-first to the floor. Gerruso had just realized that he was orphaned, that he'd lost his mother, that she was gone for all time. He tamely emerged from my grandfather's embrace and sank into his seat. Without covering his face, he began to weep silently, arms folded across his chest, his shoulders racked with sobs.

My grandfather halted Umbertino's lunge with a light touch to his shoulder, then he stared at the guy who'd talked out of turn.

"Apologize, immediately."

The guy was able to withstand that look for only a few seconds.

His friend didn't know what to do and, when in doubt, he did nothing.

Umbertino's fingers slowly, menacingly crushed the back of his seat.

The guy slipped both hands into his pockets.

"I'm sorry, kid."

He sat down, eyes in his lap.

Still, Gerruso had been unable to hear those words of apology.

The only thing he was aware of was his own despair.

Bending over him, my grandfather did his best to console him.

Umbertino had returned his gaze to the ring after one last, fearsome glare at the third row.

Carlo and Maestro Franco positioned themselves outside the ropes.

The sound of the bell marked the beginning of the last three minutes of the finals.

"Poet, how do you write a poem?"

"One word after the other."

"And what do you need to write one?"

"A pen and a blank sheet of paper."

"Afterward, will you write a poem for me, too? If my mother were still alive, tonight she's being happy if you'll win because it'd meant that I, too, was being happy."

"You got all your tenses wrong, Gerruso."

"That doesn't matter, happiness is something that goes beyond time and tenses. That's why now I'm a little happy because before long, maybe, we'll have our victory."

"Our victory?"

"Sure, I invented your nickname. Can I ask you one last thing and then I'm done?"

"Out with it."

"Win this for me tonight, too: I need it."

Ceresa had returned to center ring.

My feet let him go.

They were rediscovering the rhythm they had lost.

I let down my guard.

I had to see everything.

The Sardinian took a half step forward and my right hook, already hurtling, made itself felt on his cheekbone.

There was no blood.

There was no expression of pain.

Ceresa had absorbed the punch without blinking.

It didn't matter.

It didn't matter anymore.

If he stayed on his feet, that just meant I could inflict more damage.

It was Gerruso who passed her phone call to me. His mother had just died but still he'd thought to remind her that tomorrow I had my title bout, what's more, here in Palermo—Nina, that's something that happens, like, never.

"How is he?"

"It's been a tremendous blow for him, he's confused, he's talking crazy."

"We'll be there right away."

"No, no, Nina, my uncle's on his way, we'll take him to my house, my mother says it would be better for him not to sleep here, at least for tonight."

"How are you feeling?"

"Like someone who's going to fight for the national title tomorrow."

"Is that a state of mind?"

"Yes."

"Good to know."

"Will you come watch me?"

The seed of my anguish had been planted.

"You really don't want me to be there."

"What?"

"You need me not to be there if you want to fight your best fight. With Pullara, you only stepped in when he was trying to stab me, with Raul not until he had hauled off and tried to slap me. That's the way you are. You need to be pushed to the limit. And anyway, seeing that I'm speaking sincerely, I couldn't come in any case: I'd feel like dying if I had to watch you trade punches."

"Really?"

"Thank you for taking good care of my cousin. Try not to ruin your face tomorrow."

I hung up.

In my head, I was already in the ring, fighting.

"Is she coming to the finals?"

"No."

"Too bad. Can I come?"

"Let's hear what my mother has to say."

"Jesus, now you have a mother who tells you what to do, but I don't. Will you tell me what to do now?"

"Hold on. My uncle is coming to pick us up."

"Can I ask you something?"

"Of course."

"What does if feel like when you're in the ring?"

I looked at my hands.

Tomorrow they'd be wrapped in bandages.

"I try not to get hit."

The fingernails would be bleeding again.

The bandages would do nothing to protect them from bruises and scrapes.

"What about when you attack?"

My hands weren't suited to caressing a smooth back, I didn't have the right kind of fingers to intertwine in fine hair.

I'd been using them to punch since I was nine years old.

"A sense of peace."

Too bad I had to shut them up in a boxing glove.

"Not me. When I attend one of your fights I feel terrible, I argue with everyone else."

"You provoke those people."

"It's their fault they're rooting for the wrong side."

"Gerruso, why on earth did you ever become so attached to me?"

"It was something you needed, Davidù."

I pounded a one-two hook combination into Ceresa's side, shoving all the way, until I could feel my knuckles making contact with the ribs.

For the first time, he showed that he'd felt the blow.

It didn't knock him down, but he wasn't rebounding the way he had before.

There was confusion in his eyes.

I let fly with a cross.

Gerruso.

Come on.

Stop crying.

I landed a punch square to his eyebrow.

Lift up your head and watch this round, it'll be worth it.

Offsetting my feet, I performed the footwork of the Buttana Imperiale.

I hit him full in the forehead.

All power to you, blondie.

Being with you was a hell of a lot of fun.

You had a wonderful flavor.

Ceresa retreated to the corner.

The wind was bottled up, now it couldn't gust, couldn't rage.

My left fist smashed once more into his face.

Ceresa couldn't seem to keep his guard up anymore.

Maestro Franco was clutching at the ropes. Carlo was torturing the towel in his hands. Umbertino had come back to life and was now miming a resurgent attack. With one hand, my grandfather was pointing to the ring; with his other he was lifting Gerruso's head: look, the shark fish is savaging his opponent.

My fists were pounding faster than they ever had before.

Anguish had appeared on the horizon.

Il Negro would have been proud of me.

My father would have looked on with love in his eyes.

I was in the state of grace of one who wreaks havoc.

Bentu Maistu was a wind that had stopped gusting.

He'd stopped hitting back.

Well, all the better.

My fists centered his face seven times.

Left. Left. Right. Left. Right. Left. Left.

I wanted it to never end.

I was as calm and unruffled as the wrath of God.

"It's a way of acquiring a structured movement: you feint to the right and then let fly with a right hook."

"And then you do it over again?"

"For thirty minutes at a time."

"You repeat the same dance step for thirty minutes at a time?"

"It's called a sequence and yes, I repeat it."

"But don't you get sick of it? What's the point?"

"Gerruso, let me remind you that, in order to learn to write, you filled whole pages with *a*'s and *e*'s and all the other vowels, right? Well, it's the same thing. The same way that your hand learns the motions required to draw a vowel, so the body learns the movements needed to punch and feint through repetition."

"Are you telling me that the hand can learn things?"

"The body has an intelligence all its own. It's a piece of paper you can write on."

"Oh sure, I'll bet."

"Everything is writing."

"Everything?"

"Yes."

"Even pasta with sardines?"

"Yes."

"And women's hips?"

"Yes."

"And bombs in the city?"

"Yes."

"And just what do these words of punches and feints write down?"

"The story of my family."

My mother had woken up feeling uneasy. She missed my father terribly. Without him, the house was empty. Provvidenza was out, shopping for groceries. My mother got out of bed, without asking for help, and went into the bathroom all by herself. In front of the mirror, she came to terms with her own face, postpregnancy. She looked tired, her hair was unkempt and sweaty, there were dark circles under her eyes. She turned on the cold water and slowly rinsed her face. She listened alertly for any sounds that might come from the cradle. That short walk had exhausted her. She walked out of the bathroom and back down the hallway, bracing herself against the wall with one hand. She found Umbertino and Rosario in her bedroom. They'd crept in without making a sound. They were looking at me and talking in an undertone.

"But, are they always so little? Or is it just that this one's a midget?"

"They're small at first, then they grow."

"Me? My mother, God rest her soul, told me that when I was born I weighed eleven and a half pounds. These modern kids come into the world all sickly, if you ask me. But who does he look like, now? Your wife says he looks like Zina. To my eyes, he just looks like every other kid in the world. Oh, Zina, there you are, quiet now, the little one's asleep, let us help, here."

As soon as Rosario pulled the sheets aside, Umbertino slid her into bed.

"Now get some rest. The baby boy is doing fine. You just go to sleep. Later, Rosario will cook some fish, you need to eat something, there's a fabulous white sea bream, practically still alive, I told him to cook it *all'acqua pazza*, in water with tomato and garlic, mmmm, it drives me crazy."

He caressed her hair, brushing it out of her eyes.

"We can't lose, Zina *mia*."

He gave her a kiss on the forehead and she let her eyelids sink shut.

When my mother woke up again, she couldn't be sure whether or not she'd been dreaming, but it seemed to her that, the whole time she'd been asleep, Umbertino and Rosario had stood outside the half-closed door, watching me as I slept in my cradle.

His legs had folded beneath him.

Ceresa tried to brace himself, hold himself up with his back against the ropes.

He failed.

He cradled his head between his elbows, leaving his stomach open to attack.

I let loose with a series of low uppercuts.

He bent over even further.

He almost seemed to be on his knees.

When I hit him with my right hook, I leaped straight up on the spot, both feet in the air.

Ceresa fell to the canvas, right in front of his own corner.

The audience responded with a roar.

Gerruso, overwhelmed, gesticulated to everyone in the audience—his stump-finger held up in front of his mouth—to be quiet. His eyes were red with crying, his cheeks were on fire, his hair was matted with sweat. He was quivering. Standing next to him, my grandfather's gaze ricocheted obsessively from the ring to my uncle's eyes; my uncle's gaze mimicked the same motion.

Ceresa wasn't getting up.

I started to hop in place.

The referee took a stance in front of the Sardinian and, raising one hand straight into the air, exclaimed: "One."

Outside the ropes, Maestro Franco crammed three sticks of gum into his mouth, while Carlo bit down on the sponge.

My opponent's trainer and second both urged their boxer to get to his feet.

They were cupping their hands in front of their mouths to amplify the sound of their cries.

The referee said, "Two."

My feet came and went, flying back and forth, barely brushing the canvas, just so much water to walk across.

Ceresa wasn't getting up.

"Three."

My gloves spun through the air, in front of my pelvis.

Umbertino was clenching his fists.

"Four."

Gerruso had pulled out the sheet of paper he kept in his pocket.

He kissed it and crossed himself.

"Five."

Ceresa's manager did his best to encourage his boxer; his second kept saying "Come on, come on, come on," like someone reciting a rosary.

"Six."

Ceresa wasn't getting up.

Grandpa was clenching his teeth.

"Seven."

Umbertino was throwing punches into the empty air in front of him.

"Eight."

My breathing was calm and unhurried.

Inside my glove, my fingers still thirsted.

"Nine."

Franco gripped Carlo's arm.

The hall was filled with whistles and applause.

Umbertino and Rosario were taking turns leaning on each other and supporting each other's weight.

Gerruso called my name.

Ceresa hadn't gotten up.

Maestro Franco released his grip on Carlo.

Umbertino and Rosario looked each other in the eye.

"Ten."

The crowd was screaming.

Umbertino burst into tears and Rosario threw his arms around him.

The referee walked up to me, seized my wrist, and raised my right arm high.

Gerruso kissed his sheet of paper, yelled out "Suck it, losers!" to the guys in the third row, made his way through the crowd, and ran out of the auditorium. He found a phone booth and called my mother.

"Signora! Something fabulous has happened! I just won five hundred thousand lire on a bet! My mother would be so proud of me!"

The funeral was held in the church of San Michele.

Gerruso spent the night in my apartment, in my bed, with the trophy by his side.

"That way, if nightmares come, I can deck 'em."

I wanted to call Nina, tell her that I'd won.

I fell asleep, fully dressed, on the couch, with that thought in my mind.

My mother didn't wake me up.

"Signora, what should I wear for my mother's funeral?"

"The outfit you like best, my dear."

"That would be my pajamas, is that okay?"

"Well, let's go to your house and we'll pick it out together, don't worry."

A statue of the Archangel Michael looked down on us from on high, at the far end of the church. A long tunic, sandals on his feet, a sword unsheathed, gripped firmly in one hand. The light of the sun touched him, but it was absorbed, no reflection played into our eyes.

"What do you think?"

"*Scintillation* is a wonderful word, it accelerates from start to finish, jamming on the brakes when it comes to the end, on the *la* and then letting the *tion* gape in amazement at the spark of light that appears."

Every funeral ought to reveal a spark of light. It should remind those who are still on this side of the light that though we're caught in a fleeting stream of time, it's possible to glitter with intensity.

"What other words do you like?"

"*Quinquennial*, it sounds like a series of years clinking past in armor, the tongue has to make lots of movements just to get it pronounced, but the lips never even touch."

"I like mozzarella, it's good to eat."

"Gerruso, that's not how it works."

"No, that's exactly how it works for me, in fact it's better that way. My words are tastier: *burrata, sfincione, arancina*. Your words are different: *quinquennial*, there's nothing to eat. You may like your words in your mind, but I like mine in my tummy, too, so that means I win."

Gerruso had chosen to put on a very shiny suit, something that reminded him of Nina's birthday parties. That's how he always dressed for important occasions.

"You like it, Poet? It's the twin brother of the suit I was wearing at the fair, you remember? We all got arrested."

My mamma ironed his shirt. Gerruso put it on still warm from the iron.

"Br-r-r-r, signora, now I've got the shivers. Too bad my mother's dead, or I would have told her always to give me my shirts warm like this, these shivers are wonderful, they make me laugh."

My grandparents got out of their sky-blue Fiat 500. Rosario was clean-shaven, with a dark suit, a black vest, a white shirt, and a dark blue tie. Provvidenza, dressed in a dark brown skirt and a dark gray blouse, wore a black shawl around her shoulders. Her eyes were less lively than usual. Funerals were an uncomfortable reminder of things she wished she'd never had anything to do with. My mother had an easier time putting up with them. At the hospital where she worked, she encountered death on a regular basis.

Grandpa shook hands with Gerruso, Grandma gave him a hug and two kisses, one for each cheek.

Gerruso waited on tiptoe for the hearse to arrive: his right hand cupped against his forehead, shielding his eyes from the glare of the sun. His father, leaning against the front door of the church, was unshaven and red-eyed; no sooner had he crushed out one cigarette than he lit another. He was clutching at something to do to keep from collapsing.

Umbertino climbed up there, too, in his tracksuit.

"How do you feel, champ? Do you have a nice fat hard-on?"

He went over to Gerruso and laid both hands on his shoulders.

"Anything you need, you just ask."

"Truth be told, Signor Uncle, there is one thing."

"Go ahead and tell me."

"I'm all dressed up but I forgot my tie, could you find me one?"

Grandpa was already there. He untied his and knotted it around Gerruso's neck.

"You see? You only have to ask."

Umbertino shook hands with Rosario, who was rebuttoning his shirt and sliding off to one side again.

Gerruso's face lit up.

"You see that, Poet? Now I'm an old man."

He thrust out his chest, proud of his dark blue necktie.

A white Fiat Panda pulled up and parked. Gerruso's aunt and uncle got out, with Nina.

At last, I saw her again.

I didn't know whether to bless the sorrowful loss or curse the thought of it.

Nina's mother, who was Gerruso's mother's sister, wore black and could hardly stand upright. Her legs kept giving out at the knees. Her husband had to all but carry her by force into the church.

Gerruso greeted them with a wave of his intact hand.

Nina made an effort to stanch her tears, and was successful.

She was even prettier.

"Your whole family came, Davidù."

"And you're here, too."

"You won yesterday."

She knew.

She'd asked about me.

The hearse appeared, carrying the coffin.

Not a single cigarette survived.

Gerruso's father burst into a flood of tears.

Gerruso didn't know what to do, whether to walk toward the coffin or his father. My mother and my grandmother both hurried to his aid, each taking him by one hand. My grandmother wound up on the stump-finger side. First they walked him over to the coffin, and then into the church. With three strides, Umbertino was at Gerruso's father's side, one hand on his pack of cigarettes, the other on his lighter.

"Have a smoke, trust me."

Rosario, standing next to him, offered a handkerchief so he could dry his eyes and blow his nose.

Once again, Nina's eyes looked into my own.

"I'm sorry, Nina, for everything."

"What should I do now?"

"What we have to do."

We entered the church together.

There was no one in the church but us.

When we left the church, the sun was as intense as the traffic. Nina embraced Gerruso, my uncle and my grandfather were helping Gerruso's father along, Mamma and Grandma were walking alongside his uncle and aunt. I was walking several steps behind them, with my hands in my pockets and an urge to whistle.

In the church courtyard, we found the Dumas waiting for us.

"Eliana! You came! I'm the happiest man in the world."

For a moment, Gerruso had managed to forget about his mother's death.

The blonde went over to him.

"My condolences, Paride."

She touched his face; a long, intense caress.

In silence, she embraced Nina.

Then she came over to me.

"You were handsome in the ring yesterday, covered with sweat."

"You were there?"

She planted a kiss on my cheek, moist and delicate.

"Ciao, boxer."

She went over to her scooter, kick-started it, and left.

"Did you call her?" Gerruso asked me.

"I told her," Nina replied.

"Now, as long as we make it to the cemetery without running into any bombs or roadblocks, everything will be perfect."

Nina bit her lip to keep from crying.

Getting the coffin into the hearse was more complicated than expected. The hearse was parked perpendicular to the lanes of traffic, and cars started forming a line. A few drivers felt entitled to honk furiously. Umbertino's response was indignant.

"Who lit a fire under your ass? Come on, step out of the car and let's see if you feel like crossing that line again."

A religious silence descended.

After a few minutes, the hearse pulled away and the traffic jam unknotted itself.

We all got in our cars and drove to the graveyard.

The Rotoli cemetery, perched high on Mount Pellegrino, offers the dead a view of the sea.

I don't think I would like to be buried in the ground. I was in agreement with Umbertino on this point.

"To hell with being worm food: I'm for cremation and tossing my ashes into the sea."

Grandpa wanted to be buried in the earth.

"That way I can look up at the sky."

The coffin containing Gerruso's mother was sealed and interred. It was the first burial I'd ever witnessed. It was quick.

"Ciao, Mamma, the sun is out today, don't worry, I'm not all sweaty."

He waved goodbye to her with his stump-finger hand, while his right hand caressed his necktie.

His father poured water into a vase and filled it with a bunch of fresh flowers purchased by Grandma Provvidenza.

Gerruso came over to me.

"Jesus, Poet, now we're even, our score is one-to-one, we're each short one parent."

This time, Nina couldn't hold back her tears.

Gerruso stroked her hair with the care one would use with a newborn puppy.

"It's strange. We live on an island. Why don't we put our dead into boats, in the middle of the night? That way, the sea could carry them away into the distance, and we could stay behind, watching the flames as they vanish over the horizon of life."

"Cemeteries exist because it's a source of consolation to know that our dead are in a specific place."

"Fine, but what more specific place can there be than in our heart?"

It was midday.

Without a word, my whole family and I headed over to where my father lay.

Nina and Gerruso trooped along with us.

Mamma and Grandma removed the old flowers and replaced them with new ones, yellow and red.

My grandparents held hands; Umbertino wrapped an arm around my mother's shoulders.

"Poet, why don't you give your father the news, maybe he hasn't heard about it yet."

So many things had happened.

And I hadn't come to see him in such a long time.

I was bigger, I'd made it through another year at school, the bombs had come back.

My hands had won the battle.

In the photograph on the headstone, the Paladin was smiling.

"Ciao, Papà, this is Nina."